THE LAST PRINCE

THE LAST PRINCE

BOOK TWO OF *THE COMING OF ÁED* SERIES
THE ORIGIN STORY

E.G. RADCLIFF

Mythic Prairie Books

BISAC: YOUNG ADULT FICTION / Fantasy / General |
YOUNG ADULT FICTION / Fantasy / Dark Fantasy |
YOUNG ADULT FICTION / Legends, Myths, Fables / General

Mythic Prairie Books
154 W Park Avenue #141
Elmhurst, IL 60126

info@egradcliff.com
www.egradcliff.com

First edition

Library of Congress Control Number 2020908207
ISBN: 978-1-7336733-4-1 (pbk)
ISBN: 978-1-7336733-6-5 (pbk-Dyslexie Edition)
ISBN: 978-1-7336733-3-4 (ebook)

Edited by Kelsy Thompson
Cover design by Micaela Alcaino
Illustrated by E.G. Radcliff

The Maze

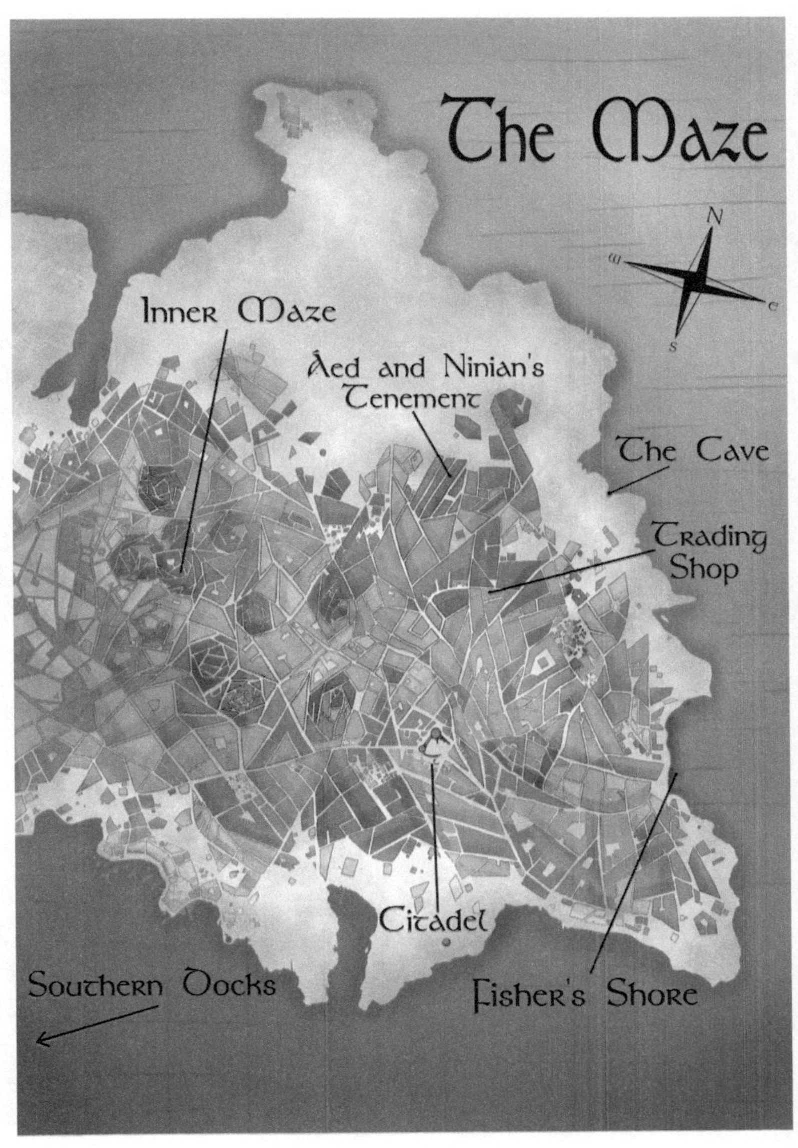

Receive a color version of the map by email: **tinyurl.com/tlpmap**

GLOSSARY

Amadán:	Fool
A thiarcais:	My goodness
Buachaill Cladaigh:	Shore-boy
Daidí:	Daddy
Cad é?:	What?
Ceann beag:	Little one
In ainm dé!:	Damn!
Mamaí:	Mummy

PRONUNCIATION GUIDE

Áed	Aid
Ailbhe	Alva
Brígh	Bree
Cahir	Care
Cuimín	Kuh-meen
Fiadh	Fee-ah
Laoise	Leesha
Máel Máedóc	My-ell My-eh-doc
Ruairí	Rory
Seoirse	Shor-sha

PART ONE

CHAPTER ONE

"Ey!" The wiry peddler's cuff landed solidly on Ninian's ear, and the boy dropped the roll of black bread he'd been trying to steal, which landed back on the peddler's tray. "Not today!"

Scowling, Ninian rubbed his smarting ear. The peddler's hand had been rough, her touch hardened by labor, though Ninian wasn't sure how a baker could have so many calluses.

The peddler wagged a finger at him. "Don't give me that look, child. You pay, or you get out o' my sight." Her face, full enough that Ninian could tell she wasn't starving, folded into a stern frown. "I've had enough o' you little street rats taking my hard work. Move on!"

Ninian growled, glancing around the bustling thoroughfare. Heads had turned toward the mild commotion. "Pig," he snarled, wishing he'd had a better insult ready. It didn't help that his voice hadn't changed yet. He still had a couple of years before he'd stand a chance of being intimidating. With the bread so close to him—he'd *held* it in his *hand*—his stomach felt like it was chewing a hole in itself.

Every vendor on this street had a wary eye on Ninian now, and he hadn't even gotten the roll for his effort. "Get on, now!" the woman urged, flapping her hands at him. "Shoo!"

He spat, and, dodging another blow from the baker, shoved through the throng of people and broke into a run down the street.

Ninian paused for a moment in a soot-painted alley, catching his breath in the midwinter air. He could never run as far when he was hungry enough to feel faint. He blinked hard a few times, shaking his head. This was the longest time in a while that he'd gone without food. Three days, he'd guess.

It hadn't been the best week.

He had been living—squatting, really—in the unused back room of a weaver's shop for the last month. The room had been warm, smelling pleasantly of wool, and Ninian hadn't minded the constant creak of the rickety spinning wheel. Once the shop owner had thrown him out, though, Ninian hadn't even been able to steal a bite to eat; he'd apparently used up all his luck.

Gathering himself, he slipped around a few men drinking in the shadows and emerged into sunlight on another street. He needed to try again, but he'd have to be more careful this time.

Slipping his hands into the warmth of his pockets, he swept his eyes up and down the road. It wasn't as busy as the first one, so he had less cover, but he spotted a ratty awning over a stand that looked promising and hurried in that direction. As he neared the stand, he peeked through the people and let out a little breath of satisfaction. The stand was draped in shriveled sausages, and the table was covered in packets of jerky and cured meats. Narrowing his eyes in concentration and ignoring the pang in his stomach, Ninian targeted a link of sausage at the very edge of the table, farthest from the woman behind the stand. He wasn't the only one; a very tall young boy and a girl with tangled dreadlocks were closing in as well.

Ninian approached the stand as casually as he could while hastening to arrive before his competition, afraid to blink for fear his sausage would vanish. His mouth began to water. When he was close enough to smell the salty smoke of the meat, he ran for it.

His fingers closed around the link, and when he pulled it free of the chain, another sausage came with it. Triumphant, he turned to make his escape.

"Not so fast!"

There was a tearing sound, and, stopped by a foot on the hem of his taupe cloak, Ninian tripped. The sausages flew out of his hand as he hit the ground hard. "No!"

He scrambled forward, ripping the edge of his cloak under the stall-owner's boot, and grasped frantically for the meat, but another hand had already snatched it up.

It was gone.

Ninian rolled over, propped on his elbows, and glared at the meat-monger while his breath shuddered in his chest. The vendor returned the look and released Ninian's cloak. "What's the big idea, boy?"

Ninian couldn't seem to form words. He'd *had* it! He'd practically tasted the salt and fat on his tongue.

He wanted to cry.

Instead, Ninian forced himself shakily to his feet and stumbled through the crowd before the meat-monger could kick him.

Where else could he go? The Fisher's Shore might be worth a try—it was always busy with fishermen, their tables heavy with glassy-eyed fare—but not only were the fishers always on the lookout for thieves, the thought of walking all the way to the Fisher's Shore made Ninian want to fall where he stood.

When he broke free of the crowd, he stopped and caught his breath. The Fisher's Shore was far, but if Ninian headed to the coast, he might find something to fill his mouth. So, he wrapped his tattered cloak more tightly around himself and set off purposefully toward the water.

He stayed on populated streets because that's where the food was. He passed a woman whose face was covered in a thousand freckles and two twin boys with hair whiter than the sun against glass. A girl with a wooden leg argued with an older man whose beard reached his broad leather belt, and someone wearing a grinning wooden mask sold withered mushrooms off a tray.

Ninian hurried past everyone not selling food. The vendors seemed wise to him—maybe he'd stolen from them in the past. He hadn't exactly kept track. Longing rose in his throat even at the sight of the masked man's wrinkled, grayish mushrooms.

"My dear!"

Ninian stopped short, somehow feeling like the call was addressed to him.

"Yes, you! With the pretty red hair!"

Turning with a frown, Ninian saw a woman standing at a table of little amulets, the sort made by knotting bits of string deliberately over and over. His eyes, searching for food, had skipped right over it.

"You need a charm, don't you, my dear? Keep away magic? Keep away fae?" She grinned a brown-toothed smile when she saw him looking. "Faeries like to steal the hearts of pretty little children, my dear."

"I'm not your dear," Ninian snapped reactively. Despite only having eleven years, Ninian hadn't considered himself a child for a long time. "And anyhow," he said, "those are a waste of perfectly good string." He pulled up his hood.

He felt lightheaded as he hurried through the splitting, tangled streets—and thirsty too. He always got thirsty when he was hungry, and it occurred to him that heading to the sea might not have been his brightest idea. Still, the nearest freshwater well was nestled deep in the heart of the city, in the courtyard of a crumbling old citadel, and Ninian was much too close to the northeastern fringes of the Maze to consider going back now. The worn-out city was true to its name, and winding through its labyrinth of streets would take longer than Ninian thought he could bear. He'd have to find something to eat on the shore, and that would make everything better.

The smell of the shore hit Ninian before he saw the ocean. He peeked eagerly between the buildings, hoping at least to spot a fisher's boat dragged up onto the coast. There was certainly no point in stealing a boat—he had no idea how to use one, and he couldn't swim—but if a fisher had been careless, Ninian might find something inside. Once, he'd found an entire fish, and bony though it was, he'd been tempted to eat it raw.

Unfortunately, as his violet eyes swept the expanse of the seaside, all he found were swells breaking against the rocky beach, sliding down ropes of black algae with a low-tide stench.

A salty wind blew Ninian's hair back and made his cloak snap as he neared the shore, and he squinted through the tears it drew to his eyes. The coast was black and craggy rock, and the Red Sea hissed as it ran back and forth between the jagged stones.

Whichever gang was in charge of this region had arranged torches on spindly poles along the coast, probably to guide the boats toward land—the only decent thing they ever did, Ninian's father had always said. Ninian suspected the gangs cared less about the fishers' safety and more about luring them in to take some of their catch, but nobody had lit the torches anyway.

The sun was sinking behind the buildings to the west, dropping over the faraway cliffs that separated the Maze from the mainland. Ninian imagined for a moment the city that sat out of sight atop those stony bluffs, doubtlessly bathed in the last warmth of the day; the sun's light would cast the White City's buildings into shades of gold. There, people would be settling in for a hot meal before turning in to sleep in downy beds. His mother had told him stories of the White City, and thinking of them never failed to spark jealousy at a life of such fabled luxury.

Ninian shook his head hard. *There probably aren't even people left up there.* All he had were old legends; he could not afford to indulge them. The way to the White City had been lost. Ninian lived in the Maze. It was the way of things.

His stomach growled, and he sat heavily on one of the rocks to avoid falling when his head spun.

Catching movement in the corner of his eye, he turned to see a cormorant preening on a spur of basalt.

Perking up, Ninian bit his lip.

It was a large bird, sooty black, and it cocked its head this way and that as it ruffled its feathers. "Hmm," Ninian mused under his breath. "It's too early for you to have a nest, right?" He'd never gotten his hands onto eggs any sooner than early spring, and it was still wintertime. The bird seemed to shake its head, shifting its weight on broad webbed feet. Slowly, so it would not see him, Ninian slid from his seat. Without taking his eyes off the cormorant, his searching hands found a rock the right size for throwing.

Aside from rats, gulls, and crows, there were very few animals in the Maze. To the west of the city, farmers raised cows, hogs, and sheep, and far off the coast, where the iron-red water became a healthy blue, Ninian knew there were fish. But in the city itself, and all along the coast, the only creatures that survived were those that could hide or fly away from hungry human hands. Storm petrels came to land sometimes in the autumn, when tempests churned over the Red Sea, and loons visited often in winter, but they were good at evading capture.

This cormorant, though, was Ninian's.

He weighed the rock carefully in his palm. He needed to hit the bird's head, or else it would simply fly off, affronted. Slowly, he crept nearer. When the cormorant was only a few arm-lengths away, Ninian squatted behind a jagged rock and took a deep breath.

With as much precision as he could, he hurled his stone at the seabird.

It struck the cormorant in the back, and the bird let out a grating screech and tumbled, surprised, off of its perch. It landed awkwardly on its feathered chest just as a wave plumed up the coast, and Ninian vaulted over his rock and ran across the shore. Water soaked up to Ninian's knees as he lunged for the flapping cormorant, but the wave was retreating, and the bird was getting its bearings. Just as Ninian reached it, its wings beat in a frenzy, and it skidded off across the surface of the water. It settled on the waves about ten yards out, making coughing sounds in wounded disapproval.

Now wet, freezing, and *still* hungry, Ninian yelled at the cormorant until he was hoarse.

It had started to rain. Ninian miserably pulled his hood up, his eyes fixed on the puddles gathering between the cobblestones and trudged through the emptying streets.

There was a spot he often went to when it was wet, a nook behind Orrin's Alehouse. It wasn't warm, but it was dry enough, and sometimes if bread got burned to the point of inedibility, or if it went uneaten long enough to grow an excess of mold, Orrin tossed it into the alley. Ninian had eaten plenty of bad bread from the waste of Orrin's Alehouse.

Suddenly, Ninian perked up his head, and his hood fell back.

Breaking into a trot, he followed a faint, enticing sound, darting through a crooked alley until it opened into a tiny, sunken courtyard.

Ninian's jaw dropped. "*In ainm dé.*"

The rain was flowing in rivulets down the gutter of the alley. It pooled in the middle of the courtyard at least as deep as a forearm.

And in the middle of the pool, there was a duck.

Cormorants and loons were one thing. They were quick birds, ocean birds, birds designed to survive through their speed. Ducks, on the other hand… "How has nobody eaten you yet?" Ninian asked it, aghast. Carefully, he unclasped his cloak for maximum maneuverability.

And he dove at the duck.

Frigid water soaked his clothes, and the duck let out a squawking racket, flapping across the pool. Ninian lunged for it, his hair plastered to his face, and the duck fought ferociously. Ninian rolled onto his back in the puddle, clutching the duck to his chest as it pecked at his hands and arms. He wrestled his hands up to its neck, and the bird thrashed desperately, quacking in terror.

He pinned it under his knee, catching his breath. If he were in one of his mother's stories—which would be only *slightly* less shocking than Ninian catching a duck to eat all on his own—this would be the part where some wicked fae trickster across the veil released the madness it had sown in Ninian's mind, revealing the duck to be a rabid rat or a hunk of driftwood. Ninian laughed exhaustedly, watching the duck struggle with fear. "Hope not."

Crack.

Panting, Ninian pushed himself to a seat in the puddle, holding the broken-necked duck. He sat there for a moment in awe, staring at his prize: it was a lovely thing, light brown with reddish streaks on its back and a precious round head.

Ninian's mouth watered.

Hurriedly, he splashed out of the puddle with the duck under his arm and quickly bundled it into his cloak. He couldn't let anyone steal it. He'd have to pluck the soft down away, and then sneak an ember out of Orrin's hearth. The alehouse kept firewood in a shed behind it, and Ninian didn't think anyone would notice if he took a bit.

Today was becoming a good day.

Full of excitement, he broke into a run toward what, for at least that night, was home.

CHAPTER TWO

Over a smoky fire of damp wood, Ninian's duck roasted on a stick. The light of the little blaze set the dead end of the alley into flickering shadow, sparks twitching into the sky, and the breeze caused the smoke to spiral around itself.

A noise came sharply from the alley's side, and Ninian looked up, instantly on guard. "Orrin," he said, identifying the source of the sound. The man had opened the tavern's back door and leaned into the night. Ninian edged away warily. "What do you want?"

The alehouse-owner shrugged. "Ain't I allowed to step outside my own tavern?" He sniffed, his rawboned face shifting into a grin. "'Specially when it smells like *this* out here."

"It's mine," Ninian said quickly, his posture growing even more defensive. "I'll kill you."

But Orrin only chuckled. "Won't be necessary." He folded his hands easily behind him and drew a deep breath of the evening air. "I got food o' my own." Squinting at Ninian, he sucked at his stained teeth. "Ain't you back here pretty often, kid?"

Ninian glared, still feeling nerves prickle over his skin. He didn't like being alone with Orrin. He didn't answer.

The truth was that before squatting in the weaver's shop, he'd been behind the alehouse every night for two weeks. There was a little overhang that kept off light rain. Since then, he'd come back often to steal firewood and old bread.

Orrin took in Ninian's still-wet clothes, ragged cloak, and tangled russet hair. "You haven't got a home, do you?"

"What's it to you?"

Orrin shrugged. "You musta done some real good praying to get a dinner like that."

Ninian's lip curled. "I don't *pray*."

"Ah. I'll bet that explains a lot." Orrin sighed heavily, the firelight making his face look craggy and wise. "You oughta try sometime."

"If I wanted platitudes, I'd find a cleric." Ninian had seen clerics before, and they were rare. Honoring the Gods wasn't exactly a profession that kept anybody fed. "Go away."

Clearly unsure what a "platitude" was, Orrin stared at Ninian blankly for a few breaths. Ninian didn't relax his defensive stance. "Well," the man said eventually. "I don't want no feral children hanging around my alehouse. Eat and move on."

"It's not your alley," Ninian shot back. "I'll stay where I want."

"Not if I make you move." He raised an eyebrow, and Ninian didn't doubt that the man would try. Ninian's lip raised in a half-snarl, and Orrin turned back inside the alehouse and left him alone.

Releasing his breath in a huff, Ninian relaxed his posture and turned back to the unevenly roasting duck with a shiver. His clothing was wet. He was freezing. He hated Orrin. He hated everyone like Orrin, especially the ones with a roof over their head and the nerve to think that life was fair. "'Pray for it,'" Ninian mocked quietly, turning the duck. He'd done plenty of praying in the past. "*Amadán.*"

He settled cross-legged a safe distance from the fire and stared at the duck's browning skin. He could imagine it in his mouth so vividly he was tempted to take it from the fire and eat it as it was, but his father had once done that to a skua his mother had been cooking—had winked at Ninian like it was their little secret—and then had vomited for three straight days. So Ninian just stared at his dead bird covetously and imagined what it would taste like once it was done.

"I don't think I'll be able to eat you all at once, will I?" Ninian mused at the duck, frowning thoughtfully. "I guess that's a nice problem to have."

The sky was a mottled, milky lavender, and darkness was gathering fast. Soon, glowing embers and the occasional tongue of flame fluttering up from the coals cast the only light—and only warmth—in the alley. Ninian wrapped his cloak around himself as tightly as he could and pulled his hood up over his still-damp hair, but the air cut bitterly. His fingers had gone rather numb, and he was shivering painfully hard. Carefully, he moved closer to the fire.

After a long silence punctuated only by the occasional gust of freezing wind, footsteps echoed down the alley.

He'd just been warming up a bit, so it was with reluctance that Ninian turned away from the cooking duck and readied himself to defend his prize. Fortunately, the footsteps were light, and there was only one pair of them.

His eyes were dazzled from staring into the embers, so at first, Ninian could see only the silhouette of his unwanted visitor. It looked small. "Who are you?" Ninian demanded.

"Oh," the figure said. It was a little girl's voice, but Ninian didn't dare relax. "I just thought I smelled..."

"It's mine," Ninian said.

"Right," the girl said, drooping.

Ninian dropped his defensive crouch as the girl's footsteps began to pad off down the alley again. Ninian squinted; he didn't think she was wearing shoes. The warm firelight made the duck's skin sparkle with drops of grease, as if the roasting bird was a beacon, but that light only set the girl into the suggestion of a shape against the night. The shadows looked like they might swallow her, and Ninian thought that if they did, she'd vanish for good.

"Wait," he said. The girl halted uncertainly with a flinch. "It's mine, but…" He looked at the dripping duck, the duck he couldn't possibly eat all at once, and felt regret turn in his stomach even as he spoke. "You can have some."

The girl turned around in a snap. Her hands splayed out in surprise. "*Really?*"

Ninian nodded, tugging at his fingers so that his joints popped. "It isn't finished cooking yet. But I'll give you some when it is."

Timidly, the girl approached the fire and, when Ninian didn't snarl at her, lowered herself into a cross-legged seat. In the closer firelight, Ninian confirmed that her feet were bare, filthy, and cracked. She was younger than he was—he'd guess six or seven—but she had the look in her eyes of someone who'd grown up fast. "I'm Kelp," she said.

Ninian blinked. "You're what?"

The girl had eyes so light that Ninian couldn't tell what color they were—the fire washed them orange, and the night sky washed them dark—and she blinked them at Ninian like he'd missed something obvious. "I'm Kelp. What's your name?"

"Ninian," said Ninian. "Your name is really—"

"Well, no," she said, uncrossing her legs and stretching her feet toward the fire. "But I saw some on the docks earlier, and I thought it looked pretty, so today I'm Kelp."

"And… what will you be tomorrow?" Ninian asked.

"Dunno." The girl shrugged. Her hair fell into her face, and she crossed her eyes to glare at it. "Where'd you get a bird?"

"It's a duck. I caught it."

"Wow." With a sigh, Kelp fixed her gaze on the duck and stopped blinking. Her focus could easily have been mistaken for worship, despite the fact that her hair wouldn't stay out of her eyes, and Ninian couldn't imagine she could see very well. "How long 'til it's finished?"

"Not long, I think," Ninian said, unable to hide the anticipation in his own voice. Now that he didn't think she was going to make off with his dinner, Ninian didn't mind Kelp's presence. It wasn't, of course, the first time he'd interacted with the Maze's network of homeless children, but they were invariably a wary bunch, self-sufficient and more mature than their small frames and big-eyed faces could attest. He'd never spent much time talking to anyone.

Night wind gusted down the alley, and while Ninian shivered, the girl huffed in frustration as her hair, the color of dandelion fluff, flew into her face. She shoved it back, muttering.

"Do you want me to braid it?" Ninian asked.

Kelp stared at him like he'd sprouted a third eye. "What?"

Ninian shook his head and turned back to the fire. "Never mind."

"No, no," the girl said. "Did you say you could braid my hair?"

Ninian nodded. Without hesitating, Kelp deposited herself in front of Ninian and crossed her legs. "Do it."

Ninian blinked in surprise at the light tresses in front of him. Most of the street children he'd met weren't nearly so quick to trust, but Ninian supposed he didn't look all that threatening. And he *had* agreed to share his dinner, which perhaps was enough for this strange girl to decide he was all right.

"Oh." He hesitated to touch her for a moment. She peeked over her shoulder, and he let out a quick breath. He started combing the girl's hair back with his fingers, feeling the dirty waves shift under his touch. Starting from the left side, he separated the hair into three and began weaving it together.

"How do you know how t'do that?" the girl asked. Her voice suddenly sounded kind of sleepy, and when Ninian leaned around to look, he saw that her eyelids had drooped with pleasure so her pale lashes lay on her cheeks.

"I used to braid my sister's hair," he said.

"Feels nice," Kelp sighed. "Where's your sister now? Are you waiting for her?"

Ninian's fingers stopped in Kelp's hair, and it was with conscious effort that he made them move again. "No. She died."

"Oh. Sorry 'bout that."

Letting out a long breath, Ninian reached the end of Kelp's hair and twisted the last three strands around each other. "It was two years ago. My parents too."

"How?" Kelp asked bluntly, and Ninian sucked in a little breath through his teeth.

"A fever," he said. "We all were sick, but they never got better." He wound up the long braid and tucked it into itself on the back of the girl's head. Examining his work, he adjusted a few loose strands and sat back. "There."

Kelp touched it and smiled. "You're good at that."

Ninian just turned his attention back to the duck, which was browned and dripping juice. He cast about for something to poke it with, located a stick, and prodded at the bird; it was firm. "I think this is done."

Kelp jumped to her feet as Ninian carefully took the bird off the fire. "Here," Kelp said. There was a ripping sound, and then she handed Ninian a scrap of her tunic. "Touch it through this, so you don't burn."

"Don't tear your clothes," Ninian said automatically, but he accepted her offering. He wrapped it around one of the duck's feet and with a solid pull, tore the leg off messily. He handed it to Kelp, who took it with her hand inside her sleeve. Grease soaked through her cuff, but she paid it no mind as, ignoring the steam, she ripped off a chunk of meat with her teeth.

After removing the other leg with similar brutality, Ninian set the bird and its skewer back over the fire before tearing into his portion.

When both of them held nothing but clean bones and a leathery foot, they set about using their fingers to pry meat off of the duck's breast, stripping it to ribs and heart and liver—a skeleton dripping innards over a dying fire that flared with each new drop of fat.

⦚

With his stomach full, weariness settled over Ninian as he sat against the wall of the alley and licked grease off his fingers. On her back, Kelp lay like a dead sea star, mumbling contentedly to herself while the fire spat fading sparks into the night.

If Ninian owned anything worth stealing, he wouldn't allow himself to close his eyes while Kelp was there—but he didn't. So, though sleep seemed disinclined to visit, he let his eyes fall shut and listened to his own thoughts.

Sometime in the night, he heard Kelp quietly leave him, slipping out of the alley into the maze of silent streets.

He kept his eyes closed and let her go.

〉〉〉

Sleep must have brushed over him at some point in the night, for he woke in the morning before the sun. Frozen dew lay over everything, sparkling in the dimness that preceded sunrise, and Ninian sat before the ashes of the fire while a new day slowly broke over the city.

He was alone again.

Eventually, he got tired of sitting with only the quiet for company, so he stood, checked the bare duck carcass for any meat he might have overlooked the night before, and headed into the streets as the sun rose. He believed in Orrin's threat about expelling him from the alley, and he didn't want to wait around.

The city was waking as he scuffed his feet over the cobblestones, watching his breath mist. There was cold fog rolling in fast from the sea, and the sunlight penetrated it, making rainbows that winked in and out as Ninian's passing eddied the fog.

Nobody's eyes stayed on Ninian for long. He was nothing more than another ragged child, commonplace and invisible. Usually, he took advantage of this to steal what he could, but for the first time in a very long time, he wasn't desperately hungry, and his invisibility just felt lonely.

He whistled quietly to himself, the noise echoing strangely until it sounded haunted. Though the weather wasn't as cold as it had been the previous day, and all that remained of the rain were puddles shining darkly through the silver mist, it didn't feel like the sky had settled. Maybe the air smelled faintly electric, or maybe the fog was just a little too still, but the longer Ninian walked through the quiet, morning streets, the more certain he became that a storm was on the way. "There's always a storm on the way," he muttered. This time of year was horrid for that. He hated the damp, oppressive clouds.

He sniffed the air and frowned. It smelled like ice, and the fog was frigid on his exposed skin, slipping under the cuffs of his pants.

Not rain, then, but a snowstorm.

It was time to find another place to stay. Maybe this time he could find one that would last—that would be nice. Now that he'd eaten, shelter was his priority, especially with a blizzard on the way. He could not be outside for that.

He didn't let himself feel his exhaustion.

He vaulted a low wall, old stone crumbling under his palms, and set his course away from the sea. If he was looking for shelter, the wettest place in the city wouldn't be his first choice.

⸹

The skeleton of what once must have been a rat peered at Ninian from a gravelly ditch, and Ninian kicked it so that the tiny bones scattered over the cobblestones. Then he broke into a jog and, skirting the edges of the noxious Inner Maze, kept moving.

He'd rarely been so far out of the city proper—it was far from everything he needed to survive. Though buildings still pressed out of the earth like ancient, manmade fungus, there were fewer people. The Maze, he remembered his mother explaining, had once been home to more people than it could comfortably hold. It had been a city kingdom in its own right, and the districts at its fringes had been just as alive as the Inner Maze.

The Maze's putrefaction hadn't been its own fault, Ninian's mother had said. It had been as glorious as any city until the White City on the top of the cliffs cut off contact with the people below and took the money with it. They left the sea for the Maze—skinny fish and salty soil.

That, and a hundred empty buildings. Turns out, skinny fish and scrawny, salted crops couldn't support very many people.

Now, at the fringes of the Maze, there was nothing to steal, nothing to cultivate, and the buildings crouched empty, as if waiting for inhabitants. "Happy to oblige," Ninian told them.

He spent a while poking his head into various tenements, trying to find one that didn't smell like death or house a colony of vermin. He wasn't picky, really, but if he could avoid rat bites, he would.

Eventually, in a tenement so far from the Inner Maze—and everything else—that Ninian was sure it had been abandoned for at least half a century, he dropped to a seat against the wall. A crooked staircase meandered upward, and the first-floor walls were covered in soot-painted pictographic graffiti, surely the markings of a long-dead gang. Dust hung all around, catching the dim light. But the air was as dry as he could hope, and there was glass in the windows, so after admiring his prize for a few moments, Ninian pushed himself up and braved the stairs. They creaked loudly under his weight but seemed solid enough.

He stopped at the second floor and tried the door. It stuck halfway, so he leaned his thin weight against it and shoved. It came unstuck with so much force that the handle flew out of his hands, and the door hit the wall. Ninian cringed. Inside, two rooms met at an empty doorway, and grayish wooden cabinets hung sadly from the wall in the corner. Ninian gave a low whistle. "This is *nice*." He wondered how long he'd be able to stay before someone else decided they liked this spot. Probably a while. It wasn't like there weren't other places to choose from.

It was common knowledge that higher floors were safer from various breakers-in, but Ninian didn't feel like checking if he'd fall through the stairs on the next flight. He crossed to the window to see the wind picking up, the fog skirting over the ground as sleet began to fall. It was going to be a stormy night, and the building creaked as if to underscore the thought.

Despite the feast of duck the night before, he was starting to feel the day without food. He'd have to get more tomorrow before things got too desperate. For now, though… "I'm not going outside tonight," he said to himself with a sigh, dropping to a seat under the window. "Fucking done with being cold." The duck had been worth the soak, but he'd shivered for so long afterward that he was actually sore.

The building groaned, the wind pressed on the old slats and crept through the windows, and Ninian flopped onto his back on the floor and crossed his arms behind his head. Lonely, yes, but safe, and sheltered, and he could stay here.

He could do that.

CHAPTER THREE

It took Ninian longer than he would have liked to find his way back from his new den, and he struggled to orient himself among the winding backstreets. The sun had begun to rise before he recognized familiar landmarks. He thought his sense of direction was all right, but… well, he supposed the city was called The Maze for a reason.

He walked quickly through the streets, which were still shining with ice from the night before. Not many vendors were outside. The sky still looked threatening, and Ninian was sure that nobody wanted to risk damaging their wares. That left a few options: the Fisher's Shore, which would be nearly empty—storms kept the boats from leaving, and if the boats didn't leave, there could be no fish—or one of the few trading shops. The trading shops weren't Ninian's favorite places. Anyone could bring anything to a shop, and if the shopkeeper thought people would want it, the trader would give the seller a few coins and vend their ware at a higher price. Plenty of people—cobblers, blacksmiths, farmers—didn't bother selling their own goods; they just sold to a trading shop where they'd have a better chance of finding a buyer. It was the way the world worked, Ninian knew, but it also meant that he didn't stand a chance of affording much of anything.

He wasn't sure how much food a trading shop would carry, but his options were limited, and he needed to try. He was definitely ready to settle for unperishable, salt-hard meat, or even a shriveled parsnip or two.

To his knowledge, three trading shops existed in the city. One was in the deepest part of the Inner Maze, a place even Ninian hesitated to go. The Inner Maze was a warzone of feuding gangs, and the poor fool who set foot on the wrong turf was sure to meet a grisly end.

Another was so tiny that Ninian wondered how the owner fed herself. He didn't think she could afford to buy enough goods to resell because he'd seen her sitting outside her shop, begging for customers on her knees.

The third, though… the third seemed promising. It was run by a giant of a shopkeeper, a man by the name of Máel Máedóc. His shop was always full—a little bit of everything moving in, a little bit of everything moving out. His reputation was terrifying, and Ninian would have liked to avoid the place, but… surely, he could slip in and out unseen. Máel Máedóc might have a giant's stature and no tolerance for thieves, but surely even the most unyielding and brutally upright of men could do nothing about what they did not notice.

His mind made up, Ninian danced around a puddle and headed in the direction of Máel Máedóc's.

⌇⌇⌇

Máel Máedóc's shop was crooked. The lintel sagged unevenly over a door that had been gradually shaved lopsided by wearing against the tilted doorframe. The shutters hung at odd angles, and the shingles of the roof skewed toward the ground, as if they were about to slide off.

Ninian took a deep breath.

He'd heard a story once, about a man who'd been caught pilfering a single spool of twine from Máel Máedóc. The shopkeeper, disgusted by the man's slippery ways, had not rested until he'd found the thief—and when he did, he'd killed the man with one blow, saying that the man's morals had been as dirty as his soul.

Ninian really hoped that story wasn't true.

Fueled by his empty stomach, Ninian turned the bent knob and slipped inside. Beyond the door, candles burned on the walls, not quite high enough to set the ceiling on fire, but too low to be safe around anybody's hair. The place was dim despite the tallow tapers' flickering illumination, and it smelled of smoke and sweat and stale bread.

Bread! That was a good sign.

Maybe because it was still early, or maybe because of the overnight storm, the shop wasn't as busy as Ninian would have liked. Haggling customers made the most reliable cover— they occupied a merchant's attention in addition to providing physical chaos. Fortunately, the inside of the shop was just as crooked as the outside. Lopsided shelves blocked the line of sight in every direction, and in a moment, Ninian had hurried into twisting aisles.

Fishnets in bundles. Sacks of oats that were far too big to steal. Scraps of tin, scavenged off of some or another roof. Ninian cracked his knuckles with a touch of anxiety, peeking all around for something he could eat. He pushed aside a couple of sheepskins hanging from the ceiling and peered into the cool darkness behind them. "Not bad cover," he whispered. There might be something hidden there that was worth taking. In a moment, he'd vanished into the shadowed hollow.

In the dimness of his woolly screen, Ninian had to stop and absorb the sight.

Clusters of rowan berries strung between the shelves alongside chains of sausages. Hard black bread, the sort that would break the teeth but never go bad. Salted fish. Pots of honey and hazelnuts. Dulse. Dried apples. Cheese. Heath-fruits. Winter-desiccated carrots and parsnips bundled together by their wilting greens.

Ninian's jaw dropped.

He'd never seen so much food in one place. His stomach growled of its own accord, and Ninian wrapped his arms around his middle. Aghast, he reached out to touch a shriveled carrot, as if he might be imagining it. "Doesn't seem quite right, does it?" he said under his breath, awestricken. "For one person to have all this?" It would have fed a whole family for months, probably even the whole winter. This stash would rot before anyone alone could finish it all.

Máel Máedóc couldn't possibly miss a little bit of it.

Before he'd consciously given himself permission, Ninian had an apple in his hand, and then an apple in his mouth and a sausage in his hand, then a sausage in his mouth and a fistful of hazelnuts in his palm. He ate without thinking. He gnawed on bricklike bread. He ripped chunks out of cheese. He drank honey like it was water.

It was paradise. The food never ran out; his reaching hands always landed on something else, and without thinking, Ninian ate. He couldn't believe that this had been here all this time, waiting while he starved in the streets… it didn't matter anymore. He was here, feasting as in a story of a grand wedding or a banquet after a glorious battle, and the voice of reason in the back of his mind went silent for the first time in as long as he could remember.

He was more satisfied than he'd been after the duck, more satisfied than he'd been since his mother and father had made him pray before meals of fish and cabbage and sloe jam. This was *paradise*. This was—

His heart stuttered.

The realization of what he'd done constricted around his chest as he set down a half-empty jar of pickled carrots.

When he stole, he stole and ran. If peddlers came after him, they just kicked him a few times, took back what was theirs, and Ninian tried again somewhere else.

This was different.

He had been distracted for too long. He had let his guard down, and he had... oh, Gods. He looked around the shelves. Empty jars. Ravaged cheese. Scattered nuts.

He had lost control.

He pressed his hands over his mouth.

He needed to run.

"Boy."

Ninian's heart plummeted to his full stomach.

Slowly, he turned around. At the last moment, he squeezed his eyes closed as if he couldn't be hurt by that which he couldn't see. As if he didn't already know the lie of such foolishness.

"Open your eyes, boy."

Ninian did. And shrank back as, once again, his heart lurched.

He had seen Máel Máedóc from afar. The man was one of the most powerful people in the whole city—*the* most powerful man without a gang behind him—and even from a distance, it was clear that he carried that power in his very being. But up close... Máel Máedóc's eyes burned a brilliant, hot blue in the light of the candle he carried, and his hair was braided back severely against his scalp.

On the left side of his face—a face that was all sturdiness and hard angles—a single scar split his dark skin.

"I'd ask what you were doing," Máel Máedóc said. "But I think it's pretty clear."

There was nothing for Ninian to say. The shopkeeper stood between Ninian and his escape, and even Ninian didn't have enough pent-up anger to hotheadedly fight Máel Máedóc. He couldn't run, couldn't fight, and wouldn't beg, and so he simply stood and stared with fear at the giant man before him.

"Nothing to say?" Máel Máedóc said, eyes narrowing dangerously.

Ninian swallowed hard. He'd die with the taste of honey on his tongue. Perhaps he couldn't ask for more than that, but the sweetness was turning bitter. "No, s-sir."

Máel Máedóc leaned back, a single eyebrow creeping up his forehead. "Did you say 'sir?'" He looked darkly amused. "What do you think you are, royalty?"

"Yes, sir." Ninian licked his lips nervously, wishing he could stop saying 'sir.' "It's old though, sir."

The shopkeeper set down the candle and let out a guffaw. "And I'm the King of the Maze."

"That's arguably true, sir," Ninian said. His voice had grown terribly small. At least he wasn't stuttering too badly; he'd struggled mightily with that when he was younger, and it still resurfaced when he got nervous— just like his proper manners. He wished he could shout at the shopkeeper, to lose his fear to blessed fury, but he had a feeling that would quickly end his life.

"Tell me, boy," Máel Máedóc said, and Ninian flinched as he saw Máel Máedóc's hand twitch. "Does *noble blood* mean you can help yourself to my things?"

Ninian shook his head. All of that food felt like it had hardened to a stone in the pit of his stomach. "N-no, sir."

Máel Máedóc leaned on the nearest shelf, which creaked and tipped to the side. For a long moment, he just stared at Ninian.

"I wonder," the giant shopkeeper said after a while, and Ninian did his best to stand tall. He didn't want to die cringing. "How many years you got?"

Ninian drew a shaky breath. "Eleven, sir."

"Eleven," Máel Máedóc repeated introspectively. He sighed. "I'll tell you something." He inclined his head toward Ninian conspiratorially. "If you were older and a little less pathetic, I would break your neck."

Ninian's breath caught in his throat.

The shopkeeper's bright blue eyes narrowed, and there was no mistaking the anger behind them. "But I'm not going to do that."

Ninian froze. And then he blinked. "W… what?"

Slowly, Máel Máedóc nodded. "I'm going to let you leave today."

It was a trap. The man was playing with him. Máel Máedóc, who tolerated no theft, whose moral code was legendary in the Maze, *had* to be joking.

Or worse… he wanted something.

Ninian took a step back, wrapping his arms around himself. "Please don't touch me."

Máel Máedóc clearly noted Ninian's expression. "I expected gratitude, boy."

Ninian shook his head. "Nothing's free. You wouldn't just let me leave."

"I'm no liar."

Ninian squeezed himself so hard it ached. His back hit a shelf, and he stumbled to the floor, where he scooted as far away from Máel Máedóc as he could.

Máel Máedóc frowned. "You're not wrong," he said after a little while. "What you've done isn't free. You can go, but I do expect to be repaid."

Ninian's eyes felt suddenly hot, and twin tears that he hadn't summoned rolled down his face. They surprised him. "Don't touch me, sir. I swear, I'll—" He hesitated, not sure if he should finish with a threat or a vow. The threat was tempting, but Ninian didn't think it would be effective, so he tripped over his words to manage "I'll do anything else you want."

The shopkeeper, through Ninian's tears, had begun to look troubled. "When I say repayment," he said slowly, "I mean money. You know that, right? Money." He lowered himself to a squat, bracing his elbows on his knees. "All I care about is the food you ate and the money you owe me for it."

It was hard to inhale normally, but Ninian focused on it until it felt more natural. "R-right."

"So here's the deal, boy. What is your name, anyway?"

He pushed himself shakily back to his feet. "Ninian."

"All right. Here's the deal, Ninian." Máel Máedóc stood as well, once again towering over Ninian like a mountain. "You get to pay me back for the food you ate." He crossed his arms and leaned forward, and Ninian did his best not to shrink back. "But boy," he said. "I don't want a single coin of stolen money."

Ninian gulped. "Then how…"

"Figure it out," the shopkeeper said flatly. "You work out how to be an honest young man, and we won't have any more problems." He extended his hand. "Deal?"

Looking at Máel Máedóc's callused hand, the alternative option hung in the air. *I would break your neck…*

Ninian shook.

"Good call," Máel Máedóc said. He stepped aside and held the sheepskins out of the way. "I'll be seeing you soon, Ninian."

There was no doubt in Ninian's mind that Máel Máedóc would enforce that.

Ninian's throat was tight, as if a millstone hung about it, and he was barely conscious of himself walking past the giant shopkeeper.

"Yes, sir."

CHAPTER FOUR

Ninian's head was empty. His palms were sweating, his heart had begun to race, and he didn't know quite why. The moment was past, and he had bigger things to worry about, but his brain was stuck on *don't touch me*.

"Focus," he muttered. He found the nearest building and squatted against it, pressing his head between his hands. "Come on, Ninian. Focus. You need money. Think about how to get money."

Don't touch me.

He shuddered and shook his head hard. No matter how deeply he breathed, his lungs didn't feel full enough.

"You're *fine*," he growled angrily at himself. "Get it *together*."

He forced himself to his feet and started walking as fast as he could so that his legs would burn and maybe it would break the cycle that kept running in his mind. He started into a run, and his breath came a little easier as the gray city raced by.

He was in debt.

Máel Máedóc owned a part of him. That's what debt was. Ownership.

Ninian wanted to throw up.

After a while, he stopped in a rare patch of sun and, with a shaky hand, pushed his hair out of his face.

"Better," he panted. "Gods."

He looked around, catching his breath and feeling the morning air scrape his lungs. This part of the city was familiar, but he didn't know it terribly well. It was full of short single-family homes in which lots of families lived at once, and ratty children younger than him watched as he braced his hands on his knees and gathered himself.

Just two years earlier, Ninian had lived in a neighborhood like this. It had been safe—as safe as the Maze could be— for it was full of families with protective parents to defend against gangs and vagabonds. Ninian remembered his father herding Ninian and his sister inside whenever danger presented itself while Ninian's mother went out to wreak graceful fury on whoever had threatened her community. When she came back in, she'd always held her children close and explain what she'd done. Someday, she'd said, it would be their turn. It would be their duty to keep people safe.

But Ninian was the vagabond now.

That period of his life was over.

Leaving the squat little houses behind, he turned back into the web of streets.

He must have unwittingly sprinted through some places he ordinarily avoided, for as soon as he was out of the familial neighborhood, the atmosphere of the city around him changed. It didn't feel as dangerous as the Inner Maze— nothing did—but it had a darkness to it from the soot that covered every brick surface. Fresh black graffiti covered older marks, wordless stories of blood and hate and desperation. This wasn't the sort of art that people scrawled harmlessly on the sides of busy streets. This was violent. Angry.

Ninian touched the closest wall with his fingertips. Soot came off in oily smudges and stayed on his skin.

Usually, he stayed away from places like this. Today, he was in no hurry to leave.

He shoved his hands into his pockets and walked deeper into the streets.

≀≀≀

Glinting, embittered eyes. Gaunt frames, even by the standards of the Maze. People glanced at Ninian like he might have something worth stealing before they turned away—Ninian knew the look.

This was not the place to find money. He reminded himself of that as he turned corner after corner, trying to get lost in the rotting streets. He couldn't run away, he knew, but the deeper he wound through the streets of the gritty neighborhood, the easier it was to ignore his situation.

He was so tired of thinking. He was so *angry*—most feelings felt better as anger, and that condensed behind his breastbone. It was safe to hate. Hatred didn't hurt.

A door opened abruptly in front of him, and a man stumbled out onto the street. He was an average man, with reddish hair and a square build. Ninian didn't know him.

Ninian turned away, pressing a palm to his mouth.

His head had begun buzzing, and his heart had started into an uneven gallop, firing icy-hot spines through his veins. "Oh—"

It was happening again. Sweat had broken out on his palms and temples, and Ninian tripped into a run. He sprinted away from the man he didn't know, feeling like he was falling.

People snapped at him in irritation as he shoved past. He barely noticed.

Damn kid.

Watch it!

Bloody—

The world looked funny, kind of yellow, and not as clear as it should be. He couldn't see anything but what was right in front of him as if the streets were closing in.

He didn't even *know* that man. But—

Someone grabbed his arm, swinging Ninian to a stop. "For Gods' sakes, kid," a man's voice said. "Watch where you're—"

That familiar heat spiked behind Ninian's breastbone, and he slammed his elbow into the man's face.

The man abandoned his grip on Ninian's arm, and Ninian tripped back, heart pounding. "What the..." The man touched his face, and his hand came away bloody. His expression darkened. "Why, you..."

Eyes widening, Ninian dodged a swing. Instinctively ducking, he launched himself up from a crouch into the man's space. Unable to land a blow at such close range, the man stumbled back, and Ninian took the opportunity to sweep his leg behind the man's ankle.

Ninian's head was clearing. As the man regained his balance, enraged, Ninian stepped to the side to let another swing go by. Once the man was off-balance with the force of the unmet strike, Ninian dropped, using the weight of his motion to drive his elbow hard into the man's kidney.

It was easier to breathe. A crowd had started to cluster around the fight, but Ninian's world had cleared to him and the stranger, and he didn't see them.

The fight had begun reactively, borne out of something he didn't understand, but this... he could handle this. Blows and dodges. That was all he needed to cope with. He didn't need to think. He just needed to move.

And he moved.

The man's fist landed on Ninian's shoulder, rocking Ninian back, and the man looked briefly jubilant.

Ninian didn't even feel it. He let the force of the impact turn him and sent his fist spinning into the man's neck. While the man choked, hands instinctively going to his throat, Ninian danced back, catching his breath.

He could feel his mother's hands guiding him, showing him where to strike and place his balance—he'd trained to fight, to defend, and maybe the man wasn't a threat at all, but Ninian couldn't stop.

This felt good. Better than the burning in his chest.

There was a sound he was having trouble processing, and as the man hacked, Ninian dared a glance around him.

The crowd.

The crowd was…

Cheering.

Ninian blinked. They couldn't be cheering for *him*, but to cheer for the man seemed foolish, if he was losing.

Ninian froze. *Wait.*

The man was losing. Ninian was fighting, and he was winning, and the man was *losing*!

A strange smile broke over Ninian's face, a too-sharp, half-mad smile that he could not dim, and without waiting any longer, he braced his foot against the curb and launched himself at the man.

The man didn't get his hands up in time. Ninian connected with his middle, driving his shoulder up under the man's ribs, and the man landed hard on his back, all the wind rushing from his lungs. He choked, rolling over and trying to inhale, but he did not get back up.

Ninian stepped back, panting, and let his hands fall.

The crowd had gone quiet. Slowly, murmurs reached Ninian's awareness, and he looked to find people gaping at him, their mouths starting to move. He blinked, trying to gather himself, and backed up a few steps before his feet hit the curb, and something inside of him went weak. He tripped and fell, and the ground swam before his eyes.

The noise of the crowd was pressing in on Ninian. He didn't know what to make of it, only that it was overwhelming and yet somehow not wholly bad, and… he was dizzy?

Somehow, the ground found its way under his shoulder. "Oh."

"Make way. For Gods' sakes, move it—let me through—oi! Kid!"

There was a new person now, a woman, and she knelt by Ninian's side. Ninian blinked at her, shuffling away as far as he could.

"Kid, are you all right?" The woman's eyes were wide and concerned, a bright yellow-green. "Are you hurt?"

Ninian swallowed drily. "I'm fine. Fine."

"Wait, wait," she said, holding out her palms placatingly. "Just wait a minute."

Using the corner of a building, Ninian struggled to his feet. The world, however, apparently wasn't done tipping, and he ended up on the ground again. "Leave me alone."

"Where are you going?"

That was a good question, actually. Ninian wasn't sure exactly where he was, but he was fairly certain that his new flat was farther away than he could walk at that moment. "Home," he said. "I'll be fine."

"Where's home?"

Ninian looked at her suspiciously. The crowd was dispersing behind her, losing interest since the fight had ended, but she didn't look like she was going to move. He made his way to his feet again, taking a deep breath to stop his head from spinning. "What's it to you?"

To his surprise, a touch of sadness entered the woman's face. "Look, kid," she said with a sigh. "I just want to help, okay?" She tipped her head from side to side like she was trying to get a crick out of her neck. "Your call, but there's a hot meal back at my place. Not much, but I'd share if you wanted it."

"I'm not hungry."

The woman looked at him skeptically. "Sure, you're not."

A drop of water landed on the ground between Ninian's feet, and then another one plinked off the edge of the roof. In a few moments, rain was spitting down, even though cold sunlight still crept through the clouds in a patchy attempt at dominance. Ninian swore under his breath.

"S'gonna rain all night," the woman said with a sigh, following his gaze skyward. "I can tell, I get a headache before it does that."

"It's *always* raining," Ninian growled.

The woman shrugged. "That's winter for ya." She fluffed the curly hair at the back of her neck. "Cold, wet, and miserable to be on the streets. You are on the streets, aren't you?"

Ninian felt himself hesitate a half-second too long. "No."

"Then I'll up my offer," the woman said. "I have a hot meal… and a roof." She tucked her hands into the crooks of her elbows as it started raining harder. "It's your choice. If you want to take me up on it, my place is the one with the green door, down this street to the right." She looked up at the sky, squinting against the raindrops. "I'm going to get inside now. Don't fancy having a bath." With a little wave, she turned away. "If I don't see you, take care of yourself."

The rain, now falling in a wind-gusted downpour, quickly obscured her retreating figure.

Ninian watched her go, and icy rainwater slid under his collar and down his spine. Already, he was shivering again.

This day had been horrible.

"Gods damn it all," he muttered.

After a few more seconds of rain-washed deliberation, he followed the woman down the street.

The green-doored tenement wasn't hard to find, though Ninian thought 'green' might have been a bit of an overstatement. It didn't look like it had ever actually been painted, but the wood was old enough to have sprouted lichen. Over the door, a bundle of rowan branches hung—it wasn't an uncommon sight, and Ninian knew it would do a better job warding off the fae than any knotted-string charm. When Ninian, lips pressed together, reluctantly rapped his knuckles on the door, it made a soft thudding sound.

It opened after just a few seconds, and Ninian found himself faced with a child maybe half his age. A little crust of snot ringed the girl's nose. "Who are you?"

"Ciara!" A voice called from farther inside, and then the yellow-eyed woman's head popped around the corner. "Let him in, Ciara."

The girl stepped aside, regarding Ninian curiously, and he slowly stepped inside. The woman smiled warmly at him and moved to close the door. "I'm glad you decided to come, dear. What's your name?"

The place was small, but uneven stairs led up to another floor. The walls were bare wood, but they blocked the wind, and the air was warm from a fire burning in a flat-stone hearth. "I'm Ninian," he said, hugging himself. He'd gotten soaked all over again.

"My name's Laoise," said the woman. "Here, I'll take your cloak, all right? Go an' sit by the fire, an' I'll bring you something to eat."

Still regarding everything with caution, Ninian shrugged off the cloak and obeyed.

Laoise hung it by the door, and, giving Ninian another smile, trotted up the stairs. The girl, Ciara, was staring at him. "What?" Ninian demanded, sitting a safe distance from the fireplace.

"You don' *look* like much," she said bluntly, scrubbing a finger under her nose.

Ninian frowned. "Neither do you."

She hmphed and followed her mother up the stairs.

Ninian let his eyes relax as he looked into the fire, listening to the ceiling creak. The warmth felt nice.

The building itself looked nicer than the tenement Ninian had found, if rather weathered, and as he looked around, he noticed that Laoise had an array of metal cooking ware hanging over the hearth and a couple of painted wooden bowls on the mantle shelf. A rug hung over the doorway, held aside by a nail, which surely helped to keep the heat in; on the ceiling, bundles of greens hung beside the occasional dried meat. Hooks on the wall held clothing and cloaks, and there was a little crate underneath them full of scarves, gloves, and hats. Laoise was definitely more well-off than Ninian would have expected anyone to be in this part of town—or in much of the Maze.

"Hey."

Startled, Ninian was on his feet faster than he could inhale.

Ciara looked surprised, and the tray in her hands rattled. "You *are* quick, though."

Exhaling, Ninian lowered himself to a cross-legged seat. "I didn't hear you."

The girl shrugged, crossing to the fireplace and setting the tray on the floor. "Bread and stew. That's beef."

"Beef?" The soup smelled heavenly. "I haven't had…"

Laoise laughed behind him, and Ninian jumped again. The woman leaned against the wall and slid to a seat inside the fireplace's circle of light. "Please, enjoy. There's more if you want it."

Ninian had picked up the spoon, but he paused, with it hovering over the stew's steaming surface. "Why are you doing this?"

The woman looked confused. "What do you mean?"

Using the spoon, Ninian poked at the bread and gestured around the cozy flat. "This. Letting me in. Giving me *beef*."

"I told you," Laoise said with a sigh, holding out her arm. Her daughter scampered under it. "I don't like t'see a child in your situation."

"I'm not the only one in my situation," Ninian said, narrowing his eyes. "Why don't you help the others too?"

"I do," she said. "When I can."

Tentatively, Ninian took a bite. He hadn't thought he could still be hungry after the stolen feast earlier that morning, but evidently, hunger was just a part of him now. He shivered as warmth filled his core.

He swallowed and looked around the room again. "Does anyone else, um… live with you?"

Laoise shook her head. "Nah. My man left us years ago."

"Oh." Ninian knew he should feel sorry, but instead, he felt a weight off his chest as if he'd been holding his breath without knowing it. "My condolences, I guess."

Laoise shrugged. "It was no great loss."

Ciara tugged her mother's sleeve. "Can I have some stew, *Mamaí*?"

"You already ate, Ra. But there's a spot more upstairs."

Grinning, the little girl ducked out from under Laoise's arm and darted up the stairs.

Laoise smiled tiredly at Ninian. "She's six," she said. "A bit of a handful." She tipped her head back against the wall. "I do worry about her, y'know? It's dangerous out there. Well, you know that. You look too young to be all alone."

Ninian gave a clipped laugh. "No such thing as too young."

"What do you mean?"

The stew steamed, and Ninian took another bite to avoid meeting her gaze. "Alone is better than lots of things," he said around the mouthful. "And I can handle myself."

"You did handle yourself very well out there, didn't you?" She looked thoughtful.

Ninian swallowed and didn't reply.

"Where'd you learn to fight like that?"

The bread was dark and rich, and Ninian tore off a piece, almost dunking in his stew before he remembered his proper manners. "My mum taught me when I was younger."

"Your mum? Taught you *that*?"

Ninian nodded.

Laoise scrutinized him. "You looked like you were dancing." A smile creased her face again. "It was something to see."

Ninian twisted his spoon in his fingers so his knuckles cracked. "Dancing and fighting aren't so different." His mother had worked so hard to raise a noble child. "Mum taught me lots of things."

Laoise licked her lips. "Well, I won't ask where she is now."

The last joint of Ninian's little finger let out a *pop*. "Good."

A few quiet moments later, Ciara came skipping back in, stew on her upper lip and bread in her hand. She nestled herself back under her mother's arm and resumed her scrutiny of Ninian. "You," she announced, "look like you're 'boutta die."

Ninian scowled at her. "Why, thank you."

Laoise cringed at her daughter's words, then shrugged in Ninian's direction. "You *do* look… a little tired."

"Your eyes have so much gray under them I thought it was dirt," Ciara clarified.

"Ciara," Laoise scolded. She turned her attention back to Ninian, who was brushing under his eyes to make sure it *wasn't* dirt. "Truly, though, when is the last time you slept?"

"Last night," he answered, a little prickly.

Laoise frowned, and he could tell her mother's intuition was about to pull apart his words. "For how *long*?"

"I don't know." He crossed his arms. "I don't need to sleep."

The sympathy in Laoise's face deepened. "Everyone needs to sleep."

"Fine," Ninian snapped, more sharply than he'd meant to. "I *can't* sleep." He looked away, feeling childish for losing his patience. "Happy?"

He heard Laoise's sigh without looking up. "No. Of course that doesn't make me happy."

Ninian chewed his lip as Laoise fell silent.

"Listen," Laoise said after a few breaths. "I know it's a little early, but… I'll get some blankets. Why don't you just try and close your eyes for a little while?"

"It…" Ninian let out a little breath. "It won't work."

"Just try," Laoise said. "Come now. Finish up your food, and I'll make you a bed."

A pang darted through Ninian's chest. He'd forgotten how it felt to be mothered.

It was nice.

Looking down into his bowl, he let out a long, deep breath.

He might be safe here—Laoise didn't seem particularly frightening, Ciara was just a child, and there was nobody else with them. There was rowan over the door and a fire in the hearth. He should consider himself lucky.

Slowly, he nodded, never breaking eye contact with his stew. "All right."

⸿

A draft drifted under the door, and it touched Ninian's face with cool air while the rest of him was blessedly warm under two blankets that Laoise had heated before the fire. Ciara lay on the other side of the little room, snoring quietly. She'd protested mildly at being put to bed so early, but in the end had fallen asleep fast. Nearest the door, as if protecting them both, lay Laoise, and the shadow of her body rose and fell with her steady breaths.

In the quiet, Ninian told his mind to relax.

He had a debt to Máel Máedóc, and he couldn't steal to pay it off. He had no doubt that if he nicked so much as a single coin, the shopkeeper would know, and he didn't know how to do it any other way. If he knew how to earn a living, he wouldn't have lived the way he did for so long.

With a sharp sigh, he rolled over. *For once*, he prayed to the Gods his parents had believed in, *just let me sleep.*

He had a full belly; he was warm, and, as far as he could tell, he was safe. *You'll never have a better chance*, he told himself. *Sleep now, and it won't matter that you won't be able to tomorrow.*

Perhaps the Gods took pity on him after all, for eventually, miraculously, Ninian felt himself falling.

He didn't land.

⸿

"Ninian."

He groaned quietly, wishing the voice would leave him be.

"Ninian! Wake up!"

Reluctantly, he opened his eyes to find Laoise crouching beside him. It was dark; the hearth was no longer glowing with embers, but he could see the woman's face in the light of the moon through a grimy window. "What is it?"

She looked worried. "You were crying and calling out. Are you having a nightmare?"

Ninian sat up, scrubbing at his damp eyes. Now that he was awake, he really did feel like crying. "I always have nightmares." He was wildly disoriented and glared at Laoise as a remnant tear from the dream slipped down his cheek. "You shouldn't have—" He shook his head, blinking hard, feeling the sudden loss of sleep with profound regret. "You shouldn't have woken me!"

Laoise pressed her palm to her mouth. "Oh, Ninian. I'm so sorry."

Ninian rubbed his eyes, trying to pull himself together. "It's fine."

Quietly, Laoise settled to her knees. "Do you want to tell me what you were dreaming about?"

"No."

Laoise folded her hands on her lap. "What's bothering you, Ninian? I know there's something."

Ninian refused to meet her eyes. "Nothing."

"Now, come," Laoise said with gentle insistence. "That's not true."

"I—" He felt his hands clench at his sides, hidden in the blanket. "I'm in debt. That's all." He'd fallen into Máel Máedóc's hands, and until he paid the man back or died, the shopkeeper would possess a bit of Ninian's freedom. His will. Him*self.*

He shuddered from head to toe.

Laoise rested her palm on his shoulder, making him jump. "I don't really believe that that's all. But it is all I needed to hear."

Ninian looked at her, still gripping the blankets in his fists. The power of the dream had faded, leaving him with nothing but faint anger and an unsettled feeling in his gut. "What?"

"Well," Laoise said, patting Ninian's shoulder with the hand that rested on it. "I might be able to help you with that."

Shoving aside the distrust that sprang defensively up at her words, Ninian sat forward. "You can? What do you mean?"

Laoise gave Ninian's shoulder a squeeze. "I'll tell you in the morning, okay? For now, try your best to fall back to sleep." She smiled. "I think I can fix this for you, Ninian, so rest easy."

"Can you tell me now?" Ninian asked. "Please?"

"Shh," Laoise said. "Don't get so excited, or you really won't sleep again. I promise, I'll tell you in the morning. Don't worry about it anymore."

She stood and, offering Ninian one more smile, crossed back to her bedding. Ninian watched her lie down.

"Goodnight," she whispered. "Sleep, all right?"

Ninian nodded and made himself lie back amongst the blankets.

I think I can fix this for you, she'd said.

Would it kill him to trust in that, just for a few more hours?

CHAPTER FIVE

The morning mist crept into the tenement, twining like soft roots over the floor. Ninian sat, wrapped in his blankets by the small fire in the hearth, while Ciara snored in the corner, and Laoise fed wood to the fire.

Ninian was dying to ask Laoise about what she'd said the night before, though part of him resisted, afraid to give in to hope.

Eventually, Laoise sat back on her heels and brushed wood shavings off her hands. "There." She looked over her shoulder to Ninian. "You slept again, didn't you?"

"I think so. A little bit." It hadn't been *good*, but he'd drifted along the border of sleep and wakefulness for long enough that he felt more rested than normal.

She beamed. "Good!" With a comfortable sigh, she crossed her legs and leaned against the edge of the fireplace, tucking her hair safely over her shoulder. "Any more nightmares?"

Ninian nodded.

"Ah, well." Laoise shrugged. "Nothing's perfect, I suppose."

Ninian tugged on the first joint of every finger until it popped. "Laoise… About what you said last night…"

"Your debt?" Laoise nodded. "I know how you can pay it back."

"I'm not allowed to steal anything," Ninian said, running his fingers over the edges of the blankets. "So if that's your idea—"

"It's not." She grinned. "Listen, Ninian. I saw you fighting yesterday. I know where you can put that to use."

Confused, Ninian cocked his head.

Laoise leaned forward. "I can introduce you to some people. I'll bet you anything that you're worth your weight in coins."

That definitely did not sit quite right. "These people," he hastened to ask, hoping she'd simply phrased it strangely. "What would they want?"

"Odd jobs, most like. A good fighter's a valuable asset, y'know? Lots of people have someone they'd rather not deal with themselves." She shrugged, and Ninian let out a little breath of relief. That sounded all right. "I won't say it's the safest profession in the city, but it sounds to me like you're gonna have some problems if you can't take care of that debt."

"I'll die," Ninian said. Something was whispering in the back of his head. With determination, Ninian forced it down. He did not have the luxury of being choosy.

Laoise clapped her hands together, startling Ciara from her sleep. "It's settled, then! When we're all sorted here, I'll introduce you to my friends. They'll take care of you."

〰

Comfortably full of black bread and wrapped once more in his cloak, Ninian followed Laoise through the street. Ciara had vanished into the tangle of streets almost as soon as they left the tenement, but the woman didn't seem worried. "She knows her way around," she said with a smile. "Say, it's brisk this morning, yeah?"

Ninian agreed that yes, it was brisk, and they went on their way without delay.

The day was proving to be a rare clear one. The fog around their ankles dissipated as the sun shone through it, and though it certainly wasn't any warmer, the light was a blessing in itself. It felt easier to breathe.

Laoise's pace was quick, and that was all right with Ninian. "How often have you been in this part of the city?"

"Um." Ninian looked around at the soot tagging the walls, the streets missing cobblestones, the alleys that ended in walls or staircases to nowhere. "Not often."

"It's not much," Laoise conceded. "This is an older part. Everything grew out from the citadel, y'know."

Ninian knew. His mother had been keen about history—*their* history. The citadel had once belonged to their family, after all, back in some golden era. It was funny how much nostalgia could accompany a time that Ninian had never lived.

Laoise was still chatting. "The closer you get to the old ruin, the older the neighborhood. Did you know that?"

Ninian nodded, and, unencouraged, Laoise eventually quieted.

They traveled through gray, graffitied streets for a long while, and it seemed to Ninian that each turn tunneled them deeper into the heart of the city. He thought that if they kept going for much longer, they would reach the Inner Maze.

After a period of the alleys getting narrower, the soot thicker, and the atmosphere of their surroundings honing its cracked, deadly edge, Ninian slowed to a stop. "Where are we going?"

Laoise smiled. "It's not much farther. Just ahead, actually—see that house with the blue shingles?"

Ninian thought that perhaps he did, but much like Laoise's 'green' door, the building to which she pointed was no more a house than a hut, and the dropping shingles were, at best, slate colored. "The hovel with straw over the window?" Ninian clarified.

"That's the one!" Laoise looked quite pleased. "Come on, let's get this done."

Ninian took a step, but then stopped again. "What should I expect?"

Laoise rolled her eyes. "Relax, Ninian. What would I gain from hurtin' you? You're just here to fix up that debt."

None of Ninian's knuckles cracked when he pressed on them; he'd been doing it too frequently since they'd left Laoise's building. No matter his uneasiness about his surroundings, he needed to rid himself of Máel Máedóc's hold.

Needed to.

After a few moments, he took a deep breath, let it out sharply, and caught up to Laoise.

The hovel looked empty when they approached. The window, which held glass in the very corners and straw in the rest, had no light behind it. But Laoise walked confidently to the door and banged on it with the side of her fist. "Oi! You better not be sleeping!"

There was a grunt from inside and the sound of someone moving around, and Ninian checked himself before he could step backward.

The door, after a bit of jerking to unjam it from the frame, opened a crack. "Who's there?"

Laoise pushed the door open with her elbow, and a figure cringed back from the light. "Let us in already. It's cold out here."

Ninian swallowed as a bleary-eyed young man poked his

head out. "Who's this?"

Pinching the bridge of her nose, Laoise pushed the man out of the doorway and shouldered her way past him into the building. "Come on in, Ninian. Ignore this *amadán*."

The young man's hand twitched uncertainly to his waist and, eyes following the movement, Ninian recoiled. Slowly, like he wasn't sure he was supposed to, the young man drew a rusty blade from his belt. "I asked you a question. You're Laoise, aren't you?"

Laoise rolled her eyes. "I sent Ciara ahead to tell you salt-for-brains I was coming. Where's Brígh?"

"Um…" The man fidgeted with his knife. "She's downstairs."

Downstairs? There had to be a cellar. Laoise stomped over to the corner, kicked aside a ratty blanket, and heaved open the wooden trapdoor beneath. "Oi!" she shouted into the darkness below. "It's Laoise! Get up here!"

A groan of complaint answered her, but footsteps followed. Then a head popped up through the opening and smiled. "Hello, Laoise." Clambering fully out of the cellar, the dark-haired woman skipped her gaze over Laoise and stopped it on Ninian. One eye was milky, a scar cutting over it from brow to lip, but the other was bright and sharp. "What'd you bring me?"

Ninian frowned faintly. The woman called Brígh seemed almost unsettlingly familiar with whatever was going on.

Laoise stepped back next to Ninian and dropped an elbow onto his shoulder, making him flinch. "This is Ninian."

Brígh shifted her weight and crossed her arms, face expectant. She had broad shoulders and muscular arms but moved with a certain lithe grace that reminded Ninian of an eel. "He doesn't look like much." Her voice was heavy and smooth, and Ninian thought it ought to be rougher, to match the rest of her.

Ninian cracked his knuckles in fists by his sides but refused to let a hint of emotion cross his face. It was a skill in which he had practice, and he knew his expression remained aloof.

Laoise smirked. "Y'know, Ciara said the same thing."

Ninian peeked at the man who'd answered the door. He'd retreated to a corner and had sunk against the wall, eyes sagging already in sleep. Ninian let out a little breath.

"Well," Brígh said, starting toward Ninian with thoughtfulness in her eyes. "What's he good for?"

In a motion quicker than Ninian had expected from the woman's previously languid carriage, Brígh grabbed Ninian's wrist and gave it a squeeze. Ninian jerked his hand back, but she didn't release him.

"He's skinny. Thieving?" She let Ninian's hand fall, and Ninian, out of pride, refused the urge to hold it defensively to his chest. Brígh began to circle Ninian, eyes raking his dirty russet hair, his fair unfreckled face, his worn-out clothes. "Could always use another cutpurse—so long as he's good."

"Not thieving." Laoise's eyes were dancing, and Ninian knew she meant to make Brígh guess.

Brígh, evidently familiar with the game, pinched her lip between thumb and forefinger. As she circled Ninian, her eyes scanned up and down his body and made him feel like he was naked. He could only stand there, uncertain and uncomfortable.

When she made her way back in front of him, she bent over and stared at his face for a good, long while, as if she were trying to analyze the exact shade of his eyes. Quickly, she reached out—Ninian cringed back, almost growling, but Brígh grabbed the back of his neck hard with one hand, and with the other, roughly pulled back his lips. Ninian let out an exclamation of protest. Brígh didn't pay him any mind, and Ninian felt the strong urge to bite her fingers as she examined his teeth, his stomach flopping in distress.

After a few moments, the woman released him, wiping her hand on her shirt. "Seems like he's healthy." She made another lap around him. "He's quiet," she said from somewhere behind him. "And pretty enough. A little *too* skinny for most tastes, but that could be fixed…"

"Not that," Ninian said, and realized his voice had cracked. He swallowed, deliberately schooling his breathing. He was pretty sure he knew what the woman was talking about, and it made his throat close to think about—he'd seen people at the docks, the ones who sold themselves to survive and paid a gang for protection. "I won't do that."

"But he says that's not it." Brígh crossed back into his line of sight, frowning. "He's not nearly intimidating enough to be a messenger. We don't need any more grunts, and he's too scrawny anyway." Her eyebrows met, sending a crease through her long scar as Ninian did his best to remember what messengers and grunts did. His father had always taught him more about the practical world than his mother had, so… messengers traveled to other gangs to deliver threats and were usually the ones to demand payment from various businesses on gang territory. Grunts upheld the infrastructure each gang needed to support their strength. They maintained roads, patrolled markets, and did the heavy lifting.

Brígh was right that Ninian would be very bad at either of those jobs.

Finally, Brígh spread her hands. "I quit. What *exactly* have you brought me, Laoise?"

At that, a broad, crooked grin cracked Laoise's face, and she squeezed Ninian's shoulder. He jumped—he'd been touched altogether too much in the past few minutes, and he wasn't okay with it. "This, Brígh," Laoise said, "is a *fighter*."

At first, Brígh's expression didn't change. Then, after a moment, she snorted blandly. "Bye, Laoise." She shook her head and turned back to the trapdoor. "Say hello to Ciara for me."

"Brígh, wait." She hadn't stopped smiling. "Give him a chance, eh?"

Grumbling, the woman turned around. "Give *you* a chance, you mean."

Laoise shrugged.

Ninian blinked. "What?"

"They have to make sure you're worth it," Laoise explained. "Don't wanna take just anyone, you know? You get killed in your first fight, that's not great."

Ninian bit his lip. Laoise sounded like she was referring to a tool that might break.

He took a deep breath—he *had* to keep his priorities straight. "If I'm good enough," he asked Brígh, trying to keep his voice steady, "you'll pay me?"

There was only skepticism in Brígh's eyes. Somehow that was almost as motivating as the money—almost. "*If* you're good enough to take on, then yes. Enough to eat and get yourself some clothes so you don't freeze. If you're useful, we don't want you dying, you know?" She leaned forward. "*If* you're useful."

Ninian's lip felt cold when he made himself stop chewing it. "What do I have to do?"

"I'd take you to the back lot," Brígh said flatly, "and see how long you last."

"I have to... fight you?" His eyes flicked over the woman's scars, her height, her thick arms.

Brígh nodded.

Ninian took a quick breath and felt his hands twitch into fists. It wasn't hard to find anger, not for this, and he held onto it tightly. "I'll do it."

Brígh closed her eyes, but Ninian could tell that she rolled them behind her eyelids. "Whatever, kid. Come with me then."

‽

Ninian followed Brígh outside and around the side of the hovel. Laoise trailed behind. She looked expectant, though Ninian thought he saw the faintest hint of worry on her face. It wasn't, he realized, for him.

"Hey, Ninian." Laoise took Ninian's arm and turned him toward her. "Give it your all, okay? You can do this."

Ninian swallowed and nodded tersely.

Brígh had opened an iron gate that barred the alley, and she held it open to let Ninian pass. Laoise waited on the other side without being told, and once again, Ninian was struck by how familiar she seemed with the process.

"Okay, kid," Brígh said, letting the gate screech closed. They'd come to the back of the building where an open lot hosted a number of dead weeds. Laoise watched through the gate as Brígh took a few steps backward, facing Ninian. She really was intimidatingly tall. "Show me what you've got."

Despite the cold, Ninian unpinned his cloak and folded it into a pile on the ground. He cracked his knuckles against each other, letting out an uneven breath.

Brígh slid her feet apart, falling comfortably into a fighting stance. "Ready?"

Ninian tried to mirror the woman's position. It felt clumsy. He steadied his breaths, letting the morning air brace him, and adjusted himself into something more familiar.

Brígh snorted. "Are you planning to dance with me?"

Ninian lowered his chin, narrowing his eyes. "I'm ready."

The woman wasted no time.

In the time it would have taken to blink, Brígh had covered the distance between them and launched a fist into Ninian's face. Ninian ducked just in time.

Brígh was a far better fighter than the man Ninian had bested on the street. She didn't barrel past with the momentum of her lunge but pivoted expertly and threw another blow with the force of her turn.

Ninian turned out of the way so that the attack grazed across his chest.

Brígh's approach was straightforward, Ninian realized, based more on power than cunning. She was direct, aware of her strength, and seemed determined to end the fight quickly.

Trusting his gut, Ninian dropped to the ground as Brígh's blow went by and swept his leg behind the woman's ankles the way he'd done with the man on the street. Brígh tripped for just a second but collected herself fast as Ninian sprang back to his feet.

Immediately, Ninian was on the defensive again, slipping sideways when Brígh threw two attacks in succession, one of them a sharp chop that would have nearly taken Ninian's head off his shoulders if it had hit him.

He needed to get inside the woman's range. Brígh was clearly very adept at using her fists, and Ninian's arms weren't long enough to land a strike from a safe distance. His mind was skipping fast, trying to recall every detail he'd ever learned—his mother may have taught him more manners than practical skills, but fighting was a stark exception. He *knew* how to do this. He just needed to *think*.

Once again, Ninian dropped to the ground. Brígh lowered her stance in reaction, but she had already begun moving forward. Ninian rolled to the side as she charged, and as soon as Brígh was before him, Ninian launched himself at the woman's knees.

Brígh stumbled, and that was all the invitation Ninian needed to rise and swing his elbow into her nose.

Brígh cursed, cupping a hand to her bleeding face, but didn't back off. With the back of her hand, she swatted

Ninian across the face.

Ninian's head snapped backward, and he crashed onto his back. Blinking stars out of his eyes, he rolled aside to avoid Brígh's kick and then darted dizzily to his feet.

That had not been good. A single backhanded blow, and his ears were ringing. He could not afford to take a direct hit.

Brígh was more aggressive than anyone Ninian had ever fought. His mother had been determined that he learn well but had been averse to actually hurting him. Ninian now found himself needing to adapt fast; some of his skills had apparently been formed with the assumption that his opponent wouldn't actually do him harm.

Blood dripped from Brígh's nose, but she didn't seem distracted. She'd fallen back into his easy stance even as her blood soaked into the dust.

She has to have a vulnerable spot. Everyone did. Everyone had to. But other than her nose, which evidently didn't bother her at all, Brígh didn't look like she had any injuries to exploit. She moved comfortably, no compensating for any weakness. So where...?

Oh.

It seemed a little dirty, but... well, Brígh hadn't mentioned any rules.

Ninian feinted like he was going to charge, and Brígh took the bait. The woman lunged forward while Ninian found his center again, and Ninian dropped his shoulder like he meant to accept Brígh's attack head-on.

Brígh's shoulders turned. A punch was coming.

Time seemed to slow. If that blow made contact, Ninian would certainly be knocked out, maybe for good. Ignoring the chill of the thought, he let gravity take over.

Keeping his legs solidly under him, he fell into a

graceful crouch.

And sprang up directly underneath Brígh.

Ninian's bony shoulder crushed upward between the woman's legs.

Brígh let out a cry and stumbled backward.

Ninian danced a safe distance away as Brígh fell to her knees, gasping. Holding his stance, ready to evade a surprise offense, Ninian watched Brígh drop her head with a groan. After a few moments, she held out a hand. "All right, kid," she wheezed, face contorted. "That oughta do it." She looked a little ill. "*Damn*, I'm glad I haven't got …"

Ninian reluctantly helped her up, and Brígh hobbled to the gate and leaned on it.

"I found a good one, didn't I?" Laoise said with a smirk.

Brígh grimaced at her. "He moves well. Though in a proper fight, I would expect him to finish me once I was down." Her gaze flicked to Ninian. "We can work on that."

"So," Laoise said, resting her head triumphantly on the bars of the fence, "we all set?"

Brígh nodded. "Go back inside and tell Fergus to give you your due."

"Fergus? The lazy kid?"

Brígh rolled her eyes. "The lazy kid. Yeah."

Ninian still stood uncertainly in the middle of the courtyard. The side of his face ached from where Brígh had backhanded him, but there was a perverse little grain of satisfaction behind his breastbone; he'd given more damage than he'd taken.

"Kid, c'mere." Brígh beckoned Ninian over as Laoise walked back to the hovel. "Follow me."

Ninian grabbed his cloak and followed Brígh around the front of the building, where Laoise was leaving, looking very satisfied as she slipped a leather purse into her pocket.

She waved to Ninian. "Good luck." She grinned, patting her pocket. "You might need it."

Ninian looked to Brígh. "What did she get paid for?"

"Hm?" Brígh's eyes followed Laoise until she turned out of sight. "You."

Ninian's brow furrowed. "What do you mean?"

Brígh waved a hand absently. "She's not one of us, but she doesn't supply anyone else. She's useful."

Ninian tugged at the top joint of his thumb. "She brings you people she thinks you could hire, and you pay her to do that?"

Brígh frowned. "'Hire' is a bit of a funny word." She watched Laoise's retreating back with a degree of coldness. "But she gets paid."

It wasn't too much of a shock, Ninian supposed, but it did sting. He'd let himself believe that Laoise was on his side. That had been foolish. His shoulders dropped a little. "I see." Served him right for trusting someone so quickly.

Still. Even if she'd been self-interested, Laoise hadn't *lied*. She had introduced him to a way to pay off his debt, so Ninian forced himself to concentrate on the immediate future. That was all that mattered.

"Anyway," Brígh said, clapping Ninian on the back too roughly to be friendly. "Let's go."

Shrugging his cloak back tightly around his shoulders, Ninian went.

CHAPTER SIX

After a little while of walking, Ninian couldn't keep biting his tongue. Brígh had been stopping people in the street every once in a while, clearly familiar with them, and everyone she exchanged words with looked at Ninian with appraising curiosity. "Who are those people?"

Brígh grinned. "Your new family. I'm just spreading the news."

Ninian pressed his lips together. "Oh."

Pieces had been coming together in Ninian's head. He wasn't stupid. Brígh's constant use of 'us.' The nearness to the Inner Maze. 'New family.'

He thought of Máel Máedóc, of the giant shopkeeper's glinting eyes and fists that would end Ninian's life. The memory of freezing terror sent a shiver down to his fingertips.

So be it, he decided quickly. He could fight on behalf of a gang until his debt was paid.

Brígh whistled while Ninian walked in silence. He made sure he kept his head up, despite the nerves buzzing in his gut.

Ninian suspected that the walk felt longer than it actually was, but the next thing he knew, Brígh had stopped outside of a gray-blue house with windows of spiderwebbed glass. Ninian raised his eyebrows at it. It was actually a proper house, with two stories, and Ninian could see furniture inside.

"Brígh!" A voice came from down the road, and Brígh looked up. Ninian saw a man with curly, honey-brown hair jogging toward them. He looked about twenty, with a compact build and an open face that easily broke into a smile; his moss-green eyes flicked between Brígh and Ninian, full of energy.

"Ah." Brígh didn't smile as the man arrived. "What's the word?"

The man was a little winded, but he grinned all the same. "I came when I heard! Is this him?"

Brígh nodded. "Did you talk to Cahir?"

"Sure. Nothing unusual." He beamed at Ninian. "Hey, there! I'm Ruairí. You're Ninian, right?"

Ninian nodded.

Ruairí's smile just got bigger. "I heard you're a fighter! Well, good on you!" Ruairí clapped Ninian on the back hard enough to knock the wind from Ninian's lungs, and Ninian flinched away. Ruairí tucked the offending hand into his pocket, but Ninian still watched him uneasily. Then Ruairí snapped his fingers and turned to Brígh. "Oh! There was one thing. Since he's kinda young, Cahir wanted to know what your call was."

Brígh's lip curled in thought, and then she sighed. "A lot of potential. Shouldn't let him go."

Ruairí's smile made Ninian wonder if Brígh's words were a good thing. "Well, then I suppose I'll see you tonight, Ninian. Try and prepare yourself, okay?"

"For what?" Ninian demanded.

Ruairí laughed. "We're a bit of a mess, so you'll have to wait to get things sorted with the boss." He waved his hand airily. "Don't worry about it, it'll be worth the wait."

"I'll get paid?"

"Once you start, yeah!" Ruairí said. "It's pretty good money, actually. Anyway!" He grinned again. "I gotta be going!"

And then he was off.

Brígh *tch*ed. "I'll never understand that guy." She sighed and walked over to where steps led to doors angled into the earth. The rust-encrusted hinges screamed as she heaved them open, and she brushed off her hands as the doors hit the ground with half-rotten thuds. "Right. In you go."

Ninian blinked. "Into the cellar?"

"Listen, kid. I know two things about you. One: you're good at fighting. Two: you need money, which means you're desperate enough to go to someone else if you think they'll do you better." She jerked her thumb toward the door. "But you lost the right to choose anything when Laoise walked away with my money. Get in the cellar."

Ninian didn't move.

Brígh tapped her fingers on the door. "It's too late now, you know. We can't have you working against us, which means you're working for us, which means you *get in the damned cellar.*"

Still, Ninian didn't step forward.

Fast as a blink, Ninian watched Brígh's patience run out. Her hand was wrapped tight around Ninian's wrist before Ninian could dodge her.

There wasn't anything Ninian could do except yelp as the woman lifted him up, turned, and sent Ninian down the stairs.

Ninian's elbow cracked against the wall, then his shin, and then his head smacked hard against the edge of a step.

The light of the doorway above him split into three. He landed on his back on the floor of the cellar, gasping for the air that he'd lost and blinking in disorientation. "Cahir would be angry if I broke you," Brígh called down from above. "So you'd better not be hurt." With a grunt, she heaved one of the doors shut, and the cellar dimmed. "See you soon."

The other door closed, and everything went dark.

Swearing, Ninian rolled to his knees and crawled blindly up the stairs. With his head throbbing hard enough to turn his stomach, he hammered on the closed doors above him. "Let me out!"

There was the sound of chains clinking through the wood, and Ninian pounded harder.

"Hey! Open the doors!"

He shoved on the doors, but they didn't budge. The clinking stopped as Brígh finished chaining the cellar closed, and then Ninian heard her footsteps move away. He gave the door one last frustrated shove before sinking to a seat on the steps. His head pounded.

Groaning, he touched the already-swelling spot on his temple. "Gods *damn* it."

There wasn't so much as a sliver of light in the cellar. It was cool and smelled damp, and when Ninian touched the wall of the stairwell, he found that it was earth. Dirt and pebbles skittered down onto the steps.

Maybe there was a different way out. He cursed to himself as he carefully felt his way down the stairs.

Anger—Gods, it was familiar, almost a relief—pressed behind his sternum. He dug his fingernails hard into his opposite forearm since there was no place else for the frustration to go.

He nearly tripped when the stairs ended at an uneven dirt floor and caught himself unsteadily on the wall.

He squeezed his eyes shut. The dark didn't particularly bother him. Once, he'd been afraid of monsters in the shadows, but he was *far* beyond that. Even so, Ninian could only surmise that he'd be trapped for a while if there wasn't another way out, and that set the anger in his chest writhing. He felt around the edges of the space, encountering nothing before he dropped heavily to a seat in a corner.

Seething, he tried to rationalize his situation.

If after all of this, he truly got paid enough for food and warm clothes… well, he went without those all the time. If he put all his earnings in Máel Máedóc's hands, surely it wouldn't take long to repay his debt, and then he'd be free. Being locked in a cellar was *not* what he'd expected, nor did he like it, but he didn't *have* to like it. He just had to go along for as long as it took to escape Máel Máedóc's hold. This was still better than being owned by debt or being dead for not paying.

He slid down the wall until he was lying on his back and closed his eyes. It was so dark, and he *was* truly tired. Sleeping at Laoise's had been such an experience; he hadn't fallen asleep like that in longer than he could remember. It hadn't been *good* sleep, but it had been incredible all the same.

There was nothing else to do in the hours until night. He rolled onto his side, pulled his hood up, and tried to remember how it had felt to slip away. He concentrated on his breathing, the chill air as he inhaled, the warm air as he breathed out. He focused on his heartbeat, and soon he didn't have to think about keeping his eyes closed anymore.

It was pleasant to force his mind blank. The darkness covered him, hid him, sheltered him away from everything outside—to neither see nor be seen was its own sort of fortress, and for just a moment, Ninian let himself relax behind the walls. He let out a soft breath. He felt himself slipping and leaned into it, feeling like he was melting through the floor.

And then he bolted upright.

His gasp caught in his throat, and he coughed, doubling over his knees and looking around frantically for a moment.

"Dammit!" he muttered, closing his eyes wearily and slouching against the wall. He'd started drifting off. "Too much to ask, I guess." One decent night clearly didn't indicate the reversal of a two-year-old pattern.

So… sleep wasn't an option. That left… no options.

He dragged the tip of his finger through the loose layer of dirt on the floor. At first, he just traced jagged, aimless scrawls, but then, blindly, he found himself tracing the shapes of words.

Fight, he wrote.

Angry.

The words started coming more easily.

Fight. Angry.

I'm angry.

His hand paused, and he shuffled his palm over the words. He closed his eyes in the dark.

I'm tired.

I'm afraid.

I'm angry.

Who was he angry at?

Máel Máedóc. That was an easy answer. *He pressed me to this.*

Brígh. Also easy. *She locked me in a fucking cellar.*

The mounting anger felt good. It was hot and alive, a sustaining force, and he welcomed it to the tips of his fingers.

Laoise, he decided, embracing the frustration swelling in his chest. *She told me she cared, and I watched that money change hands.*

Ruairí, for looking too fucking happy.

Kelp, for not staying just a little longer.

Myself, for Gods know how many things.
My uncle—and his wife too. For...
His breath trembled.

He scooted away from the words he couldn't see and clumsily kicked them out with his foot. He sat for a minute with his arms braced defensively, uncertainly. Then he rolled to his knees and pushed himself to his feet. He blindly stumbled in the direction of the stairs. He found them with his shin, swore, and then pounded up the steps.

He banged on the locked doors with the heels of his hands, as loudly as he could. "Let me out!" He worked his fingers into the crack between the doors, but the wood fit tightly together. Suddenly, he'd lost the willpower to wait—there was too much time to *think* down here, no distractions, nothing but mind and memory. Ninian had done his best not to think for almost two whole years since he'd moved in with his aunt and uncle after his parents died, and he did *not* want to start now—memory was not helpful when forward was the only direction he could go.

He just wanted to be his *own*.

He gritted his teeth. He needed to *move*. The darkness was too much; suddenly, instead of fortressed, he felt like he couldn't breathe. In the blackness, the anger was big, and it unfurled its harsh light into every dark-touched corner.

Setting his feet, he rammed his shoulder into the door. Pain splashed through the joint, and he drew back and did it again, rattling the chains.

On the next blow, his feet slipped, and he crashed back down the stairs. Without waiting, he dragged himself to his feet and tore up the steps again, not hesitating before impact. His shoulder flared with pain, and his head throbbed. Blood dripped from the cuts he'd left on his arms. "Let me *out*!"

Panting, he dug his nails into the wood. Splinters broke the skin under his nails, but chips fell away. He tore at the wood—the pain was one more thing to be angry at, and the anger was safe and familiar—until his hands, cramping with effort, refused to take his orders.

He was winded. Sinking to a seat on the steps, he pressed his palms into his closed eyes until nonexistent light bloomed under the pressure. All at once, he didn't want to move anymore.

He curled up, pressed his forehead into his knees, and sat like that while the hours passed.

$$\mathbb{C}$$

CHAPTER SEVEN

When the doors opened, Ninian looked up, then cringed away from the blinding torchlight that spilled in. Around its brilliant orange halo, he could see stars set in a velvet-deep sky.

"Hey, Ninian!" Ruairí greeted him cheerfully. "You ready?"

Ninian had calmed down out of necessity as the hours passed, but that didn't mean he wasn't immensely relieved the wait was over—not thinking took *effort*. Time to move.

He stood. "Ready for what?"

Ruairí just laughed. "I know this is a little mad, but trust me, everything will work out. Brígh said you were just in it for the money, right? She heard from Laoise that you were in debt."

Ninian scowled. "Yeah. That's right."

"Well, bear with this for a bit, and you'll get it." He put his hand on the back of Ninian's neck, seeming oblivious to Ninian's cringing. "You'll get that and more."

"Where are we going? Are you the only one here?"

"Oh!" Ruairí seemed surprised. "That's right, you probably can't see. Nah, I got one of my brothers with me. He doesn't talk, but... here." He turned so the torchlight was shaded by his own body, and Ninian could make out a second figure next to him. "We're just bringing you inside the house, that's all." Hand still on the back of Ninian's neck, he steered him toward the front door, where warm light and the sound of conversation spilled under the jamb. The silent man swung the door open and stepped aside.

All sound of conversation stopped. Ninian stood in the doorway, trying his best to see through the candlelight after his eyes had been so thoroughly acclimated to darkness.

He never got the chance to find his bearings before a wave of sound nearly bowled him over. At first, the noise made no sense, but then he realized that it was the sound of cups and fists hitting tables, feet stomping, people shouting. Instinctively, he fell into a ready stance, prepared to blindly fight or run.

He jumped when he felt Ruairí's hand on his shoulder. "Relax. They're welcoming you."

Ninian blinked. "What?"

"Go on. This is for you."

"I'm… confused," Ninian said, frowning. "You locked me in the cellar, and now you're…"

Ruairí rolled his eyes. "You think too much."

"I try not to," Ninian retorted, "but I'm not perfect. And this doesn't make sense."

Ruairí chuckled, sighing. "It's a family thing, all right? It's just welcoming. Gives you a chance to meet everyone."

With that, he gave Ninian a little push, and Ninian, off-balance, stumbled into the house. Inside, beamed ceilings and whitewashed walls held the stains of old smoke. Barrels crowded along the walls, and a fire blazed in the stone hearth; the whole place was warm and humid and smelled of ale, sweat, and wood ash. Immediately, people surrounded him, pressing in raucously on all sides.

Cupping his hands around his mouth with a laugh, Ruairí shouted. "Have fun!"

Ninian's eyes were adjusting to the light, which was good, but he couldn't tell if it was making a difference in how overwhelmed he was. He couldn't process all the people around him—people with brawny shoulders or slender curves, people his age and people whose faces were creased with wrinkles, people with sooty makeup, people with scars. They were all around him, talking at once, grinning, cuffing his shoulders, spilling ale and cider and skee as they moved.

"W-wait!" he managed, to no avail.

"Relax!" a woman said, taking Ninian's hands and spinning him in a circle. "Loosen up!"

"I—"

A man dropped an arm over Ninian's shoulders, and the bruises from where Ninian had rammed the cellar door ached. "Hey, Ninian!" He introduced himself, and Ninian promptly forgot the name. "Let me get you a drink, eh?"

Before Ninian could say anything, the man had produced a cup from somewhere in the crowd and pressed it into Ninian's hands. A cheer went up.

"That's more like it!" the man said, beaming. "Enjoy the party!"

And with that, he was gone, replaced by other people, with other smiles and other words of welcome, other pats on the back or ruffles of Ninian's tangled hair. In the chaos, he dropped his cup, but just as quickly, someone gave him another. Nobody seemed to think twice about the strangeness of the situation, and it slowly dawned on him that everyone had done this before—nobody thought it was strange at all.

He lost track of the introductions. The flickering candlelight washed everyone with the same golden highlights and inky shadows, and the effect was a disorienting whirl of movement and noise.

The energy of the crowd, he began to realize, was intoxicating. It was alive, vibrant. *It's a family thing*, Ruairí had said, and it was true: all the people *did* feel like a family. They all seemed *bonded*, somehow. It felt welcoming.

What is *this?*

Tentatively, Ninian began smiling back at people. Their grins widened even further when he did, and more people pressed in to talk to him. Everyone knew his name, which disconcerted him until he began to find it rather… nice.

After a while, a thickset man with a bushy red beard climbed onto a table and began setting up a racket with two tin cups against one another.

"Ey!" he cried. "Everyone, gather round!"

Ninian turned to the person next to him, a blonde girl with red streaks in her hair, maybe a few years older than he. "What's going on?"

She grinned. "You'll see." And then she darted away to the table on which the man stood.

"A'right, a'right!" the man shouted, letting the cups fall to his sides. They'd clearly been full when he'd grabbed them, for they'd left a spray of ale droplets in his beard. "Now, you lot all know why we're here tonight, yeah?"

The crowd let up a cheer, and Ninian could hear his name whooped in the cacophony.

"Ay, ay, that's right!" The man on the table pointed to Ninian with the mouth of one of his tin cups. "Tonight, we welcome Ninian, yeah?"

Again, the crowd bellowed. A few people pounded Ninian on the back so hard he coughed.

"Tonight is for him, yeah?" He looked around the crowd. "Who wants to start?"

Ninian frowned. *Start what?* The party looked to be raging along quite well already, and Ninian had to wonder how often the gang did this. They must not hire very many people, he decided, because if they celebrated like this for every one of them, they'd surely go broke on ale alone.

But the speaker on the table received quite a few hooted replies. "A'right!" the man laughed. "First to reach him gets the honor!"

Ninian's eyes widened as everyone in his near vicinity dove at him, followed by at least ten more elbowing through the crowd. "I got it!" Someone shrieked from his ankles, and Ninian tripped back. He couldn't fall; the people were packed too tightly. "It was me!"

"A'right!" the speaker bellowed. "Treasa's starting!"

Cheering, the crowd began to shift. They were forming a circle around him and the streaky-haired girl who looked about Ninian's age. She raised her fist triumphantly, like it meant a lot to her, and Ninian didn't understand what was happening. "Give us the cups!"

Ninian hadn't touched the cup he'd been given earlier, and most of the contents had spilled anyway. Someone took it from his hands and replaced it with a ceramic mug full of tan ale. Across from him, Treasa received a matching one and made eye contact with him, smirking. "You have to drink it all," she said. "We do it at once."

Ninian's stomach tensed. "I don't—"

The girl laughed. "Come on. Ain't you ever drunk before?"

"Yeah," Ninian said. His throat felt just a little tight. "I have."

"Well," she said, grinning. "I promise that *this* will be more fun."

Ninian pursed his lips at the beer in his cup. *It's not skee*, he told himself. It was ale, and ale wasn't *nearly* as strong as what he was used to. Would it... would it be okay?

The crowd had started chanting. *"Here's to a long life, and a merry one!"*

The girl brought the mug to her lips, and, slowly, Ninian followed. The liquid was chilly on his tongue.

"A quick death, and an easy one!"

He let the ale fill his mouth, and as the girl tipped her mug high, Ninian swallowed.

"A true family, and a happy one!"

It felt cold at first, then warm in his stomach. He brought the mug down to see the girl still gulping and, steeling himself, took another drink. He swallowed until only foam passed his lips, and then he brought the mug down with a sharp breath. The girl was laughing, wiping her mouth on her sleeve.

The crowd roared in delight. *"A decent ale, and another one!"*

Before Ninian realized it, someone had refilled his cup. Treasa was handing her mug to someone else—a bald man with a winking smile. Someone filled that mug too, and everyone cheered as the man raised it.

"To a long life, and a merry one!" he shouted, and, inclining his cup to Ninian, began to down it.

The crowd behind Ninian jostled him. *"A quick death, and an easy one!"* Someone slapped his shoulders. "Go on! Drink! He's almost done!"

Ninian swallowed. He couldn't feel the first drink at all and wondered if that was normal. Didn't it usually take a few minutes to feel it? Or was that only with skee? Did all alcohol work the same?

"A true family, and a happy one!"

Uncertainly, he started to drink.

It was gone more quickly than he'd have thought.

"To a decent ale, and another one!"

Just like that, his mug was full again.

It got easier. More and more people came through and drank with him, and while Ninian stopped being able to finish the cups, he felt fine. His chest felt lighter, and he realized he was smiling—no, *laughing*—as the crowd's cheers and chants blended into noise in the back of his head.

He actually giggled when, after drinking with a bored-looking Brígh, Ninian tripped and the crowd caught him. He blinked hard, staggering as someone poured more ale into his mug. "I've never felt like this," he confided in the stranger next to him, smiling. He felt almost giddy.

The stranger laughed, tapping Ninian's mug with her tin cup. "Glad you're havin' a good time."

Ninian tried to take a step, and the next thing he knew, he was on the floor, his ale spreading through the dust in a ring of darkness. He looked at it in bemusement, not sure how he'd gotten there. A woman with close-cropped hair helped him back up, laughing and brushing him off. "Atta boy. You're all right."

"Yeah," Ninian agreed, smiling. He *was* all right. It was surprising.

"*HEAR, HEAR!*" a voice bellowed over the noise of the crowd, and everyone fell silent. Ninian blinked toward the voice and blurrily made out a man—maybe the same red-bearded man as before—standing on a table. "My friends." Despite his smile, there was a hint of solemnity in his voice as he opened his arms. "Brothers, sisters, it is time."

There was murmuring through the crowd, and once again, Ninian found himself surrounded. This time, there were no cheers, but everyone placed a hand on him or said a few encouraging words. Ninian frowned, flummoxed and not sure why he needed encouragement. "Wha's happening?"

The man on the table cleared his throat. "Everyone," he said. "Cahir."

Another round of murmuring radiated through the people, and the sound filled the smoky room as a new man ascended to the table.

All Ninian could make out through the alcohol clouding his eyes was hair the color of red apples and a mouse-like nose among otherwise strong features. When the man spoke, his voice was smooth and full of gravity. "My friends," he said, and he didn't even need to raise his voice to command the room's attention. "Brígh has vouched for our newest brother. Make way."

At his words, the crowd parted. A path formed, and around the hearth, people backed away. Ninian saw Brígh standing next to the fireplace.

The man on the table, Cahir, nodded, and two people from the throng took Ninian by the elbows and steered him in Brígh's direction. Ninian stumbled clumsily, the world blurring around him, but his guides didn't let him fall. When they reached the fireplace, they helped him to a seat on the floor. Ninian looked around, lost, and for the first time, registered the apprehension on people's faces. "What's going on?" His words slid together.

"It's going to be fine," someone promised, but he couldn't tell who'd spoken.

Brígh knelt before him, eyes focused. Her mouth was set in a hard line, but her scar—so deep and pale, like flesh that had died—twitched with the feathering of her jaw. Without a glint of emotion in her eyes, she began pulling up at the hem of Ninian's shirt. "Take this off. There's no point ruining it."

Ninian's breath caught in his throat, and he toppled backward. "What—what're you doing?"

"Stop," Cahir said from atop the table. He looked displeased with Ninian's resistance. "Give him another drink."

Someone in the crowd spoke up at that. "I dunno, Cahir," a man's voice called. "He's young, ain't he? Don't want to kill him."

Ninian squeezed his eyes shut as, at last, a drop of fear slid into his heart. It diffused through the alcohol that filled him, reaching every pore. "What's happening?" He opened his eyes and found that he couldn't focus at all. His center of gravity slipped, and he fell to his elbows.

This was bad.

This was drunkenness, and Brígh had tried to take off Ninian's shirt.

Ninian choked and tried to scramble backward, but his body wasn't moving the way he wanted it to. He couldn't breathe right, couldn't tell if he was even breathing at all.

No, no, no, no...

He was drunk.

It was *always* when he was drunk.

He found himself prone and pushed himself unsteadily to his hands and knees. But crawling didn't work. His arm gave, and he tipped and landed on his shoulder. "Wait," he said, but then he wasn't sure if he'd said it.

Brígh was in front of him, and in the next blink, Ninian found himself before the fire again. When Brígh's hands pulled his shirt over his head, Ninian couldn't resist.

"Stop." He realized his eyes were full of tears. "Please." He gasped, but the air never hit his lungs.

"I haven't done anything yet," Brígh said to him quietly. "Breathe, kid."

Ninian couldn't. "Not again. I don't wanna do it again. I'm so sorry—"

Drinking had been a mistake—this was his fault. This was too familiar, and he couldn't breathe.

He wished he would pass out.

That happened sometimes.

That made it easier.

Cahir's voice boomed through the room. "Brígh," he said. "You vouched for our new brother, Ninian. His successes will raise you higher within this family, or his failures will lay you low." There was a wave of murmurs. "Make him one of us."

"Please," Ninian managed. "Stay away from me… please…"

A glow caught the corner of Ninian's eye, and he forced himself to find its source.

Brígh.

No.

Brígh was *holding* something.

It was black where Brígh held it, a long rod with a crescent shape at the end, and that end…

Glowed.

Ninian didn't understand.

Until people from the crowd behind him took hold of his shoulders and his hands. "Be strong," someone whispered in Ninian's ear.

"Ru… Ruairí?"

"Shh," Ruairí said. "It'll be over soon, and then you'll be one of us, okay?"

Brígh's face was a mask as she brought the glowing end of the rod closer to Ninian's chest.

"Wait," Ninian said, jerking against the people who held him, but he couldn't break the hold, and his head was swimming. "Wait!"

There was a hiss, and a curl of smoke rose from his body.

Ninian hiccupped. "Ah—"

Brígh held the brand steady, expressionless.

And then Ninian *felt* it.

Impossible. Engulfing.

"Stay strong," Ruairí murmured, and the hands on Ninian's shoulders tightened.

It didn't even feel *hot*. It was pain devoid of sensation, pure and undiluted and spreading, and the sound was like frying meat and the *smell*—

Tears poured down Ninian's face, even though the pain and his reaction seemed separate somehow. It must have been the ale, because when he finally screamed, it didn't seem like his scream, and he tried to curl inward, to protect himself. Hands held him fast.

He couldn't form the words to make it stop. Even when Brígh withdrew the glowing brand, turning away from Ninian to replace it in the hearth, the pain was there, and it bloomed over Ninian's chest like he was on fire. The crowd's grip on his arms relaxed, and Ninian careened into the ground, pressing his hands against the burn as if he could make it go away.

"Stop that," Ruairí said, and Ninian felt him pulling his hands away from the wound. "Don't touch it."

"Stop," Ninian choked. The crowd was murmuring in sympathy, and a few people kneeled nearby. Nobody pressed too closely.

"People," Cahir called from the back of the room, and he spread his arms wide. "Let us welcome Ninian the fighter as our new brother!"

There was a halfhearted cheer, but Ninian on the ground seemed to put a damper on the rejoicing.

"I didn't," Ninian whispered. "I didn't, I didn't…"

"You didn't?" Ruairí said, leaning closer. He still held Ninian's hands away from the brand. "You didn't what?"

"I didn't *want* this…"

Ruairí let out a sharp breath but didn't say anything.

"Brígh," Cahir went on. "Remember that you vouched for Ninian. He's your responsibility until he learns our ways."

"Hey, Brígh," Ruairí said softly. "Let me take care of that, okay?"

Ninian opened his eyes to see the blurry form of Brígh nod. "Don't mind if you do."

Ruairí's attention turned back to Ninian. "I'm gonna get you cleaned up, okay?" He grabbed Ninian's fallen shirt and draped it over his shoulder. "Oi, Brígh. Come with me so Cahir doesn't notice."

Ruairí hoisted him up. With Brígh trailing behind, Ruairí carried Ninian through the quieted crowd, and then wood creaked as he walked up the stairs.

It was darker upstairs, and cooler too, though Ninian didn't feel cold. His eyelids sagged as Ruairí lay him down gently, and Ninian felt rough linen under him.

"Don't…" he whispered. "Don't touch me."

"I'm just going to cover the brand," Ruairí said as Brígh watched from the corner, arms crossed. "And then you're going to sleep."

Ninian fought darkness as Ruairí dabbed something bitter-smelling onto the wound, and then covered it with gray bandages. It hurt. Ninian barely noticed new tears.

"There," Ruairí said softly. "All right?"

Ninian couldn't answer. His body felt like it was sinking into the bed, and his eyes wouldn't stay open. "Don't…"

"I'm all done," said Ruairí. Gently, he turned Ninian onto his side. That was good, Ninian knew distantly. Once, he'd passed out on his back, and he'd nearly suffocated on his own vomit. "Sleep, okay?"

It wasn't a choice. The darkness was reaching for him, and consciousness was losing its grip.

And drunkenly, painfully, he slept.

CHAPTER EIGHT

Before Ninian was even properly awake, his body was in motion. He turned fast, rolling half-off the bed, and vomited over the side.

To his surprise, it landed in a basin. He stared at it blankly for a moment, feeling his throat clench shut, and realized, as he heaved again, that Ruairí must have left the bucket there sometime during the night.

Ninian panted, trying to keep his head from spinning. His arms shook just from supporting himself on his elbows to retch.

His chest was on fire. Weakly, he dropped back down onto the mattress, caught his breath, and, with unsteady hands, touched the dingy bandages over his collarbone. Even at the lightest touch, he let out a shaky cry.

Pain was lancing through his head too, and he pressed his palms into his eyes.

Too much. Nausea lurched in his stomach, and he threw himself onto his side again and heaved into the basin. Nothing came, but he still retched until he started coughing and miserably dragged the back of his hand over his mouth. The light shining in through the window was too bright.

"Ninian?" a voice said softly, and Ninian looked to see Ruairí nudging the door open. "You awake?"

Ninian squeezed his eyes shut and turned away.

The floor creaked as Ruairí crossed over to the bed. "I brought you some water."

"I'm not thirsty," Ninian rasped.

"Liar," Ruairí said gently. "Come on, sit up. You need to drink." He sat on the edge of the bed, making the bedframe protest softly. Ninian turned to glare at him, but Ruairí didn't seem to be moving closer—just sitting. Ninian edged as far away as he could.

"I'm only going to throw it up," he said.

"You don't know that."

"I *do*."

Ruairí responded with a sympathetic sigh. "So... how much do you remember? From last night?"

Ninian swallowed and looked away again. His head was pounding, and he felt shaky even when he lay still. "I've never forgotten anything... that's happened while I was drunk."

"If you've been this drunk before," Ruairí said, "then you know you need to drink water."

"I've been this drunk before, and I know I'm just going to throw it up."

Ruairí stood, the bed creaking as he left it, and Ninian's heart slowed down just a little as he moved away. "All right. Well... I'll leave this here." There was a tap as he set the cup down on the bedside table. His footsteps crossed to the door, and he paused in the doorway. "Welcome to the family."

Ninian's throat closed again, but this time it wasn't from nausea. His eyes felt hot. "Ruairí?"

"Yeah?"

"I'm..." He inhaled unsteadily. "I'm in the gang now, aren't I?"

The floorboards creaked as Ruairí shifted his weight. "Yes. You are."

Ninian let out an uneven breath and wrapped his arms around himself, focusing on the lancing pain of his brand. It nestled under the left side of his collarbone, the size of a fist, and spread heat across his chest like the burning was infectious. "I didn't want that."

Ruairí sounded a little sad. "I know."

"If you knew," Ninian said, hating how his voice broke, "then why did you…"

"I know it's hard to understand. I do. But this is how it works. The pain is temporary, I swear. Then you'll see how good this really is." He fell silent for a long moment, and when he spoke, his voice was different. "I did."

That made Ninian pause. "This happened to you too?"

"A long time ago." He played with the doorknob, and it squeaked. "Only about half the people here joined because they wanted to. But once you're in… it doesn't *matter*."

"It's a *family*," Ninian said sarcastically. Ruairí ignored the resentment in his voice.

"It is," he agreed. "Really."

He was quiet for a minute, and Ninian heard him release a long, quiet breath.

"Please drink the water," Ruairí said finally. "I'll be downstairs if you need me."

The door clicked shut.

The stairs creaked, and then Ruairí's muffled footsteps crossed the floor below.

Gingerly, Ninian rolled back over and reached for the cup on the table. It was cool and inviting, and he was so thirsty.

Full of trepidation, he took a tiny sip. It wasn't as pleasant as it had promised to be. He quickly set the cup back down and was immediately glad he had. In the next moment, he was vomiting into the basin again. He closed his eyes, breathing hard. "Told you so."

⁂

He made himself finish the water, even though he'd been right—not a drop stayed down.

Kneeling on the bed, he looked out of the window's dirty glass. It looked like a cloudy day, but the light made even the small, dingy room look fresh. Much too bright. Ninian cast about for his shirt, found it hanging on one of the bedposts, and, swearing in pain, tugged it gingerly over his head.

He padded out of the room and looked around. There was a short hallway with tattered rugs on the floor, and a staircase cutting downward at the end of the hall. Covering his mouth like it would prevent him from throwing up, Ninian started down the stairs.

The first floor was exactly the way he remembered it. *Anything* pleasant about the night before had turned evil in his mind, and he scowled at the ale-stained floor, the disorganized table and chairs, and snarled at the fireplace.

He moved through that room quickly and continued through a doorway he hadn't passed the night before. Sunlight was pouring from windows beyond, falling over the floor in a way that made Ninian want to kick it.

Ninian poked his head around the corner. "Ruairí?" he called timidly.

"Ninian?" His head appeared from a doorway farther in the light-filled room. "Hey." He stepped into the sunshine, brushing off his hands.

Ninian bit his lip hard as he felt nausea roil in his stomach, his headache spiking, and he cast about urgently for somewhere to retch.

"How are you feeling?" Ruairí asked.

In response, Ninian stumbled to the corner and fell to his hands and knees. He heaved, and it felt almost worse when nothing came up. Groaning, he let his head droop. "Ungh."

"I'm sorry," Ruairí said, dropping to a crouch next to Ninian. He rubbed comfortingly between Ninian's shoulder blades without seeming to think about it. "It's miserable."

Ninian was too shaky to cringe away from Ruairí's touch. He nodded weakly.

"When it was me, I was too sober when they tried to take me in." Ruairí sat back on his heels and pulled aside the collar of his shirt. A shapeless, rippled scar tracked over his collarbone onto his chest, and beside it, a crescent stood bold. "I dodged, and the iron moved. They had to do it again." He sighed. "Not pleasant."

Ninian wiped his mouth. "So who vouched for you?"

"Man named Cillian," Ruairí said. "He's dead now."

"How?"

"An old injury went bad. My fault, really." He scratched absently at his forearm. "I lost a fight, so Cahir assigned Cillian to patrol the territory of some enemy gang. Cillian barely came back in one piece."

Ninian's confusion must have been evident on his face because Ruairí explained. "Vouching for someone is a way to rise through the ranks. If the new member does well, then whoever vouched for them gets a bit of the credit." He rolled his eyes, nodding to Ninian's chest. "Brígh's been trying to move up for a while. But if the new person does poorly, the voucher gets stuck with worse duties."

A rather wicked idea involving Brígh and vengeance began to sprout in Ninian's mind, but Ruairí cut it off fast.

"Don't try anything," he warned. "I ended up in almost the same shape as Cillian. The lost fight almost killed me, and Cillian gave me *hell*. It is *not* worth it."

"That doesn't sound very familial," Ninian observed with a touch of vinegar.

Ruairí waved a hand. "You rank low right now, like I did back then. It gets better fast." With a little grunt, he pushed himself to his feet. "Now, if you give me one second, I'll get you something to eat."

He returned to the other room and came back with a plate. It had a chunk of black bread and a couple of strips of jerky.

"Here," he said, offering it to Ninian. "Eat."

"I don't—"

"It'll help with the sickness, I promise," Ruairí said. "Take it slow, and I'll get you something to throw up in if you have to."

He left the plate on the floor in front of Ninian and stood again.

"Why are you doing this?" Ninian asked.

Ruairí turned around. "Huh?"

"Why are you being kind to me?"

Ruairí looked sad. "Well," he said with a shrug. "You're my brother now, aren't you?" He shook his head. "Even if you weren't," he said, "I try to treat people right." He turned away again and started walking into the other room. "Especially people who look like they need it."

"Funny," Ninian said bitterly. "That's a lot like what Laoise told me."

A little crease formed between Ruairí's eyebrows, and he looked concerned. "Was she bad to you?"

"She *sold* me to a *gang*."

Ruairí chewed his lip. "I won't say she's the most selfless

person," he conceded, and Ninian almost snorted. "But this is still a way for you to pay off your debt! So in the long run… maybe her intentions weren't great, but it will work out." He let out a slow breath through his teeth. "There's nothing I can say to make you trust me," he said. "I get that. Just… let me help, okay? I was in your shoes. I know how to make it easier."

Ninian's eyes fell to the little breakfast. There was a weight on him, a weight that had nothing to do with his nausea or his pounding head. It pressed him inward, and only something hateful inside him kept him from sinking into nothingness. "I don't need it." He pushed himself to his feet and pointed roughly at Ruairí. "I don't need a *family* or *brothers*. Not pity, not… not…"

Ruairí turned back to him and let him talk.

"I'm on my own," Ninian said forcefully. "I *am* my own."

He wasn't, though.

Another heave interrupted him, and he forced it back down. "I thought I was going to do a job and get paid. Not this." He hadn't thought he still *could* be naïve, but evidently, he'd been wrong. Anger roiled in his gut, directionless anger that seemed to affix itself to Ninian as much as it did to Ruairí, Brígh, the red-haired gang leader, and anyone else Ninian could think of. "I went along because I need the money really, *really* badly, but then *this* happened, and— and I'm tired, okay?" He pressed a hand over his mouth until the nausea subsided. "I'm tired of people thinking they can do what they want with me, because they *can't*, okay?"

Something cracked and, without warning, tears came. Because as easy as it was to say, none of it was true. They could do whatever they wanted.

Because Ninian… *let* them.

Ruairí crossed the room in two strides and enclosed

Ninian in a hug. Ninian's tears poured into Ruairí's shirt even as Ninian's hands balled to fists of their own accord.

"Don't," Ninian said, shoulders so tight they trembled. He pushed Ruairí away. "Stop it."

Ruairí looked pained. "I'm trying to help."

"No," Ninian said sharply. He couldn't stop the tears, but he could ignore them. He glared at Ruairí. "You didn't even just watch; you *held me down*. And—" His voice failed, and he swallowed his tears as hard as he could. It had been Ninian who'd let himself get drunk. He should have known that resistance after that wouldn't work. "I…"

Instead of answering, Ruairí averted his eyes. He moved into a squat and propped his forearms on his knees. "Ninian, can I… ask you a question?"

Ninian glared at him. "No." He was finished with this conversation. Clenching his fists as well as his teeth, he stomped past Ruairí. His cloak was upstairs. He was leaving.

"What happened the last time… *times*… you were drunk?" Ruairí asked quietly.

Ninian froze in the doorway as surely as if he'd met a wall. "What?"

Ruairí fidgeted. "I've been… putting pieces together. And last night, you were, um…" He bit his lip. "You were talking in your sleep."

It felt like Ninian's heart was going too fast, but only in hard, uneven beats. "That's not your business."

"Just…" Ruairí swallowed. "Well, let us know if there's anyone you need dead, okay?"

Ninian thought he was serious. Without another word, he turned and ran up the stairs.

CHAPTER NINE

Ninian didn't even bother aiming for the basin when he reached the upstairs room and retched again. Sure enough, nothing came up. His whole body felt tight and hot.

The threadbare taupe cloak felt familiarly soft as he threw it over his shoulders and turned for the door.

He jumped back.

Cahir was leaning against the doorframe.

"Where are you going?" the man asked.

His apple-red hair was pulled back by a headband made of burlap, and, up close, Ninian saw that the gang leader's eyes were two different colors, tangerine and lavender.

Ninian leveled him with a stare. "I'm leaving."

"Oh?" Cahir said. He didn't so much as shift his position. "Why would you do a thing like that?"

"Shut up," Ninian said bitterly. Deep in his head, logic whined—*you need the money, think of the money, do you want to die?*—but there was too much emotion raging over it, and Ninian couldn't think straight. "I asked for a job. I didn't ask to join your *family*."

"You came to us," Cahir said, crossing his arms. "And it's too late now, isn't it?"

"Not if I have my way," Ninian snarled.

"You won't."

Ninian fought the urge to growl as Cahir kept talking.

"But you'll come to like it," the gang leader said. "How long has it been since you had brothers and sisters?"

"I've never had brothers," Ninian said stubbornly. "And I don't care."

Cahir's eyes held something hard behind their pastel colors. "Let me tell you something, Ninian." His voice was still quiet, unaffected, but Ninian could hear the strength in it. "As of yesterday, you belong to us, not yourself." He abandoned the doorframe and leaned in close. "And you clearly do not know how this world works."

Ninian swallowed, his mouth suddenly tasting metallic.

You belong to us.

Heat raced from Ninian's gut to his face, and he felt his hands spasm to fists at his side.

In trying to take himself back, he had given himself away. *Again.*

He made himself inhale, but it didn't cool the swell of resentment and despair.

Cahir obviously noticed Ninian's distress, but he did not so much as twitch.

"It's very simple," Cahir said. "You will fight who we tell you to, when we tell you to. In return, you will have food to eat and clothes to wear. Your brothers and sisters will have your back. They would kill for you." His gaze narrowed. "But if you leave, you will have no money to pay off this debt I heard about from Brígh. You will go back to starving in the streets, only this time…" A little smile lifted the corner of his lip, and in the blink of an eye, he'd slipped a knife from his pocket and held it against Ninian's forehead.

Ninian froze as the point of the knife pricked a drop of blood from his skin.

"Every other gang who sees your scarred face will know what it means," Cahir said. "It means the crescent on your chest is no longer our protection—once you've left, it will be a death sentence."

Ninian's blood chilled. "Wait—"

"Would you like to know what I would do?"

Ninian tried to move back, but Cahir kept the knife to Ninian's forehead.

"I'd make it so your own mother wouldn't recognize you." Cahir leaned close enough that Ninian could smell his breath. "You've seen Brígh's scar, yes?"

Ninian nodded with as little movement as he could.

"Well," Cahir said with a smirk. "That's *nothing*. How would you like to have no lips?" He traced the knife down and let the tip rest on Ninian's upper lip. It felt cold. "What about no eyes?" He pressed the knife against the fold of Ninian's eyelid. "No other gang would miss the opportunity to kill someone from this family if they knew we would not stop them."

"Cahir!"

Ninian was too afraid of the knife against his eye to look up, but he recognized Ruairí's voice.

"He understands, all right?" Ruairí said. "He's not going anywhere. Right, Ninian?"

Ninian let out a shaky breath. "R-right."

Cahir beamed. "That is wonderful news. You don't need to *want* to be here, Ninian. You just need to do it anyway."

A half-cry of relief escaped Ninian's mouth as Cahir stood up and slipped the knife back into his sleeve. Ruairí stood aside to let Cahir pass, and Cahir paused in the doorway.

"Welcome, Ninian," the gang leader said warmly. "We're glad to have you."

And then he turned down the hallway and was gone.

Ninian sank to his elbows, trying to steady his breathing, and Ruairí tentatively crossed the room to crouch next to him. "Are you all right?" he asked.

A nod was the best Ninian could do.

Ruairí brushed his thumb over Ninian's forehead, wiping off the spot of blood. "I should have warned you about that," he said apologetically. "I'm sorry."

"Does he… does he do that to everyone?"

Ruairí made a so-so motion with his hands. "If he thinks you aren't *completely* committed, he'll find an excuse to. Whether you were really going to leave or not."

"I was."

"I know." Ruairí sighed, dropping to a seat on the floor.

"Was he serious?" Ninian touched the cut on his forehead. It wasn't deep, and it barely stung, but the blood on his fingers still made it unnervingly real. "Would he actually do that?"

Ruairí nodded. "He has before."

"To whom?"

"'Whom'?" Ruairí laughed a little. "Never met anyone who says that."

"*Whom* did he cut?" Ninian asked with a little more ire.

Ruairí waved a hand. "Some woman. I didn't know her well."

"What happened to her?"

Ruairí looked at Ninian with complete honesty. "She died." At the look of horror in Ninian's expression, he added, "She couldn't stay in this territory, so she left. But the entire city is *some* gang's turf, so with her face all carved up, I think she made it… a day?" He pinched his lip in thought. "No, two days."

"Why didn't she just sneak out?" Ninian asked.

"Well, why didn't *you*?" Ruairí replied. "Cahir hadn't told her the punishment for leaving, so she tried to storm right past him at the front door."

Ninian pressed his lips together.

"Don't get any ideas, though. Even if you snuck out, we'd send people after you. We'd hunt you to the White City if we had to." Ruairí's eyes softened. "I'm really sorry, Ninian. It's just the way things are." He crossed his legs and propped his elbows on his knees. "It's not a bad life at all. I really think you'll come to see that."

Ninian's fingernails had found his arms again, and he pressed them hard into the skin. When blood came to the surface, his breath came easier. "I don't even care. It doesn't matter."

Ruairí blinked. "Huh?"

Ninian focused on scratching little cuts into his upper arms. "I don't care," he said again.

Ruairí looked confused. "So... that means you won't try and leave, right?"

"I guess so," Ninian said. His head hurt. His stomach felt like an empty, half-dried gourd. His brand throbbed.

"Oh...kay," Ruairí said. "Well, um..." He scratched the back of his neck. "You left breakfast downstairs."

"I don't want it."

"You have to eat."

"Not right now."

Ruairí didn't seem to understand, but he stood all the same. "Suit yourself. Maybe sleep, then."

"Maybe."

When the room was empty again, Ninian leaned against the frame of the bed and closed his eyes.

It's not a bad life at all. I think you'll come to see that.
You'll have food to eat and clothes to wear.
Your brothers and sisters will have your back.

"Shit," he muttered.

Was there a part of him, he wondered, that had known exactly what was happening and just… hadn't wanted to stop it?

Why *did* he want to stop it?

Yes, right now, he was hurt. They had *branded* him, for Gods' sakes.

But you let it happen, said the voice in his head, and Ninian shivered because the voice made his stomach hurt. *You always let it happen.*

I think you must have wanted it.

Filthy boy.

His mother would be appalled if she could see the state of her son. He'd let so *much* happen. She who had raised him to be clean, to be honorable, would be so ashamed.

You could have stopped it.

You could've.

But you didn't.

Ninian shook his head hard. It was his fault. Could being in a gang dirty him any more than he'd already allowed himself to be dirtied? At this point, could it possibly even matter? He'd lost who he was—he'd lost the *right* to who he'd been—two whole years ago.

If this would help him live… well, he didn't have any farther to fall.

So why not?

He wanted a family. He wanted to like Ruairí, and pay his debt, and have enough to eat.

Why not?

There wasn't a reason.

There hadn't been for a while now.

}}}

Ruairí looked startled to see him when Ninian padded back downstairs.

"You're not sleeping?"

Ninian crossed to the plate of smoked meat and black bread, which Ruairí had moved to a table. "Sorry," he said quietly, not facing Ruairí. "Thank you for this."

Holding the plate, he turned to go, but Ruairí stopped him with a hand on his shoulder. Ninian flinched.

"Are you feeling better?" Ruairí asked.

Ninian paused. "I don't know," he said finally.

Ruairí let his hand slip off Ninian's shoulder.

Ninian had always carried himself upright. As his mother had taught him. As he'd been told befitted him.

He allowed his shoulders to slump.

He carried the plate to the small, quiet room, and ate with his hands.

〰

Ninian had curled in the corner of the bed and begun to memorize the pattern of the daub when, without a knock, the door clicked open.

Footsteps crossed the floor almost languidly. "Oi. Kid." By Brígh's tone, the woman didn't seem to care that Ninian wasn't looking at her. "First fight tomorrow."

Ninian absently followed a crack in the wall until it met the windowsill. "Really?" He hadn't thought it would be so soon.

"It's nothing special," Brígh said, and Ninian heard Brígh groan a little as she stretched. "Some low-level messenger. We don't need him dead *too* badly, so if you fuck up, it isn't the end of the world."

Ninian frowned, a weight dropping hard into his stomach. "Dead?"

"That's what I said," Brígh agreed with a yawn.

"I—" Ninian started, but then he stopped himself. His gut was churning, but it wasn't from the alcohol this time. What was this line, and why was he so reluctant to cross it? Had he not just decided he could fall no farther? "I've never killed anyone."

"First time for everything," Brígh said.

Ninian pressed at the back of his thumb until it cracked. "Why?"

"Lots of reasons. Maybe because they hurt our guys. Or because they have something we want, or their gang's stolen from us, or… whatever." She shrugged again. "I'm not in charge of that."

"Cahir is," Ninian said quietly.

"Yeah. And he said tomorrow's guy is a good one to start with." Her footsteps turned back toward the door. "So rest up, eh?"

She didn't completely close the door on the way out.

Ninian rolled onto his back, arms spread. This skin around the brand tugged painfully, feeling too tight, and maybe that was the only reason it was a bit hard to breathe. "Kill?" he murmured.

There was a little corner of his mind, a dark corner glistening with resentment, that wasn't opposed. *You can't get* more *disgusting,* it whispered. *This is what it takes for family. Food. Money.* It gave a humorless, bitter chuckle. *You already know how to kill.*

He did. His mother had taught him how. So that he could kill fae, not people, and make the world a safer place.

That future had broken.

Think about it, his mind whispered. *What do you have to lose?*

CHAPTER TEN

It was dark.

The moon was scarcely a sliver suspended over the horizon, and through hazy clouds, stars still glinted coldly. Ninian shivered in the windless, chilled air, holding his cloak around him as tightly as he could.

Brígh slouched against a low wall that bounded the street, cutting a dry apple and eating stiff slices off the knife. Ruairí sat on top of the wall, turning a burlap-wrapped package in his hands.

"How much longer?" Ninian asked, teeth chattering. He'd been awake when Brígh and Ruairí had come for him in the wee hours of the morning, but he'd also been warm and a little woozy, so the cold was now doubly unpleasant.

"Don't know," Brígh said, crunching another apple slice.

"He usually comes out a little before sunrise," Ruairí answered. "We've kept an eye on him for a couple of days now. Shouldn't be long."

Ninian took a frigid, stabilizing breath, and cracked his knuckles. "What exactly am I supposed to do when he comes?"

Ruairí's burlap package landed in Ninian's hands. "Here."

Glancing up at Ruairí uncertainly, Ninian loosed the wrapping and let it fall away. He gulped. "I see."

Letting the burlap slip to the ground, Ninian allowed the grip of the knife to settle into his palm. It was simple, with a blade the length of a forearm, no hilt, and a grip wrapped in stained leather. The edge was sharp, but warped, as if made from scrap.

"Do I, ah," Ninian said, turning the blade uncertainly. "Should I try to surprise him?"

"Well," Ruairí said with a shrug, "we're called *fighters,* but only because that's what usually happens. If you can take him out without a fight, that's always better."

The knife caught the faint moonlight and twisted it into something just as sharp as the steel. "Right," Ninian said softly.

Ruairí slid down from the wall and brushed himself off before grasping Ninian's shoulders. Ninian was getting used to Ruairí's touchy approach, but he didn't like it. He still cringed at the man's contact. "You can do this, all right?" Ruairí pointed to Ninian's bandaged brand. "You're one of us."

"If I…" Ninian swallowed. "If I *can't*…"

"You can," Ruairí assured him. "The first one's the hardest, but you can do it."

"If you can't, we'll take him out ourselves," Brígh said from her seat on the ground, speaking around a mouthful of apple. "And you won't get any money."

Ninian closed his eyes. "Tell me everything again."

"Sure," Ruairí said, releasing Ninian and leaning against the wall. "He's a messenger. We think he's due to deliver a sensitive message."

"What's the message?" Ninian ventured.

"We don't know," Ruairí said. "But we can't let him tell it to anyone."

Ninian stared at the building across the street, the one in

which his target was, currently, still alive.

"Ninian," Ruairí said after a few moments, "have you ever stolen anything?"

Ninian blinked. "Sure," he said uneasily. "Lots of things."

Ruairí nodded. "This is just the same."

"What do you mean?"

He shrugged. "You're stealing. That's all you're doing. You're just… taking something you've never stolen before."

Ninian's lips felt a little numb. "A life."

"It's not worth so much as you think," Brígh put in with a yawn.

"Brígh. Not helping." Ruairí turned back to Ninian with a small shrug. "She's not *wrong,* though."

The knife felt heavy and important in Ninian's hand. The moonlight warped over its surface.

Then Ninian froze.

A candle had sputtered to life in the little building. "Ah," Ruairí said. "Nearly time."

Brígh finished her apple, core and all, and tucked the small knife into her belt. She pressed herself to her feet. "Right," she said with a sigh. "Come on, Ruairí."

Ninian's heart was hammering, and his vision had started to narrow.

The candle in the window flickered and went out as Brígh and Ruairí vaulted lightly over the wall. Brígh was tall enough to see over the top, while Ruairí muttered in irritation from behind it. "Sorry, Ninian. We'll come back over if you can't do it, but if you can, it has to be on your own."

Brígh snorted. "I forgot how short you are, Ruairí."

"Shut it," Ruairí groused.

Ninian wasn't listening. The door to the little house had clicked open.

The man who came out looked to be in his thirties, with

short blond hair and a tired-looking slump in his shoulders. His lichen-blue sweater was well-worn at the elbows, his knuckles looked chapped, and he shivered a little in the brisk air, rubbing his hands together and blowing into them. Every little motion reminded Ninian just how *alive* he was.

"Brígh," Ninian hissed. The man hadn't looked up and was wrestling the old door shut again. He moved like he was trying to be gentle with it, but he wasn't succeeding. "What's his name?"

Brígh frowned over the top of the wall. "You want to know?"

Ninian nodded sharply.

"If you're sure," Brígh said, clearly not understanding. "It's Cuimín."

"Thank you," Ninian whispered tersely. *Cuimín.* He squeezed his eyes shut and then blinked fast. Cuimín was still trying to jerk the weather-warped door back into the frame, grunting with effort. Ninian wouldn't have a better chance.

His feet moved like he was in a trance, and he couldn't tell how much noise he made as he approached. *My hands are so steady*, he noticed in surprise. The moon's glint on the knife's blade slid evenly over the metal.

By the time Cuimín turned around, Ninian's knife was at his neck.

Cuimín froze, and Ninian, who was only as tall as the man's chin, pressed the glinting edge against Cuimín's throat. In the pre-morning chill, breath rose between them in silver clouds.

All I have to do is press, he thought. The knife was moving just so slightly with the force of all the blood pulsing right beneath its edge. *And it's done.*

"Who are you?" Cuimín asked. Slowly, he began to raise his hands, but Ninian held the knife more firmly and the man froze again.

"Don't move." His voice came out strangled, and he

realized that, though his hands were steady, his breaths were coming erratically.

Cuimín's Adam's apple bobbed, and as cold wind cut down the street, Ninian saw beads of sweat appear on the man's brow. "I…" he stammered. "I don't know what I did to—"

"Stop talking," Ninian growled through clenched teeth. "Stop it."

There was nowhere Cuimín could move to evade the knife, and the man seemed to know it.

"All I have to do," Ninian said, "is press."

He glared at the helpless man, but none of Ninian's anger would channel into Cuimín's wide eyes.

I have to do this before he gets over the shock. He's bigger than me, and if he's quick, he might be able to push me away. And then I'm *the one who'll die.*

"Why are you—" Cuimín managed. He'd started inching his hands upward again, and Ninian jabbed the knife into the man's throat so that a drop of blood rolled down the blade.

"I have to," Ninian said hoarsely and realized it sounded like he wanted the man's permission. "I have to, okay?"

The candle relighted in the window.

Ninian's blood iced.

"You don't… you don't live alone?"

Cuimín opened his palms, supplicating. "I have daughters. Two… two daughters."

For the first time since he had pressed the knife against the man's now-bleeding neck, Ninian's hands began to shake. "You have children."

The man started to nod but stopped himself as the blade bit his flesh.

"But you're in a gang," Ninian snarled, trying to find his fury. He needed it—where was it? "You've killed."

"I'm a messenger," the man said with a nervous smile. "It's only my job to *look* like I'll kill."

Ninian's eyes stung, and he blinked fiercely. "I don't know what's wrong with me," he murmured. The breeze carried the words away.

Cuimín blinked.

Drawing a shaky breath, Ninian redoubled his grip on the knife.

Maybe.

Without lifting it from Cuimín's skin, he traced it so that the sharp, flat tip rested beneath the man's jaw. The flesh felt soft there and very exposed.

Maybe.

"I'm so sorry," Ninian said quietly.

Ninian's eyes forced themselves shut at the last moment, and he thrust the knife upward.

Cuimín let out a throttled, choking scream and collapsed to his knees as Ninian let the knife clatter across the paving-stones. He stood in shock as Cuimín hacked screeching cries, and blood splattered over the earth from the man's mouth. It was red even in the dimness, so red that it burned Ninian's eyes as he stared unblinkingly at what he'd done.

Cuimín writhed, clutching at his throat, at his chin, and he spat and screamed until something solid flew from between his lips. Then his screams quieted; he fell to his elbows as blood poured.

The man's tongue lay glistening and red on the cobbles.

Ninian unclasped his cloak and wadded it up. Dropping to his knees, he pressed it hard under the man's chin. Blood poured into the fabric, leaching between the fibers; it turned the dusky sage the color of murder.

"Stop bleeding," Ninian ordered, as if his words could do such a thing.

Footsteps, two sets, sounded toward them, and then Ruairí's hands were ripping Ninian away from the gasping, horribly moaning Cuimín. "What are you doing? Stop that!"

Ninian fought his way to Cuimín's side again. "Leave me alone! I have to stop the bleeding!"

Brígh stared at Ninian as if he had lost his mind. "What are you *talking* about?"

"Ninian," Ruairí said, trying to separate him from the downed man. "Ninian, hey… hey. You did really well, okay? Really well, but you need to stop this—"

"*You* stop!" Ninian snapped. "Look!" He pointed to Cuimín's tongue, inert on the ground, and wrestled his way around Ruairí to press his cloak more firmly to the wound under Cuimín's chin. "I cut it out, okay? He can't talk. He can't deliver a message, right?" He was right and he knew it. Nobody in the Maze could write, and nobody could read. The message was dead.

Ruairí looked at the tongue, clearly flabbergasted. Brígh nudged at it delicately with the toe of her boot.

"He has children," Ninian said desperately, realizing that tears were flowing freely down his face. "He can't die; he has children."

Brígh slipped her hands into her pockets. "You know he's gonna die anyway, right?"

Ninian shook his head fiercely. "No! If he keeps it clean, if it stops *bleeding*, it'll heal—"

"That's not what I meant," Brígh interrupted. "I mean a speechless messenger is useless."

Now Ninian was the one staring. "Wh… what?"

Brígh looked Ninian straight in the eyes. "His gang isn't going to feed a useless man."

Ninian opened his mouth and closed it again. "But… but

he can do something else…"

"Don't be naïve." Brígh kicked the tongue into the gutter where the dust caked darkly onto the blood. "It doesn't matter, anyway. We're done here."

Ruairí's hands were warm on Ninian's arms, guiding him to his feet.

"Wait," Ninian protested.

"Leave the cloak. Come on. We'll get you a new one." He squeezed Ninian's arms. "You earned it, okay?"

"Wait…" Ninian said again. Ruairí steered him away from the increasingly still Cuimín while Ninian's shoulders started to shake. "Wait…"

But he didn't fight.

It didn't take long before Ninian could no longer hear Cuimín's moans.

By the time they reached the end of the street, Ninian could just catch the sound of a sticky door finally bursting open.

By the time they'd wound their way back into the tangled streets, the children's screams barely reached his ears at all.

He hung his head and began to sob.

CHAPTER ELEVEN

There was a point where trying to make things better required a manageable amount of action, and a point where things seemed so bad it was easier to let it all burn. And between those points, there was… nothing.

A dullness.

A vacuum.

A place where the world seemed cottony and not very important, and nothing felt like much at all.

The pouch of coins sat on the table where Cahir had dropped them… Ninian really wasn't sure how long ago. It looked filthy in stained brown leather.

True to Ruairí's word, a new cloak was draped over Ninian's shoulders. It was wool, and it was blue, and it was a little coarse, but Ninian was warm. His hands were wrapped around a lopsided ceramic mug of tea, and the steam felt good on his cheeks when he held it under his chin. In front of him, an empty plate had once held a slice of soft cheese and a chunk of black bread, and his stomach was full.

Ruairí had been rather gentle about the whole thing. The cloak, he'd said, had been his nephew's, but Ninian could have it. The cheese was a celebration. The tea was because Ninian looked shaken, and Ruairí had made Brígh do *something* to help before the scarred fighter skulked off someplace else.

And Ninian felt…

Hollow.

Wood protested as Ruairí dragged out a chair and lowered himself to a seat across the table from Ninian. He folded his hands, his eyes full of concern. "Ninian?" he ventured.

Ninian didn't answer.

"You, um," Ruairí started. "You don't want me to say good job, do you?"

Ninian hadn't done a good job. He'd placed the blade with expert skill—if it had not been into the throat of a *human*, his mother might even have been proud—but as it was, he had neither spared the man nor killed him properly. "No, thank you," he said quietly.

"Right," Ruairí said. He fidgeted with his cuticles. "So… you have money now." He tried for a smile. "That's good, right? You can start on that debt?"

That should have been encouraging news. He nodded.

"Okay," Ruairí said, rubbing his palms together. "Well… this is supposed to be Brígh's job, but I volunteered to take over." He paused. "You don't have to stay in this house all the time," he began. "You can go wherever you want. But if you don't check in within two days, you'll be punished with a whipping, which I can't say I recommend, 'specially since Cahir's got you pegged as a flight risk, and you do *not* want him to think you're trying to leave." He touched his face and traced a finger across his cheek. "Y'know." He sighed when Ninian didn't react and started counting off on his fingers. "You can't get into your own fights with someone from another gang. You can't hurt anyone from this gang. If one of us tells you that you have a fight, you have to drop what you're doing and go. If you try to run…"

Ninian couldn't focus as Ruairí listed the rules. His head felt full of fog.

Ruairí looked up as Ninian pushed away from the table, but he didn't stop him when Ninian tucked the pouch of coins into his pocket and walked silently out the door.

Outside, the air was still. Damp. Heavy. Cold. Ninian couldn't tell if it was morning anymore.

The idea of Cuimín's blood under Ninian's fingernails had refused to budge no matter how many times Ninian washed his hands, so Ninian had bitten his nails until the only blood there was his own. They stung, and the cold made them burn.

The gravel on the cobbles crunched as Ninian walked down to the street. He wanted to pick a fight, or sleep, or find the highest place he could and just… look. He wanted to run so fast he forgot everything and lie so still that time would pass him by.

But he didn't.

He went down the street because that made sense.

The new cloak was much better than the old one. It only had one hole, a frayed spot in the hem, and it kept the wind away from Ninian's skin even if it *did* seem to absorb the damp from the air and smell rather mildewed. And when Ninian put up the hood, the blue wool hid him from the city and the city from him. The gray buildings and gray sky seemed a degree further from reality, and Ninian felt invisible. He could hear crows somewhere above him, and their harsh cries blended into the human sounds of the city.

Ninian wasn't sure how long it took to reach Máel Máedóc's shop—his sense of time had cracked. The sun had set when he arrived at the crooked trading shop, and it seemed that it had done so in a matter of breaths. *Where had the day gone?* He'd killed a man at sunrise, and now that same sun was behind the horizon. Ninian blinked, disoriented.

It didn't matter. He was there for one reason, and he fished in his pocket for the coins.

It's not enough.

That was obvious. He spread open the mouth of the pouch with two fingers to see the meager glint within. "I'm so glad *this* has been my last day." He could beg for more time, he supposed, if Máel Máedóc was in a generous mood, but somehow he didn't think he'd be breathing long enough to beg once the shopkeeper saw the shortage of coin. He wondered how he'd die.

He lifted his hand and rapped his raw knuckles against the wood. "Máel Máedóc? Sir?"

No sound came from within.

He's not sleeping, is he? The shop was closed, but the sun had only just set. Perhaps the giant man wasn't home.

"Just a minute," a voice rumbled from inside.

A shiver scraped like a cold blade down Ninian's spine. *Nope. Not sleeping.*

The door creaked, and behind it, metal rasped seven times as bolts slid back from the wood. Ninian forced himself to remain still. "Who's there?" Máel Máedóc grumbled, cracking the door. "Shop's closed—oh." He opened the door further, enough for Ninian to see faint candlelight from within.

Ninian swallowed. "I... have money."

Without a word, the giant shopkeeper stepped back. A whirlpool churned in the pit of his stomach as Ninian stepped over the threshold. He followed Máel Máedóc through tipping shelves, doing his best not to trip. The shop looked alien in the dark, spidery and shadowed and disproportionate. Where shelves were weighted too heavily, they leaned at odd angles, and candle wax dribbled from brackets in ghostly stalactites.

In the back of the shop, the maze of shelves ended in a small space dominated by an overburdened table, and a door spilled warm light from cracks around the frame. Máel Máedóc cleared the table roughly, dropping its contents unceremoniously onto the nearest shelf, and then held out his hand.

Ninian set the stained little purse into Máel Máedóc's palm.

The giant man shook the coins onto the table, and in the weak candlelight, Ninian watched as he deftly sorted them into stacks by worth. The shadows ebbed and billowed about the tipping shelves, and then Máel Máedóc straightened to his full, formidable height. His face was inscrutable. "That…" he said eventually, and Ninian braced himself for the inevitable proclamation. *It isn't enough. It's over. You're dead.* The candlelight was sliding over the shopkeeper and casting shadows in the hollows around his eyes, and that was enough to send tremors over Ninian's skin. "That is more than I expected."

Ninian blinked. "What?"

"It's not enough, of course." Máel Máedóc seemed to be speaking more to himself than to Ninian, and his voice was low in his chest. "But it is more than I thought you'd bring me."

"I know it isn't everything," Ninian managed. There was a candle on a nearby shelf, more wick than wax, and its light guttered. "But if you give me more time, I can…" He pressed his lips together, trying to force speech from a throat that felt stiff as jerky. "I can get the rest." His hands curled into fists, and his raw nailbeds stung against his palms.

"You can get the rest?" Máel Máedóc repeated. Ninian

thought the man looked troubled; for a moment, the sharpness in his eyes seemed, like the candle, to gutter uncertainly.

In one sudden motion, the shopkeeper snatched the candle from the shelf and, wax running over his knuckles, held it closer to Ninian's face. Ninian cringed away sharply, but Máel Máedóc didn't let the flame touch him. Instead, he leaned closer, taking in the bruising along the side of Ninian's face where Brígh's hand had struck, the sickly darkness under his eyes, and the angry red creeping over Ninian's collarbone. "Oh, Gods, boy," Máel Máedóc murmured, and he crushed the candle to the table until the wax adhered to the grain. "*Tell* me you didn't."

Ninian didn't know how to reply to that, but it was easier to be silent anyway.

Máel Máedóc's hand found Ninian's collar, and with startling gentleness, he pulled the fabric aside.

Gasping in pain and a visceral rush of fear, Ninian jolted away with a cry. His heel caught on the leg of the table and nearly sent him to the floor, but Máel Máedóc caught him and steadied him. He held Ninian's arm too tightly, though Ninian couldn't tell if he meant to, and the blue of his eyes had turned to the color of storm clouds on the sea.

"I—I can get you the rest of the money," Ninian managed, trying breathlessly to pull his arm away. He wasn't sure where the self-preserving instinct was coming from, but it felt wrong even as the words spilled from his lips. He knew how to get money now, knew how startlingly hot blood felt, and here he was, begging to be allowed to kill. "I can, I swear."

"Ninian," Máel Máedóc said, and a strangled tone had entered the man's voice. It didn't seem like he'd been listening to Ninian's rambling. "You joined a gang."

With his collar askew, the candlelight fell over on the

loose bandage, the one doing very little to cover Ninian's new, crescent-shaped mutilation. Ninian nodded, pulling his shirt back to hide it.

"Why did you do that?" Máel Máedóc asked. "I never meant for you to do that."

At that, Ninian frowned. The shopkeeper looked appalled.

Ninian's brows met, and he almost sighed in relief when he felt anger, familiar and bright, slip into his mind. "Where else did you think I was going to find the money?"

Máel Máedóc shook his head. "Not there. From friends, or from selling rubbish, or from your family. Not from there, never there." He threw up his hands. "Hell, I was surprised to see you back at all! You could've just run!"

For one, ridiculous second, Ninian had to suppress laughter. His body was in pain, his emotions more hollow than substance, and shadows danced in the corners of his vision. Stupid, exhausted laughter clawed up from Ninian's chest. Máel Máedóc looked at him with horror and… yes. There was remorse in the shallow creases of the man's face. "I could've *run*?" Ninian's hands clenched hard onto the lip of the table like he was trying to keep himself upright. He could have run. The shopkeeper's hold had been an illusion.

An illusion for which he'd given up…

Everything.

Tears blurred his vision. "You have no right!" he managed. "No right to change the terms. You said to get the money, and I got some, didn't I? You have no right to say *now* that I can't have joined a gang, because I *did*, and it's too late now!" His voice broke. "It's too late!"

"Ninian," Máel Máedóc said, and Ninian glared at him. The shopkeeper held up his hands, his palms pale in the dimness. "I'm not changing the terms. I wouldn't do that."

"You have no idea," Ninian growled, and when his own

voice reached his ears, he sounded half-feral. "No idea what I did, do you?" He laughed, more tears falling from the corners of his eyes. "What I had to do, *have* to do—"

As if before a skittish animal, Máel Máedóc knelt. "You're right." His voice startled Ninian with its lack of harshness. "I don't know what you had to do."

"I killed a man!" His voice gave out and snapped like a line in the wind. "*That's* what I did. I pushed a knife through his throat. And the blood—" His hands twitched. "I—"

Máel Máedóc's eyes weren't on Ninian's face, and Ninian couldn't read them. Again, Máel Máedóc tugged Ninian's shirt away from the brand, but he was gentle enough for the sting to subside quickly. "This needs to be treated."

Ninian pushed Máel Máedóc's hand away and stepped back defensively. "Wh…what?"

"Your brand. It needs to be treated. It's going to get infected."

Ninian shook his head, trying to understand where the conversation had just gone.

He didn't know much about healing, but he knew the brand hurt almost more than it had when Brígh had pressed the searing iron to his skin, and that when he touched it, his fingers came away wet with blood and yellowish fluid.

"Someone already did," he snapped, unwilling to relinquish his anger to uncertainty.

Máel Máedóc's face didn't change. "I can do better." He stood. "Wait here."

And then he vanished between the shelves, the floor creaking under his bulk.

Ninian stood still, lost. He couldn't trace a line of thought, couldn't tell which tumultuous thread to pursue until one floated above the others.

So… he's not going to kill me?

He didn't think there could be a point in treating someone slated for death unless Máel Máedóc's cruel streak ran even deeper than Ninian had thought.

He was getting the feeling that Máel Máedóc's reputation did not quite match the man.

The shopkeeper returned shortly with a little ceramic vial, a bandage, and a pot of paste. Without a word, he tugged off the bandage Ruairí had tied across the burn, uncorked the bottle, and soaked the fresh bandage with it. It smelled pungent and fresh, like grass in the heat of a high summer morning, and Ninian eyed it warily as Máel Máedóc pressed the cork back into the bottle's slender neck. The shopkeeper folded the bandage over itself to make a compress. "Clench your teeth so you don't bite your tongue."

With that, he pressed the bandage to the brand.

Ninian, eyes flying open wide, let out a shriek before he could stop himself.

"Good," the shopkeeper encouraged as Ninian's voice cracked. "Steady, now." He lifted the bandage, which nearly made Ninian sob, and used two fingers to smear the herbal paste into the wound. The gritty concoction burned, and Máel Máedóc gave Ninian a tight-lipped smile and tied the herb-soaked bandage across the brand. "Finished."

"Wh…what the *hell*," Ninian panted.

"You're welcome." The giant man set the vial and the pot down before half-sitting, half-leaning on the table and folding his arms. For a few uncomfortable heartbeats, during which time Ninian gingerly rearranged his shirt back over the bandages, the shopkeeper just stared at him.

Finally, shrugging his cloak more comfortably over his shoulders, Ninian returned Máel Máedóc's gaze with a glare. "What?"

The air of the shop seemed to settle heavily with the

weight of Máel Máedóc's silence. "So you've killed."

The candle sputtered, nearly out. "What do you care?" Ninian spat. "You only told me not to steal." Ruairí's words came back to Ninian faintly. *You're just… taking something you've never stolen before.* Ninian's stomach twisted, and he winced.

Máel Máedóc looked about to say something, but then he shook his head. "The deal's off."

Ninian's heart tripped. Hadn't Máel Máedóc just said he wouldn't change the terms? Did this count as changing the terms? "What?"

"The deal. Our deal. The one where you pay back the money you owe me." Máel Máedóc opened his eyes and fixed them on Ninian's. "It's off."

Ninian froze. "I don't understand."

Máel Máedóc leaned away from the table and, turning, swept the little stacks of coins back into the pouch. He tugged the strings, cinching the mouth of the bag, and dropped it into Ninian's stunned hands. "I don't want your money."

Ninian stared at the disgusting little purse. He let his hands fall, and the purse landed on the floor with a dead-sounding *clink*. A miserable smile had crept its way back onto Ninian's lips, and he couldn't make it go away. He shook his head and swiped the back of his hand across his eyes.

"What's funny?" Máel Máedóc asked.

"I thought you'd kill me if I didn't pay you back," he said, and somehow, he couldn't quite regulate the pitch of his voice. Another horrible, breathy laugh clawed its way up his throat. "I did everything because I thought if I didn't, I'd die." His face cracked into a broken smile. "It was all for nothing, wasn't it? You won't take the money, and you won't even…" Tears had started rolling down his face again.

Silently, Máel Máedóc lowered himself to a squat, and Ninian thought he saw a glimmer of moisture in the corners of the huge man's eyes. "Ninian," he said slowly. "I still expect you to pay me back. Just not with money, okay? Not with death."

Ninian looked at him emptily. "Don't fucking touch me."

Máel Máedóc took a deep breath and looked toward the door, the one under which candlelight was creeping, and for the first time, Ninian wondered if there was someone beyond it. Máel Máedóc let out the air in a long, heavy sigh, and Ninian realized that Máel Máedóc looked almost half as tired as Ninian. "I want you to help me with something." He ran his fingers between the rows of his braids, making the beads at the ends click together. "Can you do that?"

A little broken noise escaped Ninian's lips. "Do *what*?"

The giant shopkeeper steepled his fingers. "You've taken a life, right?"

Slowly, Ninian nodded. If Cuimín wasn't dead already… he would be, soon.

"I want you to help me save one."

Ninian was sure his face was blank. "You want *me* to save someone's life."

"I want you to try."

Ninian shook his head. "I don't know how to do that." He looked up at the shopkeeper as if he could express the hopelessness of the situation with his eyes. "I've never saved *anyone*."

"There's a first time for everything."

Ninian snorted humorlessly. "That's what Brígh said when I told her I'd never killed."

"And you did *that*, didn't you?"

"I'm…" Ninian started. He swallowed hard and pressed on the backs of his knuckles. "I think I'd make it… worse."

Máel Máedóc took another heavy breath. "Then this is a good place to start," he said, exhaling in one long sigh. "Because you can't."

CHAPTER TWELVE

The light under the door glowed steadily against the dark, while outside, in the shop, spent candles sputtered and smoked. Máel Máedóc paced slowly while Ninian sat at the table, scratching at a stiff layer of wax with his fingernail.

"He's very skittish," Máel Máedóc was saying, stopping every so often to make piercing eye contact with Ninian. "Don't move quickly. Understood?"

Ninian blinked. From his tone, it sounded like the shopkeeper was describing an animal more than a person.

"And he doesn't speak, far as I can tell." The giant man rubbed at the dark scruff of stubble over his jaw. "He hasn't even told me his name. So don't go talking him to death."

"Does it seem like I would?"

Máel Máedóc didn't answer that. "Honestly, I don't expect you to get through to him. Not really. But…" He pinched the bridge of his nose. "He seems about your age, and you're a damn sight less intimidating than I am. You might be able to reach where I can't."

The wax flaked under Ninian's painfully short nails, and he flicked it away. "Where did you find this mess?"

Máel Máedóc cocked his head. "The wax?"

Ninian shook his head. "The kid."

The shopkeeper's gaze turned cutting. "You're one to talk about messes, boy. I was up by the Fisher's Shore this morning, found him senseless by the piers. The seagulls seemed to think he was dead."

Ninian couldn't imagine anyone going so far as to take in a broken street rat. "What did you want from him?"

Máel Máedóc didn't seem to understand. "Want from him...?"

Ninian nodded. "Why'd you help him?"

"It..." Máel Máedóc's brow furrowed. "It was the right thing to do."

Ninian just stared at him. "You don't match, do you? Your stories, I mean."

A faint smirk flitted over Máel Máedóc's lips, and then it was gone. He definitely knew which stories Ninian meant. "I'm an upright man. That's a frightening thing to *some* people." Ninian shook his head, and Máel Máedóc brushed off his hands. "Stay here a moment."

Ninian watched as the shopkeeper crossed to the door and opened it a crack. The man peered in, then closed the door again and turned back to Ninian.

"He's awake." He stepped aside, and Ninian stood slowly. "Remember what I told you."

"Slow, quiet, he's a wreck," Ninian muttered. "I remember."

Máel Máedóc opened the door again, leaning around the corner. "*Buachaill cladaigh*," he said softly, and Ninian was startled by the gentleness in the man's words. *Shore boy.* "I've brought someone to see you." He looked back and nodded to Ninian.

Ninian, with timidity that surprised him, moved to stand in the doorway.

The room itself was simple enough. It had streaked,

whitewashed walls, a wooden bed, and a little table covered in what seemed to be all of the shop's good candles. For a moment, Ninian didn't see anything out of the ordinary.

Then his eyes, skating over the room, landed on the boy.

He sat on the floor, his shoulder leaning against the edge of the bed. All Ninian could see were bony shoulders and sandy-blond hair. The boy didn't so much as glance up at Ninian's presence. A roughly woven blanket hung loosely about him, and in it, he seemed very small.

"Uh," Ninian said. "Hello?"

The boy didn't answer. With a quick glance to Máel Máedóc, Ninian stepped inside.

"Máel Máedóc said I'm supposed to… help you?" That sounded stupid. Ninian let out a sharp sigh and turned back to the shopkeeper in the doorway. "I don't know what I'm doing, *sir*," he said, realizing just in time that he was about to say 'sir' and quickly turning the word sarcastic.

Máel Máedóc spread his hands with a shrug.

Shaking his head wearily, Ninian walked over to where the boy sat and dropped to a squat. The boy still didn't move. "Are you *sure* he's awake?" Ninian asked over his shoulder. He shifted to his knees and leaned down to take in the boy in front of him. The boy's eyes were barely open; his gaze was fixed on the floor. He had a graceful, diamond-shaped face and high cheekbones whose angles spoke of hunger.

Ninian snapped his fingers. "Um… hello?"

The boy didn't look up, but he shifted in his seat. The blanket fell aside.

"Oh! You *are* awa—" Ninian's eyes widened. "*Oh*."

Wrapped in bandages that in no way disguised their shape, the boy's hands rested in his lap. His sleeves were pushed up, and Ninian could see deep purple bruising that crept from under the bandages up to the boy's elbows. Mottled and horrible, it looked as if he'd crushed elderberries into his skin. Ninian's eyes flicked, aghast, over the crookedness of the stranger's wrists and the ravaged forms of his fingers and palms. The bandages were stained a dark reddish-brown. Blood.

So *that* was why he was a mess.

"What *happened?*" Momentarily forgetting about Máel Máedóc in the doorway, Ninian moved to a cross-legged seat in front of the silent stranger. For a moment, he just sat and stared at the boy's arms and hands that Ninian couldn't imagine ever working again. He let his gaze wander over the light spray of freckles across the boy's nose, the darkness of his eyelashes in contrast to his fair hair, and the still defensiveness of his curled shoulders and tucked-up knees. "Who did this?" The boy didn't answer, and Ninian twisted to look to Máel Máedóc. "What happened to him?"

The big man shook his head. "I wish I knew."

Ninian set his attention back on the boy. Carefully, he slid the edge of the blanket back up over the stranger's shoulder.

That got a reaction.

The boy startled, eyes shooting wide with a little gasp, and he pressed himself against the bedpost. Ninian startled as well and leaned back in alarm.

But then it was Ninian's turn to gasp.

The boy had looked up. And Ninian... Ninian had never seen such eyes.

Where most people had eyes the color of straw, or of seawater, or of wildflowers, this boy's irises *burned*. Like... like blood on fire.

Ninian stared in shock as the stranger met his gaze, noticing the way the color danced like the glow of embers over a coal. It was darkly brilliant around the edges, licking crimson in toward the center, and around the pupil glimmered a fine circle of bright copper flecks.

It was stunning.

"Um," said Ninian, pushing himself back and trying to get himself in order. He'd never seen somebody with red eyes before. Suddenly every other color seemed drab.

The boy curled in more tightly, pressing against the bed as if it would protect him, but he didn't look away from Ninian's face. Those spectacular eyes flitted back and forth between each of Ninian's before a funny expression came over the boy's face: it was pain, certainly, but agitation too, a quiet agitation that could come from nowhere but the boy's own head.

"I'm not going to hurt you." Ninian held his hands out. "Yeah? Promise."

The boy let out a quick, shaky breath.

Ninian put a hand on his chest. "I'm Ninian. Can you tell me your name?"

At that, the boy broke eye contact. His gaze fell back to his hands with a tiny shudder.

"Yeah," Ninian said, unsurprised. "Máel Máedóc said maybe you didn't talk." He found his eyes slipping to the boy's hands, as if magnetized by the horror. He rested his elbows on his knees, unable to look away from the ruin. "That looks awful." Unthinkingly, he tugged at his shirt to make sure it covered his brand. "But it looks like Máel Máedóc patched you up, huh?"

In the doorway, Máel Máedóc cleared his throat. "I have things to do before tomorrow. Call if you need me."

Ninian nodded, and the shopkeeper, after casting one last careful look at Ninian, moved back out into the shop. Ninian heard his heavy footsteps thumping through the labyrinth of shelves.

Almost as soon as the giant man was out of sight, the boy slumped back against the wall. Ninian frowned, looking to where Máel Máedóc had stood, then at the stranger again. The pain in the boy's eyes hadn't abated, but suddenly he looked exhausted instead of afraid.

"Does Máel Máedóc bother you?" Ninian asked.

Unsurprisingly, he didn't get an answer.

"I don't think you need to be scared," Ninian said, running his fingers absently along the bandage that looped over his shoulder. "I was afraid of him too, but in the end, he's kind of pathetic… oh!" He bolted to his knees. "Oh, hell! Um—"

Tears had started to roll down the strange boy's cheeks, and he closed his eyes, beginning to shake with quiet sobs.

"Hell," Ninian muttered again. "What happened?"

The boy's head drooped, even as tears kept coming, and he leaned forward over his knees.

It was impossible not to soften. "Damn," Ninian said. *This one's damaged. Maybe as much as me. Maybe more.* For some reason, an unhappy little smile flickered over his mouth at that. He moved a little closer. "I'm really sorry. Was it something I said?"

The boy shook his head, tears still flowing, so at least he understood what Ninian was saying.

"Are you in pain?" He cringed. Of *course*, the boy was in pain. "I mean, is that why you're crying?"

He received no answer.

"Right," Ninian murmured. He looked around. "Um."

What was he supposed to do, exactly? He was no healer.

He didn't expect the boy to speak first.

He definitely wasn't talking to Ninian. His lips were barely moving, and at first, Ninian thought he might be imagining it. "Are you—?" he started, but then stopped himself.

Carefully, he leaned in closer. The boy did not shy away, but he didn't stop murmuring either. It sounded habitual, like a prayer.

I'm all right. I'll be all right. Nothing lasts if you don't let it. I'm all right. I'll be all right. Nothing lasts if you don't let it—

"Hey," Ninian said softly. Something about the boy's words stuck in his chest, like a burr on the inside of his ribs—too close to his heart, or whatever was there now.

The boy stopped whispering and looked to Ninian with eyes that were, once again, welling with tears.

"You're kind of different, aren't you?" Ninian asked, keeping his voice in that same, soft tone. Like he was talking to someone frightened or grieving. The boy, he thought, might be both. "You're…" He trailed off. The boy hadn't broken eye contact. He'd scarcely blinked. There was so much pain in his face that Ninian's breath almost seized. Even so, when the boy looked away, it left Ninian with an acute sense of loss. Ninian shook his head, off-balance, and studied the boy carefully. "You…" He stopped again and blinked hard. He wasn't sure what that feeling had been. "You look really tired." The boy glanced up again with wet, haggard eyes, and Ninian felt his face turn gentle. "Come on. Let's get you into bed."

The boy struggled to his feet, evading Ninian's touch, and then he sat on the bed, gingerly holding his hands to his chest.

"Go on, lie down." He folded the blankets away, and the boy carefully, casting nervous glances at Ninian all the while, lowered himself onto his side. Ninian settled the covers lightly over the boy's shoulders. "Sleep will make it better."

Ninian could feel the boy's eyes burning against his back as he turned to blow out the candles. He left one lit so the room wouldn't be wholly in darkness, and then he cracked his knuckles and rocked on his heels.

"I…" He swallowed. Was that it? He could tell Máel Máedóc he'd tried. That was all the shopkeeper had asked. But even as he thought it, his mouth was opening. "I'll come back, okay? Tomorrow." He looked back to where the boy's strange eyes were holding the candlelight.

The boy blinked, eyelids already drooping.

"Right," Ninian said. He crossed to the door; his hand was on the knob when he froze.

"Áed," the boy said, and Ninian turned sharply to find the boy's eyes closed. "My name is Áed."

CHAPTER THIRTEEN

Back in the flat Ninian had scouted, stars twinkled outside the window. Ninian could see them as he lay on the floor under his new cloak, which was long enough to act as a blanket.

He wondered how the boy—Áed, his name was Áed—had gotten to such a state. It hurt to imagine. He remembered how Áed's hair, golden in the candlelight, had cast shadows over his nose while those eyes burned hot and dark. It was a strangely riveting picture, even as Ninian's stomach twisted with the haunted agony written on Áed's features.

I'm all right, Áed had whispered. *I'll be all right. Nothing lasts if you don't let it.*

Ninian rolled onto his side, and then hissed as the brand tugged with the motion. He'd almost forgotten about it. The shopkeeper's medicine worked well.

He was glad he'd decided not to return to Cahir's house that evening—he had almost another day, according to Ruairí, before he needed to return. He groaned, curling into a ball on his side. It didn't seem like Cuimín's would be the last blood to stain his hands. Was this something he'd get used to? All of the stains he'd accumulated... he had thought they'd covered him already, sullied him beyond repair or recognition. But the stain he'd gained today still showed. He could sense it melting into him, moving with him. Eventually, would he collect enough to not feel each one?

The thought made him ill.

Nothing lasts if you don't let it.

"Let it…" he whispered. He stared at the dark window, but he didn't see the stars.

He remembered Áed's expression, the emptiness around the pain, and yet the red-eyed boy had whispered his words like he believed they were true.

What *willpower.*

Áed was shattered somewhere deep. Ninian was sure of that. He'd been sure of it the moment he'd looked into his eyes.

But Áed was trying to pick up the pieces.

Nothing lasts if you don't let it.

The cloak over Ninian was heavy and warm, even if it did smell a bit stale. He plucked at it, loose threads spreading between the pads of his fingers, and knew that he'd never forget why he had it.

He exhaled slowly. "You know what? I am really done with this."

Nothing lasts if you don't let it.

He had been letting it.

And the gang owned him.

"I'm done," he repeated, and felt a warm, determined rush tingle down the length of his spine. A smile crept over his face in the dark. "I am *done.*"

He pulled the hood of the cloak over his face and thought it to himself, just to hear the decision and feel it in his bones.

He was going to get out of the gang.

†††

Braiding his own hair was *hard*.

Ninian didn't have any kind of mirror in the flat, so after waking, he had fastened his cloak all the way down against the sunny morning chill and made the walk to the nearest well. All the wells in the Maze tasted just a bit salty, but given the amount of winter rain that had been filling the ground, Ninian expected it was as fresh and clear as ever it could be. He waited his turn at the edge of the square, carefully running a splinter of wood under his impossibly short fingernails to get out the dirt and—probably—blood. People chatted around the low stone well, and their voices combined with the slosh of water and the creak of the well's crank.

It was strange that now, he had to think about which gang territory he was on. It wasn't something he'd considered much before. Gangs *did* get involved with the civilians on their turf, mostly in the form of demanding dues from businesses and occasional labor from strong young folks— and, Ninian thought caustically, apparently conscripting people against their will—but Ninian had never been affected before that week.

Now, though… he touched the tidy, herb-soaked bandages over his brand. Surely nobody would bother him when the crescent was hidden. Whether it meant he was protected or not, he didn't want the attention.

He let out a sigh. He wanted to get out of the gang, and yet had no plan and a gang symbol permanently seared into his body. Whatever he tried was *not* going to be easy, and no matter what happened, he'd never be rid of it *quite* all the way.

Still.

He sighed and quit playing with the bandages.

Little red flags fluttered from the crankshaft of the well, their edges tattered. Symbols that Ninian recognized were painted in soot on each one, charms meant to ward fae from the busy courtyard. It was funny, really, how much everyone feared the fae, but nobody seemed to know how to deal with them. The fae came to the world on festival nights when the veil thinned, but that didn't mean they all left when the night was over. People never lost all their wariness, but the vast majority of the charms Ninian saw were useless.

This well sat in the middle of crumbling stone walls, where the ruins of towers reached for the sky as their own weight slowly tore them down. Crows perched at the top of the keep and the ramparts, dark against the clouds, and they watched the well with glassy black eyes and cawed quietly to each other. Ninian's mother had taken him to this citadel often when he was younger; she'd told him the gray brick walls and crumbling battlements belonged to him. Once, Ninian had imagined walking among soaring parapets and towers and turrets, like he came with some kind of ancestral memory, but that fantasy had long since decayed—the old citadel was part of the city, just like anything else.

When Ninian reached the well, he drew up the pail and splashed his face, gasping a little at the cold water, and diligently rubbed away the grime from his skin.

When he was done, he headed to the side of the courtyard to use his reflection in one of the building's windows. His reddish hair, the color of dark rust, fell on either side of his face, looking like he'd slept several restless nights without so much as finger-combing it—which was accurate.

He frowned at his reflection for a few moments before sternly dragging his fingers through the tangled russet waves. When it was workable, he started trying to weave the strands together from the peak of his forehead. It was tricky to do on himself, looking at his mirrored image, and it started falling apart once he reached the crown of his head. He quickly tied it with a bit of twine he'd found scrounging about the flat, and studied himself in the window glass, turning his head back and forth. The lower part of his hair still hung naturally down, but it wasn't in his face anymore. "It doesn't look *bad*… right?" he asked himself under his breath. He wished he had somebody other than himself to ask. The closest thing to a friend he'd had in the past year had been Kelp, who hadn't been a friend at all.

The window opened, and Ninian jumped back, startled. "Ey." A woman in a nightdress stuck her head out, looking annoyed. "Like what you see?"

Ninian felt the blood rush to his face. "What? I wasn't—I was just—"

The woman rolled her eyes. "Get out o' here." With that, she slammed the window shut, and Ninian felt his knees go weak with embarrassment. He hurried down a side street without needing to be told twice.

⁘

Máel Máedóc's shop still had dark windows when Ninian arrived, and he stood a moment at the door, catching his breath. He'd jogged most of the way there.

When he was done panting, he rapped on the door. It wasn't that early. It would be a shock if Máel Máedóc were still sleeping.

After a few seconds, he knocked again. This time, heavy footsteps stomped over to the door, and the locks scraped back. Máel Máedóc glowered at Ninian. "You're back."

Ninian blinked.

"Huh." Máel Máedóc scratched his chin. He looked a little tired, and Ninian wondered if he actually had just woken. "Didn't expect that." He turned away from the door, and

131

Ninian followed him in. "The boy's still sleeping."

Ninian nodded. "Okay." He trailed Máel Máedóc through the shelves. "His name is Áed, by the way."

The shopkeeper stopped, and Ninian almost ran into him. "What?" He turned quickly. "How do you know?"

"He told me."

Máel Máedóc was looking at Ninian with disbelief. Eventually, he closed his eyes and shook his head. "Maybe I did make the right decision." Still shaking his head, he started walking through the shelves again. "You're a very strange one."

When they got to the back of the shop, Ninian looked around in surprise. "What's all this?"

With a grunt, Máel Máedóc pushed a burlap sack aside with his foot. "New haul. Got 'em last night."

Ninian squatted next to the sack. Pinkish grains were creeping between the fibers of the cloth. "Salt?"

Máel Máedóc nodded. "Fresh off the sea, from a fellow in the southwest."

Ninian pointed at a battered crate. "What's that one?"

"Nails."

Ninian smirked as he pried open the mouth of a large linen pouch. "And this one's rowan berries." He looked up at Máel Máedóc, who had dropped to a weary seat at the table. "Are you preparing for a festival?"

The shopkeeper waved a hand, stifling a yawn. "Just stocking up. They'll all sell."

"The next festival isn't for weeks."

Máel Máedóc rolled his eyes. "You cure food with salt, build with nails, eat rowan."

"And you kill fae with all three," Ninian said, remembering what his mother had told him years ago. "Did you get anything else?"

With a sigh, Máel Máedóc pinched the bridge of his nose. He looked exhausted, and Ninian understood now. He must have traded for these packages in the middle of the night. "Why do you care?"

Ninian shrugged. "Just curious."

"Well, cut it out. You're more talkative than last time, aren't you?"

Instead of answering, Ninian took a nail from the box and turned it in his hands. It was as long as his hand, hammered sharp. Placed right, it could certainly kill. Salted and rubbed with rowan, it could kill an immortal.

Good to have.

When Máel Máedóc wasn't looking, he pocketed it. The next festival *wasn't* for weeks, but he didn't think it could hurt to be ready. His mother had told him enough that he knew to fear the creatures who visited when the veil was thin, but since he'd been on his own, he'd simply stayed in, salted the doorway when he could, and hoped for the best. Skipped excellent opportunities to pickpocket too.

"I saw that," Máel Máedóc grumbled, and Ninian turned sheepishly. The big man waved him off and pushed himself to his feet. "Keep it. I trust you know how to use it if you have to."

"Yeah." The iron was cold and rough as Ninian ran his thumb down its length, ignoring the pointedness of the shopkeeper's tone. "I think I could figure it out."

Máel Máedóc crossed to the back-room door. "Anyway. Hopefully, the boy—Áed—wakes soon. You can wait if you like." Ninian got to his feet. "Don't you wake him, though. He needs to rest."

"Yes, sir," Ninian said. He forgot to make the 'sir' into something cutting.

The door creaked as Máel Máedóc eased it open, and Ninian quietly slipped inside. "Be careful with him," the shopkeeper said softly. "Remember everything I told you yesterday." He pointed over his shoulder with his thumb. "I'll be right in the shop."

CHAPTER FOURTEEN

The little room was still dim despite the risen sun outside, and only faint light shone through the west-facing window. Ninian crossed to the chair that accompanied the candle-covered table and sat. The silence of the room was very peaceful.

Áed was curled on his side, bandaged hands tucked defensively to his chest. His gentle breaths made the blanket rise and fall.

With a little sigh, Ninian scraped curls of wax off of the nearest candle, gathering them on the back of a too-short fingernail.

Maybe it was the quiet or the mild light, but the air felt different in this room. It wasn't as heavy to breathe. His gaze darted back to Áed. The red-eyed boy's hair was just long enough to fall against his eyelids, and even in the dimness, it looked soft. There wasn't anything to do but wait for Áed to wake up, so Ninian fidgeted with candle wax and, inexplicably shy, tried not to be too overt in studying the freckles over Áed's nose. There were a lot of them, and they crossed his cheekbones like constellations.

Hopefully, Áed would talk to him. Ninian wondered what he'd have to say. Maybe he'd want to talk about whatever had happened to him. When Ninian thought about it, though, it didn't seem likely—if it had been Ninian, he knew he'd avoid the subject. Still. Even if everything was like the night before, and Áed was lost someplace in his own mind, maybe it would help just to have someone else there with him.

Of course…

Áed also might ask Ninian to leave.

Ninian shook his head hard, and suddenly the air was heavy again. For a moment, he had forgotten himself. *Fucking moron, I am.* Tidying his hair and washing his face couldn't take out the real stains. He couldn't *help.*

He tucked his knees up and wrapped his arms around them. Suddenly, he wanted to go before the red-eyed boy could tell him to.

He pushed himself up from the chair and headed for the door.

"*Mmm,*" Áed murmured sleepily.

Ninian stopped moving, waiting for Áed to slip back into a deeper sleep.

Áed shifted, then yawned. "Nngh."

Go back to sleep, Ninian urged in his head. *Don't wake up, not right now.*

There was a sleepy sliver of red iris, and then Áed was sitting up, blinking woozily in the faint light.

Ninian swallowed and turned back to face him, bracing himself. "Uh… good morning."

For a couple of heartbeats, Áed just blinked at him sleepily. He looked down to his hands, and then back up to Ninian's face.

"I was just going," Ninian said apologetically. "I'll leave now."

Áed's brows came together, just so slightly. "Ninian," he said.

His voice was hoarse.

He remembered my name. "Um, yeah." He inclined his head toward the red-eyed boy. "And you're Áed."

Áed nodded. His face had already begun to grow pained. Ninian's heart clenched in sympathy. Áed's hands must hurt worse than Ninian could imagine.

"How, uh," Ninian started awkwardly. "How are you?"

Áed's breathing had started speeding up, though his face was perfectly blank. His eyes were fixed on a point somewhere just off his hands.

"Áed?"

Áed looked up, and though his face remained empty, Ninian saw that his eyes were full. Hurt. Panic. Confusion.

"Hey, hey." Without any conscious decision-making, Ninian hurried to the side of the bed and sat gingerly on the edge of the mattress. "Um… take a deep breath?"

It was clear that Áed tried to obey, but he didn't seem fully in control. His eyes seemed almost too bright, filled with their own illumination, and Ninian could feel his warmth just from sitting beside him.

"Do you have a fever?" It would make sense. Injuries could do that if they were infected, or if they were enough of a shock. Slowly, so Áed could expect it, Ninian rested the back of his hand against Áed's forehead. "*In ainm dé,*" he murmured. "You're really hot."

Áed sucked in a little gasp and kicked himself away from Ninian. He looked afraid.

"I'm sorry," Ninian said, guilt dropping into his stomach. "I didn't mean to scare you." He stood, the mattress creaking. "I'll get Máel Máedóc. You should lie back down."

But Áed shook his head furiously, hugging his knees to his chest. Ninian squatted next to the bed, one hand on the mattress.

"Áed," he said gently. "You're burning up. You need medicine."

"No," Áed whispered. "Please."

"Why not? You'll feel better."

"I don't have a fever."

Ninian bit his lip. "I think you do."

Áed shook his head again, as if he were trying to banish something from it. "I'm so sorry. I'm so sorry." He was breathing fast and cringing into the corner where the bed met the wall. "I'll stop. It won't happen again, I promise. I'm so sorry."

He must be delirious. It was the most words in a row Ninian had yet heard Áed say, and they didn't make sense. "Áed, it's okay. You haven't done anything." He stood. "I'll be right back, okay?"

"Please," Áed managed quietly. "Don't go."

Ninian stopped dead.

What?

"Please." Áed's eyes were squeezed shut, and he was still pressed, looking terrified, into the corner, but...

With a shaky breath, Ninian lowered himself back down onto the edge of the bed. *He asked me to stay. He asked me to stay.*

"All right." His breath stole through the word and made it half a whisper.

Áed exhaled sharply. It sounded like relief.

Ninian cracked his knuckles nervously, watching how the red-eyed boy held himself. "You, um… you don't like being touched, I guess." That made sense to Ninian.

Áed didn't answer.

"I guess I spooked you when I took your temperature. I'm sorry." Ninian chewed his lip. "But… you *do* have a fever." He tucked his legs up onto the bed. "Let me get you some tea later, at least."

Áed was staring into the middle distance again.

"Áed?"

Áed looked up, and Ninian realized there were lavender

circles under his eyes. He couldn't have slept well.

Ninian swallowed. "Now that you're talking a little more… do you want to tell me what happened to you?"

Perhaps Ninian should have expected it when Áed looked away again and didn't respond. A strange emptiness slipped into his eyes.

"That's okay," Ninian said quickly. "Never mind."

Áed's gaze slid back up to Ninian. "Where am I?"

Ninian frowned. Maybe the shopkeeper hadn't told him—the man had said Áed had been unconscious when he'd found him, so it was possible that the bedroom was all Áed had seen. "A trading shop." He remembered where Áed had been found. "It's northwest of the Fisher's Shore."

Áed looked deeply perplexed. "How?"

"The shopkeeper," Ninian answered. "Máel Máedóc. He found you on the docks and brought you back." He played with his cuff. "Um… is there anyone we should try to find for you?" He'd assumed that Áed was an orphan like himself, but it occurred to him that might not be the case. Then again, Áed *had* been left to die on the Fisher's Shore, so…

"No," Áed said faintly. He looked confused, and Ninian could tell it was that self-directed, internal confusion again. "Please, don't."

"Do you want me to go?" Ninian ventured. He didn't actually want to leave—there was something about Áed that commanded Ninian's interest—but he would not blame Áed if the answer was yes.

Immediately, Áed looked up again, his gaze nearly pinning Ninian in place. "No."

Ninian couldn't help his little smile or the warmth that spread across his cheeks. It didn't mean much, of course— Áed didn't *know* Ninian—but in those moments, Ninian's presence was a good thing.

It was an incredible feeling.

It was clear when Áed was fading again. After a few moments of quiet, the look in his eyes grew distant, and Ninian noticed the red-eyed boy's breathing pick up.

"Áed?" Ninian, without thinking, touched Áed's shoulder. Áed, whose eyes had been following Ninian's hand, shuddered, and Ninian quickly withdrew. "I'm sorry."

Despite everything, the rejection stung. *Don't be selfish. You can't blame him.*

But Áed shook his head quickly. "No—please—" He gingerly held out his forearm and rested it across the tops of his knees.

Ninian cocked his head, confused.

"Please," Áed said, and Ninian realized the other boy's voice sounded confused. "Do… do that again?"

Brow furrowed, Ninian set his palm on Áed's offered forearm. The florid bruises covering Áed's skin looked horribly painful, so Ninian kept his touch feather-light. Even so, he could feel the heat of Áed's skin suffusing through his hand. It felt much too warm, almost hot, and the hairs on Ninian's arms stood up.

Áed's eyelids fluttered, and he shivered.

"Are you all right?" Ninian asked. Was it that incredible when someone's touch didn't bring pain? Áed's expression was agonized but also almost awed. "I don't want to hurt you, see?"

Áed wasn't answering, and he trembled faintly as he looked at Ninian's hand on his arm. Ninian didn't know what to do, so he scooted himself next to Áed on the bed. His shoulder brushed Áed's, and at that minimal contact, twin tears rolled down the red-eyed boy's cheeks.

"Hey," Ninian said, trying to be soothing. He hadn't meant to hurt him. "Hey, I'm sorry."

Áed cried quietly, almost noiselessly, like one who'd had practice hiding his tears. His shoulders shook, and he curled in on himself. Unsure what to do, Ninian *very* carefully put his free arm over Áed's shoulders.

Áed's breath stopped in his throat, and Ninian heard the little choke.

"You're safe," Ninian said, ready to move away, but Áed turned his head so that his cheek rested on Ninian's arm. Obeying his gut, Ninian gently turned Áed toward him, and then Áed's forehead bowed to meet Ninian's chest.

Áed felt small, even as he filled Ninian's chest with warmth. Ninian's brand smarted, but it was so easy to ignore that he scarcely felt it. Áed's tears were falling into Ninian's shirt, and with the hand that wasn't holding him, Ninian stroked the back of Áed's head. *Where are these instincts coming from?* These hands of his had driven a knife into a man's flesh only one day earlier, and now one of them was running over Áed's hair while the other traced comforting circles on his back.

It had been so long since Ninian had cared about another person.

It had been so long since he'd felt wanted.

Áed's sobs were quieting, and he was slumping into Ninian's chest. "It'll be okay," Ninian said quietly. "It will."

A sound in the doorway made Ninian look up. Still holding the broken boy protectively, Ninian found Máel Máedóc standing in the entrance to the room, mouth open. "Ninian…" Máel Máedóc looked shocked. "He let you *touch* him?"

Ninian looked down to Áed, who had stopped crying but was leaning on Ninian with exhausted, unfocused eyes. Ninian's arms were still around him. The answer seemed pretty obvious.

The shopkeeper stepped into the room and sank into the seat Ninian had vacated earlier. "He hasn't let me touch him since I treated his hands. This is progress."

Ninian laid the back of his hand over Áed's forehead. Strangely enough, it felt cooler than did his brutalized forearms, but it was still far too warm. "I think he has a fever," Ninian said. "I… also think he's afraid of you."

Máel Máedóc looked saddened but not surprised. "I don't doubt it."

"Why?" Ninian asked. "I didn't think you hurt him."

The chair creaked as Máel Máedóc stood again. "I had to bandage his hands, boy. I hurt him very, very much." He walked back to the door. "I'm going to get something for his temperature."

He left, and Ninian turned his attention back to Áed. The boy's eyes had closed. "Hey," Ninian said softly. "Are you falling asleep?"

"No," Áed murmured.

"It's okay," Ninian said. "Crying's exhausting, and…" He brushed the back of his knuckle gently under Áed's eye, where it was shadowed. "It doesn't look like you slept much last night."

Áed shook his head against Ninian's chest. "My hands…" He trailed off with an unsteady breath.

"Has Máel Máedóc given you anything for the pain?"

"There's nothing strong enough," the shopkeeper's voice came from the doorway. He sounded regretful. "Willow might help a little, but for something like that, he wouldn't even notice the difference." He held up a mug. "I brought tea."

Ninian accepted the cup as the shopkeeper settled into the chair again. It didn't seem too hot, and it smelled familiar, tart and sharp.

"Hey, Áed," he said. "Can you drink this if I hold the cup for you?"

Áed nodded tentatively. He sat up a little, and Ninian held the cup to his lips.

Right away, Áed coughed. Ninian held the mug away as Áed doubled over, and he rubbed Áed's back as the red-eyed boy struggled to inhale. After a few seconds of coughing, Áed looked up shakily. "What is that?" he asked hoarsely.

Máel Máedóc's face was strangely fixed. "It'll bring your fever down." He nodded toward the cup. "Drink it."

Áed looked at the cup suspiciously, and Ninian looked to the shopkeeper. "Are you sure?"

"Go on."

Once more, Ninian offered Áed the cup, and hesitantly, Áed drank. His face twisted in displeasure, but he swallowed until the mug was empty.

Ninian handed the cup back to Máel Máedóc, who nodded tautly as Áed made a little groaning sound. "That should do it," the shopkeeper said. He stood. "Call if you need me."

When Máel Máedóc was gone, Áed let out a faint moan. "That was awful."

"Did it taste bad?" It had smelled rather nice. Ninian couldn't place the smell, but it nagged at the edge of his memory.

Áed nodded. "I don't… feel well."

Ninian felt Áed's forehead again. It was cooler already, but clammy now. "You look a little pale."

"I don't feel well," Áed said again, but his voice sounded smaller. He winced and pressed his forearms to his stomach.

"Are you going to throw up?" Ninian cast about quickly for a basin, but there was nothing. "What kind of tea *was* that?"

"Don't… don't know…" Áed closed his eyes, which looked much less luminous. Even his freckles seemed to have paled.

"You aren't burning anymore," Ninian said. "But maybe you should lie down."

Áed cooperated as Ninian disentangled himself, and then he dropped onto his back to stare dully at the ceiling.

"Are you okay?"

Only silence responded, and Ninian's brow furrowed in concern.

"Áed?"

Is he... asleep? Áed's eyes were still a bit open, and it was unnerving.

Ninian hesitantly put a hand on Áed's shoulder. "You're okay, right?"

Áed blinked slowly, eyes sliding toward Ninian without any focus. "Hm?"

I have to get Máel Máedóc.

Ninian gave Áed's shoulder a squeeze, masking the urgency he suddenly felt. "I'll be right back."

He hurried into the shop, through the maze of shelves, and did his best to follow the sound of the shopkeeper's noise.

"Máel Máedóc?" He rushed around a corner, nearly avoided tripping, and skidded through the aisle until he found his target. "Máel Máedóc!"

The shopkeeper looked up.

"There's something wrong," Ninian said quickly. "The tea, it did something. Áed is—well, I don't know, he's sick—"

Máel Máedóc held out his hands in a 'slow down' motion. "Ninian. Ninian, relax."

"Don't tell me that!" A pop of anger sparked behind his breastbone. "There's something wrong!"

"No," Máel Máedóc said, "there's not."

"How do you—"

"He seems really tired, right?"

Ninian blinked. "Y—yeah?"

Máel Máedóc shook his head. "It's all right, Ninian. It's the tea, is all. He'll be fine. His fever's down, right?"

"Yeah," Ninian said. "You're sure—"

"I'm sure." Máel Máedóc bent to pick up a crate. "Though I'm glad you're worried about him."

Ninian bristled. "What do you mean? You told me to help him, didn't you?"

"I did," the shopkeeper said, heaving the crate onto a shelf. "But I never told you to care." He pushed the crate back and brushed off his hands. "Progress," he said, turning away from Ninian. "Progress."

CHAPTER FIFTEEN

The hem of his cloak snapped in the wind as Ninian stood outside Máel Máedóc's shop with his hood pulled up, his hands tucked as far into his sleeves as they could go. The shopkeeper stood at the doorway, bare-armed and apparently unbothered by the cold, leaning on the frame. He fixed Ninian with his cobalt stare. "Be safe," he ordered.

Ninian nodded. "That's the idea."

He was on his way back to Cahir's house. Máel Máedóc had assured him that Áed would likely be out of it for the rest of the day, and Ninian did *not* want to be late checking in with the gang, but the thought of going back sent prickly vines creeping through his stomach.

He shivered. He *had* to get out. "I wish I didn't have to."

Máel Máedóc grunted. "You do, though."

Ninian pressed at his knuckles nervously. "I do."

"Get going then."

But Ninian bit his lip. "Máel Máedóc," he said after a few moments of discomfort under the shopkeeper's expectant glare. "What should I do if they tell me to kill again?"

Máel Máedóc set his jaw and exhaled sharply. "That is a decision you'll have to make for yourself."

The house was bigger than Ninian remembered it. The siding was dingy, and the cracks in the windows glinted as the sunlight ran along them; the steps to the entrance looked forbiddingly tall.

Steeling himself, Ninian climbed to the porch and pushed through the door.

The house was quiet.

"Hello?" he called.

"Ninian?" Ruairí's voice came immediately from the kitchen, followed promptly by his footsteps as he came around the corner. "Ninian! You really cut it close! Fuck, you scared the hell out of me!" He caught his momentum in the doorframe.

"I'm fine," Ninian said. "Was just paying that debt."

"Oh!" Ruairí nodded. The energy in the room had shot up just by Ruairí being in it. "How did it go? Is everything all right? Are *you* all right? You were so broken up, I thought… honestly, I thought maybe you were going to try and run. You look better, I think?"

Ninian couldn't help but crack a tiny smile. "I'm okay. Still here." He touched his cheek, trying not to imagine Cahir's knife sliding through it. "I don't want to die."

"A good decision, honestly," Ruairí agreed. "Well, come here. I'll get you something to eat." Ninian followed Ruairí into the kitchen, where the man fetched a loaf of bread from a cupboard and began cutting it. He handed Ninian a slice, giving him a sideways look. "You did your hair."

Ninian accepted the bread with thanks and broke off a piece. "Oh. Yeah."

Ruairí dropped to a seat at the table and propped his feet on the edge. "Was there an occasion?"

Red eyes flickered across Ninian's mind. "No."

Ruairí nodded, folding a piece of bread in half and mashing it down. "Oh, I almost forgot. Since you're not living in this house, I have to ask where you're staying." He tore off a flattened piece of bread. "If you're on the streets, we'll find somewhere for you."

"I found an abandoned tenement."

"An abandoned… oh?" Ruairí popped the bread into his mouth and spoke around it. "You must be right on the edge of the city, then."

"Just about."

"Sure you don't want somewhere closer?"

"I'm all right."

Ruairí nodded and swallowed. "Suit yourself. Could you tell me how to get there?"

Ninian frowned. "Why?"

"Hey, hey, don't look so suspicious." He smashed and ate another bite. "We just have to be able to find you if Cahir decides to assign you something." He brushed the crumbs off his hands. "It'd also help to know where you usually are during the day."

With reluctance, Ninian answered his questions, aware of how much more difficult his escape would now be. He nearly found the courage to lie, but Ruairí's gaze—intense despite the tawny curls falling into his earth-green eyes—stole it away.

Ruairí looked interested when Ninian told him about the shop. "Máel Máedóc's? The trader?"

Ninian nodded, and Ruairí whistled. "Damn. He used to scare the hell out of me. What're you doing there?"

"He's the one to whom I owe—" He caught himself before Ruairí could tease him. "I mean, he's the one I'm in debt to."

A mixture of shock and respect dawned on Ruairí's face. "No kidding?" He shook his head. "I'm terribly impressed you're still alive. Nice work."

Ninian snorted. "Thank you."

In the doorway, someone cleared their throat, and both Ruairí and Ninian startled.

Cahir stood against the doorframe with his arms crossed and his hair combed back, careless and commanding at once.

Ruairí stood quickly, kicking his feet off the table. "Cahir!"

Ninian, taking the hint, stood up as well. Cahir's expression was impossible to read, but he nodded at Ruairí before locking his gaze onto Ninian. "Ninian," he said, and Ninian was struck by the gravity of his voice. "Come here."

"Um—"

"Do it," Ruairí hissed at him.

Ninian didn't want to get any closer to Cahir than he already was, but the longer he hesitated, the deadlier the gang leader's eyes became. Reluctantly, he walked around the table to stand a few feet away.

Cahir appraised him. "I heard something very interesting from Ruairí." Ninian glanced to Ruairí, who looked guilty. "Brígh, of course, didn't tell me, since she vouched for you, but Ruairí is apparently a bit more loyal under pressure." An unnerving smile bloomed on Cahir's face, and he crossed the space to Ninian in a stride.

Ninian shrank back when Cahir took him by the shoulders.

"Do you know what I heard?" Cahir asked.

"N-no."

Cahir's humor disappeared, and his words were flat and cold. "I heard that you tried to spare the messenger I sent you to kill."

Ninian's throat seized.

Ruairí looked like he wanted to melt into the floor, but Ninian couldn't have any pity for him—not when Cahir's hands were clasped like vises onto Ninian's shoulders, and he thought he might be sick.

Ninian's stomach twisted as Cahir, still holding Ninian's shoulders, slid his thumb slowly downward over Ninian's brand.

"Thing is," Cahir said quietly, tilting his head with a half-smile. "You need to know what happens when you disobey."

"Wait—"

Cahir dug his thumb into the bandages.

Ninian's chest exploded into fiery pain as Cahir ground into the brand, and Ninian couldn't stop himself from letting out a shriek. The gang leader twisted his thumb back and forth, ripping through the delicate, healing tissue, and Ninian's knees went weak.

Cahir dropped him to the floor. Ninian hit the ground hard, trembling and with tears burning his eyes.

"It was your first fight," Cahir said. "I went easy." He squatted next to Ninian and, grabbing Ninian's chin, forced him to look up. "But next time, I will not be so gentle."

He released Ninian's chin and stood, brushing his hands on his pants. Ninian tried to calm his breathing, but he was shaking. Pain pulsed across his entire chest.

"It is useless to disobey me, Ninian," Cahir said calmly. "You will pay." He leaned forward. "*Dearly.*"

Ruairí was at Ninian's side the moment Cahir swept from the room. Ninian was still gasping shallowly, his brow beaded with sweat, but he managed to scoot to a seat against the leg of the table, where he glared at Ruairí.

"Ninian, I am so sorry," Ruairí said. It was obvious that he meant it, but Ninian wasn't feeling very forgiving. "I couldn't lie to him; I'm really sorry." He twisted the bit of bread that he'd apparently never gotten rid of, and it tore in his hands. "I told him it was fine, the messenger would die anyway, but he didn't care."

Ninian ignored him, carefully tugging back his collar. The

bandages were askew, and now damp with blood and clear fluid. Grimacing with a little yelp, Ninian rearranged them back over the brand. The pain was fading slowly, but the anger wasn't. "Thank you for absolutely *nothing*."

Ruairí looked horribly apologetic.

As the burning ebbed and Ninian's heart slowed down, a weighty hopelessness settled over him.

That was Cahir being *gentle*.

It wasn't like Ninian hadn't known what lay in store if he resisted, but to feel it was another thing altogether—and Cahir's voice had held no uncertainty when he promised to know of any subversion.

Was getting out even *possible*?

Ninian bit his lip. In the very beginning, Ruairí had warned him that he'd be hunted all the way to the White City if he ran, but Ninian didn't even know how to get there, much less somewhere even more remote. If Cahir owned Ninian's life, no matter where he went…

He felt his heart sinking.

Had he really been naïve again?

"There's no way out, is there?" he asked abruptly, and Ruairí, who'd been running through a long and elaborate apology, stopped in surprise.

"You were still planning on getting out?" At the look on Ninian's face, Ruairí shook his head. "No, mate, there's not. I'd introduce you to the people who have tried, but they're all dead."

Ninian squeezed his eyes shut. He slid down the table leg until he was lying on the floor.

This was permanent.

It was his own mistake, and it was permanent.

"Ninian?"

"Leave me alone," Ninian muttered.

"I can't," Ruairí said, apology leaking back into his voice. "You have to go train."

"Train?" He opened his eyes. "What?"

Ruairí nodded. "With Brígh. Cahir wants you to start. I was going to tell you before Cahir came in."

"Brígh is going to kill me."

"She's not terribly happy," Ruairí admitted. "Cahir gave her a hard time when you didn't properly end that messenger. But she's never happy, so I doubt it'll be too different."

Ninian pressed the heels of his hands into his eyes. "Wonderful."

"Brígh should be at her place," Ruairí said. "Come on. I can take you."

CHAPTER SIXTEEN

Gray crows, hooded with black feathers, lined the brick walls around Brígh's lot, watching silently as weedy thistles *shh*ed in the wind. Their beady eyes followed Ninian as he shifted his weight from foot to foot. Ruairí tapped his toe against the gate, standing on the bottom bar with his armpits hooked over the top, and Brígh stood with a shivering Ninian in the middle of the courtyard.

"Right," said Brígh. She hadn't been wearing a cloak in the first place, but she didn't look cold. Ninian, on the other hand, was hugging himself. It wasn't doing much to combat the wind, and his cloak was hanging on the fence next to Ruairí. Brígh rolled her neck until it cracked. "You only get better by doing, I'd say." Her posture shifted, and Ninian was instantly on alert. "Good. Give it your all."

Before Ninian could even respond, Brígh was on the offensive. Ninian leapt back, cursing, and tried to find his feet. He dodged Brígh's next attack, the cold already forgotten.

"Don't be shy," Ruairí called. "Attack!"

But Ninian was barely keeping up on the defensive. He was quick, sure, but when Brígh was coming at him from all sides, all he could do was hurry backward and try to buy time.

"The lot's only so big, mate!"

Ninian swore and leapt to the side just before he hit the wall behind him. A couple of crows took languidly to the air before drifting down again, cawing quietly.

"Don't get cornered!"

Ninian didn't think Ruairí's advice was helping. Brígh's face was calm, and she took one step for each of Ninian's three, throwing accurate, deadly punches that Ninian scarcely managed to evade.

Ninian was so focused on Brígh's upper body attacks that he didn't even see when Brígh's knee swung around. It met Ninian's hip and sent him down hard, where a shard of brick the length of his palm scraped painfully down his arm. "Agh!" His back hit the wall, and he lost his breath. He couldn't feel much pain through the buzz of the fight in his head, but something warm was running down his arm.

"That's it!" Ruairí called. "Cut it out. That one's over!"

Brígh relaxed her stance as Ninian picked himself up, grumbling. She looked calculating. "For starters, quit running. I was leaving myself open, and I don't even think you noticed."

Ninian hadn't. "How am I supposed to reach you?" he asked, peeking at the newest cut. It was small and didn't look too deep. "You'd knock my head off."

Brígh beckoned him over and, reluctantly, Ninian obeyed.

"Watch. I punch with this hand, and I keep this one by my face, yeah? But if you dodge this—you're good at that, at least—then you get inside." She pulled Ninian's collar until Ninian was in the right position. "Remember this. Remember how this feels. Now." She assumed a position like she'd just thrown a punch, with Ninian to the inside of her extended arm as if he had dodged. "What does it feel natural to do?"

"Hit you?" Ninian guessed.

"Right," Brígh said. "Right here." She tapped the spot right under her sternum. "At your height and my height, that's the weakest place you'll get power to. 'Course, with a good uppercut, you can reach my chin or my throat, yeah? And, ah…" She raised one eyebrow. "There's always what you went for last time."

Ninian swallowed. "Got it."

Brígh stepped back. "Again, then."

Ninian had to fight the urge to step back when Brígh attacked. Instead, he dodged. *Dammit. Wrong side.* He straightened quickly and tried for a strike to Brígh's ribcage, but Brígh was fast, and she caught hold of his wrist. In a snap, Ninian was skidding across the courtyard, catching himself on his hands and popping to his feet with skinned palms. "Ow."

"You'll get calluses," Ruairí called across the yard, grinning. "Don't worry about it."

"Tough up those pretty-boy hands," Brígh grunted.

Ninian scowled. "I do not have… what does that even mean?"

"Means it don't look like you saw a hard day in your life." Brígh laughed.

"I never saw…?" That took a second to sink in, and when it did, Ninian felt his expression darken. "Don't talk about shit you don't know."

"You've got palms softer than a baby girl's." She wiggled her own fingers. "Life's easy for some people." She grinned. "Must be nice."

"Shut up," Ninian growled.

Brígh raised her eyebrows. "Make me."

It was obvious bait, but Ninian didn't hesitate.

He launched himself at Brígh, planless and incensed.

She batted him out of the air, looking bored.

Striding over to where Ninian was coughing on the ground, the older fighter rested her foot on Ninian's chest. Ruairí called the fight.

Ninian glared hatefully at Brígh, but she didn't even seem to notice. "That was just stupid, kid."

"Don't talk about me," Ninian spat. "You don't know what you're talking about. You haven't got a *clue*."

Brígh frowned. "Hm." She looked up. "Oi, Ruairí! What did I say? Were you listening?"

Ruairí shrugged. "Beats me," he called back. "Nothing nice, I'd assume."

Ninian blinked, frowning. "You don't *remember*?"

"Nah." Bending down, Brígh hauled Ninian up by the collar. "I just wanted you to be angry. People'll bait you, see?" She brushed off Ninian's shoulders. "And you, stupid little fuck, did exactly what they'll want you to do."

Ninian cracked his knuckles. "I thought—"

"Wrong, obviously." Brígh sighed, stepping back. "Try again."

Brushing gravel out of his scraped palms, Ninian tried to find his stance. Anger was still simmering in his chest.

He wanted to win.

He set his jaw and did his best to concentrate. There hadn't been much chance to study Brígh's finer movements, but by this point, Ninian had a feel for the woman's energy. It was a bit like dancing with a partner; he had to complement the motions, and if he wanted to change the steps of the dance, he'd have to guide it in the direction he needed. Brígh, with her directional power and her strength, would be too strong to meet head-on.

With a deep breath, Ninian nodded.

Brígh charged.

Neatly, Ninian sidestepped, conserving his momentum, and pivoted to face Brígh, who'd stopped with surprising quickness. Brígh swung the force of her charge into a punch, which Ninian dodged.

He was feeling it again.

In the fight before Laoise had found him, Ninian's world had narrowed and cleared, everything else falling away. The air had felt alive on his skin, pinpricks running over his body.

It was the dance of staying alive.

Thrill.

Focus.

A flicker of a smile crossed Ninian's face.

Every blow that Brígh threw, Ninian neatly evaded. It was almost exciting. Almost... *fun*. Entirely ungrounded as he leapt over Brígh's kick and crouched beneath a punch, Ninian landed low and sprang up inside the woman's space, just as Brígh had shown him. He bailed quickly as she threw a close-range elbow, but for all her strength, it was clearly tiring to never land a hit, and Ninian still felt fresh.

"Ninian!" Ruairí was calling, and Ninian half-listened, not daring to break his concentration. "*Offense*, mate!"

Oh, that was right. Ninian still had to *win*.

At that moment, Brígh was leading the dance, and Ninian was merely reacting. If he wanted this fight to end in his favor, he had to assert control—gracefully. He couldn't exactly block one of Brígh's punches.

The next time Brígh came at him, he dodged the punch to the outside and grabbed hold of Brígh's wrist. While she was still off-balance, Ninian dug his fingers into Brígh's shoulder and, with shoulder and wrist in his grasp, threw his weight in the same direction as Brígh's movement.

Sure enough, Brígh stumbled forward. She got her feet under herself quickly, but Ninian had never let go of her wrist. By the time Brígh had stabilized herself with a grunt, Ninian had torqued the woman's arm behind her back.

Ducking, Brígh spun out of the hold and made a grab for Ninian's arm. Ninian dropped instead and went for Brígh's thigh as the woman's balance shifted through the movement. Shoving himself upright again, he tipped Brígh backward, and she fell.

She'd gotten hold of Ninian's shoulders, though, and as she met the ground with her back, she used the momentum to hurl Ninian to the ground.

Ninian hit the dirt hard but rolled with the motion and came up on his knee.

Now, *this* was a whole new kind of dance. This was close and fast, fewer blows and more strategy, and Ninian felt his heart beat faster.

He could win this kind of fight.

There wasn't a point in attacking while Brígh pressed herself to her feet again. When her weight was low, Ninian couldn't knock her over, and he knew he wasn't heavy enough to pin her. Instead, he caught his breath and watched how Brígh moved.

"I'll give it to you, kid. You make me work for it." She wiped her mouth with the back of her hand. "A little practice, and you'll—" She interrupted herself and swung at Ninian.

Actually startled, Ninian hopped back instinctively.

Brígh laughed. "Gotcha."

Brígh advanced fast, throwing blow after blow, and Ninian was forced to guard his face with his arms, backing up. Brígh's punches cracked into Ninian's forearms, shooting hot pain up his arms, and it was all Ninian could do to keep his head safe.

Not good. Not good.

He had to stop this before he met the wall, he had to think—

Don't think.

Everything was happening fast.

Ninian swung out an arm, throwing Brígh's punch wide, and, holding his other arm like a battering ram, he hurled himself at Brígh's waist.

It didn't do much, but his body was moving on its own, and he couldn't stop it. All he could do was go low—he didn't have the strength or the weight to match Brígh's upper body, so he planted his leg between Brígh's and hooked it behind her knee. When Ninian twisted, he levered Brígh's leg off the ground, and the two of them went down. Ninian pressed his elbow into the soft place under Brígh's ribs, and when the ground rose to meet them, his momentum drove that elbow deep into Brígh's chest.

Brígh choked.

Ninian sat on her while the woman gasped for air with little *hic* noises. He dropped his hands, staring in surprise at the tear running from Brígh's right eye.

I…

Did I just win?

A grin started spreading over Ninian's face.

I just won!

He gave a little laugh and squeezed his eyes shut for a moment, trying to slow his heart rate.

And then the world exploded into light.

Pain split the side of his head, and his body met the ground.

He opened his eyes to a blur that refused to resolve.

Breathe.

Can't breathe.

Can't breathe.

The world was sideways, he was lying on the ground, and that had to be Brígh staggering to her feet.

Move.

Can't move.

Can't move.

His head felt like it was sparking, and something wet was running over the left side of his face. His side was in pain too—had he landed on something sharp? How had he fallen in the first place?

His perspective shifted dizzyingly, and then he was sitting up.

Oh. Ruairí was in front of him.

Ruairí snapped his fingers in front of Ninian's face, but though his lips were moving, Ninian could not hear what he was saying. He stared blankly.

Then Ruairí was gone, shouldered out of the way, and Brígh's face loomed in Ninian's vision. "You follow through!" the woman roared, but Ninian heard the words as if through a thick wall of wool. "The fight wasn't over; you have to *finish it!*"

"*For Gods' sakes, Brígh!*" Ruairí bellowed. Ruairí tore the scarred fighter away while Ninian watched distantly. "Hey. Ninian." Ninian recognized the words on Ruairí's lips, but they didn't make any sound. "Ninian, can you hear me?"

Ninian shook his head.

"Fuck." Ruairí's hands were under Ninian's arms, lifting him up. He pulled a hand away, looking alarmed. Ninian saw that it was red with blood.

"'M fine," Ninian mumbled. "I can walk—"

But Ruairí didn't let him go. "I'm going to deal with Brígh later," he said, and Ninian realized Ruairí must be shouting because in his right ear only, he could faintly make out the words. "I'm taking you home—"

"Máel Máedóc's," Ninian managed.

"You want to go to Máel Máedóc's?" Ruairí said, and Ninian nodded. His head felt… full. It was bubbly and frizzed. It hurt. "Right," Ruairí said. "Hang on. You're fine."

"Yeah." He swallowed. The world had been going deep red at the edges since he'd stood up. "I'm… fine."

CHAPTER SEVENTEEN

He woke with his head on a pillow.

Blinking, he opened his eyes to find a clear world. *That's a relief.*

He sat up, then winced when his head throbbed. He automatically pressed a palm to his temple to find it swollen and tender, but his mind felt mostly all right. His side stung a little bit, and Ninian touched it to find bandages soaked in some kind of herbal concoction.

Movement caught his eye, and he turned to see Máel Máedóc crossing to the bed. The giant shopkeeper pressed Ninian firmly down to the mattress again. "Don't even think about getting up, *amadán.*"

Ninian touched his fingertips to his left ear, frowning. No sound had reached him there. "What happened?" His voice sounded normal to his right ear, but his left was… silent.

Máel Máedóc sank into the chair and rested his ankle on his opposite knee. "Your *friend* elbowed you in the side of the head. The one who brought you in—curly hair, energetic fellow—said you'd just won a fight."

"Yeah," Ninian said slowly, listening to the strange noiselessness on his left side. "In a minute, I'd like to go kill

Brígh." He snapped his fingers next to his left ear. "Why can't I hear?"

The shopkeeper frowned thoughtfully. "You can't? Not at all?"

"No."

"How's the other one?"

"Fine, I think?" He frowned. "What did she *do*?"

"Hit you really, really hard." Máel Máedóc drummed his fingers on the table. "You might get some hearing back after you heal."

"*Might* get *some*?" Ninian exclaimed, ignoring Máel Máedóc and sitting up again. There was a twinge from whatever had happened to his side, and his brand ached, but he ignored it. "What the hell do you mean?"

Máel Máedóc waved a hand. "You really only need one ear anyway. Don't worry about it. Lie down."

Ninian didn't. "I swear to the *Gods* I'm going to *murder*—"

"Not on my watch." The shopkeeper gave Ninian a withering cobalt glare. "How does your head feel? You were unconscious when the curly-haired fellow brought you in."

"I'm fine," Ninian said, and surprisingly, he thought that was true. "I think I was just shocked? And *dizzy*." He touched his ear again. "I'm absolutely ready to kill—"

"Would you drop that? You're not leaving until I'm sure your head's clear." Máel Máedóc pushed himself up to his full height, and there really wasn't much Ninian could do to argue with it. "You got cut too. A bit of glass or brick, I'd guess, since your friend said you weren't fighting with weapons."

That explained Ninian's side. He remembered the sharp sliver of brick that had nicked his arm; if he'd landed on one of those when Brígh had hit him, it could definitely do damage. "Is it bad?"

"It's not deep. Ragged, though. Expect a scar." He looked at Ninian with narrowed eyes. "Re-opened your brand too."

Ninian scowled and poked at the dressings, a depressing weight settling back over him at the reminder. Máel Máedóc's herbs made his wounds feel intriguingly numb. "Trust me. I know."

"You feel all right to see Áed?" Máel Máedóc asked. He flicked Ninian's hand away from the bandages, looking annoyed. "He's been worried."

Just like that, Ninian was focused. He leaned forward. "Yeah." Then he frowned and looked around. "Wait a minute. Where is he? This is his room, isn't it?"

"No. It's *my* room. This is *my* room, that's *my* bed, and both of you boys are damn lucky to have met me." He shook his head. "The sooner you both recover, the sooner I stop sleeping on the floor." He leaned out into the shop. "*Buachaill cladaigh*? Ninian's awake." He looked to Ninian. "Hold on, I have to go get him. He's still a bit out of it."

Ninian scooted to a seat as soon as the shopkeeper was gone. He felt a little destabilized, but his thinking wasn't foggy, and he remembered what had happened—those were good signs. He snapped next to his ear again and only heard it on his right side. "*A thiarcais.*"

"Ninian?"

Ninian's attention snapped up. "Áed!" Ignoring Máel Máedóc's protests, Ninian pushed himself out of bed and made to cross the room only to find the floor tipping up to meet him. A wave of vertigo bowled him over, and Máel Máedóc's hand interrupted the fall right before Ninian's jaw cracked into the ground.

Ninian blinked, disoriented. He hadn't even gotten his arms up to catch himself. "For Gods' sakes, boy!" the shopkeeper exclaimed. "I can't manage the two of you at once!"

Carefully getting to a seat on his knees, Ninian realized that Áed was leaning on Máel Máedóc, who seemed to be supporting much of Áed's weight. Ninian pressed his palms to his eyes, trying to stop the world from spinning. "*A thiarcais.*"

Máel Máedóc gently helped Áed to a seat on the edge of the bed, then hauled Ninian up and deposited him beside Áed. "Stay put, would you? Your ear just got burst; don't be stupid."

Áed bumped Ninian's leg with his knee in lieu of tapping his shoulder. "Are you okay?" he asked. His voice was still quiet. "Where were you?"

Ninian frowned at Áed's too-pale face, the glassiness of his eyes. The red-eyed boy still didn't look well. "I'm fine." He didn't want to answer the second question. It was depressing and made him feel filthy. "Are *you*?"

Áed looked at him skeptically for a moment, then nodded. The motion made it clear his head was heavy. "Tired."

"How are your hands?"

Áed's face darkened, and his gaze fell to the bandaged appendages in his lap. For a moment, Ninian thought he would answer, but the silence stretched out until Máel Máedóc cleared his throat. "Áed," he said, and Ninian thought perhaps the man sounded uncomfortable. "Speaking of your hands…"

Áed looked up, immediately wary.

The shopkeeper actually looked fidgety. He picked at the bed of his thumbnail and couldn't seem to meet Áed's eyes. "Your bandages," he said. "I need to change them."

Áed sucked in a sharp breath and drew his hands in toward his chest. "No."

Máel Máedóc pressed his lips together. "Unfortunately, *buachaill cladaigh*, I can't give you a choice."

Ninian put a steadying hand on Áed's shoulder as Áed leaned away from Máel Máedóc. "Please," Áed said, and the fear in his voice was so palpable that Ninian's stomach flopped in sympathy. "It hurts so much."

"I know. But if I don't care for them, they won't heal." He looked apologetic. "People have died from less." He took a stabilizing breath and drew a roll of bandages and a pot of poultice from his pocket. Pulling the chair over with his foot, he set them on the seat.

Then, in one firm movement, he put a hand on Áed's chest and pinned him against the wall.

"Hey!" Ninian exclaimed, shoving himself to his knees even as his head spun. "What are you doing?"

"Moving will hurt him more," Máel Máedóc explained tightly. He shifted his bulk so there was nowhere Áed could go, even when the shopkeeper freed his hands. "Áed, stay still."

But Áed was kicking and squirming, tears already beginning to bead in his eyes. It was clear from his movements that the tea from that morning hadn't wholly worn off.

"Why didn't you do this earlier?" Ninian demanded.

"Because I wanted *you* to be here!" Máel Máedóc said. Ninian froze. "Let me be the one he hates, all right?" the shopkeeper said, still holding down the protesting Áed. "Just… just comfort him, okay?"

That felt wrong, so wrong. Bile rose sharply in his throat. "I can't just *watch* you hurt him," Ninian said, feeling his eyes grow hot with anger. Watching was no better than doing. He couldn't. "I can't—"

"Ninian, I'm trying to do the right thing. You think this is easy for anyone?" He fixed Ninian with a glare, teeth clenched. "The least you can do is be there for him."

There was a sharp lump in Ninian's throat. "Áed…" he said, and Áed squeezed his eyes shut.

"Please," Áed begged, voice cracking. "Please help me."

Ninian's chest felt tight. "It's going to be all right," he said, and he didn't even know if that was true. "I'm right here, okay?" Fighting a bit of vertigo, he crawled closer to Áed and knelt on the mattress. He didn't know why his presence should be comforting, but it felt like the right thing to say. "Right here."

Ninian could only watch as Máel Máedóc took Áed's right hand and began to unwind the bandages. At first, Áed's cries made no sound. "It's okay," Ninian said uncertainly, glancing between the shopkeeper's stony face and the red-eyed boy's terror-filled one. "It's going to be okay."

He couldn't convince himself of that.

Máel Máedóc lifted the bandages from Áed's fingers, and at the man's touch, Áed *screamed*. He bowed his head, tears dripping onto the blankets, and Máel Máedóc's face contorted even as his hands continued to unwrap the bandages. "His wrists are broken," Máel Máedóc said in a startlingly unsteady voice. "His hands, and nearly every finger. I set them as best as I could, but…"

Áed sobbed, his cries a mix of tears and screams, and his breath kept catching in his throat as inhalations turned to shouts.

"Look at that, Ninian," Máel Máedóc said woefully, but Ninian didn't need to be told. His eyes raked over the bent, uneven fingers and the unnatural crook in the backs of Áed's hands. Deep cuts crisscrossed Áed's skin, and as Ninian watched, Máel Máedóc carefully plucked out a sharp sliver of something that glinted bloodily in the light. "Someone *did* this to him." The shopkeeper set the shiny, red-stained shard on the side table. "That's glass. His hands were full of it when I found him."

Áed was shaking, still gasping, and Ninian touched his shoulder. "Áed?"

Áed leaned into Ninian, squeezing his eyes tightly closed. Ninian wrapped his arms around him and held him while he quaked.

"I've got you," he said, feeling Áed tremble in his arms. "I've got you."

Áed's cheeks were shiny with tears and drops of saltwater sat in sparkling spheres among his eyelashes. "Make it stop," he begged. "Ninian, please!"

"It'll be over soon," Ninian promised, completely unsure if that was true. He pressed his eyes closed, trying to find the right thing to do. His sister, he remembered, had been prone to night terrors; his mother had always been able to calm her. This really wasn't the same, but… with his free hand, he dragged his fingertips gently over Áed's forehead. Barely touching. Meaningless shapes, tracing across his brows, down the bridge of his nose, into his hair. Ninian grimaced to himself, certain he wasn't helping.

Máel Máedóc had all the bandages off both of Áed's hands now, and they were a gruesome sight. Red and swollen, crooked in all the wrong places… somebody must have held him down, Ninian realized, because this was not the result of any single attack. This kind of damage could only come from repeated, merciless blows, over and over and over.

Ninian thought he might be sick. "Áed, don't look." Gently, he turned Áed's head away, breaking the boy's helpless stare. "Look anywhere else, or close your eyes, but don't look there."

Tears were running down Áed's face even when he didn't blink, and the red of his irises looked gemstone-bright and a touch wild. "But I already know…"

Ninian felt a tear trace down his own cheek, and he winced with Áed's scream when Máel Máedóc began to dab herbal poultice onto the open wounds. The giant shopkeeper was stone-faced, but his eyes were damp. "Not much longer," he said through gritted teeth.

By the time Máel Máedóc tucked in the end of the last bandage, Áed had slumped against Ninian entirely. He was pale, brow slick with sweat, and both his cheeks and Ninian's shirt were wet with tears. Ninian combed Áed's hair back from his face. "You did so well," he said softly as Máel Máedóc wiped Áed's blood from his hands. It left ruddy streaks on the shopkeeper's trousers.

Áed released a shivering breath, and another tear traced down. "It's over?"

Ninian nodded. "Yeah. Yeah, it's over."

Áed held up his newly bandaged hands, and Ninian saw that they were shaking enormously. Apart from that, Áed kept flicking fearful glances at Máel Máedóc.

"I think you should go," Ninian said quietly to the shopkeeper.

The giant man nodded, beads clicking at the ends of his braids. He'd already gathered his supplies. "You know where to find me."

When he was gone, the room felt so much stiller. It wasn't a peaceful silence; it felt disturbed, like the quiet after a storm that had just reshaped the coast. "Áed," Ninian said softly. "I'm so sorry."

Áed didn't answer.

Ninian's heart twisted.

The truth was, Ninian didn't know why he cared about Áed. Ninian didn't even really know how caring *worked*. But when he looked at Áed and saw that expression...

He felt it.

He knew what Áed felt.

And it *mattered*.

"Please talk to me," Ninian whispered.

When Áed's voice came, it was full of a dullness so familiar that Ninian almost felt the words on his own lips. "What do you want me to say?"

"Anything," Ninian said. He knew that dullness so very well, knew how it felt when it crept into the cavity of the chest. "Scream. Cry. Curse. Anything."

"I've done that."

"Then…" He looked away from the glassiness of Áed's exhausted eyes. "Then lie down." He lowered himself to an elbow. "Lie down next to me."

After a moment, Áed did. The bedframe creaked as he curled inward, his forehead to Ninian's skinny chest, and Ninian put his arms around him. Áed did not tremble. He scarcely seemed to breathe.

"Just sleep," Ninian said. He didn't know how to help himself, much less another broken person, but with one hand, he cradled the back of Áed's head, and with the other, he held Áed's waist protectively. There was something comforting about the closeness of another, and Ninian hoped Áed felt it too.

Even if he could do nothing else, Ninian could make sure his touch never brought Áed pain. "Just sleep."

CHAPTER EIGHTEEN

Máel Máedóc grunted, lowering Ninian down from the top shelf alongside the dusty sack of oats Ninian had helped him reach. "Good."

"Don't you have a stool?" Ninian asked, brushing himself off. Blessedly, his balance was back—though his hearing wasn't. He felt all right, save for a sharp ache deep in his left ear and a sense of fundamentally *missing* something. His side, he'd determined, wasn't going to be a problem; the wound looked dramatic, wrapping halfway around his midriff, but it was shallow enough and fell well within Ninian's pain tolerance. The brand was back to being a numb spot doused in herbal concoctions.

The shopkeeper jerked his thumb to the corner, where a plank of wood tipped toward the ground on two legs. "Used to."

Ninian snorted, then sneezed as dust got in his nose. "What'd you do, sit on it?"

Máel Máedóc cuffed him on the back of the head, which made Ninian wince. "Funny." The shopkeeper heaved the oats over his shoulder and set off through the winding aisle. He patted the oats, sending a cloud of dust into the air. "That's all I wanted."

"You're welcome," Ninian called, rolling his eyes.

He tucked his hands in his pockets and made his way toward the back of the shop. Sunlight slanted in through the gritty windows and got lost in the forest of shelves, and Ninian could see motes of dust swirling through the beams at his passage.

The back of the shop was lovely and warm, and Ninian shuddered a little as he grew nearer. Máel Máedóc had gone out before Ninian or Áed had woken and had returned with firewood, so the hearth was crackling and making everything look uncommonly homey.

Except…

Ninian bit his lip as he reached the space behind the maze of shelves and slowed to a stop.

He hasn't moved.

Áed was sitting in front of the fire, staring into the flames.

Ninian padded into the bedroom and came back with the blanket from the bed. It was a ratty brown thing, warm, thick, and soft. He draped it over Áed's shoulders, then sat down beside him.

It was impossible to know what to say. He suspected he'd be at a loss even if tact was one of his strengths, and it wasn't. He just looked into the fire and tried to see what Áed was seeing.

He's been here since he got up.

After a while of silence, punctuated only by the snapping of the hearth, Áed spoke. "You slept better."

Ninian blinked. "Pardon?"

Áed's gaze hadn't moved from the fire, and it reflected in his eyes. "You feel better this morning. More rested." He paused. "But you're sad."

"Uh…" Ninian looked back into the fire, wondering how Áed knew.

Sad, huh?

It *was* a kind of sadness. He hadn't shaken it since Cahir had dug his thumb into that ever-permanent brand, and he wasn't sure it was the sort of thing that would ever actually leave. He had given himself away, and there was no way back.

Trapped and possessed.

"Sad" about summed it up.

"Yeah. I guess you're right." He glanced sideways at Áed. "How did you sleep?"

Áed's eyes slowly closed, then opened again to rest at half-mast. "I slept."

Not a phenomenal answer, Ninian had to admit, but it could have been worse. "How's the pain?" he ventured. "Any better?"

Áed didn't look at his hands. It was as if his eyes had locked with the fire. "I can't tell."

That tea has to have worn off by now. This heavy listlessness… it was coming from Áed himself.

"I'm sorry."

Ninian frowned, startled. "Sorry? For what?"

The firelight reflected in Áed's eyes, red in red, and he didn't respond. A log in the hearth shifted and tumbled to the grate, sending sparks whirling up the chimney like dandelion seeds on the wind. "I don't know," he said after a while. "I'm just… sorry."

There it was, Ninian noticed. Tumult through the stillness of Áed's words, a hint of chaos behind those brilliant eyes. If Ninian had heard that tumult in his mother's voice, it would have meant she was worried; in his uncle's, it would have told Ninian to be afraid. In Áed's, though… he couldn't tell. "You don't have anything to be sorry for."

Áed gave a little exhale, something that might have been a very humorless laugh. "I—" he started, and then he pressed his lips together. "I'm… confused."

Ninian folded his legs under him more comfortably. "About what?"

Áed shook his head. "Everything, I think? I don't

understand you. Máel Máedóc makes more sense, but not much. And I just—" He swallowed hard. "I can't hold a thought? Sometimes I think I'm okay, or at least I can breathe, but then everything *falls* again." His eyes shone.

The air shimmered around the fireplace, dancing in the warmth. "I think I understand," Ninian said slowly, and though Áed didn't look away from the fire, his eyebrows rose in surprise. "At least... maybe a little." He found a twig on the ground, dropped from the kindling, and rolled it between his palms. "One question."

Áed nodded.

Ninian traced the tip of the twig on the floor. "Why don't you understand Máel Máedóc and me?"

Áed's brow creased, and his teeth worried at his bottom lip. "You've..." His frown deepened. "I don't know. You've just been... nice."

It was Ninian's turn to frown. "You don't understand being nice?"

Áed cringed. "I'm sorry. I shouldn't have... I'm so sorry."

Ninian turned to face Áed more fully. Áed's gaze had broken from the fire, but the red-eyed boy was looking anywhere but Ninian. Ninian regarded him with concern. Something was dawning on him. "So... you understand Máel Máedóc more," he said slowly. His gut twinged, sensing the truth in his revelation, and he twined his fingers around the twig, threatening to snap it. "It's because he's hurt you, isn't it?"

Áed chewed on his lip and wouldn't meet Ninian's eye.

"Shit," Ninian breathed softly.

The horrible thing was, it made sense.

Hesitantly, Áed looked to Ninian's face.

"I," Ninian said, "will not hurt you." A steely resolution was forging within him. "In fact, I'd fight off anyone who *tried* to hurt you." He wanted to take Áed's hands, but instead, he rested his palms on Áed's knees. "You're my friend now." Something warm and a bit giddy was running through his fingertips, up to his heart, and back again. "I'll keep you safe."

Áed looked at him, at an utter loss. For a few heartbeats, he didn't move, and then finally, he spoke. "Why?"

Taken just a little bit aback, Ninian pouted in thought. "A startlingly valid question," he conceded after a moment. "I don't know. It's what people want to do when they care about someone."

Áed shook his head. "That doesn't make sense?"

Ninian sat back on his heels, rather deflated. A good deal of experience *did* counter that kind of idealism—in fact, he wasn't entirely sure from whence such idealism had sprung, anyway. But Áed made him feel... different. Different than he normally did. Better. Wanted. It was Áed's gentle soft-spokenness and the thoughtful glances and the way he seemed to listen. Ninian found himself wanting to respond in kind. "You're right, I guess." He dropped his fist into his palm. "Still! It can be true for you and me, okay?"

A faint almost-smile tilted up the corners of Áed's mouth. Even something so small made his whole face shine. "Okay."

Strangely pleased, Ninian relaxed and leaned on the woodpile next to the fireplace. "I haven't had a friend in a long time."

Áed looked away a little shyly. "Me neither."

"But you know what it means," Ninian said, twirling the bit of kindling between his palms again. "It means you can come to me if you're feeling... confused." He wasn't sure just what he'd do, but he'd certainly try to help.

Questioningly, Áed frowned. "What about you?"

Ninian cocked his head. "What *about* me?"

"Well," Áed said, still looking thoughtful. "It should go

the other way too, right?" He leaned forward. "When I ask if you're okay, you can tell the truth."

"Hah," Ninian laughed uncomfortably, scratching the back of his head. "You mean last night when I woke up?"

Áed nodded.

"I—" He stopped himself from saying 'I'm fine,' feeling strangely defensive. He shrugged. "I was worried about you, is all."

A little bit of color crept across Áed's cheeks. "I…" he shook his head. "I don't know if I can get used to that."

At that, Ninian grinned fully. "Well, you're going to have to."

CHAPTER NINETEEN

The day lengthened, and customers filtered through the shop. Few found their way through the shelf maze to the back, where the fire in the hearth was slowly dying. Ninian glared mercilessly at any who did, and they turned back quickly enough.

After a quiet hour of sitting comfortably on the floor by the fire—Áed had fallen back into silence as soon as the first customer came in—Máel Máedóc's voice resonated from the front of the shop. "I dunno," he rumbled. "I get a lot of people through here. I might have seen him; I might not've."

Frowning in curiosity, Ninian strained to hear a response, silently cursing his senseless ear.

"Y'can't miss him," a voice replied. It sounded like a girl's. "Hair sorta red, eyes sorta purple. Sorta cute, sorta skinny."

Máel Máedóc sounded bored. "Sounds *sorta* forgettable."

"Aw, c'mon," the girl groaned. "He answers to Ninian— funny name, sounds like 'ninny'—and he's about my age…"

Ninian frowned, and next to him, Áed made a little hiccup sound that could have been a laugh. "Ninny," he whispered, and Ninian scowled.

"You can hear them?" he asked. Áed nodded. Ninian stared pensively in the direction of the hushed conversation. "I mostly can, I think…"

"It's a girl," Áed said quietly. "She's bored but afraid of failing. Her attention wouldn't last so long if she wasn't scared of someone and…" his eyes narrowed. "She *likes* you."

Ninian blinked. "The hell? How do you know that?" He snapped his fingers next to his dead ear, frustrated. "Did she say that?"

Áed propped his elbows gently on his knees. "No."

"Then how do you know?"

Áed just shrugged. "Do you know her?"

"I don't know." Ninian tried to hear again. "I might recognize her voice, but I'm not sure."

"So you don't like her."

"Huh?" Ninian looked at Áed in confusion. Áed blinked at him, and Ninian shook his head, exasperated.

"Aw, come *on*, shop-trader-man," the girl complained. "I gotta find him. Cahir'll kill me for sure if I come back without him."

Ninian bit his lip at Cahir's name. "She's from my—" he started, then cut himself off. A low cloud of resentment stole over him. "I mean, I think maybe I do know her." He stood, his knees cracking from sitting so long. "I think I should go."

Áed looked faintly disappointed. "Oh. Okay."

Máel Máedóc was still being a hindrance at the front of the shop, claiming not to be sure of anyone named 'Ninian,' when Ninian started through the shelves. He stopped before he left Áed's sight and leaned back. "Hopefully, I'll be back by tonight."

Áed nodded. "Be safe," he said. "Please."

Ninian smiled. "I'll see you soon."

He wound his way through the shelves, watching his step around crates and burlap sacks and fallen goods until he reached the front and peeked out from behind a shelf.

A blonde girl with red streaks in her hair was arguing with Máel Máedóc and looking near her wits' end. Máel Máedóc had his arms crossed, looking disinterested.

Suddenly, the girl's eyes found Ninian, and she jumped, pointing to him. "He's right there! How long's he been here? Gods, I wasted all this time!" She marched over to Ninian and smiled, hands behind her back. "You remember me, right?"

She did look familiar, but Ninian had to shake his head. "Should I?"

The girl pouted. "It's Treasa! I had the first drink with you back when—"

"Oh," Ninian interrupted flatly. "Right. I remember."

She beamed. "Well, anyway! Now I found you, I gotta take you back to the house. Cahir wants you for somethin'."

Máel Máedóc's gaze trailed them as he followed Treasa to the door.

"What does Cahir want?" Ninian asked as Treasa leaned the door open, and they stepped into the cold air. He fell into step on her left side, so he could actually hear her answer.

"Hm," Treasa replied with a small, self-satisfied smile, wrapping her arms around herself. "It's to do with Brígh." She leaned closer to Ninian, looking pleased with herself. "I overheard Cahir talking to Ruairí about it. But..." She looked Ninian up and down. "Aren't you supposed to be hurt or somethin'?"

Ninian cracked his knuckles. He didn't want to reveal any weakness to this near-stranger, even if he thought he could take her down easily. "I'm fine."

"Huh," she said thoughtfully. "I thought Brígh knocked you out."

"She did." He wondered, a little cluster of nerves balling up in his stomach, what this could be about. Since Cahir's little punishment, he hadn't resisted anything—there hadn't been anything *to* resist. He'd just simmered, resentful and depressed. He pulled the hood up on his cloak and changed the subject. "So what do you do? In the, uh… family?"

Treasa laced her fingers behind her head. "Not much. Errands, mostly. *Treasa, fetch this, Treasa, find that.*" She rolled her eyes. "It's annoying."

"Why'd you join?"

"Huh? Oh." She kicked a pebble, looking suddenly glum. "I didn't."

That caught Ninian off-guard. "How—"

"Easy-peasy." She sighed. They'd caught up to the pebble she'd kicked, so she kicked it again. "Cahir's my *daidí*."

Ninian stopped in his tracks. "*What?*" He shook his head. "Gods, he did *not* strike me as the fathering type." Then he froze, realizing who exactly he was addressing, and remembering Cahir's knife-point at his forehead. "I mean— sorry! Uh…" He groped around in his head for dusty politesse. "I apologize for my rudeness. I'd be very grateful if you didn't inform your father of that reaction."

But Treasa just snorted. "You talk weird." She waved a hand. "Anyway, who said you had to be the fathering type to knock up a load of ladies? I got fifteen half-siblings. My old man gets around." She stuck out her lower lip. "But I'm the youngest, and I'm not really good at anything, so he won't let me properly join up."

Ninian started walking again. It didn't seem like Treasa was about to have her father carve up his face, so that was a relief. "Honestly," he said, "I don't know why you'd want to."

Clearly affronted, Treasa turned pink about the ears. After a moment of her mouth opening and closing, she started on a stream of defensive chatter. Ninian tuned her out and waited for the walk to end.

⌇⌇⌇

Brígh and Cahir were standing outside on the steps of the house when Treasa and Ninian approached, and the ball of nerves in Ninian's gut tightened. Their expressions were terrifyingly serious. "Treasa," he hissed. "What the hell's going on?"

Treasa's eyes were on the two adults as well. "Shit. Brígh looks like she wants to make sausage outta your guts." She flicked her gaze over to him. "Or maybe peel off your face."

"Thank you," Ninian muttered, stomach flipping.

"Don't mention it." She stopped before the steps and rested an elbow jauntily on Ninian's shoulder. "Found him!"

Cahir grunted. "Took you long enough." He nodded to Ninian while Treasa *hrmph*ed. "Ninian, please come in."

Full of trepidation and not a little hate, Ninian followed Cahir and Brígh into the house. Treasa gave him a supportive wave before she darted off back down the street.

Brígh immediately dropped to a seat at the table and crossed her arms with a grace that didn't match the dark chill of her expression. Cahir gestured to the seat opposite her. "Sit."

Ninian sat.

Cahir slowly walked to the head of the table. He didn't sit but leaned his elbows on the back of the chair. "Now," he said quietly, mismatched eyes sweeping between Ninian and Brígh. "I haven't all the time in the world, so let's get this over."

Ninian pressed at his knuckles under the table, eliciting a few quiet pops.

"I received word," Cahir said, his voice still quiet, "that *within this family*, a sister has injured her brother." His gaze swept to Brígh and hovered there. Brígh's scar was puckered with the force of her scowl.

Ah. Ninian relaxed just a touch—it didn't appear that Cahir was angry with *him*.

"I was training him," Brígh spat. "Like you told me to."

"Quiet," Cahir said. The steadiness of his voice made his demeanor all the more intimidating. He folded his hands. "It is forbidden for any brother or sister in this family to harm their kin without cause."

"I *had* cause," Brígh argued. "Didn't you hear me, I said we were fighting—"

"*Quiet*. I don't actually care to hear either of your stories." With a sigh, he raised his voice and called into the other room. "Come."

Ninian frowned as soft sounds crept into the room, sounds of shuffling fabric and… were those chimes? He frowned at the doorway as a figure stepped into it.

Into their clothing—a simple tunic and a cream-colored cloak—were stitched perhaps a hundred tiny bells. As the figure moved into the room, so fluidly that they seemed to be gliding rather than walking, shadows slid off their face to reveal a leather mask over their eyes.

Ninian's mouth fell open.

He knew who this was.

Their like lived in the shadows, deeper than even Ninian had ever ventured. Ninian knew stories about them that traveled around fires and along the docks, stories passed down from his mother's lips. He had never met one, but he had seen them at festivals.

Even Brígh looked a touch uneasy when the stranger, who couldn't have been more than a few inches taller than Ninian, sank to a graceful seat opposite Cahir at the table. They smiled, and Ninian swallowed hard.

"Brígh, Ninian," Cahir said, "this is Ailbhe. They speak the truth."

Ailbhe smiled again. "Hello," they said softly. There was a touch of hoarseness in their voice, but also something faintly ethereal. They looked younger than Cahir, perhaps in their late teens or early twenties, with a slender build, caramel skin, and dust-brown hair. Up close, Ninian saw that the dark leather of their mask was cut to look like sharp, elegant feathers framing their face.

"E-excuse me," Ninian said, breaking the silence that followed. His mother's warnings wisped through his mind, making his heart pound. "What... *exactly* is going on?"

Brígh grunted. "This fool is going to tell Cahir that I didn't hurt you, and we're all going to have wasted some time."

"Shut up, Brígh," Cahir grunted. "Ninian, Ailbhe is a seer. It's my custom to use their craft to serve justice."

Ninian's skin prickled. "Seers use magic."

"Yes," Ailbhe agreed mildly.

Ninian tried to crack his knuckles again, but they wouldn't pop. The very marrow of his bones was echoing with his mother's voice. *Remember what I taught you.* "Isn't that... horribly dangerous?"

"Don't worry," Ailbhe said with yet another faint smile. "I've been doing this for a very long time." They inclined their head to Cahir. "My brother grows impatient." They rested their hands on the table, palms up. "Shall we begin?"

Everything in Ninian's being resisted the thought. He pressed his lips together. Of all the ways he'd fallen, and all the ways he had, ashamed, tried to silence his mother's stubborn memory, *this*—of all things—was so deeply ingrained that it had woven with his own instincts. *Remember who you are.* Brígh had already taken Ailbhe's hand, but Ninian hesitated. "You… you draw on the fae . . ."

Brígh groaned. "Ninian, do as you're told."

But Ailbhe held up their free hand. "No, no. I don't mind easing his fears."

"I mind. I don't have all day."

Ailbhe tilted their head innocently. "Are you sure you'd like to hurry my announcement of your guilt?"

The blood drained from Brígh's face. "You—"

But Ailbhe laughed easily. "I'm teasing. I haven't started yet." They turned their focus back to Ninian. "Ninian—it's Ninian, right?"

Ninian nodded.

"Well, Ninian," Ailbhe said. "You're correct."

Shivers ran over Ninian's skin. He'd heard horror stories of magic gone wrong—jealous fae weaving illusions that left healers mad, seers walking to their deaths into the sea. There was a reason that so, *so* long ago, his family had begun doing what they did.

"Imagine magic as body heat," Ailbhe explained. There was something inherently comforting in the way they talked. "The fae… they radiate it. All I do is siphon a little bit away." A smile once again crept onto their face. "They don't notice. I promise."

Ninian chewed his lip. Despite Ailbhe's well-spoken reassurance, he didn't feel more at ease, and his stomach twisted.

"Enough," Cahir cut in from the head of the table. "Ailbhe. Do your work and go."

"Yes, yes." Ailbhe nodded to Ninian. "It's safe. Take my hand."

Ninian didn't think he had a choice.

Ailbhe's palm was cool and smooth. Under their breath, Ailbhe began to murmur strange words, the bells adorning their clothes chiming faintly with the movement. Ninian stayed perfectly still, too nervous even to blink.

After a few moments, Ailbhe released both Ninian and Brígh's hands. They sat silently for a few heartbeats, as if organizing their thoughts.

"Well?" Cahir grunted.

Ailbhe let out a soft breath. "The fight had ended." From what Ninian could see through the angular eyeholes of the mask, their expression was introspective. "It had not yet been called, but Ninian was the clear victor." They paused for a beat, mouth twitching slightly. "Impressive. It was then that Brígh elbowed him in the side of the head. Her force was… immense."

"And is Ninian wounded?" Cahir asked.

The seer interlaced their fingers. "He is deafened in his left ear and wounded in the side." They narrowed their eyes at Cahir. "Something happened to his brand too."

Cahir made a *tch* sound.

Ninian fidgeted. "I mean… I could have told you all that." And he wouldn't have needed anything to do with the fae.

Cahir shushed him. "Ailbhe. Your judgment."

Ailbhe licked their lips. "Brígh acted out of malice. The fight had ended, and Ninian had abandoned all aggression." They looked down. "It was an act of unnecessary violence."

Brígh wasted no time slamming her fist to the table. "That's nonsense. Cahir, your creepy sibling doesn't know what they're talking about—"

"*Brígh.*" Cahir's voice had gained impact, a kind of gravity. "Come with me."

She went quite pale. "Cahir—"

Cahir stalked to the doorway. "Come."

With obvious unwillingness, Brígh pushed out her seat and stood. She joined Cahir at the doorway.

"Ailbhe," Cahir said without turning around. "I've finished with you."

"Thank you," Ailbhe sighed heavily.

The feeling of the room was very different when Cahir and Brígh weren't in it.

Unsure what to do with himself, Ninian scratched at the edge of the table. "Um," he ventured after a few minutes of silence. "What's going to happen to Brígh?"

"Nothing serious," Ailbhe answered. They hadn't made any move to get up but had leaned back against their chair as if tired. "A beating, perhaps."

Ninian let out a little breath. "So she's not going to die."

"Oh, Gods no. If Cahir killed everyone who'd ever lashed out, he wouldn't have a 'family' anymore." They smirked. "I don't count."

"You're actually related, then?"

Ailbhe nodded. "He is my older brother. You wouldn't guess it, would you?"

"Not really."

Ninian thought for a moment, trying to come up with something to say. He didn't want to sit in silence, especially not next to someone with fae power at their fingertips, but he was too afraid to leave without permission.

"So... will my hearing come back?"

"Hm," Ailbhe sighed. "I can't actually tell the future. I'm sorry." They shrugged. "I can discover the truth of the past and the present, but that's where it ends."

"Really?" Ninian bit his lip. He didn't know how to reply to that. "Oh."

"Mm-hm." Ailbhe stretched, resulting in jingles and cracks. They settled their elbows onto the table. "I wasn't looking terribly hard. Nothing overly personal, I promise. But it did see, for example, that you have an iron nail in your pocket."

Ninian blinked. He did. He'd nearly forgotten about that.

The seer smiled that strange, faint smile. "It's not a bad idea, you know. The fae *are* dangerous. Protection is wise."

"I know," Ninian said. He stared hard at the edge of the table. "My mother killed them."

Ailbhe's eyebrows raised quickly behind the mask. "Your mother did *what*?"

"Hunted fae." Ninian played with the nail. "Every festival night. She said she'd teach me how, like her family taught her, and back and back." He pressed the nail hard enough to leave little indents on the pads of his fingers. "I've never done it, though."

Ailbhe looked shocked. "Is this some twisted tradition?"

"It's not *twisted*," Ninian said sharply. "My family was nobility. Heroes." He fidgeted. "They protected people. And I was… supposed to."

The seer let out a quick breath. "I see why you dislike me, then." Their eyes were shaded, but Ninian could feel the piercing gaze all the same. "The fae truly scare you."

"They should scare everyone," Ninian muttered.

"Oh, and they do." Ailbhe played with one of the bells on their cloak. "But your fear is more personal."

"I thought you said you didn't *see* anything personal."

Ailbhe sighed. "I don't need magic to see that."

Ninian chewed the inside of his lip and pressed his thumb against his knuckles in silence.

"I confess," Ailbhe said, sitting forward a bit. "There was one thing. You were thinking it pretty… loudly."

Ninian narrowed his eyes. "Oh?"

The seer nodded, folding their hands on the table. "I just…" They hesitated. "My brother should not own you. And maybe… he doesn't have to."

Ninian's eyes widened. "What?"

Ailbhe looked away, and Ninian realized they were speaking very deliberately. "It would take years," they said carefully. "And it's something that I could never do. People fear me."

"What are you trying to say?" Ninian demanded, but Ailbhe shook their head.

"Seers can't lie," they said, and Ninian thought he heard the faintest drop of frustration in their voice. "And I swore an oath to my brother, so I can't break it. Just…" Their mask obscured their expression, but deep in their eyes, there was a well of intensity. "Be patient and make friends." They raised themselves to their feet. "One day, Cahir might not own *anyone*."

CHAPTER TWENTY

Ninian hadn't realized he'd been so tense until he stepped out of the house, took a deep breath, and felt a nervous knot between his shoulder blades begin to unwind.

A thiarcais.

Ailbhe's words were echoing in Ninian's head.

Seers couldn't lie. Ninian had known that channeling magic could have an effect on the conduit—some who used magic to heal could do no harm, some who used it for their crops could eat no meat, that sort of thing. But in this case, combined with Ailbhe's oath to their brother, that little side effect was highly inconvenient.

Ninian groaned. He would have been ready to believe Ailbhe was playing with him—they were a magic user, after all, and also related to Cahir—but something in their tone told Ninian that wasn't the case.

"I have no idea what I'm supposed to take away from that," he muttered.

He shook his head. Whatever it was, it had sounded hopeful.

So until he figured it out, he could at least hold on to that.

〰

A wave of savory-smelling warm air arrested Ninian at the doorway of Máel Máedóc's shop. He closed the door behind him and stood there for a few beats. The smell was enough to start his stomach growling.

He unclasped his cloak as he made his way through the now-familiar maze of crooked shelves, shrugging the cloak off and tucking it under his arm. The back of the shop flickered with firelight from the crackling hearth, and Máel Máedóc crouched in front of it, stirring a black pot over the flames. Áed sat by the wall, eyes half-closed; every now and then, his head bobbed.

"Smells good," Ninian said softly. Or at least, he thought he'd spoken softly—Áed startled so violently he almost fell over, and Máel Máedóc nearly knocked his head on the fireplace. The shopkeeper straightened, rubbing his forehead and glaring.

"What in the *hell* was that for, boy?"

Ninian pressed a hand over his mouth. "Was that loud?"

"It was!" Máel Máedóc let out an enormous breath. "God*damn*." He twirled a finger next to his ear, seemingly oblivious to the ladle in his hand dripping onto the floor. "Is your hearing still bothering you?"

"No. My *lack* of hearing is, though." He crossed the little space and dropped to a seat next to Áed, who was taking deep, steadying breaths.

"Charming." Máel Máedóc shook his head. "You're talking too loud. Keep it down."

Ninian stretched. "Loud*ly*."

"Huh?"

"I'm speaking too loud*ly*, not loud."

The shopkeeper's face was a stone.

"Right," Ninian said, tamping down a nervous laugh.

"Never mind." He turned his attention to Áed and tucked his legs under himself while Máel Máedóc stomped off to lock the shop door for the night. "How've you been?"

Áed shrugged wearily.

"Yeah," Ninian sighed. "I really get that."

"Good talk," Máel Máedóc interrupted, returning from amongst the shelves. "Food's ready."

Ninian's eyes widened as the shopkeeper began to ladle the contents of his pot into two bowls. His mouth fell open a bit. "That's for *us*?"

Máel Máedóc rolled his cobalt eyes. "You thought I was going to eat a whole pot of stew on my own?"

"Well, I don't know!" His mood had elevated simply upon walking in the door. "You're pretty big, aren't you?"

The shopkeeper, looking exasperated, set a full bowl heavily onto the floor in front of Ninian and Áed, and plopped two wooden spoons into the thick, brown broth. "Only got two bowls of my own," he grunted, sitting back with the other in his hand. "You'll have to share."

Áed was staring at the stew with longing, but as Ninian reached for a spoon, he thought he saw a faint pinkness in Áed's cheeks and ears.

Oh. Of course.

"Here," Ninian said, trying to make it sound like it was perfectly ordinary. He filled the spoon with stew and raised it full of broth, a carrot slice, and a chunk of stringy meat. "I'll help."

Áed hesitated.

"It looks good," Ninian observed. "Smells good too."

Áed squeezed his eyes shut, but his hunger clearly compelled him; Ninian held the spoon, and Áed ate from it.

The red-eyed boy leaned back with his mouth full, face flushed, and he looked away from Ninian.

Ninian frowned. "What's the matter?" It was hard to ignore

Máel Máedóc so obviously watching, but he managed.

Even though Áed wasn't looking at him, Ninian could see the red of his ears. "I'm so sorry," Áed said quietly after he had swallowed. "It's… it's embarrassing, is all."

"You don't have to be embarrassed." He poked at the stew. "I mean, you need to eat."

Áed turned to face Ninian, even though his eyes were still fixed somewhere decidedly away. "I know," he said, and Ninian was a little startled by just how much Áed was blushing. "It's just embarrassing."

Ninian cocked his head. "Would you rather Máel Máedóc do it?"

"No!" Áed said quickly. Ninian could practically feel the heat pouring from him. "That's not what I meant—" He closed his eyes again and shook his head. "Never mind."

"Well." He thought he understood Áed's reluctance— nobody wanted to be spoon-fed—but didn't think it merited quite so much fuss. Áed was obviously hungry, after all. "Do you want more?"

Haltingly, Áed nodded, and they did the whole thing again, complete with Áed squeezing his eyes shut and turning quite pink.

Máel Máedóc slurped his own stew straight from the bowl, ignoring his spoon altogether, then wiped his mouth with the back of his hand. He set the bowl down. "You boys want to play a game?"

⸽⸽⸽

"Wait, no, no," Áed said, leaning over Ninian's shoulder. His eyes were narrowed in focus.

Ninian held the cards up so Áed could see them more easily. "What do you think?"

Across the table, Máel Máedóc was squinting at both of

them suspiciously, like he suspected they were cheating. They'd been gambling with buttons, and Ninian and Áed had collected about fifty to the shopkeeper's quickly dwindling four.

Áed rested his chin on Ninian's shoulder, his eyes focused. "Play the third card—no, from the other side. That one."

Obediently, Ninian pulled out the card and set it on the table, and Máel Máedóc groaned and ceded three more buttons. He held up the single one he had left. "Do you see this?" he complained. "I never lose at this game."

Still leaning on Ninian's shoulder, Áed smiled. "I've never played before."

The shopkeeper grumbled, staring at his cards.

"If it makes you feel better," Ninian said, "I'm only holding the cards."

"He doesn't know what's going on," Áed agreed.

"Ha!" Máel Máedóc interrupted victoriously, slapping a card onto the table. "Make what you will of *that*!"

Ninian truly didn't know what was going on, but he smirked as Áed started grinning, and the shopkeeper's face fell at Áed's expression.

"Ninian," Áed said, not even hiding his tone. "Play the card on the far left."

Ninian did. He could feel Áed's hair brushing the side of his neck, the warmth where Áed, sitting a bit behind Ninian, had dropped his chin on Ninian's shoulder, and the weight of Áed leaning on him. It turned out that once he grew comfortable enough to show it, Áed was very touch-starved. Since they'd finished the stew, Ninian didn't think Áed had broken contact with him once.

Ninian didn't mind. He'd been a bit uncertain at first—Áed's touch wasn't uncomfortable, but when the red-eyed boy had simply fit himself against Ninian's side and decided not to move, it had made Ninian strangely shivery. Áed, however, didn't even seem to think about it, and over the course of the game, Ninian had begun to relax. He started to get used to Áed's warmth and the fact that when Áed moved to look over his shoulder, his head fit very nicely in the crook of Ninian's neck.

It did feel pleasant.

"There!" Áed said. "Hand over the button."

Ninian dutifully accepted Máel Máedóc's loss.

For a moment, Áed looked happy. After the brightness faded, though, a crease nudged its way between his eyebrows, and he chewed his lip as the shopkeeper began to pack up the cards. "Are you sure you don't want to play again…?"

"And lose again?" Máel Máedóc scoffed. "No, thank you. Besides, it's late."

"Hey," Ninian said, seeing Áed's worried face. Áed's eyes flicked to his hands, and then fixed firmly on the wall. "Just because the distraction is over doesn't mean you can't go to sleep, right? I mean, what's better than sleep?"

"Yeah," Áed agreed, sounding unconvinced. Ninian couldn't blame him, but he wasn't sure what else he could say.

"Ninian," Máel Máedóc said, scooping the buttons into the pouch from which they'd come. "Did you plan on going home tonight?"

"You mean to the flat I found?"

The shopkeeper nodded, and Ninian frowned. He had thought of going back—it had been a while since he'd even dropped by—but the idea of facing the cold and the dark was suddenly supremely unappealing. "I don't know," he said. "I guess…"

"Wouldn't recommend it," Máel Máedóc said shortly. "There's going to be a gang squabble at midnight, and I'll bet anything that yours gets involved."

A cold stone splashed into the pit of Ninian's stomach.

"Right," he said quickly, glancing at Áed. "Got it." He had no problem with staying in; nobody had told him he needed to be involved with this squabble. He wasn't even surprised that Máel Máedóc knew about it, since the shopkeeper couldn't have gotten to where he was by being ignorant of the Maze's goings-on.

That wasn't the issue.

Áed had caught the most important word. "*Your* gang?" he asked. He lifted his chin to look at Ninian properly, but Ninian wouldn't meet his eyes. "You're in a gang?"

Shame curled in Ninian's stomach. He looked away. "Yes."

"I didn't know that." Áed looked troubled.

Ninian's lips were dry; when he bit them, he tasted blood. "Yeah." He hadn't *wanted* Áed to know that.

It was no doubt a product of his own emotion, but he wholly expected Áed to crack down. *What do you do? Have you ever hurt someone? What does it feel like at that moment when a knife breaks the skin, and you know you can't go back anymore? How does it feel to end a life?* He swallowed hard. What would he say? He didn't want Áed to hate him—in fact, he didn't know what he would do if Áed cut him off. He'd never regretted his lack of friends, but now that he had one… he felt a little nauseous at the thought.

"Áed—" he started, but then bit his tongue when he realized Áed wasn't listening.

The red-eyed boy was looking pensive. "Your ear. Your bruises. The bandages on your chest, the ones you keep hiding." His eyes had turned igneous. "Those are from the gang, then, aren't they?"

"Um." Ninian considered evading the question, but Áed's expression grew darker. "Yeah."

Áed was practically glowering. "They hurt you."

Part of Ninian wanted to confess to deserving it, but he was weak and said nothing.

"Ninian."

Ninian chewed the inside of his lip.

"What did they do?"

Ninian let out his breath and couldn't keep eye contact. "It's a brand. Under the bandages." He touched his forefingers and thumbs, making a circle as Áed froze. "About this big."

It was impossible to tell if Áed was even breathing until he spoke. "A… *brand?*"

Across the table, Máel Máedóc nodded. "I treated it. Nasty thing."

Self-conscious, Ninian pressed his palms to the injury. Unfortunately, he could still remember the smell of his own searing flesh.

None of the disgust Ninian expected was apparent in Áed's face. Instead, Áed's eyebrows were knit, his mouth downturned in worry. "Does it hurt?"

It was smarting under his palms. Ninian nodded reluctantly. "A bit."

"Why did you join?" Áed asked, clearly uncomprehending. "It sounds awful."

Ninian's gaze latched to the floor. There was a single oat grain under the table, and a crack in the floor shaped like the letter E. "I didn't mean to. But I…" His throat closed and stopped his voice until he swallowed. "I got drunk."

Áed looked appalled. "You decided to join a gang because you were *drunk?*"

"No, no," Ninian tried to explain. "I didn't decide." He felt his face redden, sick with himself. "I just drank, and then they… they took the iron, and then the next morning they told me that meant I was in, and if I ever try to leave, they'll cut up my face so the other gangs know they can kill me."

Áed's mouth fell open, and he stared at Ninian like he'd never seen him before.

It was Máel Máedóc who finally broke the silence. "Ninian," he said, and Ninian thought the man's voice was lower than he'd ever heard it. "I…" He pressed his lips together. "I think you should know that maybe you were naïve, but they did do you wrong."

Ninian's gut felt sharp. "It's not their fault," he said eventually. He'd been angry, yes, and he resented their hold on him, but he'd been the one who had gone along. "I mean… it's fair; I get paid. And some of them have been kind to me."

Máel Máedóc looked angry, though Ninian suspected it was just the man's interpretation of 'pensive.' "And did the kind ones watch? Did they do anything while everyone got you drunk, and someone pressed a fire-iron to your body?"

"They didn't *get me drunk*," Ninian said, and to his surprise, his voice quivered at the end in a way he hadn't given it leave to. Suddenly, he didn't feel too well. "The only way to *get someone drunk* is to shove a bottle in their mouth. There's no other way to *make* someone drink." He cracked his knuckles nervously. "Which means it's a choice. Which means that when you're drunk, whatever happens…" He swallowed. "Is your own fault."

Máel Máedóc was looking at Ninian with a very peculiar expression. "Who told you *that*?"

Who told you that?

Who told you that?

Even Ninian's deaf ear was ringing. "My—my uncle."

It was happening again. The light in the shop seemed too harsh, and his skin began to feel chilled and hot at the same time.

Áed made a concerned sound. "Ninian?"

"Sorry," Ninian muttered. He did his best to control his breathing. In-it's-fine, out-it's-fine. The last time this feeling had spiraled, he'd fought a grown man to the ground. He remembered the wild emotion, the dance of survival, and how the haze had cleared from his vision with every blow he'd dodged. But there was nobody here to fight. "I'm fine."

Áed looked skeptical. "*Are* you?"

Máel Máedóc cleared his throat. "Ninian, what kind of a man was your uncle?"

"He—he—" Ninian stopped, taking a slow breath. Áed had pressed himself worriedly into Ninian's side, and Ninian tried to focus on the warmth even as he habitually gripped his own arms. His fingernails, still bitten short, did not provide any bright relief against his skin. "H-he's—" Releasing his arms, he clapped his palms to his face. *Stupid, stupid. You haven't stuttered since you had seven years.* He put his effort into making himself speak clearly. "He was a very f-fair man."

Silence throbbed around the table. Máel Máedóc looked like he wanted to say something, but he held his tongue, and Áed tucked his head comfortingly into the crook of Ninian's neck.

"I, um," Ninian managed. The room went yellow for a moment, and he felt his hands shaking. "I don't feel…"

He startled violently when Máel Máedóc walked around the table and crouched next to him, and his heart rate spiked hard enough to ache. "Ninian," the shopkeeper said, resting a hand on his shoulder. His voice was very level. "You're safe. Take it easy."

"S-stop." He covered his face and pressed his thumbs into his eyes, but when he did that, it went dim instead of dark, and there were beams in the ceiling that didn't hold all the thatch, and the floor was uneven under his shoulder blades. He opened his eyes with a start, and he was sitting at the table again. "Stop t-*touch*—" He shoved Máel Máedóc's hand viciously off his shoulder. "Stop *touching* me—"

"Ninian, listen to me." Máel Máedóc got to his knees, tucking his hands safely into his pockets. "I'm going to breathe, and you're going to breathe with me. Can you do that?"

Ninian nodded, or he was pretty sure he did.

"Breathe in," Máel Máedóc directed, and Ninian obeyed. "Now out, nice and slow." It was harder to control his exhalation, but Ninian did it. "In again, take it easy… and out again."

It was impossible to repress the shudder that ran from his head to toes, but Ninian kept breathing. "I'm sorry," he said, and he was, but it was a sick sorry, an angry, hot sorry. "I'm so s-sorry. I'm so sorry—"

"Less talking, more breathing," the shopkeeper ordered. He'd taken Ninian at his word and had moved away.

Ninian clenched his teeth until his ears screamed with nonexistent noise.

He breathed.

Everything felt too sharp. Too acute. He could feel every pore in his body.

He breathed.

Máel Máedóc's directions were repetitive. Counting them was better than obeying them.

He breathed.

And he breathed.

Áed sounded tense when, sometime later, he spoke. "That's a little better."

Ninian wasn't sure how Áed knew, but he was right. His hands weren't shaking so much, and though his heart was still hammering, something had changed. "I'm sorry."

"Don't apologize," Máel Máedóc said. His voice was still careful. Even. "You have nothing to be sorry for."

Ninian managed to shake his head. "You don't—" He

swallowed. His tongue tripped. "No idea. Y-you have—don't have any idea."

Áed was frowning faintly. "Why do you feel so guilty?" he said quietly, so quietly that Ninian was sure Máel Máedóc wasn't supposed to hear.

Ninian stared at him for a moment. The panicky feeling was blessedly ending; he was sure of it now, but he felt shaky and sick, and Áed's words still twisted something deep in Ninian's chest. "It's r-really creepy when you do that."

Áed looked abashed. "I, um…"

I can't tell them.

He could picture the revulsion on their faces. It made his stomach lurch. His hands were still twitching.

"I'm just tired," he said, and the exhaustion in his voice validated it. That spell had been quick, bless the Gods, but it had come as strong as it had fast, and Ninian was drained and strangely jittery. "*Really* tired."

Áed shifted like he sensed Ninian's evasion, but he didn't press.

Máel Máedóc sat back on his heels. "Well," he said after a few beats. "It is late."

Ninian rubbed his eyes with unsteady hands. *I just want to sleep.* Whether or not he'd be *able* to sleep was a different question altogether, but he was weary to the marrow of his bones.

Áed stood with him when he got up, still staying close. "Goodnight, Máel Máedóc," Ninian said. "Thank you for dinner."

⟨⟨⟩⟩

Ninian couldn't close his eyes.

Áed lay next to him, curled, and warm, and quite asleep, but Ninian just lay on his back and stared at the ceiling.

Disgraceful.

Defiled.

Disgusting.

He took a deep breath, and it quivered on the way out. Next to him, the moonlight through the window made Áed's blond hair look silver.

Ninian dropped a hand over his eyes. Máel Máedóc had approached when Ninian was washing his face—scaring him to the threshold of death in the process—and had leaned on the wall nearest the basin. Áed had already been in the bedroom, but the shopkeeper had checked anyway. "You know," he'd said, "Áed has been better with you around."

Ninian had stared into the water of the basin. "I'm just doing as you said. When he's all healed…" He'd swallowed, the decision sticking hard in his throat. "I'll go." He couldn't stay. He knew that now. He would leave before Áed could come to despise him, because he didn't think he could bear Áed despising him. Why the red-eyed boy mattered so much to him was a mystery, but the facts stood.

The shopkeeper had looked thoughtfully at Ninian before examining his own rough nails. "He sees you as you are."

Ninian hadn't understood.

"I mean that you—you *right now*—make Áed happy." The giant man had crossed his arms. "You must be a strong force of good to pull someone out of darkness that deep."

Water was running down Ninian's face from the basin. "He doesn't know me."

Máel Máedóc regarded him for a few moments. "I believe," he said eventually, "that if you wanted to change that…" He folded his hands in front of him. "Call it a gut instinct, but I think you could."

He pushed himself away from the wall; the floor creaked, and a winter moth flapped around the shopkeeper's candle.

Shadows danced between streaks of orange light among the shelves. "Have a good night, Ninian."

Now Ninian counted Áed's quiet breaths, and his sleepless, exhausted mind fuzzed with thoughts. There was something lightless in the center of his core, something that had been crumbling away at him for two years; eventually, he thought, perhaps his whole person would be devoured by those widening, all-consuming edges.

I don't want anyone to see that chasm.

I don't want anyone to know where it came from.

But…

Máel Máedóc's words rolled around in his head, and he looked to Áed beside him.

But I'm so tired of falling alone.

He turned, bedsprings creaking, toward Áed, whose face was serene.

Am I actually *considering this?*

He knew what would happen. He knew why he'd never told a soul. He knew what Áed would say. But… "Áed," he whispered, too softly to be heard. Just trying out the words. Just to hear them, maybe convince himself to swallow them again. "Please." He swallowed; it was hard to say. "Please catch me."

Áed opened his eyes.

Ninian's breath choked him.

Áed looked otherworldly in the moonlight, and a slow, tiny smile crept over his face. "Okay."

CHAPTER TWENTY-ONE

Ninian wasn't really sure what happened.

It was like something had cracked inside of him; he couldn't tell if the darkness was spilling out, or if Áed's light was spilling in, but words poured, and he couldn't stop them.

He told Áed about his family's death, and about moving in with his aunt and uncle. He told him about what had happened once his uncle started looking at him sideways, and how his aunt did her sewing in the other room so she could pretend she didn't hear. He told him about always being sick the next morning, from the shame as much as the alcohol, and about agreeing to drink because he didn't want to be *there* when his uncle blew out the candles.

Somewhere in the middle, he realized he'd started crying. The pillow slowly grew damp, no matter how many times he wiped his eyes, but he kept talking.

Áed said nothing as Ninian's story emerged, even as his eyebrows knit closer together. He stayed still, simply listening.

After a long time, Ninian fell silent. The weight of fear—fear of Áed's reaction coupled with remembered dread—sat on his chest, and as the quiet stretched out and Áed didn't say anything, it became almost too heavy to breathe.

When Áed replied, it wasn't with words.

Slowly, cradling his ruined hands carefully between them, he nestled his head under Ninian's chin.

"I, um…" Ninian faltered. Áed hadn't recoiled—he'd moved closer. Did that mean… Ninian pressed his lips together. What did that mean?

As if answering the unasked question, Áed spoke. His voice was quiet, muffled by Ninian's shirt. "What are you scared of?"

Ninian's throat was tight. "I don't want—" His voice cracked. *Come on. What's a little more honesty?* "I don't want to disgust you."

Áed only pressed closer. "Ninian, does it seem like I'm disgusted?"

Twin tears traced down Ninian's cheeks, and he closed his eyes, lip trembling. "N-no?"

"That's right. Because I'm not." He shifted to look at Ninian's face. "He lied to you," he said seriously, and Ninian saw that Áed's eyes weren't exactly dry, either. "Your uncle lied to you." He closed his eyes and shook his head, the tip of his nose brushing over Ninian's collarbone. "That wasn't your fault."

Ninian simply didn't know how to believe that. "I *let* him," Ninian whispered.

"No." He let out a little breath. "This *can't* be your fault."

Tears stung as they blurred Ninian's vision. "Áed, I chose to be drunk. I *let* him."

Áed nudged Ninian's chin supportively with the top of his head, his mind clearly working through Ninian's words. "So you were vulnerable," he said. "*I'm* vulnerable. Does that mean you'd hurt me?" His voice was heavy. "You had *ten years* to his… what? Thirty? He was supposed to protect you. That's…" He trailed off unsteadily, seeming to speak to himself more than Ninian. "How could he *do* that to you?"

Ninian made a little half-throttled noise.

Áed shook his head before Ninian managed any words, and there was a decidedly new fierceness in the motion. "It doesn't matter how. Just because he *could* doesn't mean he *should've*." Everything about Áed was tense. "It's disgusting that he *did*." He looked up to Ninian. "He's disgusting. Not you. Never you."

A little cry hiccupped in Ninian's chest, and he tasted saltwater—the levies had broken properly, and tears were flowing hard and fast. "Áed, I d-didn't know what to d-do—" He broke off with a suppressed sob, because it seemed that if he didn't fight them, those tears were going to take over and he'd drown. And the words were still coming. "He—he said I was l-lucky he even wanted me, and—" He gasped, and it was painful. "I wasn't worth the g-ground I slept on, and I kn-knew I owed him, and—"

"Nin," Áed whispered. "Slow down."

It was incredible how difficult that was. "I didn't have anywhere else to *g-go*." He squeezed his eyes shut, which did nothing to slow the tears. He'd had nowhere else to go, and he had stayed in that house for an entire year. "But I… I couldn't…" He shook his head against the pillow. "I ran away." His hands were in fists, and he couldn't unclench them. He didn't know whether his uncle had ever looked for him. He had avoided that entire sector of the city ever since. "I thought m-maybe it would make me *cleaner*, make me *m-mine*—" A sob interrupted him. Ninian thought he was breathing too fast. "But it *didn't*!"

"Oh…" Áed said, and he sounded truly heartbroken. "Ninian…"

"He said I was his!" Ninian sobbed. "H-he said I was *his*…"

"You are not," Áed said, and the words were soft and firm

as he carefully put his arm over Ninian and pressed him closer. If Ninian could have cried harder, that would have made him. "You never were."

There was no point in wiping his eyes. Ninian had not cried like this in years, not the sort of crying that made it feel like the world was dissolving and him with it. He gasped, and the sobs redoubled in earnest.

Áed rested his forehead against Ninian's chest, still gingerly holding him. "You are Ninian. And you are nobody's but Ninian's." He pressed his forehead where it rested, right over Ninian's heart. "And nobody has the right to hurt you."

Ninian cried until he could not cry any longer. His whole body shook, and his face grew as drenched as if he'd stood in the rain; where the tears slowly began to dry, the skin felt stiff.

He only stilled when exhaustion's weighted grip became stronger than the force of the outpouring emotion, and, breathing so shakily that it almost wasn't breathing at all, he closed his eyes and tried to find himself.

He couldn't. It was like he had cried himself away.

Áed filled the void. "You're a good person, Ninian," he said, and the words reached Ninian as if through clouds. "I can feel it."

Maybe it was the way Ninian had seen Áed read people before, or maybe it was just the way he'd said it, but somehow, those words meant something.

I'm a good person, Ninian thought experimentally, and he listened to the words echo hollowly in his head.

It didn't feel true.

Maybe it never would.

The pitch-dark pit inside of him had been spreading for two years, and Ninian thought it might take more light to fill it than he alone would ever have.

That didn't stop him from shuddering, and it didn't stop Áed's words from sending warmth rippling over his skin.

Careful of Áed's hand still between them, Ninian hugged the red-eyed boy close. Despite his caution, Áed let out a little whimper, and Ninian relaxed his hold. "I'm sorry." He took a deep breath and released it slowly, concentrating on the control. "Áed," he said, because it was a miracle—there he was.

Not edging away, not repulsed.

He was there.

Ninian's voice was barely a whisper. "*Thank you.*"

CHAPTER TWENTY-TWO

Please don't wake him. The voice floated through Ninian's mind like a dream, and perhaps it was. *He hasn't slept right in a long time; he's so tired. Always tired.*

A different voice sighed. *Kid,* it said, and it was deep enough to be a rumble on the edge of Ninian's awareness. *It would* really *be best for you to stop announcing people's feelings.* The voice paused. *Trust me on that one.*

Ninian stretched, still not quite awake. He couldn't remember the last time he'd felt so comfortable or so heavy. Consciousness felt golden and syrupy.

He yawned, and cool air brushed over his face. Slowly, woozily, he opened his eyes.

A thiarcais. Had he... had he slept through the night? Pushing himself to his elbows, he blinked sleepily at the bright, sunlit room. Yes! He had slept not only through the night, but *into the day.* And judging by the comfortable weight of his body, the sleep had been restful. He couldn't even remember dreaming.

Stretching again and eliciting a few *pops* from his back, he slipped out of bed, tidied the covers quickly, and padded into the shop, rubbing at his eyes.

Áed sat at the table, a ray of sunlight cutting across his face and making his freckles stand out while his hair glowed. His face brightened when he saw Ninian. "You're up!" Then he bit his lip. "I wanted you to get more sleep." After a half-second's deliberation, his expression was sunny again. "But you're up!"

Ninian returned the smile. His eyes felt rather puffy. "I'm up." He sat at the table across from Áed and yawned again, hair tumbling into his eyes. He cast around for something normal to say—what was normal, again? "How did you, um… sleep?"

A cloud fell over Áed's expression. "Oh. All right."

Not fooled, Ninian studied Áed's face. "Nightmares?" He knew the look—sometimes, he thought he wore it himself more often than not.

Áed nodded. "They don't make any sense." His shoulders hunched. "They just *hurt*." He held up his hands, and Ninian saw that the monstrous bruises that crept up his arms had spread even further and taken on a sick, yellow-green hue. "I think I'm trying to move my hands in my sleep," Áed said, wincing. "I woke, and they were in fists. I thought I was going to throw up."

Ninian grimaced in sympathy. "That sounds awful."

"Mm," Áed agreed. Ninian noticed that he was moving gingerly, as if his hands hadn't been able to contain the pain, and it had spread. He fixed Ninian with a scrutinizing gaze. "Anyway," he said. "How are *you*?"

Across the room, Máel Máedóc glanced over.

A faint, tentative smile tugged at Ninian's lips. "I feel… okay."

Áed took Ninian's smile and reflected it, looking perfect, on his own face.

"Gods be damned," Máel Máedóc murmured. His eyes were creased at the corners. "I never thought that I'd see that expression on either of you." Ninian didn't think the shopkeeper was the smiling type, but the big man's mouth bent ever so slightly anyway, and he turned away.

There was a new feeling in his core. Next to the darkness, or maybe around it, it was bright: *You're a good person, Ninian,* Áed had said. *I can feel it.*

It was Áed's belief that shone there, not Ninian's, but… well, maybe for now, Áed's belief was enough.

There was something Ninian had to do that day.

"Máel Máedóc?" He fished in his pocket, fingers brushing past the iron nail until they closed around the only other thing he carried. "You know how you gave me back the money I, uh… earned?"

Áed watched the exchange curiously, but Máel Máedóc nodded.

Ninian drew the stained leather pouch out of his pocket, and the coins rattled inside. "I'd like to spend it."

The shopkeeper raised an eyebrow. "On what?"

In response, Ninian walked into the shelf maze. He heard Máel Máedóc ambling behind him, and he ducked under a curtain of sheepskins and into a cool, dry corner.

Rowan. Sausage. Bread. Honey, hazelnuts, dulse, apples, cheese, heath-fruits, carrots and parsnips—every fruit of the land or part of the beast that Ninian had ever seen.

Máel Máedóc made a thoughtful *hmm* as he ducked under the sheepskin, as if earlier events were acting themselves over again.

It was different this time.

"You wanna get food?" Máel Máedóc asked, and Ninian nodded firmly, dropping the coins into the shopkeeper's gigantic palm.

"As much as this will buy."

⦚

In the end, Ninian had to borrow a knapsack from Máel Máedóc. He stuffed it with the most nourishing things he could get his hands on—jerky, oat bread, root vegetables, whatever he could afford—and when it was full, and Máel Máedóc had pocketed Ninian's coins, he hefted the bag. It was satisfyingly weighty. The shopkeeper must have let Ninian take *significantly* more than his money's worth.

He waved to Áed, who had been drawn by curiosity. "I'll be back soon," he promised. "There's something I have to do." He offered one final grin and, hiking the bag further on his shoulders, hurried into the streets.

He remembered where Cuimín's house was. The route had seared itself into his memory, and his feet carried him as surely as if he were following a trail of blood in the dusty, damp street.

You're a good person. He felt his ears flush with the memory. *I can feel it.*

His heart was going a bit quicker than he'd have liked. What exactly was he going to say? Cuimín hadn't mentioned a partner, not anyone but his daughters… how could Ninian stand before children he himself had orphaned? He couldn't possibly apologize.

Still. This was the right thing to do. It was what a *good person* would do.

And even if Ninian wasn't one… he wanted to be.

⸝⸝⸝

Cuimín's street was quiet, and Ninian slowed his walk as he grew nearer. He carefully made sure he kept his eyes away from the gutter in case the man's tongue had not yet been eaten by rats. Rain had washed away the blood, but Ninian remembered exactly where it had pooled.

There was no light beyond the windows of the little slanted

building. Ninian approached with trepidation, slinging the pack from his shoulders.

He *would* do this.

Steeling himself, he knocked on the door.

No voices replied, but he heard movement within.

"Hello?" he called tentatively.

A little face topped with carrot-red curls peeked through the window and was just as soon pulled away.

Ninian rubbed at the back of his neck, anxious. "I, uh… I brought some food for you."

At that, quiet voices murmured behind the door.

With a measure of effort, the door opened a crack, enough to see a sliver of a little girl's face. Ninian unbuckled the bag and held up a loaf of bread. "See?"

Without further hesitation, the girl swung open the door, snatched the bread, and slammed it again.

"Wait! I have more." He bit his lip. "Do you want me to leave it out here?"

From inside, he heard a young, authoritative voice. "Oi. Biddy, stop."

Ninian listened to the house go quiet and turned his good ear to the door.

"We don't know him," the girl's voice said shakily. "We can' trust him."

A different voice—Biddy, Ninian guessed—replied. "But Aislin, he brought food."

The first voice, Aislin's, sounded a bit sharp. "You're just hungry. You have no idea if he's nice. Get away from the door."

"Uh—excuse me," Ninian called through the door. "I'm…" He squeezed his eyes shut for a moment, building up his nerve. "I'm not going to hurt you. But I'm… I'm the one who…" The words stuck in his throat like curdled milk. "I—your father—"

Dead silence fell behind the door.

Ninian released a shaky breath. "I'm sorry. I… I brought food. Lots. An apology. I know it's not enough, but…"

"Biddy," Aislin's voice came decisively. "Tell Daidí who's here."

Little footsteps pattered in response to her words.

Ninian frowned. *Tell…* "Wait. Cuimín—your father—is he…" It seemed like too much to hope for, and he feared by asking he would erase any chance of it being true, but he had to know. "Is he… alive?"

"Don' answer, Biddy!" Aislin shrieked, seeming to realize what she'd said.

Biddy's voice softly sucked in a little gasp. "What if he's here t' finish 'im off?"

"I'm not!" Ninian said. There was a bubble in his chest, and he found himself smiling. *I did a terrible thing,* he reminded himself, as if he could have forgotten. *I cut out an innocent man's tongue, when he was unarmed, without a fight.*

But Cuimín was *alive.*

Ninian had not taken a life.

It felt good to breathe, and suddenly, he noticed the sun. It was warm on his shoulders, and he felt it even through his cloak. "I'm not here to hurt you, I swear—I'll go, I'll leave this food." He bit the tip of his tongue. "Is he all right? Is he healing?"

Aislin's voice responded after a long beat of quiet. "He's not gonna die," she said. "At least, I don' think."

At that, there was a new sound.

It sounded like it was meant to be speech, a man's voice, garbled, unintelligible.

Cuimín.

"Is that…" Ninian's stomach flipped. "Cuimín? Sir?" Guilt, alongside heady relief, twined in knots through his gut. "Sir, if you can hear me, I… I am so sorry." He stooped and began unpacking the knapsack, carefully piling paper-wrapped jerky and cheese on the step. "I brought food. For your family, I didn't know how they'd—anyway, there's a lot of it—"

"D'you expect us to thank ye?" Aislin snapped. "Our daidí can't talk anymore." She sniffed, and Ninian thought she might have started crying.

Ninian stood and looked down at his inadequate offering. "Yeah. I know." Bread and honey couldn't recreate the sound of a father's words. He swung the empty knapsack back over his shoulders. "I'll go now, okay?"

Aislin sniffed again, but her voice, when choked with tears, only sounded harsher. "And don' ye ever come back!"

I have no right to argue with that. Ninian turned to leave, and he heard Cuimín's strangled half-voice again as he stepped off the crooked porch.

The door opened behind Ninian.

A girl stood in the doorway, a girl with Cuimín's blond hair, a ratty blue frock, and pink-rimmed eyes that were damp with tears. She glared at him. "Wait." She looked down and kicked at the doorjamb with her toe. "I think Daidí wants t'say something to ye."

Ninian frowned. "Say…?"

The girl listened, brow furrowing as somewhere just out of sight, Cuimín struggled to shape his mutilated words. Even without understanding his speech, Ninian could hear pain in his voice. Sulkily, Aislin repeated something back to him and apparently received an affirmative reply.

She kicked the doorjamb harder, resisting eye contact. "Now, I can' understand him too well." The jamb made dull thuds when her bare foot hit it. "But I think he says…" She looked over her shoulder to check, then went back to staring at the abused doorjamb. "He says he..."

Cuimín's voice came again, sounding to Ninian like a different language entirely, but Aislin, obviously familiar with it, scowled. Her sister ventured into the doorway to cling at her skirt.

"He's glad he's not dead." Aislin glared up at him abruptly. "Are ye happy?"

Ninian fidgeted with the strap of the knapsack. "I'm not happy I hurt him." Aislin's face didn't soften; Ninian hadn't expected it to. "But... I'm glad he's not dead." He pressed his lips together. If Cahir found out that Cuimín was alive... well, Ninian might have already been chastised for not finishing the job *properly*, but Cahir still assumed it was done. He would certainly send someone to end it if he found out the truth.

If Ninian didn't tell, and Cahir found out that he'd known, Ninian would be punished. Probably brutally. Maybe fatally. It seemed like the sort of thing Cahir would call 'lost loyalty.'

Ninian took a deep breath and let it out very slowly.

Cahir couldn't control him. So long as he didn't find out, Ninian would be okay—and so would Cuimín.

"I won't tell," Ninian said. It felt good to keep a secret. Something of his own. "I promise that you're safe."

CHAPTER TWENTY-THREE

There was a strange spring in Ninian's step by the time he reached the trading shop again. He walked inside feeling lighter than he had in years, and it was strange even to *move* with so much weight off of his shoulders. He wasn't a murderer, Áed didn't find him disgusting, and he had slept more deeply than he had since he was a proper child.

All right, he had low standards.

He wanted to see Áed again. This 'friend' situation was wonderful. He should have tried it earlier.

"Ninian?" Máel Máedóc's voice came from the back of the shop, and immediately, Ninian's buoyant mood faltered. There was something very off about the shopkeeper's tone.

"It's me!" Ninian said, already hurrying toward the back. Sounds were reaching him, sounds that were *not right*, but his single functioning ear couldn't make sense of them.

"Come quickly," Máel Máedóc said urgently.

Ninian didn't need to be told. He dropped the backpack somewhere amidst the shelves as he ran toward Máel Máedóc's voice.

He came to a stop where the shelves opened up, and

his feet skidded. He looked down, catching himself, and his jaw dropped. "What the…"

The floor was covered in salt, reddish-white grains scattered over the planks, grinding under Ninian's boots. The crate of nails had tipped over, sending iron spikes tumbling across the room, and the pouch of rowan berries had spilled. Dried fruits had rolled to every nook, and some smudges on the floor, ground in with the salt, attested to where they'd been crushed.

And in the corner, Áed was wild.

The shopkeeper was holding him to the floor by the elbows, preventing his hands from hitting anything, but the red-eyed boy was bucking and kicking, breaths coming sharp and uneven. As Ninian gaped, Áed's foot struck the empty nail crate and sent it falling toward Ninian, who dodged just in time.

"What happened?" Ninian demanded. He rushed to his knees next to Áed. "Let go of him! What are you doing!"

"Don't touch him," Máel Máedóc barked.

"*You* don't touch him!" Protectiveness had risen in Ninian, more powerful than any he'd felt before. Stronger than he'd ever felt for himself. He snarled—the lightness he had felt on reaching the shop had transformed, and his heart rate spiked. "Lay off!"

"Ninian!" Máel Máedóc's eyes, when he fixed them on Ninian's, were bright and deadly serious. "I need you to listen to me."

"Like *hell!*" Ninian dug the tips of his fingers into the soft spot of Máel Máedóc's wrist, between two tendons bulging with strain. The big man winced, but Ninian could not dislodge him. "Get off of him. Get *off!*"

"CALM DOWN!" Máel Máedóc boomed. The order

rolled through the empty shop, reverberating like a drum in Ninian's ribs.

Shocked, Ninian froze.

"There's no time," the shopkeeper growled. "I need you to take one of those rowan berries."

Still stunned, Ninian found one.

"Put it in Áed's mouth."

"*What?*"

"Just…" Máel Máedóc was sweating, and Ninian realized that the shop was warm. "Do it!"

Ninian tried. "His teeth are clenched!"

The shopkeeper swore. A drop of perspiration rolled from his temple to chin. "Then get out of here, do you understand me?"

Ninian dropped the berry, aghast. "What is going *on*?"

"Leave!" Máel Máedóc shouted. "Get out of here. Now!"

That simply was not going to happen.

"Máel Máedóc," Ninian said. He did not shout; his voice was level. "Get. The *fuck*. Off of him."

And with that, he swung his elbow sharply into the side of Máel Máedóc's head.

Máel Máedóc didn't see it coming. The giant man's eyes rolled back, and slowly, his enormous form went limp. Ninian shoved him to the side before his bulk could land on Áed.

In a blink, Áed was up.

Something was very wrong.

Áed's eyes were burning bright, and his face was tormented. Ninian realized he was muttering to himself, and that it was a constant stream of *I'msorryI'msorryI'msorry*. There was terror in his expression, and Ninian couldn't tell if it was directed at Máel Máedóc, at Ninian, or at himself.

He looked like a cornered animal.

Slowly, Ninian got to his knees and held up his hands. "Hey, Áed."

Áed's eyes snapped to him.

A shiver ran from Ninian's head to toe. "It's me, yeah?" He tried for a smile. "It's Ninian." He turned his hands, proving they were empty. "It's okay, I knocked Máel Máedóc out. Just you and me, yeah?"

Áed's breath was shaking. "Ninian."

"Yeah. That's right. I'm right here." Very slowly, he moved closer. "Nothing is going to hurt you, okay?"

"I can't do it," Áed said, his expression wild. "I can't hold it, I'm so sorry, please…"

"Shh," Ninian said softly. "Look at me."

Áed did.

"Focus right here, okay?" Ninian took a deep, slow breath, and, seemingly unconsciously, Áed mirrored him. "There you go. That was perfect, yeah?" He held out a hand, and Áed cringed away. "All right," Ninian said, holding his hands up again. "I won't touch you."

"I'm so sorry—"

"You have nothing to be sorry for. You're doing brilliantly. Just focus right on me, okay?"

Shakily, Áed nodded.

"Want to sit down?" Ninian asked. "Take it easy? We can just sit here if you'd like."

With a fluttery blink, Áed sank to a seat. He curled in on himself, and Ninian saw, when he was a little closer, that there were tears in his eyes. "My… my hands…"

Ninian bit his lip, grimacing. "They must hurt."

Áed's eyes were still too bright. They didn't hold a single shadow and looked a touch uncanny.

"Can you talk to me?" Ninian asked, propping his elbows on his knees.

Those too-bright eyes widened sharply. "Talk to me."

"Yeah," Ninian said. "Do you want to?"

"No, no," Áed said, a bit frantically. "Talk to me. Please."

"Oh!" Ninian tugged at his knuckles. *Talk*. Of course, as soon as he needed to talk, he couldn't think of a single thing to say. "Um. I, uh…" He squeezed his eyes shut. *Say something. Anything. A story. Tell one.* "H-have you heard the story of the fae crow?" It was the story of his family. As a boy it had fascinated him, but it was old now. Well-known. Easy.

"No," Áed whispered. He had closed his eyes; it looked like he was focusing very hard on something.

"Once," Ninian started, "there was a woman named Fiadh." He tried to keep his tone level to cover the spinning of his head. *Why had Máel Máedóc done that? Why was Áed like this?* "She was the Queen's sister, back when the Maze had a Queen.

"Now, Fiadh was the Queen's most trusted friend, and the two sisters loved each other dearly. They shared everything— tea, cakes, tea cakes, they had all that—and secrets too."

Áed's face was tight, and his eyes were squeezed shut so hard that Ninian knew he must be seeing spots. He modulated his voice as much as he could, trying to keep it gentle.

"So when the Queen told Fiadh that she was meeting someone on the Festival of Souls that autumn, Fiadh grew a little bit worried. Fiadh was younger, always getting into trouble, but her older sister never did anything dangerous. When the festival came, Fiadh followed the Queen through the palace to make sure she was safe.

"She hid around the corner when she heard voices and peeked very stealthily to see the Queen with a woman. The woman was unbelievably beautiful—the sort of beautiful that makes everything seem to stop, with pretty lips and long, curly hair of the most lovely copper. And the Queen was laughing and smiling, so Fiadh thought that perhaps things were all right. She went out to enjoy the festival on her own."

Áed's eyes were still closed, but when Ninian watched his shoulders' rise and fall, he thought it looked steadier. He paused in the story, ready to ask if Áed was all right, but as soon as he hesitated, Áed's body grew tight again, and his breath came more quickly.

Ninian hurried to keep speaking.

"Fiadh had a grand time at the festival," he went on too fast and then schooled his words into peaceful stability again. "So she went to find her sister, to ask how *her* night had been. She ran back to the room where she had seen the Queen with the strange woman…" He habitually paused for dramatic effect, and Áed didn't react. "Only to find inside the room were two *crows*."

It was impossible to tell if Áed was listening, but the red-eyed boy neither spoke nor moved, which Ninian thought was probably an improvement.

"Now, Fiadh was wise," he continued. "She knew all of the fae tricks. She knew that between the crows in the room, one was a faerie, and one was her sister in disguise—because fae magic can make madness in a person so clever as to deceive the human eye. But Fiadh was clever too.

"She took all of the room's furniture—all of the handsome chairs, the beautiful tables, the soft couches, and brought them to the middle of the room. And she lit them on fire."

Ninian glanced to Áed again. His face had smoothed, and Ninian let out a little sigh of relief. Maybe he *was* being helpful.

"See," he went on, "fae don't burn. So when she lit the room ablaze, only one crow began to caw. Its feathers all caught fire, and the other crow laughed and laughed and laughed. The burning crow flew to Fiadh and landed on her arm, and with that, the illusion fell away, leaving Fiadh's sister fainted in her arms.

"The Queen was sick for many days. She had no more hair, and her skin was covered in scars, but what could Fiadh have done? She knew who had to pay. So at the next festival, she found the fae lady on the streets, seducing another woman—and Fiadh knew what would happen. With her sister held in her mind, Fiadh bravely drove a nail through the fae woman's breast."

Áed made a little gasp, but Ninian couldn't tell if it was from the story or something in Áed's own head.

"The fae woman crumbled to ash," Ninian said. "When Fiadh returned to the citadel, she found her sister in good health, welcoming her home. As a reward for her loyalty and courage, the Queen gave Fiadh her crown and made her Queen."

The story was coming to an end—should Ninian drag it out, keep talking? Was it enough?

"Fiadh ruled for many years," he said slowly, trying to make the words last. "And she had many sons and daughters. All of her children learned of the cunning fae and how to strike them down as their mother had done. Her bloodline kept the Maze safe. Even after the throne fell, Fiadh's descendants were warriors." He cracked his knuckles. "And our sigil has been a flaming crow since that festival night a hundred generations ago." He swallowed. "The end."

Áed opened his eyes slowly, and Ninian thanked the Gods to see that they had abandoned their feverish, uncanny brightness. "*Your* sigil?"

"Oh!" Ninian hadn't been sure if Áed had actually been listening, or if his words had merely been a backdrop before which Áed could collect himself. He nodded. "Through my mother's side, Fiadh was my... my *many*-greats grandmother."

Áed laughed softly, closing his eyes again. "You're a prince."

Ninian shook his head with a small exhalation. "I'm just Ninian." He looked at Áed, scrutinizing until Áed made eye contact. "Are you okay?"

"I'm… better," Áed said after a moment's pause. He frowned, biting anxiously at his lip. "What, um…" His eyes flicked around the ruined room, and they widened the more they saw. "What *happened?*"

Troubled, Ninian frowned. "I was hoping you could tell *me*."

A worried expression descended over Áed's face. "I don't remember." He stared at the unconscious shopkeeper. "What happened to *him?*"

"I elbowed him in the head," Ninian said, pinching his lower lip. "What don't you remember?" He cringed as soon as he asked; that was a foolish question. "I mean, when do you start remembering?"

Áed thought for a moment. "I remember your story, starting at a room of crows." He stared at his hands, looking deeply unsettled. In fact, he looked faintly ill. "Ninian, can… can I tell you something? Please?"

"Of course," Ninian said. It seemed he would have to wait for Máel Máedóc to wake to receive any sort of explanation for what had happened. Something in Ninian's head was playing a dissonant chord, like he was one realization away from knowing something very important and not altogether pleasant. Something was wrong—and, perhaps relatedly, Ninian still wanted to break Máel Máedóc's arms. He most certainly was incapable of breaking any part of Máel Máedóc, but that didn't stop his teeth from grinding.

Áed was looking very uncomfortable. "I… I can't remember how we met."

Ninian blinked. That was certainly not what he'd expected. "What?"

"I remember you giving me some kind of horrible tea. That's the first memory I have of you. I knew I recognized you, and I knew your name, but…" He shook his head. "I couldn't—I *can't*—remember how."

Ninian was speechless.

Áed looked away. There was rowan berry paste crushed into the fabric of his trousers, and his eyes drifted to his hands again. "I've lost something." Áed squeezed his eyes closed again. Ninian's mouth had fallen open a little bit, and Áed hugged his knees to his chest. "When you ask me what happened to me, I don't answer because…" His voice trembled, and he looked away, away from his hands, away from Ninian. "Because I don't know."

The red-eyed boy's gaze fixed to the floor.

"I remember patches from before the gap. I remember that I like sewing—or I mean, I did. I know I can't anymore." He looked agitated and shook his head. "I remember my mum, but I don't want to go to her. I remember playing in the snow, but I don't know how many winters ago it was. It's like a few days ago I just *woke up*. Before then, I have nothing, and before *then,* I was dreaming. And I can feel my mind filling in pieces that I don't have, so I can't even tell what's memory or make-believe anymore—neither feels real."

Áed's words had spilled out in a rush, and he pressed his lips together, looking like he expected Ninian to be angry.

Ninian knew his shock was apparent on his face. Ninian remembered too much, always too much. What must it be like to lose entire parts of the past?

It didn't matter.

Áed had helped Ninian.

And Ninian would help Áed.

CHAPTER TWENTY-FOUR

Ninian sat with his back to the wall, and Áed leaned on him. Since Ninian couldn't see Áed's face, he wasn't sure whether the red-eyed boy was crying. It seemed like a habit for Áed to cry quietly, and the only indication of his pain was the shaking of his shoulders.

There was one image that Ninian could not get out of his head, and he looked sideways at the still-unconscious shopkeeper. Ninian had hit him well. The memory of the giant man straddling a struggling Áed, pinning him to the floor…

It made Ninian nauseous.

"Hey, Áed," he said. *There has to be an explanation*, he told himself firmly. But if there was… well, they didn't have to wait for it there. "Want to go for a walk with me?"

Áed looked at Ninian with damp eyes. "A walk… outside?"

Ninian nodded. "I'll show you where I live. It'll be nice to get some air, don't you think?"

"I—I don't know," Áed said. He looked nervous. "I don't go out much."

Ninian cringed internally, glancing around the shop again. He knew for certain that Áed's time within its walls had been far from pleasant, but he was willing to bet that Áed's last experience *outside* of the labyrinthine store had been far, far worse. "I'll be with you."

He wanted to be gone by the time the shopkeeper woke.

Áed shifted. "Are you sure we should leave?" He looked over to Máel Máedóc. "What if he needs help?"

"He'll be fine," Ninian promised. "Doesn't matter."

"Why do you want to go?"

Ninian's throat felt sharp. "Máel Máedóc did something that I… I didn't like at all," he said tightly. "And…" *And I'm feeling really, really protective. And I want you somewhere safe.*

"And?" Áed prompted.

Ninian shook his head helplessly. "*Please* come with me?"

Áed hesitated. Then, tentatively, he got to his feet.

"I trust you," he said finally, and Ninian caught a hint of pleading in his voice: *Don't make me regret that.*

Ninian scrambled up as well. "Right. Let's go."

"I haven't got a coat?" Áed said uncertainly.

Ninian lifted the right half of his wool cloak and dropped it over Áed's shoulders. "Now you have."

Together they traced through the shelf maze and pushed outside.

Wind gusted forcefully, channeled by the shape of the street, and immediately Áed shivered. "Where do you live?"

"This way," Ninian said. "It's a bit of a hike, but it's a good, quiet building. Sturdy. Out of the way."

"Sounds nice." His eyes were flitting over everything, and his shoulders were tense.

"You weren't kidding," Ninian observed, "when you said you didn't go out much."

The red-eyed boy laughed uncomfortably. "Ah—no. No, not really. And not without my mum."

"Overprotective, was she?" He watched Áed's expression and adjusted his question. "Or possessive?"

"Scared someone would hurt me," Áed said, eyes still flicking over every person who passed them. "Scared I would hurt someone." He frowned. "That doesn't make sense. I don't know."

Ninian rubbed Áed's shoulder through the cloak. "It's okay."

Áed changed the subject. "You're, um. You're in a gang, right?"

Ninian nodded. Soon, he'd be able to take the bandages off the brand. "Yeah."

"Won't people bother us?" Áed asked. He was still looking around like someone might come up from behind.

"Don't worry. The brand offers protection. People will stay to themselves."

"Aren't there—aren't there thieves?"

"Áed," Ninian said reassuringly, "*I'm* a thief. Trust me, nobody will look at us twice."

Áed shivered deeper into Ninian's cloak, mumbling. "Are you sure?"

Ninian thought for a second, and then pointed across the street. "That guy. See him, with the knapsack? His shirt is new. You can tell from the dye. Winter's almost over, and he's wearing a warm new shirt. So he has money, and he's wearing a knapsack he can't see. *That's* the kind of person thieves look for."

"You know a lot about it," Áed admitted.

"It's a life skill." Ninian tugged the cloak tighter around both of them. "I lived on the street for a whole year. I know how to keep you safe. I promise."

}}{

Ninian's flat—he'd decided that it was his since nobody else had come to squat in it since he'd first slept there—was decidedly warmer than the outside. Ninian laid his cloak in the corner, ready to be used as a blanket, and was scrounging around on the off chance that there was food in the battered cupboards.

He found a dead roach and gave up.

He crossed back into the main room and fiddled with the broken window latch. "What do you think?"

Áed was sitting next to Ninian's cloak, looking exhausted. The walk had been long for him. They'd had to take three breaks between the trading shop and Ninian's flat. Or rather, Ninian had insisted on breaks because Áed had looked like he might faint. "It's nice."

A twinge of guilt pinched Ninian's breast. "I know I haven't a proper bed. Nothing to eat, either."

"It's all right," Áed said, putting on a smile. "I'm not really hungry."

That was certainly untrue. Ninian, at least, could feel his stomach gnawing at itself. "Do you want me to go find some food?"

Áed shook his head and leaned against the wall. "Stay." His brilliant eyes were circled with darkness. Whatever had happened in the trading shop must have taken a toll on him, even if he didn't know what it was. He looked drained. "I, um," he said, clearly casting about for something else to talk about. "I liked hearing about your family."

Ninian sat cross-legged on his cloak and tugged at the cuffs of his pants. He was growing, and they were getting too short. "You did?"

Áed nodded. "Was it true? The story?"

Ninian shrugged. "I don't know if the story's true. But the people in it were real. And our crest is a burning crow, and my mum taught me all kinds of things she thought our blood should know." He picked at a sliver of wood poking from the floorboards. "Not much of it's useful." He shook his head. "My mum, she… she died before she taught me most of the important things." She had promised to show him the family art, but her breath had stopped before she had even told him how to recognize a faerie. "I mean," he elaborated, "I know what ridiculous words like 'desuetude' mean."

"And what is it?"

Ninian snorted. "It's the state of my proper grammar." He sighed, shrugging. "I know how a well-set table should be arranged. I know how to dance. I can read, I can write…"

Áed's eyes widened. "You can read?"

Ninian blinked. "I can." It was a very useless skill—nobody in the Maze could read, and therefore nobody wrote, and therefore there was nothing to read anyway. Ninian had learned from sentences his mother traced in the dust on their windows.

"Here—wait, you'll have to—" Áed stopped, closed his eyes, and took a deep breath. When he opened them again, he seemed to gather himself. "My mother left me a letter when I was a baby. Not my *mum*—my mum took me in from my proper mother. But my mum couldn't read, and I can't read—" He cut off, his face flushing. "I have it! It's the one thing from my mother… like a luck charm? I always kept it on me—but I never thought I'd know what it—well—" He took a deep breath. His face had lit up. "But could you— could you—"

"Read it for you?"

Áed's chin bobbed, and Ninian felt the blood rise in his own face. *What an important thing.* It didn't even matter that Ninian was simply useful in this situation; Áed had still decided to let him in.

"It's in my pocket." Áed looked suddenly worried. "I mean… it always is. But I can't tell, and I can't check—oh Gods, Ninian, you don't think maybe when whatever happened… *happened*…" He lifted his hands. "You don't think I lost it, do you?"

There was only one way to know. "Which pocket?"

Áed told him, and Ninian carefully extracted a very, *very* battered paper.

An immense look of relief washed over Áed's face. "Thank the Gods."

"I can't believe this is in one piece," Ninian said, almost reverently. The paper had been beaten soft as fabric, but it still held deep creases where it had been folded for years on years. Ninian opened it slowly, careful not to tear the delicate material. "You carry this everywhere you go?"

"I've never *gone* many places," Áed reminded him. "But it's definitely gotten wet a few times, and once I spilled wax on it. I hope you can read it."

Though a bit smudged, elegant handwriting swept over the page quite legibly. Without even absorbing the words, Ninian admired subtle swoops, graceful curves, reserved beauty. "*A thiarcais*, Áed," he said. "Who *was* your mother?"

"I don't know," Áed said. "But it's pretty, isn't it?"

"It's beautiful."

Áed chewed his lip, looking suddenly apprehensive. "I don't suppose the words will be so beautiful. I know she left me, so I'm not—I'm not foolishly hopeful or anything." He set his jaw. "I want to hear it anyway."

"Right," Ninian agreed. He cleared his throat. "Ready?"

At Áed's nod, he began.

"Áed—

I owe you an apology. What ought to have been a gift to me is a burden that I will not carry, and for my selfishness, I am sorry. My actions are not of your doing."

Ninian winced. Áed may have been right about the words being a bit harsher than the handwriting. Still, a glance to his face revealed Áed listening intently. No signs of distress.

"I should like to explain myself," he continued. *"I don't need forgiveness or a reason for my choice, but I want to be heard nonetheless. Child, you are the son of an animal, a glittering, half-mad animal whom I could not deter. I never expected any man to be so bold with* me.*"*

When Ninian finished that, he looked up to see Áed's face had fallen somewhat. Áed saw Ninian looking and, eyebrows creased, cast his eyes to the floor. "I see." He swallowed. "I… see." His eyes flicked up, and then away again.

"Are you okay?"

"I'm okay." He looked troubled. "But I hope my mother is too."

"I mean, it's been…" Ninian frowned. "Have I ever actually asked how many years you have?"

"Ten," Áed said. "I've ten years." His face hadn't lost its introspective look. "So it's been ten years—almost eleven." He looked up to Ninian. "Do you think she's okay? After that much time?"

"I—" Ninian grimaced internally and had to speak honestly. "I don't know. Maybe. At the very least, she's probably… moved on a bit." He *really* hoped time could heal that kind of injury. Really hoped.

But honestly, he wasn't sure.

"I see why she didn't want me." Áed's eyes lingered on the letter. "I hope that she's living her own life. I hope it's good." He breathed in steadily and blew it out. "Right," he said after a few moments. "Is there more?"

Ninian nodded and kept reading.

"Perhaps I resent you. I think I do."

Áed winced.

"Áed?" Ninian said, trying to gauge Áed's reaction. Those were hard words.

"I'm okay," Áed said in a breath. He really must have prepared himself to hear the worst. "It makes sense."

Resenting Áed did not make any sense, but Ninian tried to understand. "She was probably in a bad place."

"Very," Áed agreed.

Ninian continued.

"So I will not bring you with me, but leave you to become my revenge the way I know you will. You are as much my child as the dazzling animal's, after all."

"Revenge?" Áed said. "Revenge on whoever assaulted her?"

"I guess," Ninian said. "You don't know who it is, do you?"

Áed shook his head. "No." He looked hesitant. "I kind of hope I never do."

"Fair," Ninian murmured. "Want me to keep going?"

"Yes, please."

"I suspect you will come to hate me," Ninian read. *"I understand. I do hope that nothing truly hurts you, and that you aren't alone."*

Ninian's eyes flicked down the page—it was nearly finished.

He'd almost opened his mouth to begin the next paragraph when his eyes snagged on a word.

Blinking, certain he'd misread, he automatically scanned for context. Surely he had not seen what he thought he'd just seen.

There are things you should know, he skimmed in his head, *because I'm sure there will come a day when you need an explanation nobody will be able to give. Your father was an animal, yes, and a human one. But your mother, child, is no such thing.*

Ninian's stomach turned over.

Had he…

Had he not misread?

I'd come to this realm on a festival night and found that I couldn't leave it while I carried you. Now, I return to my home. I don't believe it's a home you can ever be a part of, not any more than you can truly belong here.

Already, denial was barricading Ninian inside his own head.

It couldn't be.

You, my son, have my blood.

Could not be.

And that blood is

Could. Not. Be.

fae.

Ninian was nauseous.

He felt his mouth move and heard his own voice before he had the chance to choose his words. "That's it," he heard himself say. His voice sounded artificial to him, but Áed didn't seem to notice. He folded the letter and set it on the floor next to Áed. "Um… one minute."

He didn't know if Áed replied. Ninian was out the door and down the stairs, blood pounding in his good ear.

CHAPTER TWENTY-FIVE

Outside the tenement, Ninian gulped clean, cold air.

It had started to snow—the first flakes startled him as they sank, heavy and damp like slow, icy rain. The snow lowered a blanket of silence as it came, and Ninian fell to a seat on the splintery wooden steps.

There was a part of him that wanted to run back up the stairs and reread the letter. As if he'd find a mistake, or as if he'd be able to think better with the words staring him in the face.

There was another part of him that knew he had committed no error.

And he did not want to—no, simply *should not*—be in the same room as Áed at that moment.

His mind was whirling, but sluggishly, like the snow.

Ninian had trusted Áed with… with *everything*. Had trusted him more than Ninian had ever trusted another human being.

And it turned out Áed wasn't even human!

Ninian took a deep breath, feeling a snowflake hit his lips. *Well. He's not entirely human, anyway.*

He was seized by the absurd urge to laugh, and he did, doubling over in the snow, shivering and gasping. He felt absurdly betrayed, which didn't make any sense—did Áed even know? It wasn't deception if Áed himself didn't know he was deceiving. And if Áed had never read his letter before, could he have found out? How much fae blood—fae *power*—could pass down to a half-human child, anyway? Could Áed weave illusions, control fire? Hell, was he *immortal?*

The wind blew, and Ninian shut his eyes as they watered. That second time that Ninian met Áed—the time Áed didn't quite remember—Áed had been burning up. Ninian rubbed his palms together, remembering the intense heat that had radiated from Áed's skin, too hot for any fever.

The longer he thought, the more that came to mind.

He thought of the way Áed read people, easy as blinking. He thought of winning at cards, and Áed's offhand comments about Treasa when the girl had come to collect Ninian. He thought of Áed's mutilated hands, how it looked like someone had tried to break him, and the gaps in Áed's memory that anything at all could fill. He thought of Máel Máedóc, looking panicked, pinning Áed to the ground while the small room grew uncomfortably warm; he thought of the giant shopkeeper shouting at Ninian to press a rowan fruit between Áed's lips.

Ninian's eyes flew open.

Rowan.

Máel Máedóc had filled his shop with rowan, salt, and iron after he had taken Áed in. And that too-hot fever! The tea that had lowered it so fast but made Áed so sick—it had smelled sharp and familiar.

Rowan.

Ninian shot to his feet.

He had already started down the street when it crossed his mind to tell Áed where he was going, but he couldn't make himself go back. As the snow flurried clumsily down, beginning to pile grimy whiteness on the curbs, Ninian started to run.

§§§

Ninian banged into Máel Máedóc's shop, out of breath and single-minded. There was noise coming from the back, and he stomped through the familiar shelves until he reached it.

Máel Máedóc was cleaning up, looking a little ill.

"Hey!" Ninian shouted, and the giant man whirled around. His eyebrows shot up.

"Ninian!" He dropped two fistfuls of long, loose nails, which scattered. "There you are! Where is Áed?"

Ninian ignored him. "You knew," he said, barely keeping his voice below a shout. "Can you read? Is that it? Or does Áed actually know? Did he tell you?"

The shopkeeper's eyes sparked with impatience. "Ninian, tell me where he is."

"*You knew!*" Ninian cried. "Can we talk about that, please?" He pointed to the rowan, to the nails, to the scattered Red Sea salt. "You knew what he was and—"

"And *what?*" Máel Máedóc snapped.

"You didn't tell me!" Ninian shouted. "I was talking to—I was *sleeping next to*—a *half-faerie*, and you didn't tell me!" He flung his arm in the direction of the door. "I told him everything, I trusted him, I trusted *you*, and—"

"And now you don't?"

Ninian had expected to cry, but his eyes were dry, and his anger fit like a well-worn glove. "How *can* I?"

"*Listen to yourself!* Do you *hear* the words that you are saying?"

Ninian's fists were balled tight at his sides.

"You're telling me," Máel Máedóc said, electricity sparking through his eyes, "that Áed, your *friend*, who has *earned your trust*, you regret even having *talked* to?"

Ninian opened his mouth, but the shopkeeper wasn't done.

"I saw how excited you were to see him every day," Máel

Máedóc said harshly. "I know how much it meant to you that he wanted to be your friend. You both improved so much in each other's company, a *blind* man could see it, and you want… what? You want to tell me that you wish it hadn't *happened?*"

"You—" Ninian shook his head. There was a lump in his throat. His fingernails dug into his palms. "You've got it all wrong!"

"Do I? Then tell it to me straight, kid." The shopkeeper crossed his arms. "And cut the righteous fury. I don't *fucking* need it."

Ninian glowered. "I'm not mad at Áed. He didn't ask for any of this."

"You did read his letter, then." At Ninian's nod, the shopkeeper looked faintly impressed. "I found it when I was first treating him. I suppose he showed it to you. I didn't know you could read."

"I didn't know you could, either. *Obviously.*" He cracked his knuckles. "I'm not mad at him. I'm mad at *you.*" He jabbed a finger in Máel Máedóc's direction. "Áed isn't the one who *lied* to me."

"I never lied."

"Omission! I—I don't know!" He looked with angry helplessness to the ceiling. "Áed is a good person, okay? He's a person I really, really like, and if I have to lose that because…" *Now* there were tears pressing hot into the corners of his eyes, but he blinked them back. He'd cried too much lately. "If I have to lose everything because I only *just now* found out what he is, then it would be better not to have had it at all!"

Already, he could feel a hole opening up inside him, like fire eating out a paper to the edges. *Oh, Gods. Not another one.* His eyes welled up properly, and he tried to force the tears from falling.

"Ninian," Máel Máedóc said firmly. "Where is Áed right now?"

Ninian blinked hard to clear his eyes and looked at the shopkeeper with painful anger. "Like I'd tell *you*. Last I was here, you had him pinned to the floor." He set his jaw. "You're one to talk about *accepting him*."

Máel Máedóc's mouth pressed into a thin line. "I confess I am not proud of that reaction." He let a breath out through his nose. "As soon as I read his letter, I suspected that he didn't know what he was. If he even knows what he can do, I think his mind is fighting it. And I don't think he's ever had the chance to learn much control. So any time he got agitated, I was ready to intervene." He swept salt into a pile with his foot. "While you were gone, he accidentally hit his hand on the edge of the table. It triggered something, I think, or maybe the pain was just too much, but he started spiraling."

Máel Máedóc pinched the bridge of his nose, and Ninian saw that the palms of his hands were angrily red where they had held Áed's wrists to the floor. Ninian swallowed hard.

"I acted on instinct," the shopkeeper said. "Which made it worse, of course. I take it that you calmed him down." Ninian nodded, and the shopkeeper sighed. "My point: where is Áed now?"

Ninian looked down, scuffing his toe on the floor. "My flat."

The shopkeeper nodded. "Right. And when you get back, will he still be there?"

"Probably."

"Do you *want* him to be there?"

Ninian's toe hit a dry berry and sent it rolling haphazardly over the floorboards. His eyes widened when, following its path, he saw darkened wood, charred where Áed had struggled, and fear swelled in his chest.

That was what Áed was. A creature of fire and magic.

Terrifying.

But he answered honestly. "Yes."

"So why," Máel Máedóc asked, "do you need to stop being friends?"

That took Ninian aback for a moment. "What do you mean?"

Máel Máedóc raised a thick eyebrow. "He's there for you. You want to be there for him. Why isn't that enough?"

"Be-because. Because he's half-fae?" The question didn't seem to make sense. Why wasn't the sun shining at night?

The shopkeeper crossed his arms. "And I'm half not-from-here, and you're half noble-or-whatever."

"But that's not *dangerous*," Ninian protested.

"Between you and Áed," Máel Máedóc said, and his voice took on a particularly hard edge, "which of you has stabbed a man?"

A rock dropped into Ninian's stomach. "That's…" He swallowed. "That's—"

Máel Máedóc leaned forward, all height and muscle and astute, lightning-sharp eyes. "Áed *is* dangerous. That's honest. If he knew himself, he could probably kill you where you stand and send an awful lot down with you. He can know every feeling you have and every lie you tell." The shopkeeper's eyes were bluer than the far-out ocean, and seven times as deadly. "He is not safe to be around."

Ninian's heart was flitting somewhere between his stomach and his windpipe, but Máel Máedóc wasn't done.

"And quite frankly, Ninian," the giant man said, "neither are you."

Something caught in Ninian's throat at that. The shop creaked like an old boat as Máel Máedóc crossed to the table and dropped into one of the chairs, resting his burned palms on his knees.

"I doubt they told you," Máel Máedóc said, watching him closely, "but you're the youngest fighter Cahir's gang has ever had. And you beat Brígh, who is the deadliest, except for a few up-and-coming bastards in the seaside territories." He leaned forward. "You beat her *twice*."

"My mother. She taught me." Ninian scowled, biting his lip. All of the violence he had learned had only ever been for only one purpose. "My mother hated the fae." He cracked his knuckles. "Our family always has."

"Did she have a reason?"

Ninian's brows met. These were things he had simply never questioned, but now, under Máel Máedóc's scrutiny, he felt uncertain. Some foundational bit of knowledge, on the same scale as 'winter is cold' and 'the Red Sea is salty' had been shaken loose and was knocking around in Ninian's head like a loose tooth. "It's just… what she did."

Máel Máedóc sighed. "Ah. Legacy." From his seat at the table, he was about eye-level with Ninian. He put a callused hand firmly on Ninian's shoulder and squeezed. "I'm not telling you to quit your family's values. They're yours to inherit if you want them. But…" His shoulders slowly rose and fell, his vast shadow shrugging with him. "You *do* get to choose. And you get to choose *which* values are your values too."

While Ninian was mulling that over, the shopkeeper glanced out the window.

"It's getting late." He stood. "Áed is probably worrying."

Ninian hugged himself, not excited for the trek back through the deepening cold and the snow. He shook his head as if he could physically dislodge his conflict. "Yeah."

The shopkeeper looked him up and down and sighed. "I'll lend you a cloak." He turned to rummage through the shelves. "With your next earnings, you can buy one from me properly. Áed needs one."

Thinking about his earnings made the weight on Ninian's shoulders feel even heavier, so he just accepted the offered cloak with quiet thanks.

Snow swirled into the shop when Máel Máedóc opened the door for Ninian.

The big man sighed. "Be careful, Ninian." His voice didn't echo outside; the snow muffled it. "But let yourself be happy with him." He squinted out at the snow. "Please."

Ninian nodded. Stricken by a thought, he reached into his pocket and pulled out the long nail. He offered it to Máel Máedóc and laid it on his hand.

Máel Máedóc held the nail up, letting its dull iron head slip into the light, and a faint smile turned his lips. "Hm." The nail slipped into his own pocket, and he gave Ninian a pat on the back. "Well, I'll see you when you need me, boy."

"See you, Máel Máedóc."

And he stepped through the snow, headed toward home.

CHAPTER TWENTY-SIX

Ninian wasn't surprised to find Áed asleep.

The red-eyed boy lay curled tightly underneath Ninian's blue cloak, his back pressed against the wall. Ninian had been gone for almost two hours—the trading shop wasn't close—and he moved as quietly as he could so as not to disturb Áed.

Wearily, Ninian pulled off his boots and padded over to the half-fae creature who now shared his home. Something about it felt strangely lasting, and it didn't even occur to Ninian that he had the cloak Máel Máedóc had lent him, so there was no reason not to sleep alone. Instead, he lay down next to Áed and draped the second cloak over both of them.

Áed made a sleepy *hm* sound and opened his eyes. "Nin…?"

"Yeah," Ninian said softly.

"You're back." Áed sounded relieved, and Ninian winced. He'd left Áed to drift off alone, in a place that was strange to him, with no warning or explanation.

"Yeah," Ninian said again. It was a very peculiar feeling, to know now what Áed was, but somehow, it was still… all right. Áed's letter lay on the floor, unfolded and pale in the snow-muffled moonlight, and Ninian's gut twisted.

Should he tell Áed the truth?

He chewed hard on the corner of his lip. The secret was Áed's, not Ninian's. And Ninian knew all too well how it felt to be lied to.

But the boy Ninian knew was not a monster. He was quiet, gentle, not at all like the nightmarish beasts Ninian had been taught to expect. He'd helped Ninian, not hurt him. He'd been good.

Surely, *that* was more important. Áed was Áed. And if Áed knew what he was, then… would he be someone else?

Ninian closed his eyes, all too aware that he was deceiving himself.

The truth was that Ninian was afraid. Afraid of Áed changing, afraid of the fire and the magic and the stories that his mother had seared into his mind. Of *course*, he was.

"I'm sorry, Áed," Ninian said. He would tell Áed, he decided. But later. When the time was right. "I shouldn't have left like that."

"It's okay," Áed replied, and his voice was muffled. Ninian thought he might be falling asleep again, for as soon as Ninian had lain down, Áed had relaxed with a barely audible sigh. "You're here."

Ninian rolled to face Áed, and it felt so familiar to tuck the red-eyed boy into his arms.

They'd done this before.

This hadn't changed.

The next morning, Ninian knew, he would have to check in with Cahir to avoid punishment. The thought made him want to hold Áed tighter. He'd prefer never to go back. He wanted to be safe, safe with Áed, safe and unbeholden to the gang that told him to kill.

Useless desires.

But…

Ailbhe's words whispered through Ninian's head. The seer had been trying to tell him something, something hopeful. Something about escape?

Ninian shook his head minutely, thinking.

Ailbhe hadn't meant escape. Ninian was sure of that. They had been talking about something that would take years and require him to make friends. Something that meant Cahir would never own anyone, ever again.

Wait.

Surely not.

Surely that wasn't even *possible*.

Ninian sat up straight, his side of the cloak-blankets sliding off of him and landing on Áed with a soft *whump*.

It would take years. He would have to connect with everyone he could, make friends, make allies. He would have to watch his back and learn to choose his battles. He would have to work from the inside.

But maybe he could do it.

If the gang owned him…

"Áed," Ninian whispered fiercely, and the fact that Áed didn't hear him did not dampen the determination that poured from the marrow of Ninian's bones. "I'm going to oust Cahir." His heart beat fast, all nerves and resolve. "I am going to take over the gang."

PART TWO

CHAPTER TWENTY-SEVEN
Seven Years Later

Ninian's hair wisped around his face, curling with the humidity. He wiped the back of his arm across his forehead, feeling a couple of loose hairs stick to the steam dewing on his face.

Out the window, the clouds looked like flax thread combed across the sky. The gray streets and gray buildings held the sunrise, briefly glowing in the generous morning light, and in the flat, warm beams spilled over the floor.

Ninian worked quietly.

He'd been a little chilly when he'd started the hearth fire, but its warmth combined with the sunshine and the steam from the softly boiling pot above the coals soon made it a bit too warm for Ninian's taste. Still, the quiet of the morning hung like dew, and for once, Ninian was glad to be up before anyone else.

Today he was going tell Áed what the letter said. It required a bit of mental preparation. He'd been planning how this day would go for… he bit his lip. A long time. He kept reaching the day he'd chosen, and then putting it off again. The truth was long overdue, and he knew it, but it had always existed to be done in the amorphous *later*.

Not anymore. He had a plan. Today was the day, and nerves swirled in his stomach.

A sound came from the corner of the room, and Ninian looked up from where he squatted before the fire.

Áed still looked disoriented and sleepy. His hair stuck up every which way, and he rubbed at an eye with a hand clad in a too-big tunic—the tunic Ninian had nicked from a tailor who'd called Áed a rude name—that fell to Áed's knees and left his hands lost in at least six extra inches of sleeve. He blinked woozily at the light. "It's early."

Ninian shrugged, getting to his feet to give Áed a hug. "Not *that* early. The sun's up."

"Mmf," Áed protested. He pressed his face into Ninian's shoulder. "It's *early*." Then he drew back a little and sniffed the air. "Smells good?"

"Breakfast."

Áed dropped to a seat before the fire as Ninian knelt in front of the hearth again and stirred the oatmeal he'd made. Reluctant to get to his feet again, Ninian awkwardly stretched to reach the chipped earthenware bowls he'd left on the table.

The oatmeal made slopping sounds as he spooned it into the bowls, and he handed one to Áed.

Áed smiled. He still looked sleepy. "Smells sweet."

"I put honey in it."

Áed took a bite with a happy little *hm*, though a slight, worried curve appeared at the edge of his mouth. "Can we afford that?"

"Don't worry." He'd saved up for a month to buy that honey. Today was a special occasion. Besides, it was still summertime, and there were always more fights for him when heat made the city restless. "We're okay."

He ate some of the oatmeal and had to stop himself from inhaling it all at once. Instead, he and Áed ate quietly, enjoying the peace of the morning. Ninian could eat more quickly, since he didn't have to brace his spoon awkwardly between crooked, uncooperative fingers, but he paced himself so that Áed didn't get left behind. When they finished, there was still some in the pot.

Ninian poked at the sweet meal with the end of the stirring-stick. "Where's our little trash child?"

Áed rolled his eyes. "Still upstairs, probably." He tucked his legs under him and set his empty bowl on the floor. "It's funny you still call him that."

"Máel Máedóc still calls you 'shore boy,' doesn't he?" Ninian answered, refilling his bowl. It only made sense— the shopkeeper had found Áed on the Fisher's Shore, and Ninian had found Ronan, a skinny thing too weak to cry, buried up to the neck in an alleyway's pile of garbage. "Ronan is my trash child." He pushed himself to his feet and stealthily added a touch of extra honey to the bowl. "Be right back."

The hallway outside the flat was darker than the sunlit rooms, but pleasantly cooler. Floorboards creaked as Ninian climbed the rickety stairs, and he knocked on the door at the top.

"Ronan?"

There were a few light thumps, and the knob clicked. A black-haired boy peered out of the crack.

"Hey, mate." Ninian offered Ronan the bowl and watched with satisfaction as the boy's big green eyes grew even bigger. "I brought breakfast."

Holding the bowl, the child threw his arms around Ninian's legs.

"Hey," Ninian said, snorting. "Don't get oatmeal on me." He ruffled Ronan's crow-dark hair. It was a shining black, almost like Ninian's mother's had been. Sometimes, Ninian could imagine her sitting Ronan in front of the fireplace and teaching him how to sit up straight, just the way she had with Ninian. She was long dead, of course, and Ninian knew he'd never have a son of his own blood, but he didn't think his mother would be disappointed by Ninian passing on her legacy to Ronan. "I'll be downstairs."

When Ronan had happily retreated back into his room with the oatmeal, Ninian went back down to the flat he shared with Áed.

Áed had started getting dressed, sitting in the nest of blankets that was his and Ninian's bed. He wore simple woven trousers—his only pair, since clothing was expensive—and was digging through the blankets looking for his shirt. He looked up when Ninian walked in. "Nin! Have you seen—"

"I washed everything yesterday. Your shirt wouldn't dry, so I hung it up." Then he blinked. "Áed, what's that?"

Áed frowned. "What's what?"

Ninian crossed the room in three strides and nudged Áed to turn around.

On Áed's ribs was a fist-sized bruise, fresh and lavender against his freckled skin.

"Oh!" Áed turned back, waving it off. "It's nothing."

Ninian was already glowering. "Who did that?" He recognized knuckle imprints when he saw them.

Áed laughed uncomfortably, looking sheepish. "Seriously, it isn't important."

But Ninian was insistent. "Tell me who hit you." He tamped down the protective aggression rising in his blood. "Please."

"Erm…" Áed fidgeted. Awkwardly, he looked away. "You did."

Ninian's jaw dropped. "I did *what*, now?" He got to his knees next to Áed. "No, I did not!" He'd sooner slit his own wrists than lay a hand on Áed in violence.

Áed held up his hands, pacifying. "Love, you were asleep. You didn't mean to."

After that sunk in a little bit, Ninian sat back on his heels. He *had* had a nightmare, he remembered that. It had been the reason he'd woken up early, after having fallen asleep only a few hours before—the dreams and the insomnia had gotten better with time, but Ninian had come to terms with the fact that some damage never quite healed all the way. It did seem possible that he'd lashed out in his sleep, but never before had Áed been the victim of such things. "That was… actually me?"

"Ninian, don't worry about it. I'm not upset." Áed got up, found his shirt where Ninian had hung it, and put it on, hiding the developing bruise. "Kind of impressed with your arm, though."

Ninian moaned and flopped over onto his side into the nest of bedding. "Áed, I am so sorry."

Áed laughed. "You're *too* sorry. Gods, come here." He dragged Ninian to a seat and gave him a hug. "Now, come on." A smile was edging its way onto his face. "I have something for you."

CHAPTER TWENTY-EIGHT

Ninian habitually grabbed his knife on the way out. It was a battered old thing, crafted from an old pike he'd found at the Fisher's Shore, but he kept the edge wickedly sharp. He hadn't left home without it for years now, not since he'd eclipsed Brígh's tally of victories. Brígh had been nearing her forties anyway, and Maze life had taken its toll. In the years after Ninian had first encountered her, the scarred fighter had taken a blow that left her with a shattered kneecap and a staggering limp. Already acerbic, the loss of her fighting ability made her downright horrid to be around. This was a shame, since Cahir, unwilling to give up her talent altogether, had placed her in control of match assignments. Ninian could never leave the flat unprepared, lest he find himself roped into a scrap without warning.

He scowled at the thought of Brígh. She knew just how badly he resented the gang and did everything in her power to make it even less pleasant for him. Little did she know how much that strengthened Ninian's resolve to rise.

Áed went down the stairs ahead of Ninian, and Ninian tugged up the collar of Áed's shirt where it slipped off his shoulder. "Why is *everything* too big for you?"

Áed shrugged, making the collar fall off again. "I'm skinny?" He brushed the edge up over his shoulder, where it didn't seem likely to stay. "And you're horrible at sewing."

"Aw, that's not fair." Ninian had been kind of proud that he'd made an entire shirt and it hadn't fallen apart, even if he was sure Áed had quietly told Ronan how to fix most of Ninian's mistakes.

"I'm teasing, love," Áed said, shoving through to the outside of the building. He had his own way of opening doors, a strategy that involved shouldering the door open with both hands awkwardly turning the knob. The method was a necessity, given his hands' impaired functionality, but it was just one of the many little things that made up Áed. Ninian had come to love it.

Áed took Ninian's hand and hurried him down the steps. "Come on!"

"Where are we going?"

"That's for me to know, and you to have no idea so I can surprise you and you'll smile."

The gray streets slid by as they walked through the city, passing familiar old buildings and crumbling tenements, dirty cobblestones and cracked windows. Despite the ordinary dinginess of his surroundings and the faint prickle of nervous anticipation in his gut, Ninian felt sunny. He dropped an arm over Áed's shoulders, unable to keep his good mood from showing on his face. Áed smiled too and held Ninian's waist.

Ninian wasn't blind to his fortune. Every day with Áed was guaranteed to be better than a day without him. But on this day in particular, Ninian really took the time to *think* about it. It hadn't been possible to define exactly when his and Áed's relationship had slipped into something decisively more than friendship, especially since Áed's naturally affectionate behavior had always pressed the boundaries of what Ninian thought 'normal' was like, so they'd agreed to celebrate on the first day they'd properly kissed.

It was always a good day.

Ninian prayed that this day would *stay* good, even after…

He shook his head, banishing the thought. *Stick to the plan. Don't think about it now.*

Changing the subject in his own head, Ninian tried to wheedle a hint from Áed again. "Where are you taking me?"

"Give up," Áed suggested.

Ninian groaned and admitted defeat.

They walked for a long time until every guess Ninian had for where they might be going had been exhausted. Finally, Áed led him down an alley, and the walls of the buildings rose above them. Clotheslines crisscrossed over their heads, devoid of clothes, and nothing but the wind sounded between the walls. "Um… Áed?"

"Just a little farther," Áed promised. "Trust me."

So Ninian bit his tongue.

Cloud shadows skidded over everything, and sunlight caught on the green edges of ivy leaves, rustling in the wind and making the buildings look alive. Empty bins clogged the alley, dull under the sky, and Áed and Ninian stepped gingerly around them. At his hip, Ninian's knife scraped the brick of the alleyway, scattering mortar dust with a quiet sound.

"Right," Áed said when they got to the end of the alley. "We're here."

With Áed, Ninian stepped past the walls. "Wow."

Áed had found an oasis.

It looked like it had been forgotten. A courtyard, not unlike the one Ninian trained in, nestled in the embrace of the tenements. It would have been like a thousand others in the Maze… but in this one, nature had found a toehold.

Ninian stepped into the sanctuary more fully, brushing his palms over the tips of tall grasses. The air smelled earthy and living, and though the plants looked a little scrawny, there were a lot of them. A woody vine crawled over a windowsill, playing host to a line of ants; yellow flowers on spindly stalks swayed in the breeze. Low to the ground, bluebells carpeted every patch of earth not covered by cobblestones or grass.

"Áed," he said, a little spellbound. The whole place smelled wonderful and green. "How did you *find* this?"

"I was being chased, actually," Áed said with a grin. "Beat some gamblers a few too many times—I should have just gone scavenging that day, but it worked out." He opened his arms and gestured around them. "Because I ended up here. What do you think?"

Ninian picked one of the yellow flowers and twirled it between his fingers before tucking it behind his ear. "It's *beautiful*."

Áed beamed. "Then come over here."

Ninian followed him to a corner where the brick of the tenements had crumbled away, leaving a little leaf-shaded cove. Ninian saw that grass had been laid out on the ground, forming a mat—Áed must have prepared. Áed sat and beckoned Ninian down. When Ninian had gotten himself comfortable, Áed transferred himself to Ninian's lap.

Broken brick dug into Ninian's back, but it had been worn by time and weather, so it wasn't sharp. On his lap, leaning on his chest like Ninian was a particularly comfortable chair, Áed was warm. Clouds wisped over the bright, blue sky, and Áed closed his eyes.

Áed reached up to run the back of one crooked finger down Ninian's jaw, and Ninian turned his head to kiss it.

"This feels so weird," Áed said softly, a little bit of a laugh in his voice.

"What," Ninian said, smirking. He kissed Áed's hand again. "That?"

Áed chuckled, and Ninian felt it in his own chest. "No, just… having a minute." He sighed contentedly. "This is so strange, Nin."

"Hey," Ninian said, playfully catching Áed's hand. With the other, he picked a dandelion, and Áed blew on it so that its seeds scattered unhurriedly to the wind. "We *deserve* a minute."

"We do," Áed agreed. He was quiet for a moment. "I wonder what Ronan's up to."

"He's fine," Ninian assured him. "There's food in the flat, and I told him to stay in." Ninian had made sure Ronan would be safe. The boy looked up to Ninian, and Ninian loved him. It made Ninian impossibly happy to raise his trash child to be whole, and happy, and… untarnished. Still, he gave Áed's waist a little squeeze. "This is *our* day, remember? You and me." Ninian had no intention of allowing a single second of time with Áed to slip through his fingers. Even sitting quietly… Gods, it was perfect. He didn't want it to change.

"Mm," Áed agreed, closing his eyes again. "Right."

Cawing, a trio of crows flapped high over the courtyard, braiding their paths across the sky. Ninian watched them until they passed out of sight over the chimneys of the tenements, and he sighed faintly.

The sun was warm.

Áed was warm.

Ninian was warm.

He didn't think Áed realized he did it, or, if he did, he never recognized it as unusual, but when he was content, the red-eyed boy made soft little humming sounds—the sort that were more easily felt than heard. It had occurred to Ninian rather early on that it was possible Áed could purr. He was doing it then; Ninian closed his eyes, just feeling it in his core. The first few times Ninian had noticed it, years ago, it had unsettled him quite a lot, but now it was impossibly relaxing.

Through his eyelids, everything was soft, dim red. Ninian didn't think of much at all and found that it was nice, so his mind wandered, Áed purred, and Ninian slowly drifted.

⸻

He woke with a start, which made Áed wake with a start.

Ninian sat up fast, nearly tipping Áed off his lap, and looked around frantically before he realized he'd actually fallen asleep. Heart hammering, he slumped back against the brick and squinted at the sky. The sun was in a different place. "Shit," he groaned as Áed, looking disoriented, slid onto the grass-carpeted ground with a little *thud*. He took his warmth with him. "I broke our nap."

Áed rubbed his eyes with the backs of his wrists and blinked. A yawn overcame him, and he arched his back to stretch his arms over his head. Ninian shook out his legs, which had fallen asleep, and Áed, like Ninian, peered out of the broken-brick cove to squint at the sun. "We slept for a *while*!"

It was true and startling. "Sorry I ruined it."

"Don't apologize," Áed said with a sleepy, satisfied smile. "It would have been sad if we'd slept the whole day away." He scooted out of the cove and stood, stretching again. "Wow! I think I needed that." He turned back to Ninian. "You definitely did."

Brushing at the corners of his eyes, Ninian stood as well, careful not to knock his head on the brick. The courtyard, with its tall grass and swaying flowers, hummed with insects and dripped with sunshine. "This is such a perfect spot," Ninian said.

"It is. I'm happy here."

Ninian knew that meant a lot more than the words expressed on their own. Áed had never wanted to stay in the Maze. He stayed for Ninian, but Ninian caught him looking to the cliffs sometimes, most certainly envisioning the city that sat atop them. "I'm really glad," Ninian answered, and didn't stop himself from smiling.

Clumsily pinching a flower off its stem, Áed tucked it behind his ear with a little laugh. "Look, we match."

Ninian's hand went to his own flower automatically—he'd forgotten about it. "So we do." He adjusted it so it wouldn't fall, and then caught Áed's eyes on him. "What?"

Áed titled his head. "Just give me a second."

"What?" Ninian ran his hands over his cheeks. "Is there something on my face?"

"No, stop it." Áed stepped close and gently pinned Ninian's hands to his sides. His eyes, catching the sun and shining like coals, flicked back and forth, looking at Ninian's.

"What are you looking at?" Ninian insisted, feeling just a hint of self-consciousness.

At that, Áed's half-smile broke into a full one. His nose always scrunched just a little when he smiled, freckles bunching together. His whole face was bright. "Come on, Nin," he said, beaming. "I'm looking at *you*." He took a step closer so he was standing against Ninian, and tilted his chin to look up at Ninian's face. Ninian stood over him by nearly six inches, though part of that was the slope of the cobblestones.

Ninian freed one of his hands from Áed's grip—it wasn't

exactly hard to do—and used it to brush Áed's sandy hair out of his face. The sun shone through it, making the lighter strands glow golden.

Gods, he was beautiful.

The kiss was patient, the sort that expects a thousand more but doesn't want to waste the time it has. Ninian felt warmth spread over him from every place he touched Áed's skin, but it wasn't troubling, too-hot warmth. It spread like honey through his veins, and his hands crept up Áed's back under his shirt.

Áed made a funny little sound and reached up to link his crumpled fingers at the nape of Ninian's neck. For a moment, he pulled away, drawing a quick breath, but then he was back, and Ninian's fingertips pressed into Áed's skin.

Ninian's heel hit an uneven cobble behind him, and he tripped backward. Áed landed on him, and after a moment of breathlessness, Áed pushed himself to his elbows over Ninian. Ninian tilted Áed's chin down toward him. Broken stems dampened the back of Ninian's shirt with sap, but he didn't care. Áed occupied the whole of his focus—how could he *not*? Blond hair and freckled skin and ember eyes, and *lips*—

Ninian couldn't carry the thought.

He wanted it to last forever.

It couldn't, of course. Eventually, Áed rolled to the side and flopped next to Ninian on the ground, grinning and catching his breath. His hair was mussed, and his face was pink about the cheeks and lips, and he gave Ninian a look like he was the only other person in the world. There were grass stains on his knees and elbows.

Suddenly, Áed perked up. "Do you hear something?"

Ninian propped himself up reluctantly and strained to hear anything beyond rustling grass and the quiet hum of insects. He'd gotten quite used to nothingness in one ear—

he didn't even notice it anymore, most of the time. But Áed did usually hear things before Ninian could, and Ninian had come to trust Áed's sense more than his own. "No. What is it?"

Áed sat up all the way, alert. "Someone's coming down the alley."

Ninian heard it, then. Footsteps, uneven ones. He groaned quietly. He recognized that tread. "Come on," he complained and dropped back to the ground. He pinched the bridge of his nose. "Not today."

CHAPTER TWENTY-NINE

Brígh was still a strong woman, all power in her shoulders and determination in her jaw. She'd lost her lithe agility with the soundness of her knee, but it didn't stop her from moving like she had places to be, people to end.

Ninian cursed under his breath as she stepped into the green courtyard and leaned on the wall of the nearest tenement. Brígh didn't bother to call Ninian's name. She knew she didn't have to.

Ninian didn't sit up. "How did she even *find* me?"

Brígh must have heard—sometimes, Ninian still talked more loudly than he meant to—because she let out an irritated sigh. "We saw you come down this street hours ago, *amadán*. I've had people keeping an eye on you all day."

Next to Ninian, Áed scooted a little closer. "Ninian—"

The scarred woman's eye fell on Áed at the motion, and she snorted. "Oh, I get it." She leaned away from the wall, looking irritable from what Ninian could make out through the tall grass. "Come on, kid," she ordered. "Ditch the distraction. Let's go."

Ninian glowered at her. "From here, *you're* the distraction. Go away."

"Ninian," Áed said, a little more insistently. "Don't make her mad; it isn't worth it."

Brígh snorted, shifting her weight off her bad leg. Ninian could see the resentment in her face, and a mean part of him relished the fact that he had surpassed her and was satisfied that she hated him for it.

Until she spoke. "Ninian," she said indolently. "Your call-boy's got more sense than you do."

Ninian was on his feet in less than a second.

Áed bolted up after Ninian, hurriedly tugging at Ninian's arm. His eyes were hot and annoyed, but he looked determined. "Ninian!" He took Ninian's chin when Ninian's gaze strayed furiously back to Brígh. "Don't ruin the day, okay?"

"*She's* ruining it," Ninian growled sharply.

"It's not done yet," Áed said. "Just go with her, win the fight, and that'll be it. Hey." He made Ninian look at him. Áed blinked slowly, and, naturally, Ninian didn't want to look away again. "Don't waste your energy on her. You're too important for that."

"Hm," Ninian said. Defensive anger still tumbled in his center, making his skin prickle, but an errant smile tugged up one side of his mouth. Áed matched it, a touch deviously. "I don't suppose I can argue with that."

"You cannot," Áed murmured, and got up on his toes for a quick kiss. Then he gave Ninian a push in Brígh's direction. "Go on."

Brígh looked repelled, and she shook her head as Ninian reluctantly ambled over. "Disgusting."

"You're jealous."

Brígh glared knives at him. Ninian rather expected to feel her palm crack across his face, but she didn't have anyone to back her up, so she kept her hands to herself. "You've got some *nerve*—" she snarled instead, but Ninian interrupted.

"You called my partner a whore," he said as they started down the alley. He could feel Áed's eyes on his retreating back, so he resisted the urge to warningly draw his knife at Brígh. "You're lucky you still have your head."

⌇⌇

Ninian stewed for the whole walk. Áed could garner patience for Brígh, but Áed was a saint—and Ninian, unfortunately, had more experience with Brígh's personality. Since Brígh had fallen from the fighter's lineup, her bitterness had become almost tangible. Ninian felt like he was walking through its murk as he followed the scarred, limping woman deeper into the city. Now and then, Brígh would look back sharply as if to ensure he wasn't pulling a knife on her, her blind eye looking like a marble in the sun.

The fact that Brígh seemed to have marked Ninian as her rival, however, definitely had more to it than jealousy. Ninian was certain she knew what he had been planning for the past seven years. Of all the people in the gang, Ninian was the greatest threat to Brígh's ambition, despite the fact that she'd been clawing her way up since vouching for Ninian… which was certainly a decision she regretted.

Ninian was going to beat her to the top.

They made it to the coast, where docks extended into the sea to be slammed by the relentless red surf. Ninian felt the salt air cool on his skin. A familiar masked figure, clothed in bells, leaned against one of the pilings, and they stood up straighter when Ninian and Brígh approached.

Ninian was rather gratified when Ailbhe greeted him before Brígh, though the seer did address Brígh after exchanging a few pleasantries. "I was told to wait here," they said, and Ninian thought they sounded a touch displeased.

"That's right," Brígh grunted. Ninian doubted she'd ever

forgiven Ailbhe for the beating they'd condemned her to all those years ago. Bruised and embarrassed, she'd been unapproachable for weeks. "Cahir needs your…" she trailed off and waved a hand condescendingly. "Whatever you do."

Ailbhe sighed. "I am not a part of my brother's '*family*,'" they said, crossing their arms. "He has made this quite clear, as have I."

"That still doesn't protect your head if Cahir decides you don't deserve to have it anymore," Brígh said. "Just do your job, hm?"

She strode by, clearly expecting Ailbhe and Ninian to follow, and Ailbhe fell into step next to Ninian. "Hello, Ninian," they said. "How are you?"

Ninian frowned with frustration at Brígh's retreating back. "I *was* celebrating my anniversary. I'd been having a rather nice day."

Ailbhe shook their head sympathetically. "Well, how's your partner doing? Áed, right?"

Ninian nodded. Ailbhe came and went through Cahir's territory, so Ninian had bumped into them enough times to get to know them better. It had definitely taken some adjusting to get used to their profession, but Ninian had already been doing lots of adjusting since inviting Áed into his home. As it turned out, Ailbhe was pleasant to spend time with, soft-spoken and intelligent, and Ninian had come to consider them a friend. "He's doing well. He's routed the imbeciles at the docks twice this month—the man can gamble, I swear."

Ailbhe laughed quietly. "Good on him."

"And how have you been?" Ninian asked. He always preferred to steer the subject away from Áed. He still wasn't sure exactly how Ailbhe's seer abilities worked, and even if Ailbhe would probably react better than most, Ninian didn't want to risk them discovering that there was more to Áed than met the eye. He'd seen how people—himself included—had acted around Ailbhe just for using magic. He knew with gut-turning certainty what would happen if Áed's secret ever saw the light of day.

"Eh." Ailbhe tilted their hand back and forth. "Been better, been worse."

"Cahir on your nerves?"

Ailbhe rolled their eyes behind the mask. "Always."

Ninian had sought out the seer almost as soon as he'd decided he would someday force Cahir from his place, but Ailbhe had quickly shushed him. They'd have to report to Cahir, they said, if they heard anything treacherous. So Ninian had kept his words vague, and Ailbhe had offered what help they could.

Ninian didn't want to kill Ailbhe's brother. He wanted to tear Cahir down, to see him fall, but he did not want victory at the cost of blood on his hands.

Which made his job a lot harder.

"I swear to the *Gods*, people," Brígh shouted back at the two of them. "You two are slower than *frozen snails*."

Ninian sighed, and he and Ailbhe walked faster to catch up.

CHAPTER THIRTY

Brígh led the way to where the docks existed in layers, built one over the other as the shore sloped downward and the high tide slapped at the bottoms of the lowest piers. She slowed to a stop and leaned on one of the piling supports, shifting her weight onto her good leg. The shade from a taller dock cast slatted shadows over her face. "Right. Here's what's gonna happen." She bent to rub at her knee, making the shadows skip over her. "One of the southeastern families just took over the territory of a smaller gang. Wouldn't be a big deal, except now we share a border, and they're feelin' all… what's the word?"

"Expansionist," Ailbhe suggested, and Brígh snapped her fingers.

"That's the one. They're feelin' a bit big right about now, and I think they wouldn't mind getting bigger. They've been a pain for years, but now, we think they might be a little more ambitious. Now!" She held up one finger, looking at Ninian and Ailbhe sharply. "One of their guys always comes down this way. Ninian, you're going to take him down—but mind you don't kill him."

"Brígh," Ninian said flatly. "When is the last time I killed someone?" He had wounded, crippled, and *soundly* terrified, but he had made a point of not killing. It had earned him Cahir's ire, but even after multiple thrashings— each of which had sent him hobbling back to Áed feeling beaten and pathetic—Ninian had refused to relax his stance. Soon, he'd made himself too valuable to harm, and from then on, he got away with it.

Brígh rolled her eyes. "Fine. Then don't start now." She turned to Ailbhe. "Seer. Once the man is down, you'll do your… your *whatever* to answer some questions." She rubbed her hands together. "Everything clear?"

Ailbhe looked irritated. Brígh got on their nerves as much as she got on Ninian's. "What exactly is my 'whatever'?"

Brígh's face grew annoyed, which, of course, was the goal. Ninian had known there was a reason he got along with Ailbhe. "Your—your creepy *thing*." She spat the word distastefully. "Your *magic*."

"Oh, *that* whatever," Ailbhe sighed.

"*Amadán*," Brígh muttered, and Ninian snorted. "Just do what you're told, both of you."

The wind was cool off the water, and Ninian watched people pass while Ailbhe skipped stones. Ninian was probably just impatient, but it felt that they were waiting a long time. Brígh wasn't helping his mood, even if she was keeping silent.

Ninian didn't feel like staying still. He paced the length of the dock, watching the shifting red water by the coast and squinting out at the blue horizon. There were a few empty bottles rolling on the waves, and as Ninian looked on, a surge bashed the nearest one into a rock hard enough for it to shatter. A few gulls shrieked father out, and on the tops of the pilings, crows perched as if surveying the area.

"Hey, Ninian!" Brígh called, and Ninian turned hopefully. If his target had turned up, he could finish his business and leave. But Brígh was still slouched against the dock-rail, not looking particularly urgent. "Come here a minute!"

Grudgingly, Ninian did. The crows croaked at him as he passed, their feathers ruffling in the wind. "What do you want?"

She grinned. "I was making a bet with Ailbhe," she said, a touch wickedly. On hearing their name, Ailbhe looked up curiously. "We need you to settle it."

Ailbhe raised their hand. "I'm not part of this."

Brígh ignored them. "We were wondering why you use a broken one."

Ninian frowned, not immediately understanding. "What?"

Brígh blinked at him, her clear eye wide and innocent. "Is he cheaper?" She cocked her head, and Ninian started to bristle. "I mean… I'm *sure* we don't pay you enough, but I didn't realize it was *that* bad—"

Ninian growled, and Brígh blinked at him. The affected harmlessness in her expression looked repulsive on her face, and then her eyes widened.

"Unless…" She pressed her hands to her mouth, looking theatrically scandalized. "Maybe you like 'em a little battered." She grinned wickedly, the curve of her lips peeking out from behind her fingers. "A bit broken in?" Her head cocked to the side. "How many had him before you?"

Ninian's stomach churned, revolted. "What is *wrong* with you?" He was sure his disgust showed on his face; that was probably what Brígh wanted. "I'll drown you, don't even think I won't—"

Brígh just laughed. Ailbhe had gotten to their feet, looking ready to do something. They didn't seem to know just what, but they didn't look happy either. Brígh leaned back easily.

"If you lay a hand on me," she said sweetly, "I'll make sure you never see your little hussy again."

It took an *incredible* amount of self-control for Ninian to lower the hand he'd instinctively lifted to strike her. "He's not a *call-boy*, and he's not a *hussy*. And you can't do that."

"Wanna bet?"

Lips pressed into a thin line, Ninian glared daggers at the scarred woman. "Why," he hissed through clenched teeth, "are you the way that you are?"

Brígh waved a hand, looking suddenly bored with the act. "Hell if I know."

"I'll tell you what *I* know," Ninian said coldly. "If you speak of my *partner* like that, even *one more time*—"

"You'll *what*?" She opened her arms. "I'm untouchable, Ninian."

"*Wrong*," Ninian spat. "You *were* untouchable."

Color rose in Brígh's cheeks. "Cahir himself put me in charge of—"

"Of something he has *literally always done himself*." Ninian folded his arms; it felt good to strike back, even if he couldn't do it with his hands, and he aimed for Brígh's weak spots. "You are unnecessary." He smiled, twisted and livid. Brígh had to know that if Ninian seized power before she did—and he was hard at work doing just that, gaining supporters at every chance he got—she would have nothing to fall back on. No reason to be important. No skills that would save her position. If Brígh beat Ninian to becoming gang leader, though, she would still need Ninian's fighting prowess if she wanted the gang to have a chance at survival. He thought she knew that, anyway. "Pitiful."

Brígh lurched to her feet, and it was Ninian's turn to

spread his hands.

"What are you gonna do?" he mocked. "I'm untouchable, Brígh."

"I'll turn you in," she spat. "Tell Cahir you're trying for his place."

"Sure," Ninian scoffed. He leaned closer, so Ailbhe could plausibly claim not to hear. "If you do that, you *know* you're going down with me."

"Stop it," Ailbhe cut in shortly. "Both of you."

"What?" Brígh snapped.

Ailbhe pointed down the boardwalk. "If you two would stop going for each other's throats, you'd have noticed our man's coming."

"How do you know it's him?" Brígh griped, and Ailbhe fixed her with a stare that very clearly communicated what they thought of that question. Brígh huffed. "Fine. You're right. It's him." She waved over her shoulder to Ninian, still obviously ruffled. "Sic him, boy."

Deeply annoyed, Ninian loped in the direction of Brígh's pointing finger. It was obvious who his target was meant to be; the space around the bony man's eyes was crudely tattooed, as were his nose and mouth, giving his face the appearance of a living skull. Ninian grimaced at it; he recognized those marks, and they weren't pretty. At least he'd gotten himself into a gang that didn't do *that*.

Ninian casually slipped his knife from its sheath as he approached, and the blade caught the sun. The light ran like a bead along the edge, so bright and smooth that Ninian half-expected it to drip off the tip of the metal. The skull-faced man looked up at the glint, and in a flash, he'd whipped a knife into his own hand.

It was difficult to tell, what with the tattoos over his face, but Ninian thought the man looked uneasy.

Well. He should.

Ninian twirled his knife so that it nestled comfortably in his palm. "Afternoon, mate," he called. He probably still sounded irritated from his exchange with Brígh, but that could serve his purposes; he didn't mind the way the bony fellow looked cowed before Ninian even got close. "You're not a fighter," Ninian said, assessing the man's stance, his white-knuckled grip on his knife, and the way his eyes flicked around and around. "Are you?"

The man didn't seem to want to reply, but Ninian was pretty sure of the answer already.

He groaned internally. This had Brígh's fingerprints all over it. Cahir's gang had several fighters, all of whom could have easily taken care of fare like the skull-faced man. To summon Ninian was, objectively speaking and without even a hint of egotism, overkill.

He gritted his teeth. Brígh was really outdoing herself, gaining the upper hand in their constant battle simply by how *many* times she'd gotten under Ninian's skin that day.

"Delightful," Ninian muttered.

As intimidating as the skull-faced man's ink was, his actions told a different story. He stood defensively, making no move to attack.

With a sigh, Ninian covered the distance between them. He struck out with the knife, gratified when his opponent swung his own blade up to block Ninian's.

With the bony man's weapon thus occupied, Ninian drove his fist into the man's stomach.

Ninian sheathed his knife as the man dry-heaved on the ground and turned back to Brígh and Ailbhe. "Are you sure this was even the right person?" he called. Even if the man wasn't a fighter, he should have been able to put up more of a struggle than *that*.

"Hold him," Brígh called, limping over while Ailbhe followed. Ninian looked back to the fallen man to see him struggling to rise to his feet. Sighing, Ninian pushed him down with his foot and then adjusted so that he pinned the man with a forearm across the throat, making sure the man could still breathe. "Just stay put." Ninian sighed while the man's eyes bugged out with fear.

"What do you want?" the man demanded, his voice reedy and grating.

"Honestly? No idea."

Ailbhe and Brígh reached them then, and Ailbhe squatted beside the tattooed man. Ninian was kneeling on the man's wrist, so it was safe for Ailbhe to touch his hand. While the seer placed their fingertips on the man's palm, Brígh leered over all of them triumphantly. "How's *that* feel?" she said, and Ninian thought it was probably directed at the man from the enemy gang, though knowing Brígh, it could have been to all three of them. She poked Ailbhe with her foot. "You ready, seer?"

Ailbhe sighed, closing their eyes with a *Gods-give-me-patience* expression. "Whenever you are."

"Right." Brígh rubbed her hands together. "I want to know what their scouts were doing at our eastern border two nights ago."

Ninian frowned. "We don't usually enforce borders." Some gangs did, but Cahir preferred to allow free passage; the more people on his turf, the more business for local merchants, and the more money Cahir could skim from the shop owners. "Why would it be unusual for them to come on our territory?"

"They were acting shifty," Brígh said. "Ailbhe, get going."

Ailbhe dutifully closed their eyes and began a half-mumbled chant, the words blurring together so that Ninian couldn't understand what they said or even which language they were speaking. The tattooed man, pinned to the ground, struggled against Ninian's grip.

"What's going on?" he asked, trying to dislodge Ninian's weight. "Hey! Hey, what's this?"

Ninian smirked. "Magic. Don't worry, won't hurt you."

The man's eyes widened. "M-magic? Wait! Wait, get off of me—stop that—"

"No," Ninian said. "Now, quit distracting them."

Eyes fearful, the man swallowed and fell still. Ninian sighed. The tattooed man might not be the best fighter, but at least he wasn't stupid.

Ocean spray misted over them, and a few seagulls chased a crow across the sky, the crow holding the remains of a silver fish in its thick black beak. Ninian watched, bored, as the gulls overtook the crow and, in an aerial struggle, wrestled the fish from its beak and sent it tumbling dangerously close to the surface of the sea. The crow righted itself, rasping out its protest, and flapped away over the buildings and inland out of sight.

Ailbhe stopped their quiet murmuring, and Ninian looked back at them. The seer sat back on their heels, looking thoughtful. "Right," they said after a few minutes. "He's not completely sure, but I think I can…" They concentrated for a moment, and while their mask hid much of their expression, a faint frown bent their mouth. "He had a conversation with his gang leader—no." They looked a little confused. "Yes…"

"*Ailbhe*," Brígh snapped. "You're supposed to be helpful."

"I'm *trying*," Ailbhe retorted, and Ninian heard a bit of snippiness in the words. Ailbhe's impressive patience was running out. "It's complex!" Without waiting for Brígh to reply, Ailbhe touched the tattooed man's palm again and muttered a few more words. After a few moments of tilting their head side to side as if trying to hear something, they sat back once more. "All right," they said, and Ninian thought they sounded a little worn out. "The old leader was just usurped. That's why they're suddenly so aggressive; there's someone else in charge."

"Who?" Brígh demanded.

Ailbhe closed their eyes. "A big man—Gods, he's huge. How does he even get enough food to look like that?"

"Focus," Ninian whispered. He didn't want Brígh's temper to break, and he'd seen Ailbhe's work enough times over the years to know the seer sometimes got a little overwhelmed.

Ailbhe took a quick breath. "Right. Anyway." They wiped their hand on their bell-covered cloak; Ninian saw that the tattooed man's palm was sweating profusely, and Ailbhe looked faintly disgusted. "He's tall and ruthless. Seoirse—oh, that's this fellow here, by the way—knew him from before he took over and was afraid of him then too."

"Stop it!" Seoirse protested. "Get out of my head!"

Ailbhe ignored him. "Seoirse doesn't know why they're acting so aggressively, but he did have a conversation a week or so ago that might help us."

Seoirse squirmed violently. "*Stop!*" He tried to knee Ninian in the back; it didn't do much, but Ninian still swore. "Get out of my *head!*"

"Sorry, mate," Ninian said, doing his best to keep the man down. "I know it's uncomfortable."

"This has nothing to *do* with me," Seoirse moaned. "I'm not even *involved.*"

"We know." Ninian watched Brígh's face and didn't particularly like the conniving expression he saw there. "Relax, I'm not going to hurt you. Stay still, though, would you?"

But the tattooed man was getting frantic. "I know I'm on your turf, but I didn't ask for *magic*. Just let me up, and I won't bother anyone—"

Brígh was observing with narrowed eyes. "Kind of pathetic, isn't he?"

Ninian rolled his eyes. "Like *you* would handle this well."

Ailbhe pressed on. "Listen," they said insistently. "This new leader is *ambitious*." They sat back on their heels. "He's not going to be satisfied with the turf of one weak gang." Their eyes flashed through the stylized holes in their mask. "He wants more."

Brígh looked intrigued. It was a strange expression to see on her face, and Ninian didn't trust it. "Right. Then who is he? This new leader?"

The seer got to their feet, dusting off their clothing, and Seoirse shot to his feet as Ninian released his hold. As it happened, both the seer and the skull-faced man answered in unison:

"Morcant."

CHAPTER THIRTY-ONE

As soon as the tattooed man shot down the street, Ninian said goodbye to Ailbhe, pretended Brígh wasn't there, and took off almost as fast as Seoirse.

Something wasn't quite right. Inter-gang squabbling was far from unusual, but Ailbhe's words had been concerning. An enormous new gang leader who'd not only taken over his own gang but had also already conquered one of its neighbors sounded a bit alarming, and Brígh had looked too pleased with the news for Ninian's taste.

She was up to something.

Exhaling in frustration, Ninian shook his head. He'd find out what she was planning, and he'd ruin it. Besides, one of his long-term strategies had another act scheduled that night, after Áed had gone to sleep; every move Ninian took toward the top was a blow at Brígh's odds. Ninian was gaining headway—and supporters.

But like he'd told Áed, the day belonged to the two of them, and Brígh had gotten in the way enough already. He wouldn't let her take over his thoughts as well as his time—especially not when he still had a very important conversation to brace himself for that evening.

He didn't bother going back to the overgrown courtyard. He knew Áed wouldn't be there. His love was the most patient person Ninian knew, but with Ronan home alone, Áed wouldn't be able to resist checking in back at the flat.

Ninian hurried back to the old tenement as fast as he could.

Ronan was in the street out front when a slightly winded Ninian got back. The boy was constructing something out of twigs, looking very focused, and Ninian paused for a moment to listen to Ronan explain that the sticks were a castle, and the gutter was the moat. The boy smiled as Ninian ruffled his thick, black hair. Ronan was always so pleased when Ninian praised him. Ninian's language of affection with Ronan tended to be teaching Ronan the ways of things, showing the boy the skills he would need in order to have a good life. He hoped Ronan knew it meant Ninian loved him, but when Ronan beamed so brightly at 'nice twigs,' Ninian did have to wonder if he'd set the standards too low. He wanted to make sure Ronan didn't grow up to be naïve—Ninian knew from experience that little could be more dangerous than naïveté—but it was just as important that Ronan knew he was loved.

Ninian smiled, gave Ronan's hair one more tousle, and bounded up the tenement steps.

Áed was in the flat, just as Ninian had expected. He was humming, Ninian could hear it through the door, and Áed jumped when Ninian turned the handle. "Hey, love!" Ninian was across the room in three strides, and in an easy motion, he'd lifted Áed to a seat on the table and nuzzled his nose against Áed's neck.

Áed laughed, pushing Ninian away and looking at the table like he was surprised. "First of all! Hello to you too. Take a deep breath." He poked the table on which Ninian had so easily placed him. "Second of all, I cannot be *that* light."

In response, Ninian just smirked, and, making Áed's eyes widen with a grin, he swept Áed off the table. Áed hooked his legs around Ninian's waist while Ninian supported his weight. "Nah," Ninian said, smiling lopsidedly. "I could be that strong, though."

"Modest too," Áed noted with a crooked grin.

Despite his big talk, Ninian did have to put Áed down after a moment, and Áed leaned on the table. The collar of his shirt was slipping off of his shoulder again, and neither he nor Ninian moved to fix it.

"So," he said. "How did it go? With Brígh?"

"Ugh," Ninian groaned, dramatically slumping against the wall. "She's the *worst*."

"So everything was fine," Áed said.

Ninian nodded. No point in mentioning Brígh's shiftiness—Brígh was always awful, and Ninian was probably overthinking. He didn't have any evidence to prove that she was up to anything more than usual. "Horribly insulting. Said she'd report me to Cahir for threatening her, so that's the fourth time this week. Oh, but Ailbhe was there—they say hello."

Áed laughed softly. "Sounds charming." He pushed away from the table and moved toward Ninian again, eyes flickering. "Glad it's done, though." He bit his lip thoughtfully and gave Ninian a look that briefly made Ninian's heart forget how it was meant to function. "Now, you *did* say this was our day. And there's still some of it left, so…" He raised an eyebrow. "What do you want to do?"

Ninian's eyes flicked to their nest of bedding in the corner, but he shook himself, dispelling the thought. *The plan. You have a plan.* "One second." He did cross to the bed, but only to grab a blanket. "Come with me?"

Áed obliged.

Ninian led the way up the staircase, and then together they kicked at the jammed door to the roof until it opened. The wind was cool, almost chilly, especially as the sun dipped lower in the sky, and Ninian draped the blanket over his and Áed's shoulders. "Wait a minute," he said, and then leaned carefully over the edge of the roof. "Hey, Ronan!" he called, and the boy, still diligently crafting his twig castle, looked up. "Go on inside," Ninian said, cupping his hand to his mouth to be heard from the top of the tenement. "It's getting dark."

"There's dinner in our flat," Áed added. "Fish and parsnips, all right?"

Ninian couldn't hear if Ronan replied, but he did see the boy make a few adjustments to his castle and then skip inside the building.

"Right." Ninian guided Áed to the western edge of the roof. He sat down, and Áed, clinging to the blanket against the breeze, sat with him. "Now for the rest of our day."

⁂

It was time.

The sun set. Ninian watched it with Áed, listening to Áed talk about an entire chain of sausages Ronan had stolen, and how Áed had found a tin mirror to trade with Máel Máedóc, and how beautiful the sky was with the clouds all red over the cliffs.

Ninian could listen to Áed talk all night.

As the air cooled down and the stars gradually began to peek between thin clouds, Áed snuggled closer to Ninian—Ninian knew Áed hated being cold, and Ninian tucked the blanket more tightly around both of them. Áed fit into Ninian's arms so well.

The plan.

Ninian bit his lip.

Áed fell quiet, as if Ninian's silence had just gotten loud. "What is it?"

Ninian closed his eyes. Of *course,* Áed could tell there was something on Ninian's mind. He could always tell. It was one of the reasons Ninian loved him—with Áed's uncanny perception came his instinct to make things better.

But there was one thing that Ninian knew Áed had not perceived.

One very, very important thing.

Ninian had planned the words for years, and he still didn't know the right way to say them. There was really no good way to go about it.

But it had to be done.

"Áed, I…"

Ninian looked away.

What would happen? Áed had doubtlessly grown up with the same awe-inspiring, nightmarish faerie stories as anyone else. How would he react when he found out those stories were *his*?

He'd probably be angry. He would have every right to be angry.

Would he be angry enough to leave?

A little shiver tremored from Ninian's head to toes. Surely Áed wouldn't leave—Ninian *had* to trust his partner more than that. Ninian might *deserve* to be left, but Áed was looking at Ninian with nothing but concern in his eyes, and guilt curdled painfully in Ninian's stomach.

He needed to say the words.

What if everything in Áed's past came back? Ninian remembered, as clearly as if it had happened the week before, that too-bright panic ruling Áed's eyes as he wrestled against something he did not know how to control. Rowan and nails on the floor. Salt between the boards. Áed still had holes in his memory—what would happen when they filled?

Would Áed break?

Or would he… change?

Somewhere in Ninian's beautiful, red-eyed love, there was a monster of magic and flame.

Ninian gritted his teeth. He knew exactly how it felt to be deceived by someone who was meant to be trustworthy, and he did not want to be that person. It was Áed's secret, not Ninian's, and Ninian done enough wrong by waiting for so long.

He just had to *say it.*

"Áed," he started. *Say it. Say it, say it, say it.*

It was such an old secret.

And Ninian was… so afraid.

Indoctrinated fear ground so far into the mortar of his being that he did not know how he could scrub it out no matter how many years he labored and loved. He had worked so hard. He loved so much.

But the truth still stuck, sharp as glass, in his throat.

"Áed," he said again, and couldn't meet Áed's garnet eyes. "I am such a coward."

Áed looked confused—confused and worried. "Nin, what's this about?"

Ninian shook his head. *I trust him. I* trust *him.*

"I love you," he said. "Áed, I love you so much." The words were true, but they weren't the right ones. "I love every single part of you. Please, please know that."

Ninian cursed himself as Áed, clearly unsure what to say, nudged himself closer. "I love you too, Nin," he said, and there was a waver of questioning to it. "But what were you *going* to say?"

The insistent voice in the back of Ninian's head was louder now. *Say it. Coward. Say it.*

Ninian could not meet Áed's eyes.

"Nothing, love," he said. "I'm sorry."

CHAPTER THIRTY-TWO

They sat on the roof and watched stars with long tails flick through the night sky, trailing white through the velvet of the heavens. Áed kept his arm firmly around Ninian's waist—he'd gotten even closer since Ninian had failed to speak the truth, clearly sensing that something was wrong. Guilt ran clammy and cold through Ninian's core, but he wanted nothing more than to hold Áed close and not let go. So, feeling weak, that's exactly what he did.

It's all right, Ninian told himself sternly. *Tomorrow. I'll tell him in the morning.* He paused in his thoughts. *Or maybe when it's the right time, I'll just* know.

Áed played with the ends of Ninian's hair, winding the russet strands around his twisted fingers. Ninian absently stroked Áed's arm.

"Áed," he said after a while. Even if he couldn't force the truth past his lips, he still felt like he needed to confess. "I'm not treating you as well as you deserve."

"Hey," Áed said, tugging gently on Ninian's hair. "You treat me like you love me."

"I *do* love you."

"And that is all I want." Áed fixed Ninian with a quick stare before Ninian could argue that no, love didn't involve secret-keeping, or at least it shouldn't. "I know there's something you're not telling me," Áed said, and Ninian's stomach flopped. "But I'm happy right now. If I'm happy not knowing, and you're not ready to tell me, then is there really any harm in waiting?"

That sounded so simple. So appealing. "Is that really okay?" It shouldn't be Ninian's choice to decide whether or not *he* was ready for *Áed* to know his own secret.

It shouldn't be his choice.

It was wrong.

"It's okay with me," Áed said, and Ninian was once again reminded that he'd found the best person who'd ever been born. "You can wait until you're ready."

Ninian wasn't sure Áed would still feel that way if he knew the truth, but the way Áed said it condemned the last of Ninian's weakened resolve.

This isn't the right time, he thought. *I* will *be ready later.*

On the roof, the world felt small and far away. They sat under the blanket, immune to the chilly breeze, and Ninian gently rubbed Áed's hands. Áed didn't always notice when the old damage was bothering him; he was too used to the discomfort. But Ninian saw how Áed touched things more gingerly, held his hands more defensively close to his body, and Ninian knew how to make it better. He pressed the tip of his thumb into the center of Áed's palm, massaging softly, and Áed let out a little groan. He closed his eyes, and Ninian felt him start purring faintly. "Do you want me to go first?" Áed said quietly, eyes still closed.

Ninian had to smile. "Sure."

They did this every anniversary. There was something about the affirmation, year after year, that was remarkably powerful. "All right," Áed said. He was still purring, which made his voice a little husky, and Ninian still rubbed his hands. Past the blanket, the wind would have stolen his words, which only made their little space feel all the more precious. "Nin," Áed said, a hint of a smile already tugging at his lips. "Ninian, who ought to be a prince."

"Stop it," Ninian groused, smirking.

"Don't interrupt." Áed opened one eye only to narrow it, mouth curving. "Wait your turn."

Ninian assented, and Áed went on.

"Almost as soon as I met you, you were my closest friend." He laughed quietly. "That was by default, since I didn't have any other friends, but it was important anyway." His crumpled fingers closed on Ninian's hand. "When I was scared and alone, you were so different from *anyone* I'd ever met. I remember—my first memory of you, actually— thinking that I liked the shape of your eyes." He let out a little breath. "They looked *kind*. And you were kind."

Áed opened his own eyes, looking down as Ninian let out a long, silent breath.

"When I realized what you meant to me," Áed said, "I wasn't about to let you go. You're brave, and clever, and strong. And *good*." His eyes flicked up to Ninian's. "I know you're not perfect." He smiled, and Ninian could have looked at it forever. "You never have been perfect. But you are deeply, fundamentally *good*." He enfolded Ninian's right hand in both of his own and squeezed it as tightly as he was capable. "And that is why I love you."

Ninian swallowed the tightness that rose in his throat and pressed his forehead against Áed's. Áed felt solid. It was strange how someone so physically slight could be so steady, as sure as an anchor.

Ninian's anchor.

"Right," he said and hoped Áed didn't hear his voice shiver. "My turn."

Áed made no move to part their bodies, and Ninian did not need to speak above a whisper.

"Áed." He knew what he was going to say. He put his free hand on Áed's and squeezed gently. "When I met you, I was… drowning. I hated. And I hurt." He closed his eyes; pain dulled, and memory faded, but the memory of pain still lived inside of Ninian, always closer to the surface than he thought. "When I met you," he repeated, "you loved me in a time where I in no way could love myself." He laughed under his breath. "Even now, there are nights when I lie awake, just… just listening to you *breathe*, and I can't even comprehend what I did to deserve you next to me."

"Ninian," Áed murmured, and Ninian shushed him gently.

"Just a little more, I promise." He turned his head so that he could feel Áed's eyelashes on his cheek. "I just wanted to say that from the *moment* I saw you, you were the brightest light in my life. I would kill for you, and I would die for you, and I'd do it because you're gentle, steadfast, patient, and by some *miracle*, you're here. With me." He lifted Áed's hand to his mouth and pressed his knuckles to his lips. He spoke against them. "You saved me. And that—among so *many* reasons—is why I love you."

"Ninian," Áed said again, so softly, and Ninian welcomed Áed's head onto his shoulder.

Ninian couldn't be sure how long they stayed that way. It didn't feel like very long, but he didn't know; he definitely wasn't thinking about time.

He knew Áed had fallen asleep when Áed stopped purring, and his breathing grew steady and quiet.

Ninian wanted to stay there all night.

But he couldn't. He had somewhere to go. Plans to enact. Strategy to execute, and supporters to win.

With a low, regretful sigh, he let himself have one more minute. Then, doing his best to move smoothly, Ninian looped the blanket over one shoulder and carefully gathered Áed into his arms. Holding him under his shoulders and knees, Ninian carried Áed to the door, and then he nudged his way inside, down the stairs, and into their dark, quiet flat.

Áed made a sleepy sound when Ninian rested him down in the nest of bedding and draped a blanket over him. "I'll be right there," Ninian whispered. "I'm just going to check on Ronan, and then there's something I have to do." He kissed Áed's forehead. "I won't be long."

He avoided the steps that creaked as he climbed the stairs to Ronan's room, certain he heard something from within. He knocked lightly on the door. "Ronan?"

The sound stopped almost guiltily. A few moments later, Ronan's little face appeared in the doorway. "Ronan," Ninian said, trying to see what had made the noise. "What are you doing awake?"

Ronan rubbed at an eye with a fist. He was wearing a shirt that had once been Ninian's, which Ninian had entirely outgrown. It fell to the boy's shins. "I couldn't sleep."

"Ah. I know the feeling." He pointed at Ronan. "Don't you dare inherit that, okay?"

The boy looked confused. "I can't inherit anything from you."

Ninian rolled his eyes. "Then don't *learn* that from me. Gods, mate." He dropped to a crouch. "Why can't you sleep?"

Ronan shrugged.

"Something on your mind?"

"No," Ronan said. He stepped away from the door, and Ninian nudged it open and followed the boy into the room. Ronan crossed to the window and pushed at it, and Ninian realized what had been making the sound. "The window's stuck."

Frowning, Ninian examined the latch. "What does the window have to do with you sleeping?"

"It's broken," Ronan explained. "I have to fix it."

Ninian sighed. "Come here. I'll show you how."

As Ninian repaired the latch—it had bent out of shape and wouldn't allow the window to move—Ronan watched with green-eyed interest. Ninian explained the process, and when he'd finished and the latch slid smoothly, he turned to Ronan.

"Now," he said, brushing flecks of rust off his hands. "Tell me what I just did."

With a hint of pride, Ronan rattled off the steps Ninian had taken. Then he pressed the window open, and a cool wind swept into the room.

Ninian ruffled Ronan's hair. "Well done, mate." He pointed to the mess of blankets in the corner. "Now, if I don't see you in that bed in *three seconds*, I'm going to close the window and jam the latch again."

With a gasp, Ronan pattered across the room and dove under the covers. He peeked out with a mischievous grin. "I'm in bed!"

Ninian smiled to himself. The moon was shining brightly, casting ghostly light over the floor. "Sleep well, okay?"

There was a rustling as Ronan adjusted his position, and then a quiet sigh. "Okay," he said. "Goodnight, Ninian."

"Goodnight, mate," Ninian said, crossing to the door. "Sweet dreams."

〰

Ninian closed the tenement door quietly, taking a deep breath of nighttime air. Áed was definitely asleep, Ronan was safe in bed, and Ninian's knife hung in its place on his belt. He cracked his knuckles.

Best to make this quick.

He tied his hair up as he walked, too tired to bother with a braid, and collected it into a thick, russet ponytail. It was getting a bit too long, almost reaching his collarbones, and he made a mental note to cut it later. In the meantime, the dark city streets had his attention, and he made sure not to drop his guard as he jogged through the summer darkness.

When he finally slowed to a stop, he looked around to see if anyone was there yet. The intersection was broad, an uneven fork where three roads met, and the center was paved with cobbles in a scalloped pattern. It did look like a good place for a fight.

"Oh! You came!"

Ninian turned to see a figure hurrying toward him from one of the intersecting streets. He was a boy of thirteen or fourteen with hair cropped close to his head and one of the widest smiles Ninian had ever seen. "Hello, Conor," Ninian said as the boy skidded to a winded stop in front of him. "Good to see you."

"Better to see you!" Conor exclaimed. "I didn't actually think you'd come."

Ninian smiled, hoping it hid how much he'd rather have been home. "Of course, I came. I keep my promises."

Conor looked like he might give Ninian a hug. Ninian took a few steps backward, just in case. "You have no idea what this means," Conor said. "When Brígh told me I had to fight some girl, I was too stupid to be worried." He shook his head remorsefully. "But when I figured out what

I was up against, I knew I was gonna die. Ailbhe told me I could ask you. I think you're actually saving my life."

"Happy to help."

The girl in question, Ninian had already learned from Ailbhe, was the daughter of some minor gang leader, and she wasn't half bad with a blade. Apparently, she was too much of a threat to tolerate. "So, um," Conor said nervously. "You won't tell Cahir you helped, right? I… I can give you my earnings."

Ninian waved him off. "Keep them. And I won't tell Cahir."

Conor's eyes widened, and Ninian suspected with chagrin that he'd just deepened the kid's boyish crush. "You're amazing."

It had been Ninian's idea to start helping a few of the newer members with their fights, and after a few tries, he'd managed to communicate the thought to Ailbhe with extreme vagueness. It felt nice to help out, but more importantly… Ninian needed to be well-liked. Not only would it smooth the transition once he finally ousted Cahir, but once in charge, Ninian needed to know he wouldn't immediately face another coup. Besides, he wanted the gang to be unified under his leadership, enough to defend itself from the opportunistic neighbors who would surely strike once they heard about power changing hands.

Really, those were the crucial elements that Brígh lacked. Planning prowess, and a soul.

"She's coming!" Conor said.

Ninian pressed on his knuckles. "Be back in a minute."

⁂

Ninian's knife made a satisfying *shnk* as he slid it back into his belt and loped back across the intersection to the waiting

Conor. He didn't think he'd ever seen anyone besides Ronan have such wide eyes.

"That was incredible!" Conor gushed. "You looked like…" He couldn't seem to find the word, and waved his arms with some accompanying sound effects, which Ninian thought was maybe meant to represent dancing.

Ninian laughed shortly. "Thank you. I think."

"You didn't, um." Conor peeked around the corner of the building. "You didn't kill her, though."

"Nor will I," Ninian said. He felt a twinge of remorse, the way he always did after a victory. "But she won't be fighting anybody else."

"What'd you do?"

It had been a long time since Ninian had been squeamish, but guilt did still get to him. "Broke her knee."

Conor blinked. "Didn't Brígh break her knee?"

"Where'd you think I got the idea?"

The boy pulled a face. "Right. Well… thank you."

Ninian nodded and offered his hand, which Conor shook. "You're welcome." He turned away from the awed young fighter, wishing he could simply vanish and appear back at his flat with Áed. "Have a good night."

When he finally made it out of Conor's line of sight, and the boy stopped staring at his retreating back, Ninian let out a breath and felt himself slump.

All this effort *had* to pay off.

C

CHAPTER THIRTY-THREE

Eyes of mismatched pastel bored into Ninian's as Cahir pressed his hands to the table.

Ninian stood his ground, despite the gang leader's stare making the back of his neck prickle. They stood in the kitchen of the gang house, sunlight battling its way through both clouds and the filthy glass of the window. Ninian dug in his heels. "I don't think you understand what you're asking."

Cahir's eyes narrowed dangerously. "Come again?"

"I don't think you realize what this would mean," Ninian said. He tapped the tabletop, where charcoal outlined a crude map on the wood. "They haven't *done* anything."

"You heard the seer as well as I did," Brígh said, looking over Ninian's shoulder. She frowned. "Actually, you probably *didn't* hear them as well as I did, but it doesn't matter." Her hands were dark with soot from tracing the map in the first place. "Morcant is a problem."

"I know," Ninian said, choosing to ignore her jab. He was pretty sure she'd meant it as an insult, but he didn't know why it would be. Brígh had been the one to deafen him, after all. "But if we don't know for sure what he's going to do—Ailbhe can't see the future, they've said so themselves—then by attacking first, we may invite retribution which otherwise wouldn't have come." Immediately, he bit his lip. The speech habits of his youth made a resurgence when he didn't pay attention, and it didn't look like Brígh knew what 'retribution' meant. "What I'm saying," he clarified, "is that right now, Morcant still might not bother us. If we invade his territory, though, he definitely will."

"That being said," Cahir mused, "it seems *likely* that he intends to be a problem. By striking first, we may have an advantage." He turned to Brígh. "Where's Ruairí?"

"He's taking care of that creep who bothered Treasa."

Ninian thought he saw a look of mild satisfaction cross Cahir's face at that. Ninian had heard about the initial incident; Treasa had been walking at night when someone took hold of her red-streaked hair and demanded the purse at her belt. The assailant had limped off with a stab wound to the gut and a broken nose, but much to Treasa's disappointment, he hadn't died. It seemed Ruairí was changing that. "Well," Cahir said. "I'm sure that won't take too long." He looked pleased. "My daughter got him most of the way dead already."

"Indeed," Brígh said, clipping the word. She had not been pleased when Treasa had finally joined the family, though Treasa had beamed when Cahir had finally called her 'daughter.' Ninian had done his best to be happy for her, but even Treasa had screamed at the brand, and Ninian didn't think fatherly acceptance could be worth the price that gang life demanded. In any case, she would *not* be happy with Ninian's plan to usurp Cahir. "Anyway," Brígh said firmly. "I don't think we need to wait for Ruairí. It's an easy decision."

"It's not," Ninian argued, but both Brígh and Cahir shushed him.

The gang leader nodded to Brígh. "Do what you have to

do. I expect to be kept informed of the details."

"Excuse me," Ninian put in, trying one more time. "I *really* think this is a bad idea."

"With all due respect," Brígh said in a tone that held no respect, "we aren't about to take the advice of a pacifist."

Ninian sighed in exasperation. "You *so obviously* don't know what 'pacifist' means." He spread his hands on the table, letting the accumulated calluses on his knuckles stand out. "I am *not* a pacifist. I *am* opposed to unnecessary death."

"Trust me," Cahir said, a chill in his voice. "I know." His tangerine and lavender eyes looked harder than their soft colors should have allowed, though they seemed to scrutinize him more thoroughly than usual. "It has posed problems in the past."

"It has not," Ninian said staunchly. "And anyway, my point stands."

The gang leader's face had begun to adopt a sharper expression, but there was something thoughtful behind it that looked almost... approving. "You're nearing a line, Ninian," he warned. "Be careful."

Brígh smirked.

Ninian huffed and dragged his hair back out of his face. He didn't have a tie with him, and a few wavy strands slipped out when he held it all at the nape of his neck. If it had only been Brígh in the meeting, he'd have mouthed off more, but unfortunately, Cahir's temper held much more weight. Brígh couldn't directly harm anyone in the gang, but Cahir could order a punishment that would leave Ninian bruised and stiff for days.

"What do you plan, then?" Ninian asked grudgingly.

A self-satisfied look slipped onto Brígh's face. "I think we ought to take out some support first, a few of their fighters—it'll be easier to end the whole lot of 'em if they can't fight back."

Cahir rubbed his chin. "You're not just thinking of defending our borders."

Brígh grinned. "Why would we stop there?" She dropped a fist onto the table with a *thud*. "If they want to expand, we show 'em that we play the same game." She pointed at Cahir. "Besides, they just took over the gang between us. They're probably already dealing with some mess there, don't you think?"

"You're not as stupid as I usually assume," Ninian said, crossing his arms. From a short-term standpoint, it did make sense to strike when Morcant's holdings were turbulent, and perhaps his grip less secure. Ninian tucked his hair behind his ear. "But even if we manage to engulf a gang the size of ours—which we won't—we will have to deal with that exact same mess on a *far* bigger scale."

"We can handle it," Brígh insisted.

As soon as Ninian saw Cahir's face, he knew it was over. The man had a glint in his eye, and his mouth was slanted in a flat smile. "Brígh," he said, looking at the map on the table with an expression of hunger. "You can get this done?"

Brígh looked smug. "You bet." She turned to Ninian and jabbed a finger into his shoulder. "You are going to be tired."

Cahir waved his hand. "Good. Brígh, use whoever you like." He raised an eyebrow at her. "Don't mess this up."

⟩⟩⟩

Ninian trudged up the stairs to the flat wearily, rubbing at his shoulder. "Áed?" He slouched inside, grouchy. Brígh had wasted no time—as soon as Cahir had dismissed the two of them, she'd dragged Ninian to the edge of the territory and set him on two of Morcant's fighters.

Ninian thought he understood things better now. As he'd handled both opponents at once, Brígh watching from the shade, the realization had almost distracted him enough to take a knife in the face.

The fact was, Brígh didn't have the social backing to ascend peacefully. Which meant that she needed to take over by force, from the inside.

She didn't give a damn about expanding their territory.

She wanted to spread them thin.

Deliberately dispersing their own resources would weaken the gang, and Brígh would use that to claw her way to the top with as little resistance as possible. The problem was, once she was at the helm, the fighting she'd have encouraged wouldn't miraculously cease, and Ninian had no confidence that an impaired gang with Brígh at the helm could survive a war.

Everyone would be killed or absorbed into a new group.

Either way, Ninian would lose seven years of progress. And the thought of that...

He shuddered, nausea rising momentarily.

He could not cope with that.

He needed a plan. Just as Brígh couldn't rat out Ninian to Cahir, Ninian couldn't inform the gang leader of Brígh's treachery—it would result in Ninian's downfall just as surely.

Conflict might be inevitable, given Cahir's lust for land. Brígh would thrive on it. Brígh would use their own gang's losses for her gain.

So that meant... Ninian just had to make sure they won. He'd have to make sure that they emerged victorious over Morcant's gang, and he'd have to do it while impeding Brígh's bids for power.

He groaned quietly to himself. He really *was* going to be tired.

"Áed, you home?"

Áed's head popped around the corner. "Hey!" He looked

like he was in a good mood. "Come here; I have something I want you to see."

"Sure," Ninian said. He'd planned on being rather dramatic about his new bruises to distract himself from his realizations, but Áed looked excited, and Ninian decided he was much more interested in that.

"I was scavenging today," Áed said, leading Ninian into the other room. "Couldn't go back to the docks yet, the gamblers are still sore. But I found *this*." He picked something up from the table and held it out to Ninian with a bit of a flourish.

Ninian's eyes widened. "*A thiarcais.*"

"Right?" Áed put it into Ninian's hands. "Here."

Ninian held it up to the light. It was a knife, not unlike Ninian's, but it had been painted in an intricate, tessellating pattern: bones on bones, skulls and ribs and fingers in fine black strokes over the whole of the blade. "This is…" He turned it, watching the bones seem to shift with the light on the metal. "Where did you find this?"

"Between the Fisher's Shore and the old citadel. It was stuck into the ground—looked intentional. Honestly, I wasn't sure if I should touch it." He shrugged. "But I did. We'll get a coin or two for that, huh?"

Ninian was still examining it carefully, a weight sinking into his stomach. So much for distracting himself from his realizations. "Actually, I think I want to take this to Cahir."

Áed looked taken aback. "You want to *what*?"

The blade rang when Ninian flicked it with a fingernail. "You found this right at our border," he said with a hint of chagrin. "And these bones…"

"No *way*," Áed protested. "If we can sell that, we'll have food for *days*." He held out his hands, and Ninian reluctantly parted with the knife. "Have you seen how skinny Ronan is?" Áed dropped the knife back onto the table, looking at

Ninian narrowly. "He's supposed to be growing, Nin. He needs to eat."

Ninian cracked his knuckles. "I know."

"What would Cahir want with it?" Áed demanded. "Does he actually need to *have* it?"

"Ehm," Ninian said, looking away. He would not have brought the blade to Cahir out of any semblance of loyalty. He just wanted the man to be able to prepare. He wanted as few people to die as possible. "Well… I suppose I could just tell him I saw it."

"What is it, anyway?" Áed squinted at the blade, which, under the swirling black paint, was shiny enough to reflect his eyes. It made the bones look bloody. "I assumed it was just a knife, but by your reaction—"

"It's a threat," Ninian said grimly. "Well, more of a declaration." He picked up the knife and ran a thumb carefully along the blade. It drew blood at first contact. "Bones are the mark of the gang to our east—the one that holds the docks. Led by a man called Morcant." He put the knife down again and licked the blood off the pad of his thumb. "And as of today," he said, "we're at war."

CHAPTER THIRTY-FOUR

Cahir was eating when Ninian knocked on the doorframe to his personal room at the house. "Excuse me," Ninian said. He entered at Cahir's wave.

The gang leader wiped his mouth. "Ninian?" He put down his knife, which had a piece of poultry speared on it. "Rare for you to seek me."

Ninian folded his hands behind his back, ignoring how the sight of Cahir's food made his stomach grumble. "Morcant has declared war."

Cahir frowned. "And how do you know this?"

Ninian would not bring Áed into gang business, so he took credit himself. "I found their knife. Painted in black bones and planted on our border."

That was enough to make Cahir look concerned. "And where is the knife now?"

Ninian squared his shoulders. Honesty, he'd learned, was the best choice when dealing with Cahir. "I sold it."

Both of Cahir's eyebrows rose up. "You *sold* it."

"I have a family to feed," Ninian said. "You don't need it. You just need to know that I've found it." He pressed his fingers gently backward until the joints popped. "And now you do."

"Ninian."

Ninian grimaced. Just because honesty was the best choice didn't mean it was actually any good. This wasn't about to go well for him. "Yes?"

Cahir pushed aside his chair and stood. His face had a hard, thoughtful look. "You disagree with everything I do."

"Well." Ninian bit his lip. It wasn't exactly a secret. "Just about."

"You aren't quiet about it," Cahir said. "I know it's true."

The gang leader didn't usually talk very much before dealing out a punishment, so Ninian kept quiet. It could be that the man was building up to something else, or it could be that he was about to snap entirely. Ninian *had* decided to sell a declaration of war, after all.

Cahir nodded. "You know, it's the people who disagree with you that are the most trustworthy."

That had not been what Ninian had thought the man was going to say. He wasn't sure how to respond, so he settled for, "Oh?"

"If someone only ever agrees with you, then you know that at least sometimes, they are lying." Cahir laughed shortly. "You have never agreed with me."

Ninian scrutinized Cahir. "You've had me beaten for it more than once."

"Well, you are quite obstinate." He took a long, slow breath. "I can be honest too." He placed his palms against each other and tilted them forward. "Honestly, I don't like you very much."

Ninian raised an eyebrow. Should he confess to the feeling being mutual or would that be a mistake? Probably a mistake.

"But," Cahir went on, "I can appreciate your talent. You are, somehow, my best fighter." He shook his head. "Sorry state it is when my *best fighter* won't follow through on a kill." Leaning on the table, he folded his arms. "Whatever the case, you are my best. And I have slowly come to see that nobody is more dedicated to this family than you are."

Ninian blinked, taken aback. "What?"

The gang leader smirked as if he'd discovered something Ninian had been trying to hide. "You speak against every decision that could lead to this family losing lives. And," he said, the smirk growing, "I know that you've been helping the new fighters with their assignments."

A pang of ice darted through Ninian's veins.

"Ailbhe told me." Cahir laughed and waved a hand at Ninian's expression. "Oh, don't look so betrayed. I asked them why fights kept ending with carefully placed injuries, but not a single death. Ailbhe has to answer if I ask directly; they swore me a loyalty oath when they were too young to know better." He crossed his arms. "You had been careful with your words. They said they didn't know anything, so I had to ask if they had any *idea*."

"You didn't punish them, did you?" Ninian said, taking a step toward Cahir. "You can't—"

"I could," Cahir said. He was still staring at Ninian with cutting eyes, judging Ninian's reactions. "They tried to keep something from me."

"But—"

"But I did not." Cahir tilted his head. "Nor did I punish any of the fighters who were cowardly enough to ask for help."

Ninian froze. That was... incredibly out of character. "Why?"

"Because you care about them. And I don't want to punish *you* for caring about your brothers and sisters."

He waved a hand. "Not counting Ailbhe, of course. I only didn't punish them because they threatened to curse me."

"Lovely." Ninian swallowed. He hadn't thought Cahir could still surprise him, and he didn't like it. "Glad that's sorted. But shouldn't we be preparing for war?"

"Oh!" Cahir said. "But we are." He walked around to the front of the table. "Whether I like you or not, Ninian…" He folded his hands. "I trust you."

Ninian kept his expression *very* carefully schooled, so he didn't react to the foolhardiness of that. Clearly, he had done a good job in his seven years of dedicated climbing if even *Cahir* trusted him.

"Based upon the scale of Brígh's plan, as well as what Ailbhe's told me of Morcant, this war will claim lives." The gang leader's tone had become heavier, somehow, and yet more delicate. "I would like to ensure that if it claims *my* life, this family will still have a future."

Ninian's eyes had started to widen.

Was this going where he thought it was going?

"Ninian," Cahir said, and he looked like part of him couldn't believe the words were leaving his mouth. "If I die, you will take my place."

The air around Ninian—namely the air in his lungs— seemed to have stopped moving. "You're joking," he managed.

Cahir smirked coldly. "I am not." He gestured to the door. "I have already told Brígh, Ruairí, and the rest of the closest family. It is final."

This was impossible. This was… this was *huge*.

This was the step Ninian needed.

Even if it took years more, this was *certainty*.

Ninian would be free.

Ninian would be his *own*.

But Ninian shook his head. That could not be it. Cahir would never name a successor—to do so would invite death. The man was a gang leader, not some royal, and all of his heirs were killers and thieves.

Deliberately, Ninian drifted his hand to the grip of his fisher's pike knife. "What's to stop me," he asked, carefully watching Cahir's face, "from offing you, here and now?"

But Cahir only smiled and spread his hands, like he was inviting Ninian's blade to his undefended heart. "Another reason I chose you, Ninian," he said. "I know that you don't kill."

CHAPTER THIRTY-FIVE

Dust stirred in the street as Ninian moved with deliberate slowness, and across from him, Ronan mirrored his defensive positions. "Good," Ninian said, dropping his stance with a sigh. Ronan was not the most coordinated of children. Ninian had tried to teach him to dance too, with questionable results. He moved to stand behind Ronan and adjust the boy's posture. "Better."

Ronan looked uncomfortable. "This is right?"

Ninian bit his lip. "Uh… everyone is a bit different." He crossed his arms. If anyone tried to attack Ronan, Ninian wanted the boy to be able to defend himself. He'd been giving Ronan lessons here and there, but with the stress of the impending war pressing heavily on Ninian, it was all the more imperative that Ronan be able to take care of himself. After all, he had a relation to Ninian, and Ninian was ingrained deeply in what would soon doubtlessly be a conflict to remember. Aside from that…

Ninian didn't like to think about it, but the fact that *Cahir* had a strategy in case of his death made Ninian uncomfortable. Cahir wasn't even a fighter. If the gang leader had such dramatic contingency plans, it only made sense for Ninian, who spent much more time at risk, to prepare the ones he cared about.

Just in case.

It was, however, pretty clear that Ronan would never be a fighter, and Ninian wasn't sure how to teach combat instinct. "What feels right?"

Ronan adjusted his stance questioningly.

"That won't work," Ninian said, a little exasperated. "If I pushed you, you'd fall over."

The boy's green eyes were bright with frustration. "What am I doing wrong?"

Ninian didn't even know. "Maybe you just need practice?"

In truth, Ninian couldn't quite focus on sparring with Ronan. He couldn't stop thinking about Cahir's declaration.

It felt like a victory.

He knew, logically, that being Cahir's successor didn't change anything. As long as Cahir was in charge, Ninian was under his hold, and he still wasn't going to stop fighting for the opportunity to force the gang leader out. The difference was that now, success was so much closer. Even if it took ten years, it *would* happen.

He just wished that Brígh didn't know about it. If he'd thought their rivalry had been intense before…

Ugh.

From his seat on the tenement steps, Áed got Ninian's attention. "Nin," he called. "Incoming."

Ninian followed Áed's gesture to see a silhouette approaching. It didn't limp, and Ninian recognized Ruairí's easy, strolling gait. The man hailed Ninian as he approached.

Ninian sighed. "Ruairí."

Ruairí grinned at Ninian and waved to Ronan. Ronan moved to hide behind Ninian's legs, and Ruairí laughed. "Sorry, I didn't mean to scare you." He addressed Ninian. "Training a new family member?"

"No."

"Of course not. I should have known better." He said hello to Áed on the steps, and Áed waved back politely. Ruairí turned to Ninian again. "Anyway!"

"Brígh has an assignment for me?" Ninian guessed. He still had bruises from his last fight, but he'd handled much worse before and expected to do so again.

"Not until tonight," Ruairí said. "She wants you to meet her on the eastern coast; you know the place." He shook his head. "Nah, right now, I'm here on a favor for Ailbhe."

"Oh?" Ninian put a hand over Ronan's shoulders when the boy didn't move from behind him. "What's that?"

"They wanted to let you know that Brígh is up to something," Ruairí said. "When she heard about you and Cahir, evidently she got really strange and vanished for hours. I mean, it's sort of an open secret that she's a climber, you know? And now you're properly in her way."

Ninian sighed. "This war is too good for her," he said. Brígh wasn't stupid, as much as Ninian insulted her, but until recently, Ninian had always thought the woman was too straightforward for real conniving. From his experience, her planning approach had always been like her fighting style. Direct. Intentional. Efficient.

Now, though… conflict was her comfort zone. There were an uncomfortable number of ways she could use the chaos in her favor.

"I don't think I'd worry too much." Ruairí shrugged. "Even if she has the nerve to go for Cahir in his sleep or something, there's no way she can take *you* on herself—and nobody likes her enough to back her up." He tucked his thumbs into his pockets. "This doesn't change much for me, I guess. I'm just fighting who I'm told to."

"Well," Ninian said, pressing at the center of his forehead. He was getting a bit of a headache. "I don't suppose there's anything else we *can* do, at the moment."

"Fight or be killed," Ruairí agreed, and Ronan, who'd edged out timidly, looked rather alarmed. "Ah, well. I don't envy you. You're Brígh's favorite."

"Funny."

But Ruairí just laughed. "No, I mean it. Next time you're fighting, just glance at her. She'll practically be drooling."

Ninian made a face. "That's disgusting."

Ruairí waved his hands. "Not like *that*. I just meant that… well, you're better than she ever was, you know? Even I love to watch you fight—you're so smooth it's terrifying." He folded his hands into his opposite sleeves. "But when Brígh watches, she gets to admire the beauty and hate you at the same time. It's apparently pretty heady."

"That *is* disgusting."

Ruairí's head tipped back when he chuckled. "Anyway. Be on your guard."

"Right," Ninian said. "Well, thanks, Ruairí."

"Don't mention it." He shook Ninian's hand, then waved to Ronan again. "See you, mate." He saluted casually to Áed. "Goodbye, all."

When the man had left, Ronan slumped. "Can I be done fighting?"

"Yeah," Ninian said, secretly relieved. Ronan was talented with little things, fragile things, detail. He liked to use his hands, just in a different way than Ninian, and Ninian didn't really know how to teach something that came so naturally to him. "Sure."

On the steps, Áed stood, looking concerned. "What do you think Brígh's planning?"

Ninian shook his head. "She can't do anything to me herself." If he'd been truly worried about Brígh harming him directly, he'd have tried to prepare Ronan much more seriously. Ninian only had to worry about himself if the whole gang fell to the enemy, and he was going to endeavor with all his might to prevent that from happening. He had support, support he had literally fought for, and if Brígh dispersed the gang, Ninian would unify it. He was determined to. "Don't worry about it."

"I don't know," Áed said, crossing into the street. "She could make anything look accidental."

"I'll keep my eye out," Ninian assured him. He'd been injured in fights before, just through the normal course of events, and both he and Áed knew how to handle it. "Besides, you'd patch me up if something went wrong."

Áed let out a little breath, accepting Ronan under his arm as the boy migrated over to him. "Just promise me you'll be careful."

"I'm nothing if not careful," Ninian said, tossing his hair over his shoulder.

Áed snorted. "Then you're nothing." He poked Ninian's chest as Ninian feigned woundedness. "Nin, I'm serious. Watch your back."

"All right," Ninian ceded. "I'll be careful. Promise."

Áed rolled his eyes. "You lie as badly as Ronan."

Ronan frowned. "I don't lie."

"Liar," Áed and Ninian said at once, and Ronan smiled sheepishly.

"I don't lie to *you*," the boy amended.

Áed raised an eyebrow. "Do you want to tell me about the hazelnuts I found in your room the other day?"

While Ronan stammered out an excuse that *didn't* involve stealing them, Ninian found himself staring down the road. He had to go to the east shore that night, and, as always, the new order made him resentful. To Áed, Ninian had done his best not to complain about gang life. He whined about his bruises and occasional scrape, but when his fight money kept Áed and Ronan fed, it had never felt right to voice his deeper bitterness. Once he took over, he'd be able to provide for his family better than ever before—or hell, maybe he could hand the gang leader's mantle to someone else, and the three of them could leave the Maze, as Ninian knew Áed wanted. Now he held on to that more tightly than ever. But until then…

He rubbed his temples, trying to work out the headache before it got worse. He'd been patient for seven years. He could hold out a little longer for his reward. Lack of stamina was not one of Ninian's flaws. "Hey, Áed?"

Áed looked up from where he'd been teasing Ronan. "Hm?"

Ninian pointed over his shoulder with his thumb, gesturing toward the tenement. "I'm going to go inside. I have to leave before sunset."

Áed's face fell just a little bit. "Ah. All right."

Ronan looked more openly disappointed. "Another fight?"

"Not sure," Ninian sighed. "She might just be paying me." It was always good to get paid, even if he had to endure Brígh when it happened, but Ninian didn't really want to leave that night. So much war on his mind was making him crave a moment of security, and even if the walls of the tenement provided only the illusion thereof, there was nowhere Ninian felt safer than Áed's arms. He turned toward the tenement, and Ronan took his hand. Áed smiled at that and followed them in.

"Do we have food?" Ronan asked, swinging Ninian's hand as they went up the stairs. "I'm hungry."

"We should." Ninian glanced to Áed, who had been to the trading shop to sell the bone-painted knife. "Right?"

Áed nodded. "And Ronan, you have those *hazelnuts*."

Ronan looked away guiltily, and Ninian snorted. Áed gave Ronan a hard time, but Ninian knew neither he nor Ninian would ever actually do anything to stop Ronan from feeding himself. Ninian's fight money was enough to support one person, not three, and Áed's earning opportunities remained limited by the state of his hands. He scavenged for Máel Máedóc and sometimes brought home a gambling haul from the docks, but there was never a time when money wasn't painfully tight. Anywhere Ronan could get his hands on food—provided he was careful—was all right with Ninian.

Ninian unbuckled his knife and dropped it, sheath and all, onto the table when he got inside. Immediately feeling twenty pounds lighter, he crossed to the cupboard, where he found a reasonably fresh loaf of bread, a spot of soft cheese, and some carrots. While Ronan checked all the latches on Ninian and Áed's windows, explaining to Áed that he could fix them if they broke, Ninian tore the bread and spread it with cheese. He divided up the carrots into two portions for Áed and Ronan and settled for a bit of bread himself.

Áed smiled at him as he accepted the food and gave Ninian a quick peck on the cheek.

"Thanks, Ninian!" Ronan said, bouncing a little as Ninian slid his portion over. "Hey, why is Áed the only one allowed to call you 'Ninny'?"

Áed choked on a bite of bread.

Ninian answered a little more smoothly. "Because it's a stupid nickname," he said, "and Áed's the only one who can't annoy me."

Áed swallowed his bread with some difficulty and looked up innocently. "I can't annoy you, Ninny?"

Ninian snorted. "It wasn't a challenge."

Laughing, Áed set his attention back on his meal, and Ronan, apparently satisfied with the exchange, inhaled another bite of carrots.

It didn't take long for Ninian to finish off his own bread,

and then, quashing his disappointment at having to leave when all he really wanted to do was lose to Áed at cards, maybe chase a giggling Ronan around the flat until the boy was tired, and end the quiet night early, he picked up his knife again. "All right," he announced to the room as a whole. "I'm off."

"Be safe, Nin," Áed said, leaning away from the table. "Remember what I said. Please."

"I'll be careful," Ninian promised. He ruffled Ronan's hair and blew Áed a kiss on his way out the door.

CHAPTER THIRTY-SIX
Áed

Áed was uneasy, and by this point in his life, he was experienced enough to trust his gut. So when Ninian walked out of the flat and Áed was left with nothing but a swirl of nerves in his stomach, he couldn't seem to ignore it.

When Brígh had interrupted Áed and Ninian's anniversary, Ninian had immediately bristled at the woman's approach. Áed hadn't been surprised by that reaction, especially after Brígh had insulted Áed so openly, but while Ninian had grown endearingly defensive, Áed had been scrutinizing Brígh. The woman was bitter—and hateful too. She definitely resented Ninian for his skill. But there was more to it than that.

Brígh was not just acerbic.

Brígh was *ambitious*.

There wasn't anything inherently wrong with that, except for Áed's sinking certainty that Brígh's ambition involved others' downfall. And it was pretty clear to Áed that Ninian was high on the list of people Brígh planned to trample. His intuition was sparking in a way he'd learned to trust, and it did nothing to set him at ease.

"Hey, *ceann beag*," Áed said, addressing Ronan by the boy's nickname. "When you've finished up your dinner, I think it's probably time for bed."

Ronan pouted. "It's not even dark yet."

Áed sighed. "It will be soon, mate." Out of habit, he started tidying the table, but Ninian had already left it quite clean. "At the very least, I'd like you to go upstairs. I'm going out, and I want you inside while I'm gone, okay?"

Ronan sighed, popping another carrot slice into his mouth. "Okay."

Áed smiled. "Thanks, mate. I don't want to worry about you."

"You don't have to worry about me," Ronan said around a mouthful of food. "I go around the city all the time."

"I know you do," Áed said with a sigh. He didn't love that fact. He'd seen Ninian's attempts to teach Ronan self-defense, and he had to admit the results hadn't given him much comfort. "Not at night, though. Not until you're older." Ronan looked disappointed, and Áed chuckled. "You aren't missing anything. I promise."

After Áed shooed Ronan upstairs, he stood in the flat for a few minutes, gathering himself. Unlike Ronan, Áed knew how to defend himself if he had to but going out at night was still far more dangerous for him than it was for Ninian. He needed to make sure his head was on straight.

He wasn't sure exactly what his plan was, except that he didn't want to be apart from Ninian right then.

Ninian's friend Ruairí—at least, Áed thought they were probably friends, since Ruairí hadn't seemed unpleasant— had mentioned the eastern coast, so Áed knew about where to go. The eastern side of the Maze's peninsula was honeycombed with sea caves, and Ninian had mentioned meeting in them sometimes; in fact, he'd told Áed about trying to live in one, back in his homeless days, though he said he'd never felt safe in the eerily dark, dripping stone caverns. At this time of night, some of the caves would be underwater, so Áed hoped that he could simply wait on the coast without checking each one.

He tucked his hands into his pockets when he stepped outside. Doing so had become something of an instinct. It wasn't shame that prompted him to hide their deformity—he'd never found any reason to be ashamed—but safety. Revealing that his hands were nigh useless *definitely* exposed too much weakness. Showing weakness in the Maze, especially at night, was foolish.

The air was much cooler than it had been during the day, and under the moon, the streets sparkled with dampness. It was protectiveness that hurried him forward, Áed realized as he walked. His stride was purposeful; he was walking fast, and it wasn't just because he was feeling clingy. No, this was worry, the need to make sure Ninian was okay.

He shook his head hard. There was no reason to believe Ninian wouldn't be okay. The man could take care of himself; he'd proven it over and over.

Still.

When Áed had been lost, Ninian had found him. When Ninian had hurt, Áed had done his best to heal him. They had kept each other safe and loved since they'd been young, and Áed wasn't about to stop now.

The cobblestones of the street ended unevenly at an ocean overlook, where the tips of the waves still held indigo glow from the sun's last breath, and Áed walked to the rocky bluff. The caves were hidden to any looking down. The only indications of their existence were the places where the surf, instead of crashing into the rock and spraying back, trailed foam and ropes of seaweed into the land itself. Ninian was in one of those caves, somewhere close.

The moon hung over the water, glinting brightly, and Áed was glad of its light. It shone on craggy stones, fish skeletons, and other oceanic detritus, and Áed took a deep breath of the briny, low-tide air.

Nothing to do but wait. He found a spot by the side of the road and sat, feeling his legs burn from walking so quickly to the east. That trip should have taken at least half of an hour, but he must have made it in half that.

Gods, he wanted Ninian.

He took another slow breath, tasting the salt in the chilly, humid breeze. "Relax," he told himself, trying to squash the feeling in his gut. He hated how he couldn't seem to push aside this particular uneasiness. "It's *fine*." Ninian led a dangerous life. He had for as long as Áed had known him, and Áed *always* fretted when anything unusual happened. It was stressful enough when Ninian came back from some or another fight with a black eye marring his face, or a knife cut that Áed had to tell Ronan how to stitch, and that sort of thing was just routine. Áed shouldn't be surprised that any additional threat made him nervous.

The ground was covered in cracked seashells, and he dragged the side of his hand absently over them. They clinked, occasionally throwing light off their milky nacre undersides. He found one that was whole and picked it up, admiring the way the inside shone in the pastel colors of a sunrise despite the cold white moonlight. The outside was dull brown and covered in long-dead algae, but if Áed brought it back home and had Ronan help to polish it, he could give it to Ninian; it was pretty, and Ninian deserved pretty things. It could be a good luck charm.

He slipped it into his pocket, deciding. There was enough going on that any way he could protect Ninian—even if it was superstitious, a seashell and nothing more—he would.

But it was going to be okay. He would work for that—
he always had. And Ninian was strong, capable, and had
promised to be careful.

So it was going to be okay.

Everything was going to be okay.

Thank you for reading this book!

If you enjoyed this book, you can be an author-reader
matchmaker by leaving an honest review on your
preferred book-buying platform.

Post a picture of the book on Instagram, Facebook or
Twitter and tag **@egradcliff**!

ACKNOWLEDGEMENTS

I'm going to be honest: *The Last Prince* was hard to write. I started it three separate times, each differently, and went so far as to complete half of the book before scrapping that draft entirely and starting over. And yet, through it all, I had a team of wonderful people by my side, without whom I surely would not have been able to come so far.

First and foremost, I'd like to thank Erin Radcliff. Her steady dedication to my writing career has not wavered since I first penned *The Hidden King*, and as I launched into production of *The Last Prince*, the enthusiasm with which she supported the project simply reaffirmed how invaluable she truly is. Besides contributing her exemplary tech and administrative skillset, I always knew I had her ear, and that meant the world to me.

Tim Radcliff, my unconditional rock, was there for me even as I struggled to motivate myself, even as I failed, even as I deleted my progress again and again. His faith in me, when I struggled to have faith in myself, represents the kind of love that I pray to be able to emulate. I'd also like to thank my magnificent friend Blake, who never hesitated to show up with lime tortilla chips and peach tea, ready to talk story arcs or character development. Blake is a true writing compatriot. And of course, I wish to thank my wonderful beta readers, Mimi Black, Mark Reed, Woody Ward, and librarians Alyssa Murphy, Michelle Haller and Erica Drumm, all of whom took time from their busy lives to read *The Last Prince* and share their honest thoughts. The importance of good betas cannot be overstated, and to find such a collection of generous and insightful people is truly a gift.

Beyond my narrative (and emotional!) support squad, I want to recognize Máiréad Ní Chatháin Uí Chonchúír, who again helped with the Irish Gaelic expressions which make up the language of the Maze. The team of professionals helping bring this book to market includes my extraordinary developmental and line editor, Kelsy Thompson, who proved once again to have a genius eye for storytelling, and her input on the dynamics of *The Last Prince* helped me tweak the plot so that the beats fell rhythmically, and the story flowed freely. She was patient and encouraging, lifting compliments and critiques from the pages. Finally, the incredible Micaela Alcaino was my cover designer extraordinaire. Her breathtaking talent is only made more stunning by her professionalism and flexibility, and I count myself lucky to have been able to work with her.

The supportive writers and bloggers in the bookish Instagram and Twitter communities who were generous with support and advice, I am forever grateful to you.

ABOUT THE AUTHOR

E.G. Radcliff is a part-time pooka and native of the Unseelie Court. She collects acorns, glass beads, and pretty rocks, and the crows outside her house know her as She Who Has Bread.

Her fantasy novels are crafted in the dead of night after offering sacrifices of almonds and red wine to the writing-block deities.

You can reach her by scrying bowl, carrier pigeon, or @egradcliff on social media.

CONNECT WITH E.G. RADCLIFF

www.egradcliff.com
info@egradcliff.com

@egradcliff

Join the mailing list from **www.egradcliff.com** for news about upcoming books in the series, giveaways, blog updates, and limited edition book swag!

BOOKS IN
THE COMING OF ÁED TRILOGY

The Hidden King
The Last Prince (the origin story)
The Wild Court (a sequel)
"A powerhouse conclusion to a sensational series... a blockbuster finale."

www.ingramcontent.com/pod-product-compliance
Lightning Source LLC
Chambersburg PA
CBHW020919110726
47900CB00001B/215